Gunnerson's Gunners

Michael O'Gara

Michael O'Gara

CHAPTER 1 – DANGEROUS INSTINCTS

It was an instinctive reaction. There was no question of bravery or fear. It happened too fast. One moment Raif was making sure the pack on their mule was well tied down. The next he heard it.

Raif looked up at the sound of the shot and saw his father fall to his knees in the middle of a street. Another shot sounded and dirt flew up a foot in front of his father.

Raif turned to his father's horse and drew his father's prized Jennings lever action rifle from its sheath. He ran out from between their animals. He entered the street cocking the rifle and putting a round in the chamber. A man was aiming at his father who Raif knew was unarmed. Raif aimed and fired. The attacker fell almost straight back dropping his pistol.

Two other men were running forward and, when they saw their companion fall, they drew their side arms and fired at Raif. It was too far for accurate pistol shots and the morning sun was directly in their eyes. For Raif with a rifle, the men might as well have been at point blank range. Raif was used to shooting fleeing rabbits for fun and food with a rifle of much less quality than his father's prized Jennings repeater.

Raif worked the action so quickly the second man did not get off another shot before he fell dead. The third man was dead before he realized he'd been shot. Raif still had the rifle to his shoulder scanning the street, but now the busy street was deserted and quiet as a grave yard. Raif saw no other danger and went to his father.

Raif bent over and it was obvious his father was dead. Raif was still acting on instinct. He took off his father's money belt and put it on. He then took his father's pocket watch.

Raif walked over to the closest assailant. He was dead. Raif took the man's holster and two side arms. He put the

1

man's holster over his shoulder. He searched the man and found some money which he took. He repeated this with the other two men. He went to his father's horse and put the holsters he'd taken on the saddle horn. One loose pistol he stuck in his waist band.

The man from the general store poked his head out.

"If'in I were you boy, I'd skedaddle. The first un ya shot was a Keefer brother. His kin will be lookin' ta kill ya."

Raif said, "They killed my father. He wasn't even armed."

"No matter to thet lot. They's evil through and through fer sure."

Raif sighed and asked, "What about the sheriff?"

The shopkeeper shook his head, "Bought and paid Keefer man. He gits ya ur goin' ta hang. Best make tracks 'n fast."

Raif looked at his father, "Why'd they do it?"

"Probably after ur pa's poke."

Raif looked at the shopkeeper, "If I give you money, will you see my father gets a pine box and a proper burial?"

The man nodded. Raif's father had been doing business with him for years and so Raif figured the man was honest. Raif gave him money and looked one more time at his father lying in the street. Raif's father had taught him that life was for the living. His father had made sure his son's survival instincts were strong because they lived in a harsh land.

Raif asked, "How long do you think I've got?"

"I reckon if'in ur lucky a couple hours. Half hour for someone to ride hard out to the ranch 'n the same back. Depends on how long it takes 'em ta gather."

Raif mounted his father's horse and led his horse along with the pack mule out of town.

Raif travelled as fast as he could leading the mule and an extra horse. Half way to the crew's camp he switched horses. As he rode, it finally hit him and he cried over the loss of his father.

It was almost evening when Raif got to camp. Ross the lead hand and the four permanent hands who'd been on the cattle drive came to meet Raif.

Ross asked, "Where's ur pa."

Raif sighed as he dismounted, "Dead. Murdered."

Ross asked, "We goin' for revenge?"

Raif shook his head no, "They are dead."

Ross looked at the holsters on the saddle horn, "Ya kilt 'em."

Raif nodded yes then said, "His kin will come for me. I'm headin' north to tell my father's family. You boys go back to the ranch. Travel through the night. The ones after me will follow my trail."

Ross said, "We can fight 'em."

Raif shook his head no, "Nothing to be gained in that. I'm going back to the railhead and take a train to my father's family. You take my horse and pa's. I'll take two of the spare horses saddled. With two I can easy outrun them."

One of the hands said, "The boss is dead."

Ross said, "Raif's the boss now."

Raif was removing the saddle from his father's horse, "Ross, I'll give you money to raise another herd. You keep the ranch going until I get back. It may be some time if father was right and a war is coming."

Ross just nodded, "Sure thing, Raif."

Ross looked at the others and they all nodded.

Within a half hour, Raif was headed northeast and the crew was headed west by the light of the full moon with the mule and most of the provisions. Raif rode through the night switching between horses. He rode for two days without seeing anyone following him. Raif did not understand why he was not being followed.

The Keefer clan had made a major mistake. They had taken out after the crew thinking a mere boy would not head out by himself. They caught up to the crew on the second day. The crew had stopped in a place where the Keefer's could only approach in the open. It would be a dangerous undertaking.

The elder Keefer, Elroy, looked through an old navy spyglass.

"There ain't no young un there. Them boys is hardened ranchers and they's all got rifles. It would be a nasty business to take 'em in the open and the boy ain't there no how."

Elroy's oldest son Beau said, "The boy musta traded with 'em fellers and lit out. We best back-track."

Elroy nodded. The group turned and headed back the way they came.

Ross watched the Keefers leave and said, "They won't catch Raif now. They reckoned wrong and the trail will be cold after the rain last night."

The crew mounted up and headed west.

By the time the Keefer clan got back to where Raif had left the crew, the trail was cold. The Keefer's were unable to pick it up. They were cutthroats and robbers, not man trackers.

Raif crossed the state border and with no sign of being followed, he stopped in the first decent size town he came to. The main street was really not much, but there was a general store. Raif stopped, took his provision bag and rifle, and then went inside to buy provisions.

The man at the counter said, "Afternoon, son."

Raif looked at the man and sized him up. Raif said, "Good day,' then gave the man his order and put his provision bag on the counter.

The shopkeeper asked, "You got money to pay?"

Raif looked the man in the eye, "I wouldn't order if I couldn't pay."

The man went about gathering the provisions. Raif did not let go of his rifle, but walked around the store looking at what the man had for sale. Raif stopped where the man had a number of used and new weapons. Most were of poor quality. Two well used holsters in a display case caught his attention. They were very unusual.

Raif said to the man, "How much you want for these holsters?"

The man smiled, "They's specialty items and fetch a goodly price."

Raif said, "More likely they're not something you'll easily sell. I'll trade you for four you can easily sell." Raif pulled back his duster showing the four holsters.

The shopkeeper looked at them.

"Two dollars more."

Raif said, "Not necessary. I'll trade you even and you don't have to pay me extra."

The man said, "I reckoned you'd pay me two dollars."

Raif shrugged and said, "Your loss and mistake."

He watched the man finish his order. The man gave him a total.

Raif said, "I think you calculated wrong."

The man smiled, "How ya figure?"

Raif rattled off what he'd ordered and the prices calculating the total as he went. At the end the total was fifty cents less than the man had said.

The man said, "Give me the extra fifty cents and I'll trade ya fer the holsters."

Raif nodded agreement. Raif kept a small amount of the money in a button pocket and it was from that he paid the man. He was not about to let anyone know he wore a money belt.

Raif transferred his weapons and ammunition to the new holster belts and shoulder harness. He put them on and adjusted them.

Raif asked before leaving, "Is there a respectable boarding house here?"

"Only place is Miss Ruby's. It's on the street behind here at the north end. Big two story place."

"A place to keep my horses?"

"Miss Ruby has a horse barn."

Raif said, "Thank you," and left the general store with his purchases.

Miss Ruby's place was a large wooden house that was not much to look at on the outside. Raif tied his horses out front and took his rifle and went toward the door. It opened before he got to it.

A fat grey haired woman stood blocking the door, "It's twenty five cents in advance and the same for each horse. No liquor or women allowed."

Raif watched the woman pick a flea off and squash it between her fingernails. He turned and walked away. He would rather sleep in the open again rather than sleep in a flea infested house. He mounted his horse and rode out of town.

That evening he slept propped against a tree in its shadow with a small fire burning nearby. His father's sleeping roll was laid out and Raif had made it look as though someone was asleep there.

Raif woke to the sound of restless horses. He saw the two men approaching the campfire.

Raif stood slowly in the shadows and faced the men his rifle cradled in his arms. When they were twenty feet away from his father's bedroll, he called out, "Only men with evil intent approach a man's camp in the dark without announcement."

One of the men was holding a wicked looking knife and the other pulled a hog leg. Raif shot him and then immediately shot the other man. It was almost sunrise so Raif found the two men's horses and tied their bodies over them. He broke camp and headed out.

Raif rode for five hours to the railway town. It was a
large town with a population of several hundred people.
The town had been built around the railway station and it
was where Raif's father brought their stock to sell. He and
his father were known here.

The town sheriff's office was in the middle of the main
street. Raif rode through town drawing a lot of attention.
The sheriff was waiting on the jail's porch

Raif nodded to the sheriff and dismounted, "Good day,
Sheriff."

The sheriff tipped his hat, "What you got here, Raif."

"Two bushwhackers that came to my camp last night
and tried to kill me."

"Reckon they had a bad night."

Raif said, "The worst."

"Where's your pa?"

"Dead and buried."

The sheriff sighed, "Sorry about that. Ur pa was a
good honest man."

"Yes, sir. Too good to be shot down like a dog and
him unarmed."

The sheriff came off the porch and pulled each man's
head up and looked at them.

"I knows of these two. They's wanted dead or alive.
Ya got reward money coming. Guess ya is lucky two
ways."

Raif asked, "How you figure, Sheriff?"

"They's killed many a good man, so ya's lucky ya
outlived them and ya's lucky there's reward."

Raif nodded.

The sheriff asked, "What brung ya here. Ya's young
to be travelin' alone."

Raif looked at the dead men, "Not too young."

The sheriff smiled, "I reckon not."

"I'm headed to see my kin in Pennsylvania and let
them know about father's passing."

The sheriff said, "Ya got a piece to go."

Raif said, "I'm taking the train."

"Best way to travel if'in you can afford it."

Raif nodded.

The sheriff said, "I can give ya papers to have the reward paid ta ya."

Raif nodded, "Thank you, Sheriff. Is there a place to rest my horses and sleep in a bed?"

"There's a nice hotel at the end of the street. Good eats there. They'll stable ur horses out back."

Raif nodded.

The sheriff said, "If'in ya give me ur particulars, I'll arrange the reward."

Raif nodded agreement and followed the sheriff into the office.

The sheriff asked, "Where's the hands?"

"Headed back to the ranch. Somebody's got to run it."

The sheriff said, "Ya's pretty smart fer a young feller."

Raif said, "Just practical. I'm after all a Gunnerson of the Pennsylvania Gunnersons. My people are merchants and very practical people."

The sheriff said, "Ur not no merchant."

Raif said, "No. Like my father, I'm a rancher."

The sheriff said, "Seems to me you are as much a shootist as a rancher."

Raif didn't think about that statement then, but he would many times afterwards.

When he was finished at the sheriff's office, Raif went to the railway station and bought a ticket to go north. The next train would not arrive until the next afternoon.

Raif booked a room at the local hotel and then went to the sales yard and sold the four horses and three saddles for a goodly sum. He kept his father's saddle. It would be hard to replace as, like the rifle he'd inherited, it was of unusual quality.

Raif bought himself a suit of city clothes to travel in. He also bought a new wide brim high crowned hat. It was tan with a black hat band. Raif thought it was the most handsome hat he'd ever seen. He had the hotel wash his tan duster.

That evening Raif treated himself to a hot bath and then ate a good meal in the fancy hotel dining room. It was after all his fourteenth birthday. His father had taught him to enjoy life's simple pleasures like a hot bath, a good meal, and a good wine. Raif had not, however, acquired a taste for the cigars his father had loved.

When Raif finally got to lie down in the soft bed, he was a little excited about again seeing his uncle James and the rest of the family. He'd been only six when he'd last seen his uncle. Raif had been on seven drives since then and was trail capable beyond his years. Like his father, Raif would be a tall man. Even at his age, he looked several years older than he was.

That night Raif dreamt about the good times he'd had with his father. Raif rose early the next morning. He put on his new clothes and went out for breakfast. He returned at mid-morning after a long walk and packed his cleaned trail clothes and arranged a wagon ride to the train station.

Raif had to change trains twice and he only had one incident. He was sitting against a station wall beside his saddle and rifle waiting for a late train when a stranger approached him. Raif had his hat down over his eyes, but was aware of the man's suspicious approach.

The man was looking around when Raif said, "If you think I'd be easy pickings you'd best think again."

Raif pulled his duster aside revealing the pistols he had in each hand. The man turned on his heel and walked quickly away. Raif put his guns back in their holsters. He pulled his duster closed.

The station at Raif's destination was very busy. Raif got off the train carrying his saddle over one shoulder, his rifle and saddle bags in the other. It seemed to Raif, who was used to being in wide open places, as though the world was converging here. Raif walked through the station into the street. There were several for hire carriages waiting to be employed.

Raif went to plainest and handed the driver a note, "How much to take me there?"

The man gave him a price and Raif nodded, threw his saddle up and climbed in.

The driver asked, "You kin to the Gunnersons?"

Raif just nodded.

"You don' look like those rich folks in spite of your fancy clothes. Too weather worn to be a merchant. That ain't no merchant's hat and merchants don't wear all them guns you got hid under that strange coat."

Raif said, "I'm from the rancher Gunnersons."

"Explains it."

The carriage driver followed Raif's lead and said no more. Finally the carriage arrived at the destination and went up the lane of a large estate. It stopped under a covered entranceway to a grand house. Raif got out and unloaded his gear and said, "Thanks," while paying the driver.

The driver left and Raif went to the door and knocked. A man answered the door, "May I help you, sir?"

"I'm Raif Gunnerson and I'm here to see my Uncle James and Aunt Pauline."

The man seemed taken aback, "Yes, sir. Come in and I'll send for Mr. Gunnerson."

Raif entered the house's large entrance way.

The man said, "I'm Henry, Mr. Gunnerson's house manager. May I take your hat and coat, sir?"

Raif took off his duster and hat, "Yes, please. Thank you."

A woman suddenly appeared behind Henry. Raif handed his belongings to Henry who handed them to the woman. She curtsied and left to put the clothes away.

Henry said, "If you'd care to wait in the parlor, I'll let Mrs. Gunnerson know you are here."

Raif nodded and followed the man. He sat there quietly for several minutes examining the room. Raif thought the house was larger than any reasonable man would want. It had changed little from what he could remember.

A woman came into the room followed by Henry and Raif stood, "Aunt Pauline."

The woman stood looking shocked, "It is you, Raif. You've grown so." She came to Raif and took his hands and looked up into his eyes. "You look much like your father. How is he?"

Raif regretted the way he said it as soon as it was out of his mouth, "Dead."

His aunt said, "Oh, my," and Raif thought she would faint. He held her up and helped her to a chair.

Henry rushed to her side, "Are you alright, Madame?"

"Please bring me a libation, Henry."

Henry hurried away.

Raif said, "I'm sorry, Aunt Pauline. I have been too long among men and I was unthoughtful."

Pauline smiled, "Your father has seen to it that you speak well. Do you cipher and read as well?"

Raif smiled, "Yes, ma'am. Reckoning is a required skill for ranchers, as are contracts, so reading well is necessary."

Pauline nodded and Henry brought her a small glass which she sipped. Raif sat down near his aunt. Henry stood nearby.

Pauline said, "I suppose you came to us for help?"

"No, ma'am. My father has left me a very successful ranch. I just came in person to tell you about my father's death. I thought Uncle James should hear about it in person. I plan to stay only for a short visit."

Pauline said, "How rude of me. Would you like a libation?"

"No thank you, ma'am. I don't take strong spirits but only the occasional glass of wine."

Pauline nodded understanding, "Just like your father. I suppose you disdain those who drink spirits?"

"No ma'am. Most of my hands drink and they are honest hard working men."

Pauline smiled, "In that you are more like your mother, God rest her soul."

Raif said nothing for he had never known his mother. She had died giving birth to him. Aunt Pauline was the closest thing to a mother Raif had known. She had raised Raif with her children until he was six when he went to live with his father.

Pauline said, "You act much older than you are, Raif."

"Yes, ma'am. Our, I mean my way of living requires it." Raif looked down at the floor.

Pauline sipped at her glass, "Yes, I suppose so."

Raif heard the front door open and his Uncle James came rushing into the room. Raif stood and his uncle embraced him heartily. He stood back and said, "You are armed."

"Yes, sir."

To Raif's surprise his uncle said, "A good practice in these times. I suppose you know how to use them."

"Yes, sir."

The men sat down and James motioned to Henry and pointed to Pauline's glass. Henry nodded and hurried away.

James asked, "Is your father here?"

Pauline interjected, "Raif has serious news."

Raif looked his uncle in the eye, "Father is dead. Murdered."

James turned to Pauline, "It may be best my dear if you leave us men to talk."

Pauline nodded agreement, "Yes, dear," and got up and left.

James said, "I'll do what is necessary to help you avenge your father."

Raif said, "It will not be necessary," and proceeded to tell James about his father's murder and his encounter with the Keefer brother and his two men. He told it without any drama and in a very matter of fact way. When he finished his uncle looked at Raif. He asked, "There is more isn't there?"

Raif told his uncle about the two wanted men he had killed and how he had handled the maintaining of his ranch.

James said, "I need to consider all this. We will talk more. Please promise me that under no circumstances will you tell anyone your age. Please promise."

Raif nodded agreement.

"We will invite your Uncle Edward and Aunt Mary as well as your cousins and their husbands to dinner. Henry will show you to your room so you can rest up from your trip."

Raif said, "Yes, uncle."

James looked at Raif and nodded. Henry came and Raif followed him. Raif enjoyed the luxury of a second hot bath in a week. Raif wore the same suit as he only had one, but he had on a clean shirt. He went downstairs and Henry met him. Henry led Raif to the library where his Uncles James and Edward were talking. Raif was not wearing his hip holsters out of respect for his uncles. He could not bring himself to go unarmed so was wearing his shoulder harness with two pistols.

Raif smiled as he entered the room and greeted his uncle, "It is good to see you, Uncle Edward."

Edward stood and embraced Raif. He stood back and said, "Do you always go about armed?"

13

Raif made no apology and said, "Yes, sir, but usually more so than presently. I feel naked without them."

Edward smiled. Raif knew then that he was accepted as a man in spite of his few years.

James said, "Please have a seat, Raif. We are talking about the prospect of war. What do you think, Raif?"

"War is inevitable. Stock prices will go through the roof. Father was planning for war."

Edward asked, "What do you think about slavery."

Raif shrugged, "Ranchers have no use for slaves. It seems to me slavery is inherently wrong though it has made a lot of families wealthy. I can't see fighting a war over it but we will."

Edward asked, "Who do you think will win?"

Raif shrugged, "I agree with my father's view. Both sides will lose, but one side will lose more than the other. It will be a close thing at first. If it goes on for any time, the north may win because its ability to manufacture is greater."

James said, "Then we are all in agreement."

Raif was aware his Uncle Edward was looking him over. Raif did not shy from the stare.

Edward broke the silence unexpectedly, "How did you feel when you killed those men?"

Raif sat back, "It was not a matter of feeling, but necessity. It was instinctive."

James asked, "Has your conscience bothered you?"

Raif looked at James then Edward before saying quietly, "No."

Edward said, "I ask you to come with me tomorrow. I have something to show you."

Raif said, "Of course, Uncle."

Edward said, "Then it's agreed. Your uncle James will lend you a horse and we will leave at sunrise."

Raif just nodded.

James said, "Let us go join the others."

14

Raif enjoyed the family dinner. He had not seen his cousins in some time. It was good to see them. He listened intently to the conversation but didn't say much. He found the husbands of his female cousins very citified. They probably wouldn't last a week on a drive.

After the meal, the men went to the library for cigars and a drink. Raif was the only one who declined a cigar and libation. He did take a glass of nice wine to sip.

Curtis, who was married to Cousin Constance, said, "I suppose you are too young for cigars and liquor."

Raif just shrugged.

Curtis couldn't leave it be, "Probably afraid of your shadow as well. War is coming and you're not the kind we'll need."

Raif smiled and refused to be baited, "We'll see, sir."

Curtis said, "At least you recognize your betters."

Raif looked at his Uncle Edward who was watching the exchange and Raif just shook his head gently. Raif said little and listened to the men. He realized his uncles were the only serious men in the room.

Raif retired early and in the morning he instinctively dressed for the trail and left the house with his saddle, rifle, and gear. He wore his duster as it was a cool March day. James was in the stable when Raif entered.

James said, "Good morning, Raif."

"Uncle."

"You have your choice this morning."

Raif said, "Thank you," and went looking into each of the stalls. There was a lot of good looking horseflesh. Raif did not find what he was looking for at first. He found the right mount standing in the paddock. Raif brought the horse and saddled it.

Raif was waiting when Edward arrived. Edward had a young man with him.

Edward said, "Good morning, Raif. Raif, this is Charles Bleeker. Charles this is my nephew, Raif."

Raif walked over and offered his hand which Charles shook. Raif returned to his horse and mounted. Without another word, the men rode off leaving James behind. They rode for half an hour. They arrived in a broad open field where a group of men were assembled. Edward rode to a hill overlooking the field.

Raif and Charles were on either side of Edward, who said, "These men are being trained to be foragers and scouts. I'd like your thoughts, Raif. You've spent a lot of time on the trail."

Raif watched from the hill for fifteen minutes. He then followed his Uncle on a tour. They came upon Curtis training a group of men to dismount and shoot, then remount, and charge ahead.

After the demonstration, Curtis approached smiling, "Pretty good aren't they."

Edward looked at Raif, "What do you think, Raif?"

"It's all wrong."

Curtis smirked and said sarcastically, "I suppose you could do better."

Raif looked at the targets Curtis's men had fired at. Raif said, "Reset the targets and have your men move to the side."

Curtis looked at Edward who said, "Do it."

Curtis arranged it while Raif moved further away from the targets. Edward and Charles followed him.

Raif took off his duster and asked Charles, "Will you please hold that for me?"

Charles laid it over his saddle in front of him. When the targets were reset, Raif drew his repeating rifle and spurred his horse forward the reins in his mouth guiding the horse with his knees as he repeatedly fired at the targets until his rifle was empty. He quickly slid his rifle into its sheath and drew two pistols and emptied them, holstered them and drew two others and discharged and holstered them and drew his pistols out of his shoulder holsters and emptied them as he was close to the target. He finally drew the single pistol from his back holster as his horse reared and he fired point blank at the targets. He then rode away from the targets at right angles hanging on the side of the horse shielded from the targets. Raif circled around and reloaded his weapons quickly. The charge had taken less than two minutes and he was entirely reloaded within five.

Raif walked his horse to where Edward was sitting.

Edward said, "That was impressive."

Raif said, "Imagine thirty or forty men in such a charge."

Charles handed Raif his duster which Raif laid across his mount in front of his saddle. They rode down to the targets.

The men there snapped to attention. One of the men had been closely examining the targets and was standing next to them.

Edward asked, "What do you think, Boyles?"

"He done as much damage as we all done sir. I'd rather be on his side," Boyles said with a grin.

Curtis was standing there red faced and said, "It's different when men will be firing at you."

Raif looked at Curtis and said, "It is. You are more focused because your life depends on your aim. Scaring them with firepower throws an ordinary man's aim off, but accuracy kills."

Edward said, "There aren't many of those repeating rifles around and they're expensive."

Raif said, "True Uncle, but foraging and scouting should be mostly close up fighting and the firepower of pistols on the move would be large. Pistols are plentiful. The men should be able to shoot rifle or pistol from the saddle."

Edward asked, "Why did you pick that mount."

"Speed is useful, but in a fight endurance is everything."

Edward looked at Raif, "We need to talk more, nephew."

Raif said, "Yes, uncle."

Edward said, "Give me a minute gentlemen."

Raif and Charles rode off toward the hilltop. Edward leaned over in the saddle and said to Curtis out of hearing of others, "I wouldn't push Raif too far, Curtis. He is a natural born shootist like his father. Those who crossed him found out the hard way. He's pulled bounty on some very bad men. Fair warning."

Curtis glanced in Raif's direction and said, "Yes, sir."

Edward rode up the hill and said, "Let's head home."

On the ride back Edward asked, "What do have planned this afternoon, Raif?"

"I thought to explore the town Uncle. May I have the loan of this horse?"

"Of course."

Raif looked at his uncle, "Are there many preparing for war?"

"Yes and no one will be safe until the issue is resolved. The slave states are talking secession. Those states think the Europeans will intervene because of cotton. I think that is short sighted. The federal government does not want war, but I think the issue will be forced."

In the afternoon, Raif rode through town. He noticed that hardly any of the men went armed. If war came that would change. Raif thought things were different here.

Raif stopped by the sale barn where a horse auction was taking place. There was a stout black stallion in the paddock and Raif stopped to watch him. He could tell the horse was half wild. He watched the men who were trying to handle the horse and it was obvious they did not know how to deal with the high spirited horse.

Raif went to where the bidding was taking place. When the bidding for the big black stallion was called for, there were no takers. Raif bid what he thought was a ridiculous price and the auctioneer immediately declared the horse sold. Raif saw the men laughing and pointing. They thought he'd been taken. A half hour later as Raif gently led the stallion away, the men had changed their minds. At his uncles, Raif turned the stallion loose in the paddock with instructions to the help to leave the horse alone.

Raif continued his exploration of the town. He found a gun shop and found a matched set of pistols he wanted. After much negotiation, he traded in two of his older pistols and paid the difference.

That evening only Raif and his two uncles and aunts were at dinner. Aunt Pauline, as always, was the consummate hostess. Halfway through dinner, she shocked Raif with a casual remark she made to Edward's wife Aunt Mary.

"I think we need to start thinking about a wife for Raif."

Mary nodded agreement and said with a broad smile, "Yes, with war coming a man needs someone to keep the home fires burning."

Raif said, "I appreciate the thought Aunt Pauline, but I'm not in the market for a city wife. You forget I'm a rancher and when the time comes I'll need a wife fit for a rancher."

Mary said, "Your mother was a city born woman and she was a rancher's wife. Besides, your father wasn't always a rancher."

Edward said, "This is woman's business, Raif, and best left to them."

Raif said, "I was brought up to think a man should defend himself when attacked on any front."

Mary smiled broadly and Pauline did as well.

After dinner, the three men went to the library. Raif knew his uncles were up to something. Once the cigars were lit and the uncles had a drink Edward started the conversation.

"The men here have no knowledge of how to fight the way James and I have in mind. We are financing the composition of a unit for raiding, scouting, and foraging."

Raif said nothing, but made note of the order of the stated goals.

James said, "You know how to fight the way we will need this unit to. We want you to take a commission as an officer and train the men. We will provide the money to equip and mount the troop."

Raif said, "I have a ranch to run."

Edward said, "You have a man who knows ranching and we have people who know business. We will send a businessman to help your lead hand and keep an eye on finances. We'll also send a couple of men to guard your home. These men are a little long in the tooth for the army, but capable of fighting off a few raiders or rustlers."

James said, "We could use you, Raif. We have something special in mind."

Raif said, "I do not want to be cannon fodder and I'm too young anyway."

Edward said, "Not for the army, but theoretically to be an officer and that's what we plan. We will lie about your age. You are seventeen. You will not be the only young captain going to war and you are more capable that most of the men that will be going off to fight."

Raif asked, "Who will command?"

"Charles. He is a graduate of the Virginia Military Institute. He, like some other graduates, is against the slavers. He will be accepted by the regular military officers."

Raif asked, "Why should I take sides? My ranch is in the territories."

Edward said, "Raif, everyone is going to have to choose sides, even the territories. Our name is already associated with the north and the outcome of the war will put you on our side unless you fight for the slave states."

Raif said, "I'm not about to fight for slavery."

James said, "There you have it."

Raif said, "I need time to think about it."

Edward said, "Of course, nephew."

The conversation turned to more pleasant things and Raif told his uncles about his purchase of the stallion. The men found the story amusing.

CHAPTER 2 – THE END OF WAR

The sergeant came into the tent, "Major, me and Bill found somethin' you'd ought ta see hurry up quick."

The major knew his men and if Cracker said it was important, it was. The major followed the sergeant who had already saddled the major's horse. The three men rode out together. It was only about a mile and a half outside camp. Cracker led the way down into a heavily treed gully. At the bottom was a ruined wagon and the skeletons of horses and two men. The wagon had obviously fallen down the ravine and rolled over.

The three men dismounted. The major went to the wagon and saw the boxes. They had Confederate markings.

The major ordered, "Bill, find something to pry these boxes open with."

Bill said, "Yes, sir," and hurried away.

Cracker watched his major inspect the boxes. Cracker had followed this man through most of the war and respected him as a leader. He had kept most of his men alive by cunning, negotiating with more senior officers, and practical soldiering. His men had followed him willingly because they trusted him. He was not a man to be reckless with the lives of others and his men knew their chances with him were better than those of most men in the war. They had also sent a lot of valuable items home.

Bill came with a hardwood spoke from one of the wheels. The major took it and easily pried one of the boxes open. It was Confederate currency wrapped in oil cloth.

The major looked at Cracker, "It's worthless. Let's look in the others. Get some more levers and pry them all open."

They had opened all the boxes but one and found only worthless Confederate money. The last box was different. The major pried it open and found four bags. He grabbed one of the large ones and opened it and smiled. He showed the contents to his companions. It was full of silver coin.

Cracker exclaimed, "Damn if we didn't hit the mother lode."

The major smiled and handed the bag to Cracker, "You fellows each take a larger bag and I'll take the two smaller. Bill, fetch my saddle bags."

Bill said, "Yes, sir," and hurried off.

Bill came back with three sets of saddle bags and he and Cracker put the money bags in their own saddle bags.

The major said, "Now listen."

The two men listened intently for they knew the major well and when he spoke like this there was danger. They knew they needed to listen carefully.

"The war's over and we are going to be discharged. Don't let anybody know you have all this or your life will end quickly and badly. When you get back, deposit the money in different banks or find some hides. Don't spend large sums at one time. Spend only a little at a time. Understand?"

Cracker asked, "How much can we spend or put in one place?"

"No more than a man who is tight with his money and in a foraging unit could save in four years of service in the army."

Bill said, "That's a right good sum if a man was rightly a tightwad."

Cracker added, "Which we ain't, but can pretend like."

Bill said, "I s'pose so."

Cracker looked at Bill, "Remember what the major told ya. Bein' a rich dead man don't do ya no good. Sides, we done already sent stuff home."

The major said, "Right, but this isn't like the house silverware I helped you send back so be careful. Stay close to me until we get back home. Don't even look at your bag. Keep it tucked away out of sight."

Bill and Cracker hurried to their horses. The major put the two small bags into his saddle bags and in the process he noticed there was an irregularity in the small box's floor. He quickly put his finger in and pried up a false bottom. He found Union paper currency. He quickly stuffed it into his saddlebags and went to his horse.

The three men returned to camp. The major's unit broke camp and went to the nearby rail station. They travelled home by train with their horses in cattle cars. They arrived back in Pennsylvania without fanfare. When they claimed their horses and assembled, they were all given their discharges. Many men came to say goodbye to the major. Their losses had been less and their accomplishments more than most units. The last three to leave were Cracker, Bill, and the major. They shook hands and headed out.

When Raif arrived at his uncle's house, Henry welcomed him and Aunt Pauline came outside to greet him before he was dismounted. He hugged his Aunt although he had his saddlebags and rifle in one hand.

Pauline said, "It's so good to have you back. You stink. Henry, have a bath drawn for Raif and clean clothes set out."

Henry smiled, "Yes, ma'am."

Pauline said, "Your uncle will be glad to see you."

Raif smiled.

The bath felt good and after shaving, Raif dressed in some of his uncle's clothes that had been left out for him. Raif had become heavier as he had matured and put on muscle. His uncle's clothes looked good on him except they were more form fitting on him and he could not do the neck button up. He decided the clothes he'd been wearing were not fit to wear again. He had them thrown out.

For the first time since he'd found them, Raif took the money bags out of his saddle bags. He had been a good example to Cracker and Bill and resisted the temptation until now. As he opened the first one, he was taken by surprise. The smaller bags contained gold coins not silver ones. Raif sat for some time considering what to do until there was a knock at the door.

Raif put the bags back into his saddlebag and said, "Come."

Henry opened the door, "Your uncle sends his regards. He would like you to meet him at the Merchant's Club at four. A family dinner is planned here at seven."

Raif nodded, "Thank you, Henry."

Raif took out his pocket watch and looked at the time. He had about three hours before he was to meet his uncle. He gathered his saddle bag and went to town on one of his uncle's horses. His horse needed a rest. At the largest bank, he put a portion of the gold coins in his safe deposit box and deposited a large amount of the paper currency in his account. The ranch profits had been deposited there. Raif then opened accounts at smaller banks and made deposits. He also rented another safe deposit box.

Raif arrived at the Merchant's Club a little before four. He put his horse into the care of a club stable hand and entered the club carrying his saddlebags.

The stiff little man at the door looked him up and down. It was obvious the man thought the battered cavalry hat and long hair did not suit a gentlemen. He said, "May I help you sir? This is a member's only club."

"I'm here to meet my uncles."

The man asked, "What is your name, sir, and who are your uncles?"

"I'm Major Gunnerson and my uncles are James and Edward Gunnerson."

The man changed his attitude and smiling said, "Of course, sir," and motioned to a young man who rushed over.

"Please show Major Gunnerson to the library."

The young man said, "Right this way, sir."

Raif took his hat off and followed the man to a room. The man left closing the door behind Raif as he entered. Uncles James and Edward put down their cigars and rose from their chairs. Raif went to them and they all embraced.

Edward spoke first, "You look good, Raif. It seems you have grown stronger in war." He motioned for Raif to take a seat.

Raif said, "War does change a man."

James said, "That is all in the past. Now we must plan for the future of the family. Would you like a drink?"

Raif said, "Please. It has been some time since I've had a good wine."

James rang a bell on the table next to him and a waiter rushed in and took his order.

Edward said, "Your ranch has done well. It seems your father left you quite an inheritance and the cattle business is very profitable. The losses of the stock confiscated during the war was but a temporary setback."

Raif nodded agreement. He had been exchanging letters with Ross throughout the war and knew exactly what was happening at the ranch.

James asked, "What are your plans now?"

There was a knock on the door and James said, "Come."

A waiter brought Raif a glass of wine and left.

Raif sipped the wine and said, "Very nice." He paused and said, "I don't know what I'm going to do. I guess I should go back to being a rancher. It's what I know. On the other hand, the war changed me."

Edward said, "Good. It would be a waste for you to be a rancher. We have a proposal."

Raif looked at his uncle, "What is it?"

James said, "We have learned a lot from your ranch operation. We think there is a fortune to made in cattle moving east on the transcontinental railway system when it is finished. The movement of cattle to eastern markets will be extremely profitable. We are invested in railroad shares of a spur line as part of the long term strategy. The railroad acquired rights to build a town at one of the stops and it's in a location that will service other investments we plan to make related to the cattle market."

Edward added, "There is one problem you can help us with. We have identified what we think is a key future area. The problem is there is no rule of law which is necessary for business to prosper."

Raif nodded understanding, "I see."

James added, "We have enough influence to have a sheriff appointed for the county and of course he can appoint deputies. Part of the agreement is, as the major land owners in the county, we will pay for the deputies."

Edward said, "We just need a leader to recruit, organize, and command."

Raif waited, "What would be in it for the leader?"

James said, "If the leader was a man of substance, he could get in on the ground floor as an investment partner in the railroad. We also have large tracts we purchased which are ideal for ranching. We are prepared to deed you a third of the land for a third of what we paid. We almost stole it. The territorial council wants it settled."

Edward said, "Your work as a forager was very profitable for both the army and your men. The confiscated items you sent to us for safe keeping are by themselves worth a fortune. Then there are the accumulated profits from the ranch. You could be a partner in our investments and lead the local lawmen. We'll continue to have our man help you with the management of your father's ranch as we have in the past."

James added, "Your greatest contribution would be establishing and keeping the peace in our area of influence. I would think you could delegate most of the duties."

Raif asked, "How long will I need to serve?"

Edward added, "At least until the territory achieves statehood. That may take a decade, but fortunes will be made in the meantime."

Raif said, "Let me think about it."

Edward said, "Of course."

Raif asked, "How are the cousins doing?"

James said, "They are well. It's time for our daughters to provide us with lots of grandchildren."

Raif asked, "How is Curtis's widow, Cousin Marjorie doing?"

James said, "She has remarried. Her husband is a banker some years her senior. He's a serious man."

Raif said, "Good. I didn't think Curtis would last long once the fighting started. Arrogance can lead to carelessness in war. I never liked the man."

James nodded, "I think Marjorie is better off with her new husband."

Edward smiled, "We'll see you at dinner and you will meet him."

Raif nodded, rose, shook hands with his uncles, and left.

Edward looked at James, "Do you think he'll do it?"

James said, "I think so. I hope so. I can't think of anyone as capable who we could trust as much as Raif. He's probably going to decide what he must have and wants, then he'll negotiate with us. I could hardly believe the reports about his exploits at first. He seemed to be very adept at leveraging money into survival and negotiating to get what he wanted from senior officers."

Edward nodded and said, "His talents as a fighter and negotiator could make us all much richer."

Raif left the club and walked down the street examining the stores as he went. He found a barber and had his hair cut. He then went to a gentlemen's clothier and purchased new shirts, suspenders and two suits before returning to his uncle's home.

Raif was sitting in the parlor reading a newspaper when Cousin Marjorie came sweeping into the room, "Cousin Raif, it is so good to see you." Raif rose and Marjorie gave him a hug. She added, "Let me introduce you to my husband Connor. Connor, this is my cousin Raif."

Connor offered his hand and Raif shook it, "I'm pleased to meet you, Connor."

Connor smiled. He was not what Raif expected. He was a fit looking man who Raif guessed was in his mid-thirties. He was tanned and had the look of an outdoorsman and not a banker.

Marjorie took her husband's arm and said to him, "Let's sit down, dear."

They took seats and Marjorie said, "Raif, you and Connor have something in common."

Raif looked at his cousin, "What is that, Marjorie?"

"The army of course. Connor was in the 83rd Regiment, Pennsylvania Volunteer Infantry. He was a paymaster or some such."

Raif smiled at Connor who returned the smile. Cousin Marjorie was ill informed and probably intentionally to ease her worry having already lost one husband to the war. One just had to look at Connor to know he'd been in the field and the 83rd had been in most of the eastern engagements.

Marjorie said, "Cousin Raif was some kind of store man. He was responsible for provisioning troops."

Connor broke into a broad smile and Raif thought his cousin was very naïve, but perhaps that was best for an eastern wife.

Raif asked, "Do you come from a large family, Connor?"

"Yes. I have three, had three brothers, and a sister. Two of my brothers died in the war. Perhaps you could come and meet some of my family?"

Raif said, "I'd like that."

Marjorie changed the subject, "Are you staying in Pennsylvania, Raif?"

Raif said, "There's not much call for ranchers here, Marjorie."

"But surely there are other things you can do."

Raif smiled, "I suppose so."

Marjorie said, "But surely you'll stay for a while."

"Of course."

Uncle Edward and Aunt Mary entered the room.

Edward said, "Raif, I see you've met Connor."

"Yes, Uncle."

Raif got up and hugged his aunt, "Good evening, Aunt Mary."

James and Pauline came in before Raif got seated and everyone exchanged greetings. They were followed by cousins Constance and Helen and their husbands Gary and Dennis.

Raif took a seat and listened to the family chatter. He caught Edward looking at him and smiled. Edward nodded. The family had a formal, but pleasant dinner. Raif talked a little with Gary and Dennis. Raif determined quickly that he had little in common with them. Raif thought they seemed like sound middle class city men. Gary was a lawyer and Dennis was a shopkeeper. There was something about Gary that Raif didn't like.

After dinner, the men retreated to the library to smoke and drink. There was some discussion of local business matters but nothing that much interested Raif. After a half hour, Gary and Dennis took their leave and went to rejoin their wives.

Connor got up and closed the library door.

James sighed and said, "They are nice men and good husbands to my daughters but they are not serious men."

Raif knew his uncle meant he did not expect they would do anything of economic or social significance.

Edward said, "They will raise your grandchildren close to home."

James said, "There is that."

Raif asked, "Where is Cousin Paul?"

Edward said, "He's away overseas on business. I don't expect him back soon."

James looked at Connor, "How is your father doing?"

Connor shook his head, "Not well. I fear he is not long for this world."

Edward looked at Raif, "His father was almost forty when Connor was born. His father was ambitious and did not marry until late in life."

Raif nodded in acknowledgment.

James asked, "Will you change how the bank does business?"

Connor looked up, "No need. What we do works and my father trained me well."

Edward nodded agreement and simply said, "Good."

Connor said, "Marjorie will be telling the women she is with child."

James said, "Congratulations."

Edward added, "Yes and may there be more."

Connor nodded, "It is my hope as well."

Edward looked at Raif, "You will need heirs as well."

Raif said, "My life is a harsh one."

James said, "Then you will need an unusual woman, but you must leave heirs otherwise what's it all about."

Edward added, "There is no future in consorting with whores, Raif."

Raif said, "I know nothing of whores."

Raif had never paid for the company of a woman though he had been with three. Two of them had been widows.

Edward asked, "Is that so?"

Raif said, "Always seemed an ugly business to me."

James said, "I suppose with your looks there were sufficient volunteers."

Connor rescued Raif by changing the subject, "You must come to our country place for the weekend, Raif."

Raif said, "I would like that."

Connor said, "We'll leave tomorrow afternoon about three."

Raif noticed Edward and James exchanging looks. He wondered what that was about. He supposed he'd find out.

In the morning, Raif purchased some new country clothes. He also had his riding boots shined and his cavalry hat cleaned. When Connor and his entourage arrived Raif had his horse saddled and his gear ready.

Marjorie waved as their carriage came up the lane. It was followed by a horse drawn wagon with two people who Raif assumed were house servants.

Connor did not get out of the carriage but called out, "Come along."

Raif mounted up and rode up beside the carriage asking, "How far is it?"

Connor smiled, "About an hour's carriage ride."

Marjorie said with a broad smile, "Connor won't let me ride a horse now that I'm with child. He insisted on the carriage. He's so sweet to me."

Raif said, "It's because he loves you, Marjorie."

Marjorie had a satisfied look on her face, "I suppose," she said as she put her arm through Connor's.

Marjorie told Raif all about their home and also the country place as they rode. She talked about the family and brought Raif up to date on what had been happening in the cousin's lives. The ride seemed to pass quickly.

The summer home was on a hill overlooking the river. Raif could feel the cool breeze and imagined it would flow through the house in summer, cooling it. The house was surrounded by mature trees that would shade it from the summer sun. It was a beautiful spot.

The little party stopped at the back of the house. A man came out of the house and took charge of the carriage as Connor helped Marjorie down. Raif dismounted and led his horse to the stable. Connor soon joined him.

Connor said, "Always the cavalryman."

Raif said as he unsaddled the horse, "Where I come from a man's horse is as vital to survival as his rifle."

Raif rested his saddle on a rail and led his horse into a stall where he removed the bridle. He then fetched a bucket of oats.

A man came and said, "I will brush your horse, sir."

Raif said, "I'm Raif, what is your name?"

"Jeremy, sir."

Raif said, "Jeremy, you best wait until he finishes his feed. He's touchy when he's eating. He's reassured if you keep your open hand on him."

The man smiled, "Yes, sir."

Raif took his rifle and saddlebags and headed with Connor toward the house. At the door a maid came, "May I take your hat and coat, sir?"

Raif said, "Thank you," and took off his duster and hat. Raif thought the young woman was stunning, a real beauty. He asked, "What is your name?"

"Miriam, sir."

Raif said, "Thank you, Miriam."

The woman smiled and walked away with his hat and coat.

Connor led Raif through the house to the river facing hall and said, "Your room is up the stairs, third room on the right. I'll wait for you on the veranda."

Raif nodded and went upstairs. He put his rifle in a corner and took off his waist holsters. He unpacked his saddlebags and laid out his shaving kit, clean shirts, and extra pants before heading back downstairs. In the hall he met a very attractive young woman.

Raif said, "Hello, I'm Raif."

"I'm Kate."

Raif motioned her ahead, "After you, Kate."

Kate smiled, "Thank you."

Raif followed her downstairs and out onto the veranda.

Marjorie said, "Hi, Kate. Have you met my cousin Raif?"

Kate took a seat, "Yes."

Raif stood looking at the river and said to no one in particular, "It's beautiful here."

The maid came out onto the veranda, "May I get you something, Miss Kate?"

Kate said, "Lemonade please."

The woman asked Raif, "You, sir?"

"The same please, Miriam."

Miriam smiled, "Yes, sir."

Kate asked, "How do you know Miriam?"

Raif looked at Kate and smiled, "She was kind enough to take my duster and hat so I introduced myself."

Kate turned her head slightly looking at Raif out of the corner of her eye as though with a different perspective she would see something different. Ralf looked directly at Kate which seemed to cause her some discomfort. Raif thought Kate was very attractive and noticed she was not wearing a wedding ring which he found curious given her obvious womanly qualities. These were evident even in a plain country dress.

Kate had obviously noticed his looking for a ring and laid her hand flat on the chair's arm.

Raif stifled a light laugh which caused Kate to purse her lips. Raif found this quite amusing and laughed lightly.

Marjorie was watching the silent exchange.

Kate said to Raif, "Do I amuse you, sir."

Raif nodded yes and said, "Oh, yes indeed, Kate. Please call me Raif."

Kate said, "I do not know you well enough, sir."

"Oh yes, you do. I expect Marjorie has told you all about me. I know how you women conspire."

Marjorie laughed, but Kate ignored her. Raif went and sat down beside Kate.

Marjorie said, "I think this will be an interesting weekend."

Connor came onto the veranda, "What's interesting?"

Marjorie smiled, "Kate and Raif. How's your father?"

Connor said, "He is asleep. The nurse said he had a good day. He even spent some time outside here in his wheelchair reading."

Kate sighed and looked away. Raif could tell her father's illness was weighing on her.

A woman Raif guessed would be in her early fifties came onto the veranda and Connor said, "Mother, this is Raif Gunnerson, Marjorie's cousin."

Raif stood and bowed his head slightly, "I'm pleased to meet you, ma'am."

The woman said, "Please call me Ellen."

Raif smiled, "Yes, Ellen. Thank you."

Ellen took a seat and addressed Raif, "I hear you, like my son, fought for the Union."

"Yes, ma'am."

"I hear you were a store man."

Raif did not want to mislead this woman so said, "Like your son was a paymaster."

Ellen laughed and Marjorie looked a little confused. Ellen quickly changed the subject.

"I hear you are a rancher."

Raif said, "Yes, ma'am, since before the war."

"What are your mother and father like?"

"My mother died having me and father was murdered."

Ellen asked, "Were the villains brought to justice?"

Raif looked at Ellen, "They paid with their lives."

Ellen studied Raif and he figured she knew what he meant.

Raif volunteered, "My lead hand has been running the ranch while I was in the army. He was helped by a businessman my uncles arranged."

Ellen asked, "How big is your ranch?"

Raif said, "Just a little over twenty thousand acres."

Ellen looked at Raif, "That's a lot of land so I suppose you have a big herd."

Raif nodded, "Yes, ma'am."

Ellen looked at Kate, "Take note dear that Raif is not only handsome, but a man of means."

Raif looked at Kate who was blushing and he shrugged. It seemed to make her more comfortable.

Ellen got up, "Please walk with me, Raif."

Raif got up and Ellen took his arm and led him off the veranda and down the path toward the river.

When they were out of hearing by the others, Ellen said, "I am a straight forward woman, Raif. Always have been. We've been looking for a match for Kate. Problem is she is a strong willed woman."

She looked at Raif and smiled.

Ralf nodded.

"She intimidates the young men around here because she's bright and strong. She has a mind of her own. She's like that half wild stallion you ride. You don't break its spirit because that's its strength, so you partner with it. I imagine it's not your first half wild horse."

Raif said, "I see you are well informed."

"I was like Kate, so ended up marrying a mature man who could accept me as I am. I have had a happy marriage. The problem is I will live out my last years alone because of our age difference. I don't want that for Kate."

Raif said, "I understand but life has no guarantees. I lead a dangerous life."

"Yes but there is a difference between a chance and a near certainty."

Raif said, "That's logical."

They reached the river bank and stood looking at the water.

After a moment Raif said, "I'm interested, but I don't know your daughter yet or she me. You may not want your daughter to consider marriage to a man like me if you knew the dangerous path I follow. I also do not know if Kate is suited."

Ellen said, "My husband and your uncles are very close both personally and as business partners in the railroad. My husband told me our family stands to gain if you are successful. The danger I fear for Kate is the breaking of her spirit, which is worse than death itself."

Raif shrugged and to avoid a commitment said, "Then shall we see?"

Ellen looked at Raif, "Yes, let's do."

They walked back up the hill to the summer house without further conversation. When they got back to the veranda, only Kate was still sitting there. Raif went and sat by her and her mother went inside.

Kate asked, "What did you and mother talk about?"

Raif smiled, "She was matchmaking."

Kate sighed.

Raif said, "She seeks your best interests."

Kate said, "I won't be forced into a match."

"Of course not. That would result in hell for both parties."

Kate seemed stunned, "You think I'm that bad?"

"As yet, I have no way of knowing."

Kate smiled, "You are certainly different from the other men who have tried to court me. Different good or different bad, it's too soon to tell."

It was Raif's turn to sigh, "You are certainly a challenge."

Kate laughed, "Am I not worth the bother."

Raif smiled, "That's yet to be seen."

Kate said, "That's not very gentlemanly."

"I never said that I am a gentleman."

Kate said, "You walked mother down to the river. The least you can do for me is the same."

Raif got up and offered his arm which Kate took. They started down the path.

Kate asked, "Do you always go about armed."

"Where I come from it is wise. I am usually better armed."

Kate paused then asked, "Do women carry and use guns out west?"

Raif said, "If they are wise."

"Really?"

Raif nodded, "It is after all the frontier. The worst thing that can happen is to need a weapon and not have one handy."

Kate said, "Tell me what it's like out west."

Raif did and Kate had a lot of questions. Raif found her questions very revealing. They told him something of her character and interests. Some of what she revealed was not good.

As they were coming back to the veranda Kate said, "It sounds as if life out west is challenging."

"Challenging and rewarding for the strong."

Kate asked, "Is it always dangerous?"

"Not always, but it has it times. It is those one must be prepared for. It is not an easy life."

They had come back up the veranda steps when Miriam came out, "The evening meal is about to be served."

Raif opened the door for Kate and they went in. It was a pleasant and informal meal. Ellen arranged for Raif and Kate to sit next to each other near the center of the table. There they could talk easily with each other and most of the family. There was a lot of small talk which Raif enjoyed listening to.

After dinner, the family sat on the veranda talking. About nine o'clock, Raif excused himself and turned it. He slept well and rose early. The sun was coming up when he went out onto the veranda. A man in a wheelchair was sitting there looking at the sunrise.

Raif said, "Good morning, sir."

The man turned and looked at Raif, "It is indeed."

Raif took a seat next to the man and said, "I'm Raif Gunnerson," and held out his hand which the man shook more firmly than Raif had expected.

"Peter Patterson."

Raif nodded in acknowledgement.

Peter said, "They all think I'm dying."

"We all are. We just don't know when."

Peter laughed and coughed up phlegm.

The men sat there without saying anything for a few minutes. Peter broke the silence, "I think I might just fool them. I'd like to live to see Kate bring grandchildren."

Raif continued looking at the sunrise and replied, "Indeed that would be worth living to see."

Peter said, "The pneumonia is diminishing. I can tell. I think I'll live a little while longer yet."

Raif said, "Good. Your family is very worried about you."

Peter said, "I am a selfish man. I didn't care about the burden my age would eventually put on Ellen. I love her so I just had to have her."

Raif said, "You are a lucky man. It is a burden she willingly accepts."

Peter looked at Raif, "I suppose it is."

"It is. Ellen is that kind of woman. She obviously loves and is devoted to you." Raif paused, "And the children."

"They are hardly children anymore."

"No matter how old they are, they will always be Ellen's children. It's been my observation it's like that with mothers."

Peter smiled, "You notice a lot for such a young man."

"I hope so, sir."

"Has my wife been trying to be matchmaker?"

Raif smiled, "Yes, sir."

"Peter, please, Raif."

"Thank you, Peter."

Peter coughed up some more phlegm. His coughing was loud this time and the nurse came outside to help him. When he finished, she went back inside.

Peter said, "Your uncles tell me your father was the maverick of the family."

Raif thought for a moment before replying, "He was no maverick. He just realized he wasn't the merchant type. I don't think it was rebellion as much as finding his place in the world. He found it. He was a good rancher, a good father, and he taught me what I needed to know."

Peter asked, "What did he teach you?"

"How to be a man. He also taught me to read, cipher, speak well, be a rancher, ride, and shoot."

Peter just nodded and looked at Raif's shoulder holster harness. The men sat there quietly for a few minutes before Ellen came out.

She leaned over and kissed Peter on the cheek and said, "Good morning, dear. You are looking much better."

Peter smiled, "I think the pneumonia is lifting. I may live to torment you a little longer."

Ellen laughed and said, "Delightful."

Miriam brought tea out and Raif said, "Good morning, Miriam."

"Good morning, sir," and poured the hot drink into cups.

When Miriam left, Ellen asked, "Do you always socialize with the hired help?"

Raif said, "The only difference between me and them is an accident of birth or circumstances."

Ellen made a "humph" sound which Raif assumed indicated her displeasure with what he'd said. Raif realized that as much as he liked Ellen, she was very conscious of social class. Some would say she was a snob. He would. Raif still liked her. He never expected his friends to be perfect or else he would have none and would never be anyone's. He knew he was far from perfect.

He looked at Peter who smiled. Peter seemed to know what Raif was thinking.

Connor came out, "Good morning, father, mother." Connor kissed his mother on the cheek then took a seat saying, "You look very well this morning, father."

"Thank you, son. I think I'm on the mend."

Connor said, "Good," then turned to Raif, "Good morning, Raif."

"Good morning, Connor."

Miriam came out and asked Ellen, "Should I prepare breakfast ma'am?"

Ellen asked, "Anyone?"

The men declined so Ellen said, "Perhaps later," and Miriam left.

Raif got up, "If you'll excuse me, I think I will go see how my trusty steed is doing and perhaps exercise him."

Raif got up and went to the stable. Raif went into the stall and petted his horse and spoke to him. He got a rope and led him out of the barn and walked the horse along a path that ran parallel to the river. It wound around and down to the river. At the river Raif found a quiet inlet that was obviously suitable for swimming. He tied his horse and stripped off his clothes and went into the water.

Raif enjoyed swimming and stayed in the water for some time. It was just cool enough to be refreshing. He did not however stray far from his guns and clothes that were on a nearby rock. After fifteen minutes, Raif came out of the water and air dried then put on his clothes and headed back to the house. He turned his mount out in the paddock. He was leaning against the fence post when a female voice said.

"He's a beautiful horse. What's his name?"

Raif turned to see Miriam and said, "Night."

Miriam smiled, "Because he's as dark as?"

"Yes."

Miriam came to the fence and looked at the horse, "My brother tells me he's half wild and needs the right handling."

"Your brother?"

Miriam said, "Jeremy is my brother."

"I didn't know."

"He's good with horses."

Raif said, "Must be. Night hasn't maimed or killed him."

Miriam laughed.

A stern voice came from behind Raif, "Miriam, you're not paid to socialize with our guests."

Miriam turned around and said, "Yes, miss," and scurried away.

CHAPTER 3 – TROUBLE AND DOUBLE

Raif had turned his head and was watching Kate. He realized she was angry. It dawned on him that Kate had a mean jealous streak. It was not an endearing trait. He watched as Kate suddenly got control of her temper.

Kate said sweetly, "We are having tea on the veranda and mother sent me for you."

Raif nodded and walked toward the house. Kate came and took his arm though he had not offered it. All of the family except Peter was on the veranda having tea.

Raif and Kate sat down and joined the others.

Connor said, "Mother and I are going fowl hunting. Would you like to go Raif?"

Raif asked, "Are you going, Kate?"

Ellen said, "Kate can't abide guns." There was a pause because Ellen realized she had put her foot in it.

Kate said, "I'll walk along with you mother. I might learn something."

Raif said, "I think I will stay."

Kate suddenly had a smirk on her face. Raif wondered what that was all about, but said nothing. Kate stopped the smirk as soon as she realized Raif was watching her.

After tea the little party set off. Raif remained on the veranda. After ten minutes, Peter was wheeled out by his nurse.

Peter said, "I am getting better. This is the first time I've felt like being out twice in one day."

Raif said, "That is good."

"Indeed."

Peter turned to his nurse and said, "Please have Miriam bring me some of her herbal tea."

The nurse said, "I'm sorry, sir, but Miriam has been discharged. Your wife has sent for a replacement from the big house, but it will be a while before she gets here. I will make you some tea if you'd like."

Peter shook his head no.

Raif looked at Peter, "Please excuse me, Peter. I have some business I must attend to. I will return."

Peter said, "Of course."

Raif went to the barn and saddled Night. He caught up to Miriam and Jeremy about three miles down the road. They were walking toward town. He rode up beside them and dismounted. Jeremy took up a position between Miriam and Raif. Raif thought that was a brave thing to do. Raif was not only the bigger man, but he was armed and Jeremy wasn't. Raif noticed Miriam was angry.

Raif said, "Jeremy, I'm afraid an innocent exchange between your sister and I led to her discharge."

Jeremy asked, "Are you trying to apologize?"

Raif said firmly, "No. I have nothing to apologize for and neither does your sister. Aside from that, I would like to offer you employment."

Jeremy paused then said, "Is this because," Jeremy paused again obviously to choose his words carefully, "you are fond of my sister?"

Raif smiled, "If your sister was as homely as a wart hog, which she is not, my sense of fair play and your industrious and pleasant natures would lead me to make the same offer. You are the first groom that Night has tolerated. That means you are good with horses. Where I come from that is a talent much in demand."

Jeremy said, "But you admit to being attracted to Miriam."

Raif sighed, "What man in his right mind wouldn't be. You have my promise though that I will act honorably."

Jeremy said with some disdain, "A gentleman's promise."

Raif smiled, "No, a warrior's promise."

Jeremy smiled, "Much better. What is the pay?"

Raif smiled and the two men negotiated. When they finished, Jeremy spit in his hand to shake with Raif, but before they could Miriam intervened.

"Just a minute!"

The two men looked at her.

Miriam looked at her brother, "What right do you have to commit me. I am a free woman here and not bound by the customs of the old country."

Jeremy stood open mouthed.

Raif started laughing.

Miriam shouted, "You think this is funny!"

Raif couldn't stop laughing and just vigorously shook his head yes.

Miriam threw her hands up in the air. She and Jeremy waited for Raif to stop laughing. When he did, Miriam spoke, "I will not work for that Kate woman again. If you intend to wed her, I will not accept."

Raif said, "I will not be wed to her."

"I have one other condition."

Raif asked, "What is it?"

"If you are going to take us west you first learn us to shoot and give us weapons. If I find a suitable husband, you agree to release me from employment."

Raif said, "Agreed."

He shook hands with both Miriam and Jeremy. He then said, "Go to my uncle's house. You know where that is?"

Jeremy said, "Yes."

"Ask for Henry. Tell him I have hired you and ask him to find housing for you until I return."

Jeremy nodded, "Yes, sir."

Raif gave Jeremy and Miriam some money, "This is for your upkeep until I return. I don't expect to be away but another day or so."

Miriam smiled, curtsied and said, "Yes, sir."

Raif smiled, mounted Night and rode back to the Patterson's summer place. He arrived before the hunting party had returned. He unsaddled Night, fed him, and put him in the paddock. He went out on the veranda to find Peter asleep in his chair and the nurse reading. Raif nodded to her and took a chair. He started planning in his head and drifted off.

He woke to a female voice, "I see you lay-abouts are enjoying yourselves."

Raif looked up and said, "Hello, Ellen."

Peter was now awake, "Did you have a good hunt, dear?"

"Yes. We shot three grouse. We'll have them for dinner once they age a bit."

Peter smiled and looked at Kate, "Kate dear, would you make me some tea?"

Kate said, "Let the help do it."

Peter smiled, "It seems we don't have any at the moment."

Kate turned a deep red, but got up and went into the house. Peter turned knowingly to Raif and smiled. This was not lost on Ellen. Connor and Ellen told Raif and Peter about their hunt as Peter sipped his tea.

After a while, Kate turned to Raif, "Would you like to go for a walk, Raif."

Raif did not want to be rude so said without much enthusiasm, "Of course."

He stood up and Kate took his arm. She led him to the path leading to the river that he had walked in the morning. Along the way Kate had to sidestep one of Night's droppings.

"Nasty things, horses."

Raif said nothing. Kate chattered as they walked and Raif dutifully listened. At the river Kate said, "This is a great place to swim. Shall we?"

She ran to the water's edge and started stripping off her clothes. Raif turned and marched back to the house. Kate took the silence behind her as admiration and imagined Raif was watching her intently. She knew she had the kind of body men lusted after. Her mother had suggested this ploy. After Kate had gotten naked, she walked slowly into the water and went in up to her shoulders. When she turned around, much to her dismay, Raif was not there.

Raif arrived back at the house and sat on the other side of Peter away from Ellen.

Ellen asked, "Where is Kate?"

Raif said nonchalantly, "She decided to bathe and it would be ungentlemanly of me to watch, so I came back."

Peter started laughing and then coughing. His nurse came to help him, but all he needed was to get rid of the phlegm.

Raif saw that Ellen was sitting almost pouting and said, "I think it best if I leave for my uncle's this evening."

Ellen said gruffly, "I suppose it would be best."

Raif turned to Peter, "Peter, it has been the utmost pleasure to meet you, sir. I hope, when you are better, we can share a meal together at the Merchant's Club."

Peter smiled, "I would like that."

Raif rose and shook Peter's hand. Ellen sighed.

Raif said, "Ellen, I do not expect my friends to be perfect and I hope we two imperfect people can be friends. I'm sure your match making skills will eventually show fruition."

Peter again started laughing and coughing.

Ellen could not help smiling. She simply said, "Friends," and offered her hand which Raif took.

When Raif had left, Peter turned to his wife, "He is an old soul and wise beyond his years. You must not hold that against him."

Ellen smiled, "I suppose."

Peter added, "My dear, you should accept our daughter Kate is not a strong willed woman as you were at that age. She is more a willful girl. You sought to build a life, but she seeks to marry a life. Your matchmaking will go better if you accept this."

Ellen just nodded agreement.

Raif went and packed, saddled Night, and headed for town. He did not plan to see Kate again. He took his time enjoying the ride. He arrived just before dark and Henry met him at the door. A man came and led Night away.

Henry said, "Good evening, Major. Your new employees are housed in the loft above the stable."

Raif said, "Thank you, Henry."

A servant came and took Raif's things.

Henry said, "Both your uncles are in the library."

Raif nodded and went to the library and knocked on the door and waited for the invitation.

A voice responded to the knock, "Come."

Raif went in, "Good evening, uncles."

Edward said, "We did not expect you so soon."

Raif said, "The matchmaking attempt failed."

James choked on the drink that was partially down.

Edward asked, "Would you like a drink of wine."

"Please, uncle."

A bell was rung and wine was brought for Raif.

James asked, "What do you think of the Pattersons?"

"I like them. Peter and Connor are serious men, Ellen is a force to be reckoned with, and Kate is a beautiful girl."

Edward asked, "Girl?"

Raif smiled, "A willful and spoiled beautiful girl. She needs a citified man who will cater to her whims and be content to have her on his arm for other men to admire."

James laughed, "I think he has assessed the situation correctly."

Raif said, "If I am to marry, it will be to a hard-working tough woman up to the trials of western life."

Edward asked, "Have you given consideration to our proposal?"

Raif said, "I have," and the negotiations began.

Early in the morning Raif went to the stables as the sun was rising. He found Jeremy mucking out Night's stall.

Raif said, "Good morning, Jeremy."

"Good morning, sir. Night is in the paddock."

Raif went to the paddock and found Miriam brushing Night and talking to him.

"You horses are better listeners than men folk. You just accept what is said. You understand tone even if not the words. Tone is important."

Raif interjected, "Indeed."

Miriam looked up and said, "Good morning, sir."

"Good morning, Miriam. I see you have made a friend."

"It was easy once he reckoned I had no desire to dominate him."

Raif smiled, "Now you know Night's deepest secret. He rebels against domination."

Miriam said, "Most of us are like that."

"So true. When you finish what you're doing, come fetch me. I have to talk to you and your brother."

"Yes, sir."

Raif went and got coffee and came out back and sat on the grass his back against a tree. He'd been there about ten minutes when Miriam and Jeremy came to him. Raif motioned them to take a seat on the grass.

"Can you both ride a horse?"

Jeremy said, "Yes, sir."

Raif looked at Miriam and asked, "Sidesaddle?"

"Gracious no. That ain't no practical riding. I ride like a man."

Raif said, "My uncle is lending me two horses and saddles. Choose two of each. I'll meet you here in half an hour."

Miriam and Jeremy got up and rushed off to make preparations. When Raif came down to saddle Night, he found him ready to mount. Raif figured he might get spoiled if he wasn't careful.

Raif said, "We are going on a shopping trip."

They mounted up. Raif noticed Miriam was showing quite a bit of leg when she was mounted. He liked what he saw, but knew it would be a temptation they did not need to flaunt. He dismounted.

Miriam asked, "What's wrong?"

Raif said, "Miriam, please dismount."

She did.

Raif decided to be direct, "You are a beautiful woman and in the saddle with what you have on, too much leg is showing. It is an invitation to trouble where I come from, perhaps here also. Until we get you suitable riding clothes, we'll take a carriage."

Raif was surprised that Miriam was smiling. Jeremy was too. They all unsaddled their horses, hooked up a carriage and got in. Miriam sat between the two men. Raif felt his pulse race a bit being this close to her.

Jeremy asked, "What are we shopping for?"

Raif smiled, "Necessities."

Miriam looked at her brother, "He's goin' to torment us and not tell until we're there."

Jeremy said, "I suppose them that pays makes the rules."

Raif smiled, "It's not nice for the two of you to try to gang up on me."

The three of them talked as they rode. Jeremy had a lot of questions about the horses used in the west. It didn't seem long until they arrived at their destination, a clothing shop. Raif got out and held out his hand to help Miriam down, though she didn't really need a helping hand.

It was like static electricity passed between them when Miriam took his hand. They both felt it and looked at each other, but said nothing. Jeremy was tying the team up and had not noticed.

They went inside the general store and bought Jeremy clothes suitable for western living. They then went shopping for Miriam. When Raif asked for what he wanted the woman clerk gave him a strange look. Raif drew a picture. The garment looked like a skirt but really was a skirt divided and made into half pants. This allowed a woman to look as though she was wearing a skirt, but be modest on a horse.

The clerk said, "We have no such thing, sir. I ain't never seen such either."

Miriam was looking over Raif's shoulder and said, "I've never seen such, but it is practical for a woman rider."

Raif smiled at Miriam, "I suppose we could have some made like that." He turned to the clerk, "Can you recommend a seamstress or leather worker?"

Raif bought riding boots for Miriam and Jeremy and new blouses for Miriam. Raif also bought her a loose fitting pair of men's pants for her to wear under her dress for riding. That would work for the time being. The merchant did not have suitable hats.

They went to the seamstress who agreed to make what Raif described. She took Miriam in back to measure her. They then went to a leather worker and arranged to have lined full leather versions made that would fit Miriam.

When they got in the carriage, Raif realized he was getting hungry and said, "Let's find a restaurant where we can have lunch."

Miriam said, "I've never eaten in a restaurant."

Jeremy added, "Me neither."

Raif said, "Well, there's a first time for everything."

They found a nice place and went in to eat taking their parcels and belongings with them. It was a pleasant lunch which Miriam and Jeremy seemed to enjoy immensely.

When they had finished eating, Miriam said, "So that's what it's like on the other side of things."

Raif smiled. He paid the bill and left a tip.

Back in the carriage Miriam asked, "Why did you leave money at the table?"

"Was the server pleasant and did he do a good job?"

Miriam said, "He did."

"It's sort of a reward and my showing appreciation for a job well done."

Miriam said, "I've been in the wrong business."

Jeremy and Raif smiled.

Their next stop was at a gunsmith's shop. Raif got out and again held out his hand to help Miriam down. The result was the same as the first time. Jeremy tied the horses to the rail and the three of them went in.

Raif was wearing all his weapons and carrying his rifle when he went in. The gunsmith took one look at Raif and came to meet them.

"Hello, folks. I'm Jed Miller, proprietor and gunsmith."

Raif said, "I'm Raif Gunnerson and these are my friends Miriam and Jeremy."

Miriam and Jeremy exchanged looks.

Jed asked, "Are you Major Gunnerson of Gunnerson's Gunners?"

Raif said, "The same."

Jed said, "I'm truly honored to meet you, Major. How can I be of service?"

Raif smiled, "Maybe, just maybe, you can sell us some weapons. We are looking for practical weapons and not the fancy things city folk like."

The man looked at Raif's rifle, "I suppose you've had that Jennings repeater for a while?"

Raif nodded.

Jed said, "I got four of the newer Henry's. They's expensive, but I think you'd like one. Quality weapon."

Raif said, "I've only seen one. I had the pleasure to fire a few rounds from it."

Jed went and fetched a rifle and brought it to Raif. He explained about the rifle and Raif examined it.

"How much?"

Jed told him and Raif nodded then said, "I need side arms." Jed went behind the display case and brought out some new high quality pistols, "These are the newest and best."

Raif examined them intently then said, "How much?"

The man told him.

Raif said, "May I look at one?"

The man said, "Of course."

The man gave it to Raif who turned to Miriam, "Take it and hold it out like this," and demonstrated.

Miriam did. She held it there for some time before her arm started to quiver. Raif then took the revolver from her.

"Good. You are strong enough."

Raif took one of his pistols out and asked, "Have you got a holster that will fit Miriam and hold two pistols this size? One straight down and one cross draw."

Jed handed Miriam a belt but her waist was too small for even the smallest belt Jed had in stock.

Jed offered, "I can have a new one made to specification."

Raif again asked how much.

Raif finally asked, "How much for all four of the Henry's, four of the new pistols, two holsters for my friend Jeremy, and the special holster for Miriam. The stock of one of the Henry's will have to be cut down to fit Miriam. You take my Jennings in trade."

Jed looked stunned, but started figuring. Raif already knew the original total he'd been quoted. Jed quoted a price for everything that was discounted two percent and Raif knew the trade in value for his rifle was too low. The negotiations started. The men finally came to agreement on price for everything and delivery of the special items.

Raif said, "Write it up and fit Miriam, but be a gentleman. I'll also need a large quantity of ammunition."

While Jed was gathering the ammunition Raif noticed it and asked, "How much for that coach gun?"

Jed told him and Raif said, "I'll take that as well and I'll need shells for it."

Raif and Jeremy had to make two trips to the carriage with their purchases. Once they were loaded up and started the ride back, Miriam spoke.

"I didn't know guns were so expensive."

Raif said, "Quality usually costs. You'll think it's worth it if you ever have to use them. You'll need to pack in the morning. We are going to my uncle's summer place for a few days."

Jeremy asked, "May I ask what are we going to do?"

Raif said, "I'm going to teach you to strip weapons, clean weapons, and shoot, first on foot and then on horse."

Miriam said, "That will be a challenge."

Early the next morning, the trio loaded their gear, weapons, ammunition, provisions, and three saddles in the carriage. They tied three riding horses behind the carriage and set out. They arrived well before lunch.

Raif took out a key to the house.

"Uncle James said there are three guest rooms on the third floor. Unload our gear and get the horses stabled. I'm going to find a place set up a practice range."

When Raif returned, he found Miriam and Jeremy sitting under a tree drinking lemonade.

Miriam jumped up, "I'll get another."

Raif said, "Why don't you bring bread and cheese and we'll eat before we practice."

Miriam nodded and rushed off.

Raif sat beside Jeremy. They sat resting and did not say anything. Miriam brought Raif a glass of lemonade and was carrying food in a cloth. She took out cheese and bread.

Raif pulled out his knife out of its sheath and it occurred to him. He said, "You'll both need one of these. They come in handy."

He cut the bread and cheese splitting it between them.

Miriam took a bite of the cheese and said, "This is the best I ever had."

Raif took a bite and said, "It is good."

The three of them sat eating the cheese and bread.

Jeremy said, "I never ate with an employer before."

Raif said, "Things are different out west. If I have a hired hand who is good after a while you come to depend on each other and get familiar. Sometimes friendships develop."

Miriam asked, "What do your employees out west call you?"

"The ranch hands call me boss."

Miriam nodded.

That afternoon, Raif found out that Jeremy was good with a rifle and Miriam was better than he expected a woman to be. She did not flinch when the weapon went off. He expected she would improve considerably when she got the fitted stock and a little practice in.

Raif was first to fire a pistol. He took two of the new ones and fired alternating hands. He found the new pistols improved his already high level skills. When he finished, he found Miriam and Jeremy staring at him.

Jeremy said, "I see why they say you're a natural shootist."

Raif said, "Who says that."

Miriam said, "Everyone who's heard the stories about Major Gunnerson and his Gunners."

Jeremy said, "About everyone in these parts."

Raif said, "Now it's your turn."

Miriam took naturally to the pistol and was hitting half the targets after the first fifty or so rounds. Jeremy was not so good. Beyond fifteen feet, he had trouble hitting anything. They expended a couple of hundred rounds each before Raif called it a day. They went back to the house and Raif instructed them how to strip and clean the weapons.

Raif said as they were assembling the weapons, "Jeremy you are already good with the rifle. With a little practice, you'll become very deadly. We'll get your accuracy up a little and work on your speed. Miriam, you will be good with a rifle, but I think you will be a deadly pistolero."

Miriam said, "What's that?"

Raif smiled, "A pistol gun fighter."

Miriam laughed and looked at Raif. He had a serious look on his face. She stopped laughing.

"You are serious?" she asked.

Raif just nodded.

That evening they fried up steaks and beans. They ate it with bread. Raif explained this was typical ranch food. Jeremy and Miriam expressed their appreciation for ranch food.

For two days they practiced shooting. Jeremy became fast and deadly with the Henry rifle and Miriam gave a respectable account of herself with it. Miriam's talent was with the pistol. She became deadly with it and though Jeremy improved somewhat he would never be good. It was because of this that on day three Raif handed Jeremy the coach gun.

Jeremy said, "What's this?"

Raif said, "Your close in weapon. The pistol will be your last resort."

Jeremy put two shells in, aimed the weapon, and let go. Four targets were shredded. Jeremy smiled.

Raif took two shells and showed Jeremy how to hold them so he could fire two and quickly reload two more. Jeremy loved the coach gun.

Raif said, "We'll get you a bandolier for it."

Jeremy looked confused.

Raif said, "It's a shell belt that goes over your shoulder so you have shells handy."

Jeremy smiled.

On day four, the trio went to town. They picked up Miriam's special riding clothes and the special holsters. While Miriam was trying her new holsters, Raif saw something unusual and motioned quietly to Jed.

He pointed and asked quietly, "How much?"

Jed told him and Raif said almost in a whisper, "Wrap it and slip it to me."

Jed nodded and took it away.

Jeremy called out, "Here's a bandolier."

Raif went and looked at it. He said, "This one's poor quality," and explained why. He showed Jeremy what to look for. They bought one that was used, but would last.

They bought more ammunition and left. They ate lunch for the second time in a restaurant. After lunch, they went to a bank and Raif said, "Wait here while I do some business."

Raif was not gone long and came back and said, "Ok, one more stop."

They went to Raif's uncles' warehouse and again Jeremy and Miriam stood guard at the carriage while Raif went inside. He was not gone long. Afterward, they headed back to the country.

They arrived back dusty and tired. They put the carriage in the barn and turned the horses out.

Jeremy suggested, "Let's go down to the river."

The three of them went walking. The river was quiet and Jeremy without warning stripped off and went into the water. Raif was shocked when Miriam did also. Raif stood gawking as she ran into the water. They both called out to Raif.

Raif shrugged and stripped. They could both see his state and Jeremy called out, "I think he likes your look, sister."

At a distance Raif could tell Miriam was blushing then realized he was too. He ran and dove in. Raif enjoyed the water, but was careful to keep some distance between him and the object of his lust. The cold water also helped. It didn't take long and they were cold and got out and dressed without a word.

Miriam said as they started walking back to the house, "I'm not brazen. It's just me and my family never had any shyness about being naked. We were so comfortable with you, I guess we forgot you weren't family."

Raif just nodded.

Miriam said, "I really ain't' brazen. I ain't never been with a man. I was kissed once when I was twelve. Jeremy always protected me."

Raif asked, "How old are you?"

"Sixteen."

Raif said, "I thought you were older."

"I didn't think I looked old."

"Not old, just older. Perhaps nineteen or twenty. You seem too mature for a sixteen year old."

Miriam smiled, "I guess that's a compliment."

"It is."

Jeremy was a little ahead of them. He slowed down so they could catch up. When they did, Miriam scooted ahead.

Jeremy said, "You lusting after my sister?"

Raif said, "Not to worry. I'm no thief. I won't take what I don't have claim to."

Jeremy smiled, "Good. You are too good a fighter and I'd have to kill you sly like. My conscience would bother me a little about that."

Raif looked at Jeremy and smiled, "But just a little."

Jeremy laughed, "Ya. Then we'd be unemployed again."

That evening Raif taught Jeremy and Miriam how to make tortilla bread and stuff it with good stuff. They said they really liked it. After washing up, they all went outside to drink coffee.

Raif said, "I have a little present for you Miriam," and handed her a little package.

She opened it and said, "It's a little gun. How's it work?"

Raif showed her, "It breaks open like this and two shells go in here. It's only useful up close, very close."

Miriam said, "Strange holster."

Raif said, "It's a woman's holster. It goes on your thigh inside your skirt hidden away. Some man tries to steal what he has no right to, you use it to blow off his privates or stop his heart."

Miriam looked aghast. She paused for a moment and had a thoughtful look. She then said, "Very practical. Thank you, boss."

Raif smiled and said, "You're welcome."

Jeremy looked at his sister, "By that you can tell his intentions are honorable."

Miriam looked at Raif and teased, "I'd better test fire it first to make sure it works."

Raif smiled broadly, "I'm learning you good."

The next morning they went to an open field with the horses. They started practicing shooting from horseback. First stationary, then at the gallop. Raif was pleased at the start.

When they stopped for lunch, Miriam said, "I think I will really like western life. Do women get to go on cattle drives with their husbands?"

Raif said, "Those that can sometimes do. There's no law against it, though some hands are superstitious and think bringing women along is bad luck."

Miriam just nodded.

In the afternoon, they practiced some more then put the horses up and cleaned the weapons. Miriam cooked the evening meal which consisted of beans, ham, eggs, and fresh bread. Raif thought it was very good. It was the type of food he had at home.

After the meal, they were sitting on the porch drinking coffee. Raif took something out of his pocket and handed it to Jeremy who said, "What's this?"

"Your pay. It's Friday."

Jeremy said, "You didn't deduct for lodging and food."

Raif said, "Where I come from wages is wages and hands get chow and a place to sleep. Usually it's in the bunkhouse."

Miriam asked, "What's a bunkhouse."

"Sort of a barracks."

Miriam was horrified, "I'm going to have to share space with a bunch of men?"

Raif shook his head no, "Women folk usually stay in the main house in their own room or in a small cabin. In your case it will be a small one room cabin."

Miriam said, "Thank goodness. By the way, where's my pay?"

Raif handed her coins.

Miriam said, "I could get used to this. I never before had so much money. I'm rich."

Raif asked, "Didn't the Patterson's pay you?"

Jeremy said, "Yes, but there weren't much left over after deduction for lodging, board, and clothing."

Raif said, "Seems unfair to me. Not much better than slavery."

Miriam said, "Oh, we could leave anytime."

Raif said, "And go where? Do what? Do you think the Pattersons would give you a reference?"

Raif could tell Miriam was studying on what he'd said. She was very quiet.

After a bit she said, "I'm going to turn in now," and went inside.

Jeremy said, "She is young. She doesn't fully understand the way of the world. I was worried one of them rich young no goods would get her aside. You know?"

Raif said, "I understand. Innocence lost cannot be regained."

"Yes. As you said boss, a man should not take what he has no claim to."

Raif said, "Let's turn in."

It turned out Raif could not sleep. Images of Miriam naked tormented him. He finally gave up trying to sleep and got up. He put on his pants and his shoulder holsters. Bare chested and bare footed went out on the veranda. He was surprised to find Miriam sitting there in night gown. She had a pistol in her lap.

Raif sat down, "You couldn't sleep either."

She sighed, "No. My mind was too busy."

Raif said, "Me too."

Miriam said, "I guess I never thought about how easy my life could be broken. What you fretting about?"

"You. Thoughts of you are tormenting me."

Miriam said, "I'm sorry. I truly am. I'm really not brazen."

Raif said, "I believe you. You know, you going out west as my employee is not going to work."

"I know." Miriam sniffled a little.

Raif said, "I guess then you'll either have to wed me or I'll have to find you other employment."

Miriam said, "You are too far above my station."

Raif said, "Out west that kind of thing doesn't matter. It's a person's character that counts."

Miriam sighed, "I must admit I been wondering what it would be like married to you, to share your life, your bed, to have your children."

Raif said, "Are you willing?"

"Yes."

Raif said, "You'd best go back to bed. I don't trust myself with you. We'll talk with Jeremy in the morning."

Miriam got up and leaned over and kissed Raif then rushed off. Raif found his pulse was racing.

Raif went to bed and slept until the sun was coming up. He rose and went out to the well and pumped some water. He heard Jeremy working in the barn as he shaved, but he didn't see him. Raif went back inside and put on his shirt. He went out on the veranda. Shortly he smelled bacon cooking.

Jeremy came out and said, "Good morning, boss."

"Good morning, Jeremy. Please have a seat."

Jeremy asked, "What's up."

Raif asked, "Do you have other family?"

Jeremy shook his head no. "Ma and Pa died a few years back of fever. Me and sis went into service to the Pattersons'."

Raif said, "So it's just you and Miriam."

"Yes."

"Then you are man of the family?"

Jeremy said, "I suppose."

"What would you think of Miriam and me being wed?"

Jeremy said, "Only trouble comes from marrying too far above your station. I don't want that kind of trouble for my sister."

Raif smiled, "Where I come from people don't care about such. Your character and what you do is what counts. You would still work for me. It's not unusual for family to work for family."

"If what you say is for sure, I don't have no fault with it."

Raif said with a smile, "Good. Miriam wouldn't have been happy if I had to shoot her brother to marry her."

Jeremy smiled and said, "It seems my sister is carrying a torch for you."

Miriam called out, "You two get washed up. Breakfast is about ready."

The men did as asked and came to the table. They all sat down and Raif said, "This I could get used to, but I'd bloat up like a city banker."

Miriam smiled.

Raif said, "Miriam, your brother has no objections to our being wed."

Miriam said trying not to laugh, "Good. You won't have to shoot him after all."

Jeremy choked on the food he was swallowing.

Raif said, "Before it's all agreed, you need to know what I have planned. I'm going west to organize lawmen to bring peace and the law to a place that has none. The sheriff appointment is so we can tame the area. We will be going far afield. It will be dangerous for me and maybe for you. I will start another ranch and maybe some other businesses with my uncles. It could make us very rich if I pull it off."

Jeremy said, "I thought you were rich."

"There's rich and then there's very rich. The rolling in money kind of rich. For me though, it's also doing something worth doing. It's leaving a family and a legacy."

Miriam said, "I recently found out how fragile my life is so I'm willing to be the pistolero that watches her husband's back."

Jeremy asked, "What would I do?"

"The deputies will need horses and horses are the lifeblood of a cattle ranch. We'll need to keep a good reserve of good horses and keep the horses healthy and well trained."

Jeremy said, "I can do that."

Raif said, "Then it's settled."

He pulled a ring out of his pocket and slid it across the table, "That, my dear Miriam, is your engagement ring."

Miriam put it on her finger and said, "It's gorgeous."

Raif knew its history. It had once belonged to the wife of a plantation owner for whom it had been specially made.

Miriam got up and came around the table, sat in Raif's lap, and kissed him passionately.

She was flushed. She said, "I will make you a good wife. That's a promise."

Raif smiled and said, "I expect so. Now let's finish eating and get back to practice. Time is short. This afternoon, I need to go talk to my uncles."

Miriam asked, "Are you going to tell them about our wedding plans?"

"Yes, but I mostly expect it will be business. They had some things they have to do on their end. I will get my aunt's advice about the wedding."

Jeremy asked, "Then we will stay here?"

"Yes, until I return."

They practiced some more that morning. Jeremy and Miriam promised to continue practice while Raif was away. That afternoon he rode back to town and arrived just before he expected Uncle James would return from work.

Henry greeted him, "Good afternoon, sir."

Raif inquired, "Is my Aunt here, Henry."

"Yes, sir. I'll see if she's available."

Raif went and sat in the parlor. When Pauline came into the room Raif stood and embraced her.

Pauline said, "How are things at the summer house? I heard rumors you have been making quite a racket."

Raif said, "Shooting practice. The west is a dangerous place."

"So your uncle has told me."

Raif said, "It is other kind of danger I need your help with. You have been like a mother to me and I need your help."

Pauline smiled broadly and asked, "What is it, my dear?"

Raif waited for Pauline to sit and then he sat back down.

"Well as you know, in the west there is no class distinction. Out there character and achievement define a person. A woman who would be a suitable wife here would not last long out there. There a man needs an independent, hardworking, healthy, and strong woman. In short, a working partner. That is not a role women here would find acceptable."

Pauline said, "I think I see. I suppose you have found such a woman and she is not your social peer, but the type of woman you need."

"Exactly. To complicate matters she and her brother worked for the Pattersons."

Pauline said, "Oh, dear. Ellen will be beside herself. She had thought to marry you to Kate."

Raif said, "I know. If I married Kate, I could not go west. She would not last a month out there and she'd come crying home to her family."

Pauline said, "I expect so. From what I know, I would not fit in there."

Raif said, "It is as true, Pauline, as is the fact buffalo do not live in Pennsylvania."

Pauline smiled, "Interesting comparison."

Raif shrugged, "I need your advice on how to manage the wedding so there is no problem with its recognition if something should happen to me."

Pauline said, "You expect heirs."

"Of course. Is not a family legacy what we are working for?"

"Yes, it is. Let me consider this and with your permission I'll talk with Mary."

"Please do."

Pauline smiled, "Leave it to us, dear. We'll figure it out. Will I like your future bride?"

Raif said, "Maybe and maybe not."

Pauline smiled.

Raif added, "What's important is, I do. She is a woman I will be able to rely on. She will work at being a good ranch wife."

Pauline rang a bell and Henry came into the room. She said, "Henry have someone take a message to Mary that I need to meet with her soonest."

"Yes, ma'am."

Raif said to his aunt, "Thank you."

Pauline knew it was sincere.

CHAPTER 4 – PREPARATIONS

Raif arrived back at the summer house Monday at mid-morning. He could hear shooting and went directly to the practice range. He watched from a distance and noted the improvements. His students were doing well.

Miriam saw him first and came galloping over. She pulled up alongside of Raif and leaned over and kissed him. They both smiled.

Jeremy came riding up, "Welcome back, boss."

"Hi, Jeremy. Let's go to the house. We have a lot to talk about."

They rode the short distance to the house and took care of the horses then went inside. Raif put his bags down and took out a small wrapped box.

Raif went into the parlor and took a seat on the sofa and Miriam sat beside him. Raif motioned to a chair and Jeremy took a seat.

Raif looked at Miriam, "We are going to have a society wedding and all my family will be present as well as a lot of distinguished guests. Jeremy will give you away."

Miriam only got, "But," out before Raif held up his hand.

"It is necessary. If something happens to me, I want no challenge to the validity of your or our children's' claims as heirs. Do you understand?"

Miriam nodded, "I understand."

"Good. My aunts are going to take you in hand and tutor you on what is to be done. This once we must fit in. After we leave here, we can be ourselves again."

Jeremy chuckled.

"We will be married in two weeks' time. As my fiancée, you will stay with my Aunt Pauline and Uncle James. Jeremy, it will be necessary for you and me to stay with my Aunt Mary and Uncle Edward. My Aunt Pauline advises it would be unseemly for me to stay in the same house as Miriam. Jeremy, as part of the wedding party you will stay in the room next to mine. Everyone will know you are in my employ, but they will be told you are my station manager. No one will know what that means nor will they likely ask. If they do you say you manage the livestock operations."

Jeremy asked, "Will I have to wear a suit?"

"Every day for the next two weeks. Clothes will be delivered in the morning. Then we will escort Miriam to town."

Raif handed the box to Miriam. "You will wear some combination of these at all times. They are symbols of your new status."

Miriam opened the solid silver box and sucked in a deep breath. She took the pieces out one by one and examined them.

She looked at Raif, "They are beautiful. I suppose they are worth hundreds of dollars."

Raif smiled, "No thousands."

"I can't wear these."

"You must. Think about me when I wear all my side arms. It is intimidating to most men. It's a signal I mean business. This display of wealth will have the same effect on women."

Miriam said, "Wearing these, I intend to go about properly armed."

Raif smiled, "Consider them my wedding gift to you."

Miriam said, "At least with two guns."

She leaned over and kissed Raif, "Thank you, future husband."

Jeremy said jokingly, "What gift did you bring me?"

Raif said, "It's the medium parcel next to my bags. The larger one is for Miriam."

Jeremy went and fetched the parcels and was undoing his when he came back into the room. He sat down and finished unwrapping the paper.

"What the?" Jeremy recognized what it was, "Well doesn't that beat all?"

Miriam asked, "What is it?"

Raif answered, "A broad shoulder sling for the coach gun. He can hide the gun under a duster with that."

Jeremy said, "Thank you, boss."

Miriam said, "Hand me mine brother."

He did and she unwrapped it. She looked at it and quickly figured it out. She slipped it over her head.

Raif said, "It's called a poncho. It's water proof and will cover the fact you are armed. If the time comes you just slip off the hook and sling the side back over your shoulder leaving your holster clear. It will keep the rain and dust off. In winter you wear a long wool or fur jacket under it and it will keep you warm and dry."

Miriam stood up. It hung down covering her to mid-thigh. She flipped it up easily and then moved her arms as though holding a rifle. She smiled, "I think I like this better than the jewelry. Now mind, I'm keeping that too."

The next day went as planned. The clothes were brought by two of Aunt Pauline's servants. Raif did the introductions. The woman who brought the clothes for Miriam helped her get dressed and pack her things. When all the belongings were packed in the carriages, they left for town. Raif and Jeremy rode on horseback and one horse was tied to the back of one of the two carriages.

When they arrived at Pauline's, Miriam's things were brought to her room, but Miriam held on to her jewelry box. Raif and Jeremy went in with Miriam.

Henry met them at the door, "Good afternoon Major, Miss Cole, Mr. Cole. You are expected."

Raif said, "Thank you, Henry."

Miriam had watched these people enough she thought she could imitate their actions to a large extent. Pauline got up and came to greet them, "Raif, my dear," she said as she hugged her nephew.

Raif said, "Aunt Pauline, may I present my fiancée, Miriam Cole, and her brother, Jeremy Cole."

Pauline offered her hand to Miriam who took it and shook it lightly, "Raif has spoken very lovingly about you. I am so pleased to have the opportunity to finally meet you."

Pauline smiled. She looked at Jeremy who nodded slightly once and slowly. Pauline said, "Please everyone, have a seat. Would you like some wine?"

Miriam knew it was too early for wine, "No, thank you, but some tea would be nice."

Pauline smiled, "Of course" and looked at a servant who hurried off.

Raif said, "Thank you for helping us."

Pauline looked at Miriam and said, "This will be easier than I thought. You have been observant."

Miriam said, "Yes, I have, thank you. I'm sure you can teach me much and I will be forever grateful."

Pauline laughed, "You are so pretty and such a charmer."

Miriam said, "And it will be our little secret that I can shoot very well and ride like a man."

Pauline looked at Raif who just nodded.

Pauline said, "The family has much to gain by your success. I will do everything I can to help you and Raif establish your branch of the family and its legacy."

Miriam said, "And I will do everything in my power to be a good wife and partner to Raif and to do honor to your family."

Pauline raised an eyebrow and looked at Raif then back at Miriam.

"You are very young, my dear."

Miriam nodded, "I have many child bearing years ahead of me."

Pauline smiled broadly and said, "Good answer. I think you and I will get along famously."

They drank tea and made small talk for a bit before Pauline looked at Miriam, "I'm sure, Miriam that you and your brother would like to freshen up and get settled."

Miriam knew it was more than a suggestion and said, "Yes, please."

Pauline said, "Henry, please have Miriam shown to her room and see Mr. Cole gets refreshments."

"Yes, Mrs. Gunnerson."

When they had been left alone, Pauline said, "She is very pretty and very bright, Raif."

Raif nodded agreement.

"Yet, so young."

Raif smiled, "Aunt Pauline, have you forgotten my true age?"

Pauline looked at her nephew, "Yes, I have as a matter of fact. I see your point."

Raif asked, "What do you have planned?"

"I will spend a lot of time with her regarding social matters and all things ladylike."

Pauline heard a scream. She looked at Raif. One of Pauline's new girls came running down the stairs and out the door. Miriam came gliding calmly down the stairs.

Pauline looked at Miriam, "I assume there was some unpleasantness."

Miriam came into the room and calmly said, "I think you may wish to consider replacing one of your servant girls. I caught her rummaging through my things."

Pauline asked, "Rummaging or unpacking?"

Miriam smiled, "I know the difference better than most."

Pauline just nodded and looked at Henry, "Please take care of that unpleasantness."

Henry smiled, "Yes, Mrs. Gunnerson."

When Henry left, Pauline motioned for Miriam to sit which she did after Pauline was seated.

Pauline asked, "What did you do to frighten that poor girl so."

Miriam said, "I simply put a pistol to her head and told her if she didn't put my jewelry back, leave, and not come back, I'd blow her brains out."

Pauline said, "I suppose she thought you meant it."

Miriam said, "I did."

Pauline couldn't help herself and laughed lightly, "Oh, my dear, you are so delightful. A delicate balance of beauty and deadly resolve."

Miriam smiled, "Thank you for the compliment."

Pauline looked at Raif and said, "Wise choice. You may leave her in my capable hands. But only if she promises not to shoot my servants."

Miriam nodded, "I promise as long as they stay out of my things."

Pauline smiled, "By the way, we will be having a social gathering here Friday evening to introduce your fiancée. You had best leave us, nephew, so we can get started."

Ralf got up and kissed Miriam on the cheek, "I will see you later, my dear."

Miriam said, "Yes, love."

When Raif left, Pauline asked, "Bad?"

"Very. The very thought of him torments my nights."

Pauline smiled, "You are a very lucky woman. We have much to do, so let us start."

Raif found Jeremy waiting outside for him with the carriage. Night was tied behind. Raif climbed into the carriage, "It's off to Uncle Edward's."

The week passed quickly as Raif had a lot to do and much to arrange. Jeremy helped him arrange the buying and crating of goods to be shipped by rail. On Tuesday and Thursday the two of them stopped by to have lunch with Pauline, Mary, and Miriam. It seemed Miriam was fitting in nicely.

When Friday evening rolled around, Raif and Jeremy showed up formally dressed. Raif was used to such wear, but Jeremy was struggling not to show his discomfort. They arrived in the carriage and climbed down. A servant took it away. They entered the house to a formal greeting and went to the ballroom. Many guests were already milling around.

A quartet started playing and a young woman approached Raif, "Good evening, sir."

Raif said, "Good evening, Miss."

The young lady said, "Rayborne."

Raif repeated, "Miss Rayborne, I am Raif Gunnerson. May I present Mr. Jeremy Cole?"

The young woman offered her hand, "Mr. Cole."

Jeremy shook the hand lightly and said, "Miss Rayborne."

Miss Rayborne turned back to Raif, "So you are the famous Major Gunnerson, the man about to marry the guest of honor."

Raif just dipped his head slightly.

Miss Rayborne asked Jeremy, "Are you some war hero as well sir?"

"No miss. I work for the Major."

Raif said, "He is my stock manager and body guard."

Miss Rayborne smiled, "You must be a dangerous man Mr. Cole if you are body guard for the major."

Jeremy said, "Not dangerous at all to a fine pretty lady as yourself."

Miss Rayborne said, "Oh, you are most definitely dangerous."

An elderly lady came and took the younger woman's elbow, "Come along Rose, your father wants you to meet someone."

Rose said, "Good evening, Mr. Cole."

As soon as the women were out of hearing, Raif said, "I told you that you looked distinguished."

Jeremy said, "I guess I could get used to it if I get to meet such pretty young ladies."

Raif smiled, "You'll do better out west."

Jeremy said, "Really?"

"No."

Jeremy said, "It isn't funny, boss."

A young man came over and stood beside Raif and Jeremy. It was obvious he'd already had too much to drink.

He said, "It's a farce, sir."

Raif asked, "What is?"

"Having such an affair for a low class slut."

Raif asked, "Who would that be?"

The man said, "That Cole woman of course."

Raif turned to the young man and leaned forward and said in a low voice, "I'm Major Gunnerson and Miriam Cole is my fiancée. You have a choice between a death duel and leaving right now. Your choice."

The young man turned ashen. Raif pulled his jacket back just enough so the grip of one of his pistols showed. The man made a hurried exit.

Jeremy said, "Nicely done."

"There's always that sort at these things."

Uncle James came in with Aunt Pauline and Miriam. Raif thought Miriam was a vision of beauty and went to meet her. She was wearing a very striking scarlet gown against which sat a necklace of precious gems which were reflecting the light of the ballroom chandeliers. The matching earrings seemed to catch fire with every turn of Miriam's head.

Raif walked up to her, "Good evening, my dear. You are a vision of beauty."

Miriam offered her cheek which Raif dutifully kissed. He then said, "Good evening, Uncle, Aunt Pauline."

Pauline kissed her nephew on the cheek.

Miriam took Raif's arm, "Let us dance."

During the dancing, Edward and Mary appeared and came onto the dance floor. Raif and Miriam enjoyed the dancing. They danced with each other and with the relatives of the opposite sex. It was a delightful time.

At one point, while Miriam was dancing with Edward, Raif noticed Ellen Patterson standing and talking to a woman Raif did not know. Raif went to Ellen.

"Good evening, Ellen."

Ellen smiled, "Good evening, Raif."

"May I have the pleasure of this dance?"

"Yes, of course."

Raif offered his arm and they went to the dance floor. A waltz had just started.

Ellen said, "Kate is quite put out with you."

"Her pride with heal."

"Of course. It was a surprise to learn you were marrying the hired help."

Raif smiled and said in a low tone, "I believe you've forgotten that not much more than a generation ago both our families were poor immigrants."

"I haven't forgotten and neither have a lot of others here. This kind of thing just stirs up the history."

"Why Ellen, I never thought you were one to care about what others thought." Raif changed the subject, "How is Peter doing?"

"He is getting stronger each day. He is walking around the downstairs but he's still weak and uses a cane. He wanted to come this evening, but the doctor told him it was too soon. Peter always was fond of Miriam and he is the only one in the family who truly approves of your choice."

Raif looked Ellen in the eye, "Yes, but you probably understand better than anyone."

Ellen gave Raif "the look." It was not common knowledge, but Ellen had been a young shop clerk in New York before she married Peter.

Raif asked, "May I come and visit Peter?"

Ellen said, "Of course. He will expect you to bring Miriam which will drive Kate to distraction. I can't guarantee her good behavior."

"I think Miriam will be able to deal with that."

Ellen said, "Then come tomorrow afternoon."

Raif said, "With pleasure."

The music ended and Raif walked Ellen back to her friend.

"Thank you, Ellen. Please give my regards to Peter."

She smiled, "I will."

Raif went to Miriam who took his arm. There was a break in the music and James and Pauline went to the middle of the floor.

James said, "The Gunnerson family is so happy you could all come to the engagement party for my nephew Raif and his soon to be bride, Miriam Cole. Miriam we are so pleased you are to be a part of the family. Please everyone, take a glass."

Servants brought trays of crystal flutes filled with champagne.

James waited for people to get one then said, "A toast to Miriam and Raif."

Most repeated the toast, "Miriam and Raif."

James said, "Let's celebrate."

The music started again.

Miriam said, "Let's get some air."

Raif escorted Miriam onto the patio. Other couples or small groups were nearby talking. The couple found a marble bench and sat.

Raif asked, "How are you doing?"

"I'm holding my own. I think Pauline and Mary are truly accepting of me, though I think it will be some time before we are close friends. Until we have children, my acceptance is conditional. Some of what they are teaching me I'm sure will be useful even out west. So many people are so phony it drives me crazy. I am learning things about the rich families I didn't know. Most of them are new rich and the old rich look down on them. There's so much social pushing and shoving. They are like school children."

Raif smiled, "I think you are very insightful, my dear."

Miriam smiled and said, "Oh, what I do for you, my love."

Raif said, "And I am pleased and grateful that you do. We have been invited to visit the Pattersons."

Miriam seemed shocked.

Raif answered, "I talked with Ellen. I want to visit Peter and he will expect me to bring you. He is fond of you."

Miriam smiled and said, "He is a gentle heart."

"Ellen said she could not guarantee Kate's good behavior and I told Ellen you could handle Kate."

"Indeed."

"We are expected tomorrow afternoon. I will come for you at one o'clock."

Miriam nodded, "I'll be ready, dear. We'd best go back in before we start gossip."

The evening ended on a pleasant note.

The next afternoon, Raif arrived at his uncle's at just about one o'clock. A servant took charge of the carriage as Raif got down and said, "Thank you," then went to the door. He was brought to the parlor where Pauline and Miriam were waiting.

Raif said as he entered, "Good afternoon, ladies," then went and kissed his aunt on the cheek first and then Miriam.

Pauline asked, "Did you enjoy the evening, nephew."

"Yes, I did."

Pauline said, "I also noticed you did some fence mending with Ellen."

Raif smiled, "We'd mended the fence before last night."

Pauline was surprised and said, "I see," though she really didn't. She turned to Miriam and said, "You didn't tell me."

Miriam smiled, "It never came up."

Raif asked, "How has your student been doing."

Pauline sighed, "Beyond my expectation and to my surprise, I find Miriam and I have much in common. I think we are becoming friends."

Raif said, "Good. It will make it easier when she brings the children to meet the family."

Pauline smiled, "Blackmail is not necessary my dear."

Miriam said, "Behave yourself, love."

Raif smiled and nodded, "As you wish, my dears."

The women exchanged looks and Miriam asked, "Has he always been such a tease?"

Pauline said, "Always."

Miriam and Pauline spent some time sharing their plans with Raif. After about twenty minutes, Raif said, "I think it is time we left. We are expected."

Pauline said, "Of course," and walked them to the door.

It was a pleasant drive to the Patterson's summer home. They went in a formal carriage driven by one of James' servants. Along the way, they enjoyed the scenery and talked about the home they would build when they got out west. They arrived about two thirty. Raif got out and helped Miriam down.

They were met at the door by a new servant girl who said, "You must be Major Gunnerson and Miss Cole. Mr. and Mrs. Patterson are expecting you. They are on the veranda. Please follow me."

Miriam took Raif's arm and they went out onto the veranda. Ellen stood and shook both their hands and said, "Welcome."

Peter also stood, "It is good to see you again Raif," and the men shook hands.

Peter said, "Hello, Miriam."

Miriam smiled, "Sir."

Peter opened his arms and Miriam hugged him gently and politely.

Ellen said, "Let's all sit."

They did.

Raif said, "It is so good to see you so healthy, Peter."

Peter smiled, "Not as good as it is to be healthy again, but thank you, Raif."

Miriam smiled broadly and Peter noticed it and nodded to her.

Ellen looked at Miriam, "I hope there are no hard feelings."

Miriam smiled, "Of course not, Mrs. Patterson. A mother's second duty, after duty to her husband, is to protect her children."

Ellen smiled, "I'm glad you understand."

Peter was smiling and said, "I told you, Ellen, that Miriam was a gentle heart."

Raif said, "Miriam said the same about you, Peter."

Peter smiled, "That so?"

Miriam smiled.

Ellen said, "He really is, Miriam. It's one of the things I love about him."

Miriam said, "And why a strong woman fit well into his life."

Peter laughed and Ellen smiled.

They had not noticed Kate standing at the screen door. She opened it and everyone looked at her. She came and took a seat near her father.

Kate did not greet the guests, but looked at Miriam and said forcefully, "Just because you are about to marry Raif and become rich doesn't change anything."

Miriam looked Kate in the eyes and said in a quiet voice, "It changes everything, Kate."

Kate had not expected this response and was speechless.

Ellen jumped in, "Kate, don't be rude. You have not greeted our guests."

Kate looked at her mother, got up, and left without another word.

Ellen said, "My apologies."

Miriam smiled, 'None necessary. You did nothing wrong. You have been very kind."

Ellen looked at Raif and said, "I now understand your choice."

Raif said smiling, "She can also shoot and ride like a man. That will be a huge asset out west."

Ellen looked at Miriam, "I expect you will act much differently out west."

Miriam said, "When in Rome."

Ellen asked, "Do you know what that means?"

Miriam smiled, "Not really."

Ellen laughed, "Oh, my dear, you are something else."

Peter and Raif were smiling.

Ellen said, "Let's have lemonade and talk."

The four of them spent an hour talking about the business plans out west. Miriam said little and listened intently. Raif had shared with her, but the size of the plans now really hit her. This would be a massive undertaking.

Near the end of the visit, Ellen asked, "What do you think, Miriam?"

Miriam said in the most serious tone she could, "The risks and initial hardships will be great, but the rewards greater. It will be a challenge to manage the businesses and raise a family, but I believe it can be done."

Peter said, "Well put, Miriam."

Ellen asked, "When will you start?"

Raif said, "We intend to go recruiting right after the wedding?"

Ellen looked at Miriam, "You are going with Raif?"

"Yes. I want to meet the men who will have my husband's back. We will be dependent for our lives on the men chosen."

Ellen looked at her husband who smiled.

The visit had taken longer than expected, so Miriam and Raif were invited to stay for the evening meal. It was late and after dark when the couple headed back to town. They had only gone a short distance when two highwaymen came out of the bushes aiming guns at the carriage. They didn't have a chance.

The gunfire was almost immediate. Raif drew his pistols quickly and shot the man on the left and Miriam slipped her gun from her purse and shot the one on the right. One of the men's shotguns went off as he fell and hit the horse which staggered. Miriam and Raif realized what was about to happen and jumped free. The horse collapsed and the carriage tipped onto its side. The driver was thrown and injured.

He was moaning so Miriam went to him. She called out to Raif, "He'll live, but his leg's broken."

Raif was making sure the attackers were dead.

Miriam went to the horse and shot it to put it out of its suffering.

Raif came to Miriam and handed her some extra shells and she reloaded her pistol. Raif said, "I'll make sure there are no other scoundrels around and then I'll go for help."

Miriam nodded.

Raif was gone a half an hour. He came back with a wagon and two saddled horses, Ellen, her carriage man, and woman servant. Ellen came to where Miriam was sitting with the driver's head in her lap comforting him. Her night shawl was covering him.

Raif pulled some wood from the wagon and using a pocket knife cut his vest into strips. He came, and with Ellen's help, splinted the driver's leg, then, with the help of Ellen's man and Miriam, lifted the driver into the wagon.

They took the injured man to the closest doctor and Ellen sent her servant to fetch a constable.

When two constables arrived, Ellen sent her man to tell Raif's family what had happened and that the couple was alright, but the driver was injured.

The driver had been treated by the time the constables arrived. They asked Raif and Miriam to wait outside while they took a statement. It was early morning and still dark when Miriam and Raif were at the site of the attempted robbery with two constables, two of the undertaker's men with a wagon, Ellen, and her servants. Miriam and Raif explained what happened for the second time.

The senior constable said, "Well it's clear what happened. It seems a good thing you knew how to use a pistol, Miss. Everybody's in agreement. I guess it's bury these buggers and get on with it."

The constable tipped his hat, "Sir, Miss, I'm sorry you had to go through this."

The undertakers' men started to load the two bodies.

Ellen said, "Well, I suppose you'd best come back to the house. Peter will be worried."

Raif said, "Thank you, Ellen."

It was getting close to sunrise when they arrived back at Patterson's summer home. Ellen put her help to work preparing breakfast. Peter wanted to know what had happened. Raif and Miriam sat in the parlor drinking tea and telling Peter about the adventure. Kate was standing at the door listening.

When the story was over, Peter looked at Miriam, "What was it like to shoot a man. I've never done such a thing."

Miriam sighed, "I didn't think. I just did. It was necessary. Afterward I thought what a horrible waste the scoundrel had made of his life. The poor horse had no choice in the matter and yet I had to put him down. Shame that."

Peter just sat looking at Miriam and sipped some tea. Miriam did the same.

Ellen came in and sat down, "Food will be ready soon."

Miriam said, "I'm hungry. Thank you for your kindness, Mrs. Patterson."

Ellen said, "You may call me Ellen."

"Thank you, Ellen."

Ellen looked at her husband, "I've never heard of such a thing in this area in recent times. I suppose we should bring an extra man with us. I think I'll keep my shotgun loaded."

Peter said, "It wouldn't hurt."

The four of them ate breakfast together, but Kate did not join them. After breakfast, they went out on the veranda to drink tea. Some men came to the door and were brought to the veranda. One of the men was Henry.

Henry said, "Good morning Mr. and Mrs. Patterson. Good morning, Major, Miss Cole."

Peter said, "Good morning, Henry. What brings you out here?"

"Mr. Gunnerson sent us to fetch the carriage and arrange disposal of the horse carcass. We brought horses for you and Miss Cole and your riding clothes and your gear. Mrs. Patterson was certain you would want them."

Henry looked at Miriam and winked.

Miriam said, "Thank you, Henry."

Henry smiled, "You're welcome, Miss."

Raif said, "You go on ahead, Henry. We'll be along in a bit."

Henry said, "Yes, Major," and left.

Ellen said, "Miriam, aren't you afraid to ride back?"

Miriam smiled and said, "I think word about last night is already spreading and it is likely anyone who might wish us harm will keep their distance."

Raif said, "I expect so."

A half hour later Miriam and Raif had changed into their riding gear. When Miriam came downstairs, Ellen gave her a strange look.

Ellen said, "Is that what you are going to ride in? You are really going to town looking like that? And with that holster on?"

Miriam said, "Of course."

Ellen said, "I have to see you mounted in that skirt."

Miriam smiled and they all went outside.

Ellen gave them both a hug and Raif shook hands with Peter. Ellen watched as Miriam went to the horse, put her foot in the stirrup, and swung her leg over the saddle.

Ellen exclaimed, "I have to have one of those!"

Raif said, "They are common for women's use out west. They are very practical."

Ellen said, "I can see that. Delightful." She went over and had a closer look, "It looked like a skirt until you mounted."

Ellen backed away. Raif and Miriam turned their horses and started down the lane. Miriam turned in the saddle and waved to Ellen.

Peter said, "I think they'll do it."

Ellen said, "I expect so. If we were younger we'd probably go with them."

Peter said, "You know that's not true. We are city people."

Ellen said, "True."

They went into the house holding hands. For them that was an unusual display of public affection.

As Raif and Miriam rode, Raif said, "I haven't told you that you did very well last night."

Miriam said, "I was afraid that when the time came I might not be able."

"There should be no doubt now."

Miriam said, "True."

They rode in silence for a little while then Miriam asked, "Will you give me some money."

"Just tell me how much."

Miriam told him and Raif said, "Of course. He took money out of his pocket and handed it to Miriam."

She said, "It's too much."

"Use what you want. Soon all I have will be yours too."

They attracted a lot of attention the closer they got to town. They encountered a constable and stopped to talk.

The constable tipped his hat, "Good morning, Major. Miss Cole. You know, Miss Cole, you are suddenly quite famous. Your adventure with the Major is already the talk of the town."

Miriam smiled and said, "Thank you for the forewarning, Constable. You are too kind."

"My pleasure, Miss. Have a good day."

Raif nodded and they rode off.

Miriam said, "Interesting."

"Yes. I see my Aunts' hands in this. I suppose they wanted to shape the story to our benefit."

Miriam smiled, "That was good of them."

A few people came out to the street to wave to them as they rode through town. Miriam found it quite amusing and enjoyed waving to everyone.

Raif said smiling, "If women could vote, I suppose you would run for public office."

Miriam laughed.

They arrived at the house and were met by Jeremy as they dismounted. Jeremy said, "Little sister, you are already the toast of the town." Jeremy looked at Raif, "You not so much, boss. They seem to expect that sort of thing from you."

Raif did it without thinking. He punched Jeremy on the shoulder playfully. Jeremy smiled.

Pauline and Mary were waiting when Miriam and Raif came into the house.

Pauline said, "Miriam, you must come in and tell us all about it.

Raif said, "If you ladies will excuse me, as I'm not needed, I will go to Uncle Edward's and sleep."

Mary waved him away and the women sat down. Raif went out, got back on his horse, and rode away. He wanted sleep and at Edward's he went to bed.

He tried to ignore the knocking on the door. It kept on.

Raif said, "Go away. I'm sleeping."

A male voice said, "Major, your Uncle said to, and I quote, get your lazy butt out of bed, get presentable, and be downstairs for dinner in forty minutes, unquote. We are having guests, sir."

Raif said, "Alright," and rolled his legs out of bed and sat up on the side. He went and got his pocket watch and looked at the time. He'd been asleep for five hours.

Shaved, washed, and dressed in clean clothes, Raif came downstairs. He heard voices in the parlor and went in. All the family was there as were the Pattersons, a young man Raif did not know, his beloved Miriam, and Jeremy.

Edward teased him, "Welcome back to the land of the living. Too bad you don't have the stamina of your fiancée."

Raif smiled and bowed slightly, "Good evening, all."

The conversations resumed. Raif went and kissed the cheeks of his aunts and then Miriam. Raif realized all over again just what a beauty Miriam was.

Pauline patted the sofa between her and Miriam and Miriam moved slightly and Raif sat down. His thigh was touching Miriam's and he sighed.

Pauline leaned over and whispered, "Control yourself, Nephew."

Miriam heard and stifled a laugh.

Pauline sat back smiling broadly.

Peter was sitting in a chair close to Raif. Raif said, "I'm so glad to see you out and about, Peter."

"Thank you, Raif. I guess I just needed a little excitement to motivate me to full recovery."

Raif smiled, "I'm glad we could help."

The group had a pleasant dinner and Raif soon realized the purpose of the gathering was to celebrate Peter's recovery. After dinner, the men retired and Connor approached Raif.

"It seems you and your fiancée have touched my mother and father. Thank you."

Raif smiled, "No need. I really like Peter."

At the same time, the women were talking and drinking tea. Miriam found the opportunity to get Ellen to herself. They were sitting in a corner away from the other women.

Miriam said, "You have been so kind to me. I have a gift for you."

Miriam took the little package from her purse and gave it to Ellen. Ellen unwrapped the present and looked inside. She seemed puzzled. Miriam looked around to make sure no one was looking and hiked up her dress on one side so Ellen could see. Miriam quickly slipped her dress down.

Miriam said, "It is two shots, over and under, and only good at close range. If you need to use it, it would be at close range."

Ellen looked at Miriam and laughed. Some of the women looked in their direction. Ellen put the item in her purse and said, "It is the best practical gift I have ever received. I expect when Peter sees it, he may be somewhat excited with this dangerous woman who is his wife."

Miriam smiled.

CHAPTER 5 – IMPLEMENTING PLANS

The wedding was a gala affair on the grounds of the Gunnerson mansion. Everyone who was anyone in the county attended. After a formal reception, the newlyweds left for their honeymoon. They headed to the summer home where Miriam had learned to shoot. The plan was she would learn to love there as well. There would be no servants there and they would have the house to themselves.

As they got to the house, Miriam leaned over and grabbed Night's reins and led her husband to the river bank. It was a moon lit night. Miriam tied her horse to a tree and started undressing. Raif did not need encouragement. If a river could boil, that night it would have.

After they had made love in the water, they lay naked in the grass in the light of the moon. Raif was happy and Miriam was content. Raif's gentle snoring woke Miriam and she shook him.

He opened his eyes and she kissed him. She thought they would set the grass on fire. To her it seemed they did. Afterward Miriam said, "Let's go up to the house and sleep in a bed."

They dressed and went to the house. They put the horses up and went to bed. Miriam woke to the sun streaming in the window and a light breeze blowing across her naked body. Her husband was lying on his side propped up on an elbow staring at her.

She smiled.

He said, "You are so beautiful," and kissed her. She knew he was ready again.

She stroked his face and said, "Please, no. Love, I am sore. I am new at this."

Raif smiled and put his arms around her. She felt so good. They lay there for a while before Raif had to get up. Miriam dressed and went downstairs to cook breakfast.

The three days they spent at the summer home were the happiest days of Miriam's life up to that point. On day four, they packed up and rode to town. They arrived about lunch time.

Henry met them and said, "Welcome, Major and Mrs. Gunnerson."

Miriam smiled, "Thank you for that greeting, Henry. It's the first time."

Henry nodded, "I'll have your things brought to your room. Major, your things were brought over and are in your room here. Mr. and Mrs. Gunnerson are out. Mr. Cole is out on your business. Would you like me to have a light meal prepared?"

Raif said, "That would be nice, thank you. We'll eat on the back veranda."

"Yes, sir."

Jeremy returned before they had finished eating and was brought to them.

Miriam saw him coming and said, "Hello, Jeremy."

Jeremy smiled, "Good morning."

Raif asked, "Have you eaten?"

"Yes, Major. I think I have found what you are looking for."

Raif said, "We'll go look after we finish here."

An hour later Raif and Miriam were at a horse breeders place. Jeremy showed Raif and Miriam the horses he had chosen and Raif examined them. He also arranged to ride them.

After the rides, Jeremy asked, "What do you think?"

"You are right. They are well bred and well trained."

Raif turned to Miriam, "What do you think?"

"It is hard to choose between them."

Raif nodded, but asked, "However, you must. Which do you prefer?"

Miriam told him, "I like the personality of the chestnut."

Raif asked, "And you Jeremy?"

Jeremy made his choice. Raif went and bargained with the owner. Miriam and Jeremy now had their own riding horses. Next Raif bought tack. They then went back to the house.

Pauline was home when they returned. Jeremy took the horses to the stables while Raif and Miriam went to Pauline on the veranda. After greetings, they sat and lemonade was brought for them.

Pauline said, "I suppose you'll be leaving soon."

Raif said, "As soon as my parcel arrives, we'll go recruiting."

The expected parcel arrived the next day. On the following day the little party took their leave and headed out. The first day they travelled thirty miles and were able to stay in a hotel. The second day they made the other twenty and arrived in the area they were looking for. They made inquiries. They arrived at Cracker's place about four in the afternoon.

Raif had expected something else. Cracker's place was run down and seemed deserted except for a man sitting on the porch. He had a rifle nearby. They approached slowly. The man stood up and was cradling a rifle. When they got closer, Raif stopped his little party.

"Hey, Cracker," he called out.

"Is that you, Major?"

"Put that rifle down, Cracker. You are making my wife nervous and she might shoot you."

Cracker put his rifle down and yelled, "Come on in."

The little party approached, dismounted, and tied their horses to a hitching rail. Raif walked up onto the porch and shook hands with Cracker slapping him on the back.

Raif said, "Cracker, this is my wife Miriam and her brother Jeremy."

They all shook hands.

Cracker said, "Well you gone and done it, Major, but at least ya got ya a real looker. Y'all sit."

Raif and Miriam took the other two chairs on the porch and Jeremy sat on the step.

Raif said, "I expected you'd be better situated."

Cracker sighed, "I come home to find my ma and pa died and my woman run off with another man and the money I sent home to pa. My pa was right, the gal was prone to whoring. And to think I was goin' to marry her proper when I got back." Cracker looked at Miriam, "No offense, ma'am."

Miriam smiled, "None taken, Mr. Cracker."

Cracker smiled, "Mr. Cracker. Don't that beat all?"

Raif looked at Miriam and said, "Cracker's real name is Carl Cummings. Cracker is a nickname that stuck."

Miriam looked at Cracker, "How did you get the nickname."

Cracker smiled, "The black folk took one look at my white skin and white hair, the mule whip I had, and called me cracker. The fellers thought it was a hoot and it stuck."

Raif said, "You don't seem to have done much with the place since you got back."

Cracker shrugged, "Guess I just didn't see no reason to do much."

Raif said, "Well at least you didn't get lost in a bottle."

Cracker said, "Well you know how it always bin, Major. I ain't much for liquor."

Raif nodded.

Cracker asked, "What brung ya?"

Raif said, "I'm going out west to establish a group of lawmen to bring law and order to where there isn't any so as to allow me and my uncles to start ranches. I came to ask you if you knew where some of the fellows were. I was going to try and recruit a few of the best."

Cracker nodded, "I understand some of them have had a hard time adjusting."

Raif just nodded, "To be expected."

Cracker said, "Were ya planning on askin' me."

Raif said, "I'd be more than glad to have you, but I had figured you'd be well situated and not interested."

Cracker waved his hand in a broad arc, "Ain't nothin' to keep me here. I've got some money as ya know right well, but nothin' I want to spend it on. I jist might as well make a new life elsewhere. Maybe find a good woman, get married proper, and start a family. How much does it pay?"

Raif told him the arrangement.

Cracker smiled, "Them's good wages. I think you'd get some good ole boys who'd be as willin' to go. I would."

Raif said, "Then if you want the job as my sergeant, it's yours."

Cracker smiled, "Done. How many boys ya lookin' for?"

"Twenty five to thirty. Thirty would be better."

"Does they have to be from the Gunners?"

"No, but I want dependable experienced men of even temper and smart about fighting."

The men spent some time talking about potential candidates and who might be available. In the end they came up with thirty potentials and decided on the order. It was getting late.

Cracker said, "It's getting late. Major you and the Mrs. can stay in ma and pa's ole cabin there. There's room in the barn for your horses. Jeremy can sleep on the floor in my cabin. I'll fix some grub."

Miriam said, "If you'll let me, Cracker, I'll cook us all a meal so you men folk can go on doing your reckoning."

Cracker smiled, "That would be real nice, ma'am. I ain't had no woman cookin' for some time."

Miriam looked at Jeremy, "Brother, how about you get the horses and gear put up and I'll get to cooking."

An hour later, Miriam had a meal cooked mainly using the provisions they had brought with them. They all sat down and Miriam served the men and sat with them.

Cracker started eating and said, "Ma'am, this is some good eatin'."

Miriam smiled, "Thank you."

Cracker said between bites, "I seen ya got one of them Henry rifles, ma'am. Ya know how to use it?"

Miriam smiled, "Yes, Cracker."

Cracker just nodded, "Figures, ya bein' married to the Major and all. I s'pose you can use them pistols ya wear?"

"Yes."

Cracker looked at the Major who nodded agreement. Cracker changed the subject. After dinner, Jeremy helped Miriam clean up as Raif and Cracker talked. It was finally decided as they all sat and drank coffee.

Raif said, "It's agreed then. We'll do the nine and you do the rest."

Cracker nodded and added, "I s'pect most of the boys will have fallen on hard times. I'll need money to outfit 'em."

Raif said, "I'll provide it. They can pay me back for their gear out of their wages. Half each month."

Cracker said, "That's more 'n fair."

Raif said, "I have expectations on how our men will dress. Same hats and dusters or the like."

Cracker said, "I suppose so folks will know what's what when we's around."

Raif smiled, "Yes."

It had been a long day and they all retired early. Miriam and Raif went to the old cabin. They laid their bed rolls out on the floor. Raif was afraid the old bed would collapse as it was in poor condition.

Miriam asked, "You and Cracker serve a long time together?"

"Yes. The entire war. We saved each other's lives more than once."

Miriam just nodded.

Raif said, "You don't mind sleeping here like this."

Miriam said, "My love, you are here aren't you?"

Raif smiled.

The next morning, Miriam made a meal with Jeremy's help. After eating, Raif asked Jeremy to bring the case. Raif took out a paper, wrote something on it and signed it. He handed the paper to Cracker with a badge. Cracker looked at the papers and read them. He did not read well and asked about a few words and their meaning.

Cracker said, "So's the paper makes it official like and the badge tells folks I am."

Raif said, "Yes. Thing is, I'm paying not the government. The deputies are to take and sign the oath. We'll do that when we all meet at the railway station."

Cracker signed the enlistment paper and oath, then handed it to Raif.

Raif took out a packet of money and handed it to Cracker, "You have to account for the money so keep a reckoning for everything. Spend it like it was your own."

Cracker nodded.

Raif said, "We'll head out and meet you in thirty days."

Cracker put out his hand and they shook. Cracker looked at Miriam and said, "I is pleased to meet ya, ma'am."

Miriam smiled, "You watch my husband's back, hear?"

Cracker smiled broadly, "Yes, Mrs. Major."

Cracker was taken aback when Miriam came and hugged him lightly. She moved back and said, "Cracker, you smell. You'd best clean up. You won't find a respectable wife smelling like that."

Cracker chuckled and said, "Yes'm."

Cracker waved as Raif's little party rode away. That evening the trio camped in the open. They arrived the next afternoon in a fair size town and booked rooms in a respectable boarding house. They ate a pleasant meal then went making inquiries. As a result, a constable showed up.

The constable approached, "Good afternoon. Guns are not allowed to be carried here."

Raif said, "Good afternoon, Constable. I don't think that applies to us."

The Constable asked, "It applies to everyone?"

Raif pulled his jacket back showing his badge, "I'm Raif Gunnerson, territorial Sheriff, and this is Deputy Jeremy Cole. The lady is my wife and because of the business I am in, it is necessary for her protection that she carry weapons."

The Constable asked, "Are you the Raif Gunnerson of Gunnerson's Gunners?"

Raif smiled, "Yes."

The Constable said, "Well it's a pleasure to meet you, Major. May I help you?"

Raif smiled, "That is very kind of you. We are looking for Tim Waters. He served in the Gunners. Do you know him or his whereabouts?"

"Yes. He works in his father's feed store. It's on the west end of Shop Street."

Raif said, "Thank you, Constable."

The Constable tipped his hat and smiling went on his way. They had no trouble finding the store. They went in and asked for Tim. An elderly man asked, "What do you want with Tim?"

Raif said, "I served with Tim during the war. I want to talk with him."

The man said, "I'm Tim's father."

Raif smiled, "I'm Major Gunnerson, this is my wife Miriam, and my associate Jeremy Cole."

The man said in a sharp tone, "Tim's out back loading a wagon, but he has work to do so don't keep him too long from it."

The trio went out back and when Tim saw Raif a broad smile came across his face, "Major, what are you doing here?"

"I've come to see you."

Raif did the introductions then said, "I came to offer you a job."

Tim said, "Anything would be better than workin' for my pa. He expects me to work for hardly no wages 'cause I'm kin. If he weren't my pa, I probably would have kilt him by now or at least beat him senseless."

Raif told him about the job, the dangers, and the wages.

Tim said, "I'm in. When are you leaving?"

"In the morning."

"If it's the same to you, I'd like to leave with you."

Raif asked, "You have your own horse?"

"Yes, but she ain't much and she's old. If I don't push her too much she'll do."

Raif said, "Meet us in the morning at eight at the boarding house."

Tim's father came out, "Get back to work, Tim. I ain't payin' you to jaw with your friends."

Tim said, "You ain't hardly payin' me at all, pa."

His father ignored the remark and went back inside.

Tim turned to Raif, "I'll be there."

Three came to town and four left. It took them three weeks to make the circuit to the last man on the list. Of nine possible recruits they had visited, seven had accepted.

Raif figured that was pretty good. Bill Wasserman had used his money well and as a prosperous merchant was one of those who did not accept.

Raif's party of ten arrived at the meeting place a week early. They would have some down time. They checked into a hotel and stabled their horses. Raif, Miriam, Jeremy, and Tim went to eat at the restaurant. They were half way through their meal when two men showed up.

One stood nearby and the other came and sat at their table.

Raif said, "I didn't invite you to join us."

The man pulled back his jacket to display his badge, "I didn't need it. When armed men are in my town, I will find out why."

Raif smiled and said, "Put them away."

The man seemed surprised when the three people with Raif, including the woman, made movements suggesting they were holstering weapons.

Raif pulled back his jacket slowly to show his badge and said, "I'm Sheriff Raif Gunnerson, and these two gentlemen are Deputies Cole and Walters. The pretty lady is my wife Miriam. We just arrived. I had planned to pay you a visit, but you seem to have beaten me to it."

The man held out his hand, "Cole Banner."

They all shook hands.

Cole asked, "What are you doing in our community?"

"A group of us will be heading out west to bring law and order to the frontier. There will be close to thirty lawmen in town by the time we leave on the train. In the meantime, if there is anything we can do to help, we are at your service."

Cole said, "You don't have any jurisdiction here."

Raif said, "That's true. We won't stick our nose into local affairs unless our help is asked for and we won't cause any trouble. My men are all professionals."

Cole said, "Good to know."

Raif said, "May I buy you and your man a meal."

Cole smiled, "We never turn down free food."

The group had a pleasant meal. During the meal the man with Cole asked, "Are you any relation to Major Gunnerson of the Gunners."

"The same."

The man looked at Cole and said with a smile, "It's a good thing he's on our side of the law."

Cole said, "Dan here fought with the 83rd."

Raif asked, "Do you know Connor Patterson?"

"Yes, sir. I was his sergeant. Good officer, Captain Patterson. Hard but fair."

Raif asked, "How did you end up being a lawman?"

"Needed a job and this provides two squares and a room."

Raif nodded understanding. The little group finished lunch. Raif and his group took their leave and left the restaurant.

Raif said to Jeremy, "See if you can help Tim find a proper mount. I'll advance the money."

Tim said, "Thank you, Major."

Miriam asked, "What now?"

Raif said, "I think I'll send Connor a telegraph."

Raif and Miriam went to the telegraph office and sent it. They then went to meet the afternoon train. They were expecting a shipment. As it turned out, the shipment arrived. Raif had it moved and when Tim and Jeremy arrived they were given responsibility for safeguarding the shipment.

A day later, Raif received a reply to his telegraph. He went to look for Dan. Dan was patrolling when Raif found him.

Dan tipped his hat, "Good afternoon, Major."

"Hello, Dan. Have you had lunch yet?"

"No, sir."

"Let me buy you lunch at the hotel."

Dan smiled, "I would like that."

"I'll meet you there in ten minutes."

When Dan came in, Raif was already there. Dan came and sat with him. They ordered and were drinking coffee waiting for their meal.

Raif asked, "You have any serious problems around here?"

"Nah. The odd drunk, the odd barroom brawl, petty theft, and such. Mostly minor stuff."

Raif said, "Would you consider being one of my deputies?"

"Tell me more."

It didn't take much persuading. The pay increase alone was enough to entice Dan. So it was Dan would be added to the unit's roll.

Cracker showed up two days before the agreed time and came looking for Raif. He found him at the railway station. Raif saw him coming and went to meet him. They shook hands.

Raif asked, "How many?"

"Seventeen."

Raif smiled, "Good. I have eight. That will give us twenty five plus you and me."

Cracker asked, "That include Jeremy?"

"No, he'll mainly be looking after my business and the stock."

Cracker nodded.

Raif said, "I have one from outside the Gunners. He was a sergeant with the 83rd. I know his captain and he comes highly recommended. Name's Dan Bleeker."

Cracker said, "The 83rd saw hard action."

"Yes, they did."

Cracker asked, "Where is everyone staying until we pull out?"

"We've got army tents up on the hill just east of town. I hired a couple of cooks to prepare meals. We'll only be here a few days."

Cracker said, "I assume the tents will be going with us?"

"We'll need them until we have quarters built. There's no town there yet. In fact, we'll be there before the railway line gets there."

Within two days, everyone had arrived at the camp. All of the deputies were sworn, given their gear, badges, and issued clothing. They would all be wearing tan hats and dusters. The group spent some time getting used to using their new rifles. In no time, they were able to use the Henry rifles to quickly and accurately hit targets. Each man was also issued two of the best pistols money could buy. Their old weapons would be secondary. Each deputy was expected to be heavily armed.

The day before they were to leave, they broke camp and packed up. Their gear was loaded on a box car and their horses put in a corral until they would be loaded in boxcars. The men slept in railway passenger cars on a siding. Miriam and Raif shared the inconvenience with the men.

The travel across country took several days. They arrived at their destination in midafternoon. The deputies were quite a sight getting off the train. They drew a lot of attention with their matching hats, dusters with badges, and their fancy rifles. When Miriam got off the train she seemed to draw more attention than the company. Many of the workers stopped to look at her.

The temporary rail camp was a bustle of activity.

Raif yelled to Cracker, "Get things organized, Sergeant."

Cracker yelled back, "Yes, sir, Major."

Raif called to Dan, "Sergeant Bleeker."

"Sir."

"Three men and come with us."

"Yes, sir."

Raif and Miriam with the four deputies headed for the station tent. Raif found the station clerk. He had a black eye, cut lip, swollen jaw, and had obviously had some teeth knocked out.

Raif asked, "Are you Ray Dunn?"

The clerk nodded his head. It was obvious talking would be painful.

Raif asked, 'Who did this to you and why?"

The man's speech was slow and tortured, "T'was Bernie Boyle and his gang. They took some wagons and teams I was told to put aside for ya. He said he had more need of 'em and if'in ya had a complaint, he'd deal wit ya."

Raif said, "Where's the security man, Kyle?"

"Dead. Boyle kilt him and another when they tried to stop him takin' the wagons and the teams."

Raif asked, "Why'd he want the wagons."

"He needed 'em for contract work on the railroad."

Raif asked, "Where's Boyle and my wagons."

"The railhead."

"How many men has he got?"

"Maybe twelve to eighteen. Depends on if some of 'em are out thieving."

Raif looked at Dan. They walked back to the train. Cracker and the men were unloading. Raif motioned to Cracker.

Cracker came over and Raif said, "It seems a fellow named Boyle has stolen our wagons. I'm going to take Dan and ten deputies and go fetch them back. You get things organized here."

Cracker said, "Will do, Major."

Raif looked at Miriam, "Dear, please stay here with Cracker."

Miriam nodded agreement.

Ten minutes later, Raif, Dan, and ten deputies rode out. The railhead was not far ahead of the temporary camp. It didn't take long for Raif's men to find it. Raif looked through his field glasses. Boyle's men were obviously using the teams to help in the building of a small trestle.

Raif looked at Dan, "Horse thieving and murder are capital offenses. We'll ride 'em down."

Dan nodded in acknowledgment. This was hard country and the safest way to resolve the matter was to just shoot the culprits out of hand. Raif's men started down the hill toward the rail end. Boyle's men recognized trouble had arrived and started shooting too soon. The rail workers took cover.

Raif's men drew their rifles and sped up. They started shooting while the rode and Boyle's men started to panic as their number started to dwindle. It became a slaughter. Boyle's bullies were no match for trained men. It was over almost before it started.

All but three of Boyle's men were dead. Dan went to one of the men who was lying wounded and disarmed, "Where's Boyle?"

The man spit at Dan and Dan hit him.

The man screamed.

Dan said, "Where's Boyle?"

The man shook his head no.

Raif walked up to the man, "You might want to rethink your actions. Horse theft is a hanging offense. It doesn't matter if it's a horse team or a riding horse. You tell us where Boyle is, we send you to trial for stealing the wagon. You go to prison. You give my man a hard time, you'll be tried and hung for horse thieving. Your choice."

The man said, "He ain't here."

Dan said, "I can plainly see that. Where is he?"

"There's surveyors up ahead. He took two wagons to bring 'em back here."

Raif said, "More likely to kill the surveyors and rob 'em. Leave two men to guard these three. The rest of us will go after Boyle."

Boyle had been in no hurry and had been travelling slowly. It did not take long for the deputies to catch up to him. Boyle saw them coming. He and five of his men who were on horseback lit out leaving the wagon drivers to fend for themselves. Raif pointed and two of the deputies set out after the wagons.

Boyle's men were not good horsemen and their horses were no match for the deputies' mounts. Boyle's men outran the deputies at first, but their faster horses started to tire quickly. The deputies kept coming because their horses had been chosen for stamina.

Boyle knew he had no choice, but to stand and fight. He and his men stopped, dismounted and drew their rifles. It was open country. The deputies pulled up and simply shot Boyle and his men from a distance. It wasn't much more than target practice for the deputies.

It was evening when the Raif and the deputies got back to the temporary rail camp with the wagons and teams. One of the wagons was full of the bodies of Boyle and his men. The word quickly spread through camp. Everyone came to see for themselves. Raif pointed to the railway clerk who came forward.

"Have graves dug for these scoundrels. I also want the blood washed off my wagon."

The clerk said, "Yes, sir."

The bodies were taken from the wagon and laid out on the ground for everyone to see. The prisoners were chained up in a lean-to.

Raif and his men took the rest of the wagons to load their gear. That night they camped out in the open on the hill overlooking the rail camp. Raif and Miriam were sitting in campaign chairs when two men came up from the main camp.

The clerk said, "Major, Sir, this is Terry O'Malley, the foreman on this job."

Raif said, "Mr. O'Malley." Raif turned to Miriam, "This is my wife, Miriam."

Terry said, "Ma'am."

Raif said, "What can I do for you, Mr. O'Malley."

"Major, sir, if you could see yourself clear to leave a couple of deputies stay with us to keep the peace, I'd be much obliged. The work'll go faster if men and womans aren't worried 'bout being kilt in their sleep or worse. Boyle's men treated some of the whores real hard. Others are thinking they can do the same."

Mr. O'Malley looked at Miriam, "No disrespect, ma'am."

Miriam nodded, "None taken."

Raif said, "I will leave four deputies, Mr. O'Malley. In return, I expect you to keep me informed to what's afoot."

"Yes, sir. Thank you, sir. By your leave."

Raif said, "Of course, Mr. O'Malley."

When the men left Miriam asked, "Why do women become whores?"

"Some are too lazy to do other work, some are forced, and some by circumstances have no choice if they don't want to starve or die at the hands of an abusive man."

Miriam sighed, "There is so much I don't understand or know."

Raif said, "The key is to change what you can and not try to do it all at once."

Miriam nodded.

The next morning Raif, Cracker, and Dan were discussing who to leave at the rail camp. They decided they'd rotate the duty. They left the most temperate men for the first rotation. Tim was one and would be in charge. The rest of the company packed up and moved out.

CHAPTER 6 – BUILDING A NEW HOME

Raif sent a pair of men ahead to find the survey camp. By the time the wagons and the rest of the company arrived at the future town site, the chief surveyor was waiting. Raif dismounted and introduced himself, Miriam, Jeremy, Cracker, and Dan.

The surveyor said, "We have finished the town survey. The stakes with the blue cloth are the lands on your deed, Major. They are on the hill there just visible from the town site," and he pointed.

Raif said, "And the land for the sheriff's office and barracks?"

The surveyor pointed and said, "The red flags outline that land on that closer hill. Both your land and the sheriff's are outside the town proper."

Raif nodded.

The surveyor continued, "The streets are laid out with black flags and the commercial lots are laid out with green flags. We kept the entire town site to the east of the creek. We have proper survey markers sunk, but the layman probably couldn't find them easily. I have prepared a site map and I have two copies for you. The deeds and surveys have been registered."

Raif nodded and asked, "What about the ranch land?"

"The parcels are very large and we used coordinates for the deed. Now we're working on dropping survey markers. If you want to come out in the morning, I'll show you the general area."

Raif nodded, "I may just do that."

The surveyor held out his hand, "I'd best be back to my work. I'm finished the work for the railroad and you and your uncles don't pay me to laze about."

Raif smiled and nodded. As the surveyor left, Raif turned to his sergeants.

"Tell the men it is important the flags not be moved or interfered with. That hill there is the land for the sheriff's office and barracks. Have the men establish camp to the east side of the land. Miriam and I will set up a couple of hundred feet to the west. Tomorrow, we'll schedule patrols. For the time being, it will be along the rail line as it's our life line."

Cracker said, "Yes, Major," and he and Dan left.

Raif turned to Jeremy, "Take the wagon drivers and set up our camp."

Jeremy said, "Right away, Major," and went about his business.

Miriam said, "It looks as if the surveyors laid out broad streets."

Raif nodded, "And the lots all slope to the east so the rain will run off. The streets may not become mud holes. Let's look at the plans."

The two of them studied the street map.

Miriam suggested, "Let's get a feel for how the streets are laid out by riding them."

Raif agreed with the idea. They knew the town was to be large, but riding the layout gave them a better feel for just how big. They went to their personal site and rode the markers.

Miriam remarked, "It is a big site and it has its own spring."

"Yes. We will build a small town house here later. First we'll build a modest cabin at the new ranch. In time, once we're successful, we'll build a bigger house at the new ranch."

When they finished the tour, Miriam went and helped with the setting up of their camp. They would be staying in the tents for some days and she wanted it set up properly. They had three personal tents, one for the cook tent, one for her and Raif, and one for Jeremy and his two helpers. The tents were all fairly large military surplus. While Miriam and Jeremy were finishing their personal site, Raif walked over to the deputies' camp.

The men had the tents and the folding military cots up. Two horse picket lines had been set up and the horses were being fed. Raif thought one of the advantages of having ex-cavalrymen on the payroll is they knew what needed to be done without being told. Of course there was Cracker and Dan if telling was needed.

Cracker came over to meet Raif, "We are just about set up, Major. Who's going to do the cookin'?"

"You'll have to do your own for the time being. I have cooks coming with the carpenters, masons, and laborers, once the track is laid this far. They'll be cutting timber from nearby."

Cracker asked, "How long you figure it'll be 'till they get rail this far?"

"Two or three weeks if we can keep trouble away. We won't let them set up camp here. They'll have to keep about a half mile to either side until they move past."

Cracker said, "We'll set pickets out at night."

Raif nodded, "Tomorrow, we'll start sending teams of two out to scout the area out a half days ride. Once we're familiar with the area close in, we'll expand our scouting. We'll also ride the rail line."

Cracker nodded.

Raif said, "Carry on," and walked back to his camp.

The next morning Miriam, Raif, and four deputies along with a pack horse rode out to where the surveyors were working. They topped a hill and they could see for a long distance. They were about a half hour's ride from the railway right of way.

Miriam said, "Where's our ranch going to be."

Raif said, "You're looking at it. The valley is the ranch and a small river runs through it."

Miriam stood up in her stirrups looking off in the distance. She said, "It goes on for miles."

Raif said, "Yes," and took a pair of military binoculars out and searched the distance. He handed the glasses to Miriam and she looked through them. She could just make out the surveyors camp in the distance.

Raif said, "Tom, you and Bert keep those surveyors safe, hear."

Tom said, "Yes, sir," then he and Bert started down the hill with the pack horse. They knew the plan was to relieve them in four days.

Miriam said, "We not going?"

Raif said, "Distance here is deceiving. Tom and Bert will be lucky to get to the surveyor's camp in three or four hours."

Miriam said, "I'd never have guessed."

"You'll get used to it. Let's head back."

That evening, after Miriam had cooked dinner and cleaned up, they sat in camp chairs outside their tent to drink coffee.

Miriam asked, "How is it you got all that land?"

"It was the price for me to take this job. I'll have to invest a large portion of our wealth in the railway undertaking and maintaining the deputies and getting established here."

Miriam said, "Until I met you, I would have thought two hundred acres was a kingdom size piece of land. I really didn't realize how vast this country is."

Raif nodded, "Most people back east have no idea. Our future is here. We just have to make it."

For the next two weeks the deputies kept patrolling further and further out. They ranged for miles in all directions and became familiar with the area. The men who policed the temporary railway camp were the only ones who actually did any law enforcement.

The time had come to move the camp and they moved everything by rail and wagon to two miles east of the town site. The rails were now to the edge of the town site but

Raif had no intention of having the survey stakes messed up. Four deputies patrolled the town site day and night and two more deputies were now patrolling the railway camp. At night the music and noise could sometimes be heard where the deputies were camped.

It was the middle of the night on Saturday when Cracker called from outside Raif and Miriam's tent, "Major. Major. You're needed."

Raif came out barefoot, shirtless, wearing just pants and holding his Henry.

Cracker said, "There's big problems in the camp. I think we need to go."

Raif said, "Get the men ready."

Raif went and started getting ready. He said to Miriam, "Get dressed and ready for trouble."

Miriam did not need to be told a second time. She dressed for battle and checked her weapons. She and Raif came out to find Jeremy and his two helpers waiting. Jeremy's two men had rifles ready and Raif's horse was saddled.

Jeremy's helpers had single shot rifles, but they were better than nothing. Raif thought he should have gotten them pistols.

Raif said, "Jeremy you stay here with Miriam. Keep watch. Find cover."

Raif mounted up and leading the deputies, headed for the railway camp.

Miriam started giving orders. They pushed one of the wagons next to their wood pile where split wood was stored for the cook stove. They had cover between the three foot high stacked wood and the wagon. Miriam ordered canteens brought and blankets. The evening was cool but Miriam and the three men were not too cold. Miriam could see flames in the distance. Miriam thought this could not be good.

About that time, Raif and his men were topping the hill overlooking the railway camp. It was under attack. Raif didn't have to give the order. The men spread out in a skirmish line and charged toward the camp.

The attackers saw them too late. The deputies started to cut the raiders down. Some tried to counter attack and were cut down. Soon the raiders were running for their lives. The deputies set out in pursuit and shot several more before a few survivors slipped away into the darkness. Raif and his men got back to the camp to find some of the tents and equipment in ruin. His deputies had got most of the railway workers behind the train and held the raiders off.

Raif yelled, "Sergeant Crocker."

"Sir."

"Send four men back to secure our camp and police the camp for the wounded and round up any surviving raiders."

"Yes, sir."

"Sergeant Bleeker."

"Sir."

"Take some men and see to the railway people."

"Yes sir."

Raif did not know that back at his camp another conflict was about to break out.

Miriam said, "Horses are approaching."

Jeremy said, "They don't sound like ours. They aren't shod."

Miriam said, "Get ready men. Don't fire until I give the word. She rested her rifle barrel on top of the wood pile.

Several attackers were racing up the hill. Miriam waited until they were almost too close and yelled, "Fire!"

She and Jeremy laid down a fierce fire from their Henry repeaters. Several of the attacking riders were shot from their horses or were killed when their horses went down under the withering fire. Miriam had emptied her rifle and now drew her pistols. Only two of the attackers were still coming and they were now on foot.

It was instinct. Miriam spun around and saw three men on foot running toward her from the rear. She stepped out from behind the wagon. One was drawing a bow and she shot him before he could release the arrow. The other two were screaming as they charged. One was waving what seemed like a small axe and the other had a long spear. Miriam ignored the dramatic gestures and coolly shot them.

She turned around to find the three men staring at her and asked, "Are the rest down?"

Jeremy said, "Yes."

They heard more horses. Miriam handed her Henry to one of the men and said, "Reload," as she hurriedly reloaded her pistols. The horses were getting close.

Jeremy said, "I think they are ours," then yelled, "Who goes there?"

Jeremy recognized Tim's voice, "It's Tim. We're coming in. Don't shoot."

Miriam holstered her pistols and put her hand out for her rifle and it was handed to her.

Miriam said, "Thank you, Hiram."

Hiram smiled, "You're welcome, Mrs."

Miriam came out from behind the wood pile to see the deputies getting off their horses. They began checking the attackers. There were several gunshots. Miriam assumed at least some of it was wounded horses being put out of their misery. After what she'd been through, she didn't care if it was only horses or not.

Miriam went to look at some of the attackers. She had never seen people like these. There was only partial moonlight, but she could tell they were strangely dressed and dark skinned. They didn't seem to be as dark as the people from Africa.

Miriam asked, "Who are they?"

Tim said, "Indians. I don't know what tribe."

Raif came riding up the hill and said, "They hit here too?"

Tim said, "Ya. Miriam's group finished them off before we got here."

Raif smiled, "The moral to this story is don't mess with the major's wife."

Tim started laughing and the other deputies did too. Miriam figured it was nerves.

Raif said, "This does not make sense."

Miriam bent over one of the dead attackers. She examined the man's rifle and held it up for Raif, "Is it military?"

Raif examined it, "Yes. I'd like to know where it came from." Raif turned to Tim, "Collect their weapons. I want to examine them."

The men searched the area. Nine attackers had died charging Miriam's position. It was reckoned that some wounded attackers might have escaped as blood trails indicated the possibility.

Raif went around looking at the bodies and then said, "Tim, you stay here. I'm going back to the railway camp."

Miriam said, "I'll go with you."

Raif looked at her.

"There may be some who need doctoring and I may be able to help."

Raif nodded agreement. They set off for the railway campsite. Miriam was shocked with the condition of the camp. Tents were smoldering and there were several bodies lying in the open. Some were attackers' bodies and some were those of railway workers.

She and Raif arrived at the railway cars. Half of the deputies had taken up defensive positions and the other half were either helping the wounded or scouting through the town for survivors.

Raif asked, "Who was on duty when the attack started."

Bob stepped forward, "Me and Jess was."

"What happened?"

Bob spat out chewing tobacco, "We was ridin' patrol to the north when they come over the hill. There was twenty or so. We started right out after 'em and dropped three of 'em so they veered off. I guess the shots alerted Tom and Hank and as the injuns headed toward the town they had to veer off as Tom and Hank started layin' down fire and dropped a couple more. We chased 'em but they split up and we couldn't run 'em all to ground. Some got away but not before they kilt some civilians. Tom was shot in his leg, but it's went through. It's still bleedin' though. Should be ok if it don't git all pus filled and if the bleedin' stops."

Cracker had appeared and Raif asked, "How many civilians wounded?"

"One and he's gutted bad. He'll be dead within minutes. His innards are spilled out. Seven killed. The attackers got the worse of it. The boys are gatherin' the bodies."

Raif said, "I want their weapons collected. Some of the one's that attacked at our camp had military rifles. I want to know if this lot had some."

Cracker said, "Yes, sir," and left.

Miriam got off her horse and asked, "Where's Tom."

Hank said, "I'll show ya, Mrs."

Miriam followed Hank and Raif followed them. Tom was sitting on a box in rail car and his leg was still bleeding.

Miriam said, "Get him on the floor. Get me something to prop his leg up with and something soft to lay his head on. Don't you know nothing about injuries?"

The men hurried to do as she asked.

Miriam pointed to one of the deputies, "You, go find me the hardest liquor you can."

The deputy stood looking shocked.

Miriam almost yelled, "Now! Move it!"

The deputy hurried off. She looked at another, "Go have someone find me sewing needle and thread. Find some clean white petticoat cloth. Someone get a blanket over Tom."

A crowd was gathering by the open boxcar doors. Miriam was kneeling and inspecting Tom's wound when the things she had demanded started arriving. The deputy who brought the liquor took the cap off and was about to give Tom a drink. Miriam grabbed the bottle.

"It's not for that!"

A deputy brought needle and thread. Miriam cut a piece of thread. She threaded the needle and then poured liquor over it and the thread and then over her hands.

Miriam said, "Some of you hold him and this leg still. This is going to hurt like the dickens."

Several men came forward and held Tom. Miriam poured liquor on and into the wound. Tom screamed and fainted. Miriam then went about sewing the exit wound on the leg first for it was larger. She then proceeded to sew up the entry wound.

Cloth was brought to her and she tore it into strips and soaked it with what was left of the liquor and tied it over Tom's wound. Tom was now unconscious on the floor.

Miriam said, "Someone needs to stay with him. If he starts to fever then we'll have to cool him down. Keep a barrel of water close and cloth."

A woman standing in the door said, "Tom was kind and respectful to us women. I'll stay with him."

A man grabbed her shoulder and the woman winced with pain as the man sneered, "Ya got whoring to do."

Miriam was angry and before the man realized what was happening, Miriam had jumped up, drawn her pistol, and was standing in the boxcar above him. She had the barrel of her gun against the top of his head. Miriam almost spat the words.

"You are a boil on the butt of mankind. You don't use the brains God gave you and I'm about to take them away from you if you don't leave this place."

The man looked into Miriam's eyes and what he saw there frightened him.

He said, "I'll go."

Miriam waved with her pistol and he left. The bystanders were taken aback. There was dead silence for a moment. Miriam heard a commotion. Two men came carrying a woman and one said, "She's still alive, but she's cut up bad."

Miriam looked at the woman who was covered in blood.

Miriam said, "I'll need a lot more thread and lots of the strongest liquor you can find."

Men rushed away to get it. Miriam called for women to help.

Miriam ordered, "Some of you fellows fetch some of those boxes outside and a two doors or such. I need to make tables in here."

It was done quickly. One of the camp women showed up and Miriam had the railway car doors shut. She and the other woman lifted the victim onto the makeshift table and stripped the victim's clothes off. They washed the blood away and Miriam started to work. It took her almost two hours to sew the woman up. Miriam was worried because she'd lost a lot of blood. They covered her up and Miriam said, "Let me know if Tom or this woman start to fever."

One of the women said, "Her name is Loretta."

Miriam nodded, "I'll come by to check on Tom and Loretta later. If they get thirsty you can give them water."

Miriam left the rail car and leaned against it. Raif was nearby and asked, "How is she?"

"She's lost a lot of blood. It's a flip of the coin if she'll make it. You've got another problem though."

Raif asked, "What."

Miriam said, "It wasn't the raiders who did that. She was tortured and it took some time in the doing. She has rope burns on her wrist and ankles and she was gagged. All the marks are still there. Her woman parts are all torn up. She was raped and rough."

Raif said, "This isn't good."

Miriam said, "I'd start with her pimp."

Raif said, "I bet after the way you threatened him, he's already lit out. More so now that news has spread about you shooting all those attackers. It seems you killed five or six."

Miriam shrugged.

Raif said, "I didn't know you could doctor."

Miriam said, "Up to now it's just been critters. Mostly horses."

Raif said, "I see."

Miriam said, "I'm tired."

Raif said, "Come sunrise, I'll be leaving with most of the deputies to track down the raiders who got away. I'll send a couple of the boys after Bully. That's what they call the pimp. The rest of the company will stay here with you to guard the camp and the workers. I'd appreciate it if you'd help stand guard with the deputies during the day while the crews work. Jeremy has already said he would help. I gave him a badge."

Miriam nodded, "Alright."

Raif said, "We're going to put up in that rail car." Raif pointed. "It's empty now. Jeremy, Hiram, and Horatio and a couple of others have gone to get our things from the camp."

Miriam nodded then started toward the rail car. She climbed up, sat in the corner, laid her rifle in her lap and leaning against the end of the car fell asleep. She woke to the sound of work. She stood up and opened the car door. Jeremy and his helpers had piled their camp necessities by the door.

Miriam jumped from the car and Hiram came running. "Good morning, Mrs."

"Good morning, Hiram."

"Mr. Jeremy told us to set up when ya was woke."

Miriam smiled, "Well, then you'd best get to it."

Hiram smiled, "Sure enough, Mrs."

Horatio was coming on the run. The two men started loading the camp goods. Miriam went to the car where the patients were. She knocked and the door was opened and she went in. Tom was sitting up eating. Someone had put up a rope and blanket divider between him and Loretta.

Miriam went first to Tom, "How are you doing?"

"I'm sore."

Miriam said, "You'll have to stay off that for a bit. Hopefully, you'll not get infected."

Tom said, "I don't want to have to put you through the bother of cuttin' off my leg."

Miriam said with a smile, "Then see you don't."

Tom smiled, "Yes, Mrs. Major. And thank you fer what you done."

Miriam said, "You're welcome."

Miriam looked at Tom's leg. Someone had changed the bandage. Miriam undid it and examined the wounds. They were not too swollen nor did they seem infected.

She redid the bandage and said, "It's looking good, Tom."

Miriam went and looked at Loretta. She was pale, too pale. A woman was sitting next to Loretta wetting a cloth and putting it on Loretta's head. Miriam asked, "She have a fever?"

"No, ma'am. I just find it gives her comfort."

Miriam nodded and said, "I'm Miriam," and offered her hand. The woman shook it.

"I'm Mable."

Miriam said, "Pleased to meet you."

Mable said, "I was wonderin', seein' hows ya run off Bully, are we going to work for you?"

Miriam was surprised by the question but said, "No. I don't do that sort of thing. Why don't you band together and hire your own protection."

Mable said, "Meanin' we keep what we git for layin' with the fellers."

Miriam said, "Yes."

Mable said, "Ya don't approve though."

"No, I don't. But then, I don't know your circumstances."

Miriam checked Loretta's wounds and bandages. She said, "It seems there is no bleeding inside and so far no sign of infection."

"She's in bad shape though ain't she?"

"Yes, she is, Mable. She lost a lot of blood and was badly used."

Mable said, "You knows."

"Yes and the deputies are looking for Bully now."

Mable said, "He done it afore, but not as bad. He kilt one little gal, but nobody did nothin' jist 'cause she was a whore. The security men was as afraid of Bully as they was of Boyle."

Miriam said, "That isn't right."

Miriam left the car and met Raif who was on his horse. He said, "We are heading out now. How are the wounded?"

"Tom's doing well. Loretta is not so good."

Raif said, "Be careful. I'll see you in a few days. Cracker is in charge of the men here." Raif leaned over and said in a low voice, "But I expect he thinks highly of

you and would heed what you might have to say if it comes
to it."

Miriam said, "Be careful," and put her head up so her
husband could kiss her. He did then rode away.

Cracker came over, "The work is still being done in
sight of the camp here so we are going to keep the workers
and support people together so we can keep everyone under
guard until the major gets back."

Miriam just nodded, "Thank you, Cracker."

"For what, Mrs.?"

"Paying me the courtesy of letting me know the plans."

The wagons and the engine pushing the flatcars with
the rails on them started down the track the quarter mile to
where the track ended. Miriam spent the day watching the
distance for any signs of danger. In the distance, she saw a
rider partially hidden. She went and stood beside Cracker.

She asked, "You see him?"

Cracker said, "Yeah. Where?"

"To the west just at the tree line."

Cracker said, "Yeah that's the one."

Miriam walked to the water bucket and took a drink.
She went to the other side of the track and looked south.
She saw movement but could not make out what it was.
She waited a couple of minutes and went back to Cracker.

"I saw movement to the southeast. I couldn't make out
if it was human, but I don't hold with that being a chance
thing."

Cracker said, "I agree."

They had no more sightings that day. As it was getting
to be dusk, Miriam approached Cracker, "What do you
think?"

"They may come at us tonight while the rest are
away."

Miriam nodded, "Maybe we could ambush 'em."

Cracker said, "You think like a soldier. I still wish we
had more riflemen."

Miriam smiled, "Maybe we can have the next best thing." Miriam explained and Cracker said, "It can't hurt."

Miriam asked, "How would we go about setting an ambush?"

When they got back to the tents, Miriam went to see Tom and Loretta. Tom was alright and Loretta's color seemed a little better.

Miriam said to Tom, "We expect an attack tonight. I need your Henry. Any killing you do will be close up so here are two extra pistols we took from the raiders."

Tom looked up, "Cracker and ya got a surprise awaitin' them raiders don't ya?"

Miriam smiled, "Oh, yes."

She took Tom's rifle and went outside and gave the Henry rifle to Hiram and said, "Put it to good use, Hiram, and stay close."

"Yes, Mrs."

Miriam went to the meeting. There were eight women beside Loretta and Miriam in camp. There was the ole Bessie the cook, the railway clerk's wife, and six whores. Miriam figured these were hardened women and if they weren't they now needed to be.

Miriam asked, "How many of you would still like to be living in the morning?"

They looked at each other and Mable was the first to say, "I do."

The others agreed.

Miriam said, "Then this is what you will have to do during the attack we expect tonight."

Miriam told the women what was planned then opened the tent flap and Horatio brought in the captured army rifles and pistols wrapped in blankets. Miriam started teaching the women how to load and load quickly. They would be working in tandem with a shooter. The faster they could load the extra rifles and pistols the more fire could be brought to bear on the attackers.

As they were finishing their practice one of the women asked, "What if our shooter gets hit?"

Miriam said, "What do you think?"

"I'd better take to shootin' if'in I want to live."

Miriam said, "It could be necessary. Let's hope it doesn't get to that."

Mable said, "What about Loretta?"

Miriam said, "Tom will be guarding her. He has four pistols and he's good with them."

Mable just nodded, "I guess if you can do it, there's no reason we can't."

Miriam said, "That's the right thinking. Each of you take a pistol and hide it in your dress. Horatio will see the rifles are at your position along with ammunition."

That night the camp seemed to follow its natural course. At three in the morning there were but a few lanterns burning in the camp. Bob watched as the enemy took the bait. An arrow flew into what appeared to be a sleeping sentry. Bob thought in the dark and at a distance the straw man seemed real.

There were seven and they were almost to the picketed horses when they were cut down by rifle fire. It lasted only seconds. The second group rushed the camp, screaming and throwing torches into the empty tents. The fire lit up the night sky. The attackers were now easy targets and the counter fire began.

Cracker had expected a bigger party, but there appeared to be less than a dozen raiders in the camp and they all fell.

Cracker yelled out, "Everyone keep your places. Stay put! Stay down!"

The men and women did nothing to deal with the fire in camp. The tents burned completely. Everyone stayed put under cover until sunrise when they heard horses leave. Cracker sent three deputies to scout. Only Hank returned.

Hank came to Cracker, "There were only two riders. They were keepin' the horses for the attackers. Probably just kids. They won't get far."

A report was brought. One of the railway workers had been killed. The woman with him had shot the attacker. Miriam knew it had been Mable. She'd been with that shooter. Miriam felt relief that there were no wounded for her to treat. She knew she should feel guilty for that thought, but she didn't.

Cracker had the dead collected and this time they found only two old rifles. The rest of the weapons were fairly primitive except for the knives, one old revolver, and one sword.

Miriam looked at Cracker, "They were willing to risk their lives for our horses and guns?"

Cracker said, "More than not likely they was after provisions too. They is pretty skinny."

Hank said, "In the two attacks we kilt a bunch. Their band has got to be thin on fightin' men."

An hour later, two deputies came back with a string of Indian horses, one body, and one bound captive. The youngster could not have been much over twelve.

Miriam was a realist. She knew that in spite of his age, he would kill any of them if given the chance. He was taken and chained to the axle of one of the rail cars.

The camp salvaged what they could and everyone set to preparing food. Cracker had guards posted.

The foreman, Miriam, and Cracker got together to meet.

Terry said, "Mrs., I suggest we not work today and have everyone work on making the best we can of what's left."

Miriam looked at Cracker, "What are your thoughts."

"I guess the money part is your decision since the major is away."

Miriam said, "Cracker, please, I want your thoughts."

Cracker said, "All our tents is burned. All we've got left is a couple ah boxcars, a partially burned railcar, some cargo tarps, and some trestle lumber."

Miriam looked at Terry, "How far until we need to build another trestle?"

"Thirty miles."

Miriam said, "Alright then. Ration out the lumber to make lean to shelters and the same with the tarps. The partially burned out rail car strip down to use the wood. Make it into a flat car. We'll cut trestle wood when the carpenters arrive. They should be here before you get to the next crossing."

Terry said, "It'll work."

Miriam said, "Well then, Terry, get them to it. Cracker, I leave the setting up of our camp and the security to you."

Cracker smiled, "Yes, Mrs. Major."

Miriam nodded.

That afternoon, two deputies came in with the surveyors. They reported to Cracker who immediately came to see Miriam who was changing Loretta's bandages. Miriam came out to talk to Cracker.

Cracker told her, "The boys brought the surveyors in. They was attacked by a small band. They killed four attackers, but one of the surveyor's helpers was killed. The boys thought it best to come in."

Miriam nodded.

Cracker said with a smile, "The good news is the surveyor's tents is packed on their wagon."

Miriam said, "Let them keep one, use one for the deputy's, and I'll claim the smallest one."

Cracker said with a smile, "Seems fair. Specially since everyone knows ur family owns most of the railway."

Miriam said with a broad smile, "Gossip."

Cracker said with a smile, "It ain't gossip if'in its true."

The next day two deputies came to camp with Bully slung over his horse. He was dead. Cracker took a report from the deputies then sent them to get some sleep and arranged Bully's burial. Miriam was informed Bully had put up a fight and been killed.

The camp settled into a new routine, but everyone was still on guard and nervous. New track was being laid at a good rate. Three days after the last raid, Raif returned with the deputies. They had caught the rest of the raiders and killed them.

Raif immediately came looking for Miriam at the rail head. She saw him coming from a distance and mounted her horse and went to meet him. They kissed on horseback.

Raif said, "I missed you."

Miriam said, "I missed you too, but I have to tell you dear that you stink."

Raif laughed, "But you still kissed me."

"Love conquers all."

That evening Raif washed in the stream and changed into clean clothes.

They had eaten and were sitting in their camp chairs when Miriam said, "I was asked if I was going to boss the whores since I ran Bully off."

Raif looked shocked.

Miriam smiled, "Relax. I said no. I suggested they hire their own protection so they could keep their earnings."

Raif said, "Unusual, but maybe workable."

Cracker came up the hill with a couple of deputies.

Raif said, "Evening."

Cracker spoke, "Evening, Major. May we speak with the Mrs.?"

Raif motioned to her.

Cracker took a unit shoulder flash out of his pocket and handed it to Miriam, "The boys says you're now an honorary member of the Gunners for yar bravery and service to our company."

Miriam's eyes watered up and she said, "Tell the company I am greatly honored and thank them."

Miriam got up and shook hands with each of the three men. They were all smiling.

Cracker said, "With your permission, Major, we will take our leave."

Raif said, "Dismissed, Sergeant."

Cracker snapped to attention and said, "Sir."

The men did an about face and walked down the hill.

Miriam asked, "You know about this?"

"Yes, but I was sworn to secrecy."

It was two days later that the parts for the new water tower and the tradesmen and the materials showed up on a train. Raif received a telegram that had been sent to the closest telegraph office then brought on the train.

Raif looked at the message which read, "Judge not coming. Stop. Use own discretion. Stop. Contract nullified. Stop. Strange happenings. Stop."

Raif knew this telegraph was a code he had to figure out. He found Miriam and showed it to her.

Miriam said, "Strange message."

"It is. Let's find a private place to talk."

They walked to where no one could hear them.

Miriam asked, "What is going on we don't know about?"

Raif had a serious look on his face, "I don't know. We have to figure out the telegraph."

"Well it's important and urgent or they would not have sent it this way."

"Agreed. The message didn't say the judge was delayed, but not coming. My uncles are very precise in what they say. The cancelling of the judge is political so that's the message there. "

Miriam said, "So there is political danger and perhaps betrayal."

"It would seem so."

"What's the part about the contract? What does nullified mean?"

Raif said, "It means the deal's off?"

"Which deal?"

Raif thought for a moment, "So far we have it's urgent, political, and we need to make a decision because the deals off. I'd say the rug has been pulled out from under us by the politicians."

Miriam asked, "How important is political support?"

"In reality, it's everything where the railway is concerned. It does not affect the ranch."

They stood thinking.

Raif said, "The strange happenings probably means that people with more political clout and money are trying to take over the railroad."

Miriam asked, "Can they take away the land?"

"Not the house site or ranches. The railway and commercial sites are owned by the railroad as is the right-of-way."

Miriam said, "So because of politics, someone else will get rich on that."

"Maybe. We could sell the railroad shares and concentrate on the ranch, but if the railroad can charge whatever they want, we would be at their mercy."

Miriam asked, "If this spur charges too much is there some place else we could take the cattle."

Raif thought for a moment and said, "Of course. It's only sixty miles to a main line. We could drive the cattle there. We'd still have options."

Miriam asked, "What will happen to the deputies."

"They might be decommissioned. The railroad could hire its own security."

"That wouldn't leave us vulnerable because we're paying the men anyway."

Raif said, "You're right."

"How much do we have invested in this?"

Raif said, "About a third of our wealth is in the railroad, the land, and future wages for the deputies."

Miriam said, "What are the options."

Raif said, "Sell the railroad shares and leave to cut our losses. We still have the other ranch. Alternately, we sell the railway shares and use the money to concentrate on the new ranch here."

Miriam said, "Or keep the shares and if the commissions are revoked, we just keep the men on and concentrate on ranch operations."

Raif said, "That's a good option. Security has always been the important part of our plan."

"How much of your money do your uncles and others probably think you have invested in this?"

"They probably think I'm all in."

Miriam said, "So whoever is behind the treachery probably thinks you don't have any options."

"Yes, and my uncles probably can't put more into this without putting their other businesses at risk."

Miriam said, "So someone is trying to push us out. They are probably trying to get your family to sell the railway shares at a loss and maybe the other land as well. It's possible they know something we don't."

"That would be logical. If we are right, it might be to our advantage for them not to know we aren't out of money."

Miriam asked, "If we sold my jewelry wouldn't that serve to make others think we are desperate? How long would that keep us going?"

Raif said, "Maybe two years. You won't actually have to sell yours. I have more jewels. Word will get out that you are selling your jewels. We can keep the real extent of our wealth secret."

Miriam said, "Then it will buy enough time to get the new ranch up and running?"

"Yes. The sale of gems will be misdirection and will not raise any alarms. Those trying to push us out might just try to wait us out thinking we will run out of money and they'd pick up the pieces."

Miriam smiled and said, "So our enemies, whoever, might try to wait us out rather than risk coming at us directly."

Raif said, "I can use the profits from the other ranch to get this one up and running and we'll still have our money in the bank."

Miriam said, "We'll need to move quickly."

Raif nodded, "Agreed. The train will be leaving day after tomorrow."

They developed a plan then met with Cracker and Dan and explained just the part of the situation they needed to know. A meeting with the deputies would be held that evening.

When Cracker and Dan had all the deputies together Raif and Miriam came into the tent. They had a plan.

Raif asked Cracker, "Is everyone here?"

"Yes, Major."

Raif said, "I have something to tell you."

The men were looking around.

Raif said, "I have reason to believe the sheriff's authority here might end."

There was a lot of murmuring.

Raif looked at Cracker who said, "Quiet. The major has more to say."

Raif continued, "I think the chances of that happening are a toss of the coin. As you know, I own a lot of ranch land and Miriam and I will be concentrating on that. We will still need your help and we will continue to pay you for two years as promised whether we keep our badges or not. Those who can learn skills on the ranch can stay on past that. If you work for us for five years, we'll give you two acres on which to build a house."

Raif looked at Miriam who said, "Some of you might want to take a wife though I don't know many women who would want any of you lot," and smiled broadly.

The men were smiling or chuckling.

One of the men said, "What's the pay?"

Raif said, "Same as promised and what you're getting now for the first two years. After that, regular ranch hand pay. If you marry, we'll build you a cabin and after five years we'll deed you the two acres."

There was quiet in the room.

Hank asked, "What work will we do?"

Raif said, "Same as we discussed when you were hired. Whatever needs doing. The deputy thing is to help us tame the area. Remember we're really here to build a ranch."

Miriam added, "And a future."

Another of the deputies said, "What if we leave after two years?"

Raif said, "You leave. This is a free country."

Cracker asked, "How long we have to reckon?"

Raif said, "I need to know in the morning. I need to make arrangements if anyone decides to leave. Any other questions?"

"What happens if we decide to leave?"

Miriam said, "We'll buy you a train ticket back to Pennsylvania. Of course the gear and horse we provided stays here. You may keep the clothing."

There was silence for a minute so Raif said, "Let Dan or Cracker know your decision."

Raif and Miriam left the tent and went to their own. They slept well that night and rose early. They were drinking coffee sitting in camp chairs when Dan and Cracker came walking up.

Miriam said pointing the pot over the fire, "We have fresh coffee. Help yourselves."

The men did and then sat down.

Cracker looked at Raif and said, "Two want to go back. The rest want to stay with you and the Mrs. Two other of the men are married and want to bring their wives out."

Raif said, "Good. Miriam has to go back to Pennsylvania to take care of some business. Dan, I'd like you to go with her with a man of your choosing. The wives can return with you so they aren't travelling alone."

Dan said, "Yes, sir."

Raif added, "The rest of us will load up and go to the ranch site and start work."

Miriam, Dan, and Hank, along with the two returning home boarded the train when it arrived. They took the prisoners including the Indian with them to turn over to authorities. At the first depot with a telegraph, Miriam sent a telegrams to the uncles. It read, "Miriam on way for visit. Stop. Short stay. Stop."

The prisoners were handed over to the closest jail which was reluctant to accept them but did on Miriam's insistence.

When Miriam arrived at her destination, she was dressed for the city as were her companions. They hired a carriage and went immediately to James' home. Hank stayed in the carriage and watched their gear as Dan accompanied Miriam to the door.

A servant opened the door and said, "Good afternoon, Mrs. Gunnerson. You are expected. Please come in. I will fetch Mr. Henry."

Miriam led Dan into the parlor. Henry came in and said, "Hello, Mrs. Gunnerson."

Miriam got up and did something inappropriate. She gave Henry a hug.

"It's good to see you, Henry. Henry, this is my associate, Dan Bleeker. I have another associate, Hank Durant waiting in the carriage."

Henry said, "It's a pleasure, Mr. Bleeker."

Dan nodded and held out his hand, "Mrs. Major seems to hold you in good stead, so that's good enough for me."

Henry smiled and shook Dan's hand.

Henry said, "Mr. Gunnerson directed we were to send for him and Mr. Edward as soon as you arrived. I'll have your things taken upstairs. Perhaps you'd like to get settled and refreshed after your journey?"

"Please."

Miriam was sitting in the parlor sipping lemonade when James and Edward came into the room.

It was James who said, "Miriam, my dear."

Miriam got up and embraced James, "It is good to see you again, James," then hugged Edward, "How are you?"

Edward said, "Well thank you. It's good you decided to come."

They all sat.

Miriam said, "What is happening?"

James said, "The smaller investors were bought out. We no longer control the railway. We therefore no longer control the right-of-way. In fact, our political influence has been compromised."

Miriam said, "We reckoned that from your telegraph. What do you intend to do?"

Edward said, "We were considering selling. We could recoup our investment."

Miriam paused then asked, "Have you considered there must be a reason someone is trying to squeeze us out? They must know something we don't."

James asked, "Don't you understand, if you don't control railway rates the transportation could become so costly to make your ranch lands unprofitable."

Miriam said, "The railway does not have that leverage. It is a simple thing for us to drive our cattle to another rail line. There are two competitors much closer than the railway is from our other ranch."

Edward was stunned and paused before saying, "So they can't strangle our cattle venture."

Miriam smiled, "No. We plan to hang on to our railway stock as we expect it will yield a good profit. We also plan to go ahead with our cattle ranch. We suggest you consider keeping your range lands for the same purpose."

James said, "We were counting on the merchant trade."

Miriam said, "There must be more at stake here if someone is spending all this money and effort to drive us away."

Edward said, "It will get nasty. They may take away the authority of a sheriff and then send in trouble makers."

Miriam smiled, "Raif considered that. All the deputies have as well. All but two of the men have agreed to continue to work for us no matter what happens with the badges. It may take a lot longer to get the ranch established than we thought."

James said, "How will you manage to finance your operation without income?"

"I am here to sell my jewels. They are worth a large fortune if sold in New York or Philadelphia. They will fund our fighting company for a couple of years at least and by then no one will be able to stop our progress."

Edward said, "What do you want from us? We can't afford to invest more without putting our present businesses at risk."

Miriam said, "Raif knows that. We ask only that you just hold on to your railway stock and the range land. We jointly hold enough stock not to be shut out of shareholder meetings and to have one of you on the board. It would help if you could refer me to someone to see about selling my jewels."

Edward said, "I know a gem broker who can assess and another man who can arrange the sales for a commission."

Miriam and Edward discussed the sale of the jewels.

James asked, "Do you think there will be danger and trouble?"

"There already has been. We expect another attempt to drive us out. We believe there are fortunes at stake."

Edward asked, "Who are the men with you?"

"Bodyguards. Dangerous and honorable men."

James asked, "Soldiers from the Gunners?"

Miriam nodded, "Most of our fighting men are from the Gunners or the 83rd."

James looked at Edward who nodded. James took the lead, "We will hold on to our stock and range as long as you hold your lands."

Edward said, "And I will stay on the board and be a thorn."

Miriam said, "Good. The railway will not be able to challenge us openly. Individuals may work against us, but I reckon we will be successful because we seem to be natural shootists. I think we'll all end up much wealthier."

James and Edward smiled. That evening the family had a formal dinner together and Miriam got caught up on the family happenings. The big news was that cousin Marjorie was with child. After dinner, the men and women divided.

Pauline was the first to ask about life in the west. Miriam told about the Indian attack and how she'd had to doctor Tom. She left out the part about Loretta. The women sat listening intently. When Miriam finished the story, Mary spoke.

"Did you shoot any Indians?"

Miriam simply said, "Yes."

Marjorie asked, "How many."

"Several. Some with rifle and some with pistol."

Constance said, "I couldn't do that."

Miriam said, "You'd be surprised what you could do to protect your loved ones and friends."

Pauline changed the subject to Marjorie's upcoming birthing. Miriam sat listening and realized that these women really did lead very sheltered lives. They had no idea about the broader world, nor did they want to. They enjoyed being in their safe little cocoon.

The next morning Miriam, with Dan and Hank, went to James' office and retrieved a small strong box out of his safe. Miriam had the key Raif had given her and she removed the needed items.

Dan had asked around and was referred to a respected gem merchant. Miriam wanted options. They went to see the man who had agreed to assess the jewels. At his offices, they were led into a small room and after Miriam sat, he entered. Miriam had expected a man who looked like a clerk. This man looked like an aristocrat. Miriam decided to assert higher social status and remained seated.

The man said, "I am Aaron Ben-David."

Miriam smiled, "I am pleased to meet you Mr. Ben-David. I am Mrs. Gunnerson," and offered her hand which Aaron shook gently.

Aaron took a seat.

Miriam said, "As arranged, I have brought the stones for you to appraise."

Miriam took out the first small bag and poured the gemstones out onto the felt pad on the table. She knew, because Raif had told her, they had been removed from the gold that had held them in necklaces, pendants, and earrings. The gold had been smelted and now was in small bars in a safe deposit box.

Aaron said, "Stunning." He took out a jeweler's glass and examined the stones for some time before saying, "The gems are flawless."

Miriam just nodded agreement. One by one she took out the little bags and let Mr. Ben-David examine the stones. Many were quite large. With each one, he scribbled notes and made positive comments. After two hours, the appraisal was completed.

Mr. Ben-David said, "In all my years I have never seen such a collection. I now wish someone else had appraised them. The commission on this sale will be very large."

He handed Miriam a signed paper with a description and price range for each group of stones and a total. Miriam looked at the total and it was a staggering figure. Miriam had to fight to maintain a calm composure.

Miriam asked, "Why can't you sell them for me?"

"It would be unethical for me to give you the value and then sell them."

Miriam said, "I like you Mr. Ben-David. What if I were to have another independent appraisal? Would you then be willing to sell them and for what commission?"

She talked with the man for some time. He offered to take a much smaller commission percentage than Edward had told her would be necessary. He would also deduct his appraisal fee from the commission. Miriam knew Mr. Ben-David was motivated by the amount he estimated the jewels would sell for. She pressed him and he lowered the commission rate. She paid him for the appraisal and left with her bodyguards.

Edward had arranged the afternoon appraisal. It took about the same amount of time. The estimate of value was about ten percent less than Mr. Ben-David had calculated. That difference represented a lot of money.

After the appraisal, Miriam returned the jewels to the safe. She and her bodyguards went back to James' home.

It took almost three weeks for Aaron Ben-David to sell the gems. They went for more than he had estimated. During that time, Miriam was busy making purchases.

Miriam's party went back west with a boxcar full of purchases and two deputies' wives with their meager possessions. As they travelled, Miriam explained about western life, that in the short term it would be rough living and in the long term things would get better. She learned the women were used to hardship and hard work. They came from families of subsistence farmers.

They were less than a day from their destination when a man introduced himself. He started with, "Are you Mrs. Gunnerson?"

Miriam saw Dan move his jacket so he could get to his gun.

Miriam said, "Yes, I am."

"I'm Will Parker. I'm to replace your husband in building the railway town."

Miriam smiled, "Mr. Parker, you are misinformed. My husband never worked for nor does he work for the railroad. It is true we have a substantial share in the railroad, but the building of the town has little interest for us. We are ranchers."

Mr. Parker seemed confused and said, "I'm sorry. I was misinformed and mistaken," then walked away.

Miriam thought that Mr. Parker was no town site manager.

When the little party arrived at their destination, Miriam had changed into her local clothes. She no longer looked the part of the city socialite. She no sooner stepped off the railway car than Raif picked her up twirled her around and kissed her. Miriam was smiling broadly.

"I missed you too."

Raif put her down.

Miriam noticed Raif had eight men with him including Horatio and Hiram.

She asked, "Trouble?"

"Maybe and maybe not. Things seem to be coming to a head. I'll tell you about it after we unload and get on the way."

Miriam looked around. Only four buildings had been started and they were just partial frames. They did not look well built.

Miriam said, "Not looking too good."

Raif smiled, "They don't really have anyone to oversee the work. There is really no reason to build a town yet."

Miriam said, "They sent a man named Will Parker to supervise here. He was on the train. He doesn't look like the manager type, more the breaking heads and shooting people type. Come, I have two ladies I want you to meet."

Miriam introduced Raif to the wives she had travelled with. She then helped stand guard with Raif while the men loaded the wagons. Raif had brought five large wagons and they were piled high when the rail car was unloaded.

They set out in late afternoon.

As they rode Raif asked, "How much did you raise?"

Miriam told him and he said, "That's a lot more than I expected."

It was dark when they arrived at the campsite. The wives were met with enthusiasm by their husbands. The married men had their own small tents up. Several buildings were in various stages of construction. The men had been busy. Even in the dusk, Miriam could see there was a large pile of dressed logs. The horses were unhitched and put in a corral the men had built.

The late arrivals ate a cold meal of cheese, bread, butter, and coffee. Miriam was happy to be home. That night she showed her husband how happy she was to see him. As she lay there afterward, she heard the sound of running water from the nearby river. She found it soothing and drifted off.

At sunrise the camp was busy with the sound of the company getting ready for the day's work.

A hot breakfast of fried salted pork, fresh eggs, and bread was served. After breakfast, Raif took Miriam for a walking tour. The site was on top of a hill overlooking a broad meadow on the north side and the river on the other side. The site overlooked where a spring fed creek ran into the river.

Raif said, "This will be the main house facing the south." He pointed, "The west will be anchored by a bunkhouse as will the North. The small houses and the barn will be on the east side of the compound."

Miriam asked, "Do the cattle run free?"

Raif nodded, "Yes, but eventually we'll fence. And this is ideal because the valley is sheltered, there is lots of grazing, and the spring fed river provides water. We don't have to pump the water using wind mills."

Miriam looked at the houses under construction. They had stone foundations and floors and were constructed of long dressed logs. She watched the logs being notched and fitted and how the seams were packed. Miriam asked a lot of questions and met the carpenters, masons, and laborers who had been hired to help with the building.

They walked past where the barn was being built. On one side was a chicken coop and the other a paddock fence was being put up.

Miriam said, "The chickens are a good idea. I like eggs."

Raif smiled, "They're also likely to squawk if there's something around at night. I have two border collies coming. They are good herders and they'll raise a ruckus if a stranger is near. We will have dairy cows so we can make our own cheese. We'll have a garden."

Miriam asked, "Will we only eat beef for meat?"

Raif said, "There is game in this valley. We'll have all kinds of other meat. We'll put up fences to keep the cattle within a certain area. We'll also brand the cattle. The trick is to build the herd by breeding. They have everything they need here. It is not an overnight process. When the houses are finished, we'll start stringing fences."

Miriam asked, "How does beef get shipped to the cities?"

Raif said, "Nowadays, the most efficient way is to ship beef sides in refrigerated box cars. The cars have double walls that are packed with ice."

Miriam said, "So where is the slaughter house?"

Raif said, "Ideally, it's close to the railway siding."

"Is that what you planned for here?"

"Yes, but I didn't mention it to anyone. We'll see what happens. I'd better get to work."

Miriam took the metal plates to the creek to clean them. It seemed more practical then bringing the water to the camp. She was rinsing out a plate when she saw it. She thought she knew what it was. She kept on until she had a small pile in her handkerchief. She left the stream and found Raif. She motioned to him and he knew something was up.

She said, "Come walk with me."

Raif asked, "What's up?"

Miriam said, "Let's walk further and took her husband's hand. When they were over the hill out of sight and sound of the others she said, "I know why others want us gone."

Raif gave her a puzzled look.

She showed him the little pile of gold nuggets and dust.

Raif asked, "How?"

"I was rinsing the dinner plates. It stayed in the bottom. I just kept doing it. It is what I think, isn't it?"

Raif said, "Yes, and this changes everything. We have to figure out how to handle this and quickly. This won't stay a secret long unless we take care."

Raif looked up the hill, "The spring is near the top of that hill. That means it's washing down from there and it's all on our land."

Miriam said, "Let's see how much we can pan and how quickly."

They panned and talked the rest of the day. They filled Miriam's hat to the brim and had developed a plan before the sun started to set. They headed back to camp and Raif had to carry the hat with his left hand under the crown to keep the weight of the gold from collapsing the hat. A handkerchief was hiding the contents. Dan came out to meet them and was smiling broadly.

"The single men have been glancing on and off all day toward where you disappeared. The married men snuck off for a while."

Raif said, "Dan, please go get Cracker and bring him to our tent."

Dan knew something serious was up and hurried off.

When Dan and Cracker were in the tent Raif said, "When are the stone masons and laborers leaving?"

"They left this afternoon. The floors and foundations is all done and logs are all ready for our fellas to put in place."

Raif said, "Good. Go fetch the carpenters."

The two carpenters showed up. Raif said, "Would you fellows like another couple months work? You'll have to agree to stay here in camp the whole time and not leave."

They both agreed to stay because Raif was paying top wages.

Raif said, "Good, you may go back to your tent."

The carpenters left, and Dan and Cracker were waiting for Raif to tell them what was going on.

Raif said, "I don't think we'll be raising any cattle here for the time being."

The men sat silently waiting for the explanation they knew would come.

Miriam took the handkerchief off the hat sitting upside down on the camp table. The men leaned over and looked at it.

Dan said, "Can I touch it?"

Raif nodded. Dan picked up a small nugget and examined it.

Cracker said, "You gathered this just today?"

Raif nodded.

Cracker and Dan looked at each other.

Raif said, "When this gets out, we will have our hands full. The trick will be to keep it secret for as long as possible. The spring washes down from the hills and it's all on our property. There may be serious mining in our future."

Dan always the practical one asked, "What are you going to do?"

Miriam said, "Well this is what we thought. We want to know if you think it will work." Miriam told them the plan.

Cracker said, "I reckon it'll work. We have enough provisions to stay hold up here for at least a month. I think the boys can keep this secret 'cause they'll have somethin' to lose."

Raif said, "Then we'll all meet first thing in the morning. Until then, don't speak of this."

Cracker nodded and Dan said, "Yes, sir."

Raif said, "Get some rest."

Miriam found a large bowl and they poured the gold dust and nuggets into it. Raif kept the largest nugget out. Neither Raif nor Miriam slept well that night.

The next morning their group, including women, met in the meadow out of hearing of the carpenters who were already at work.

Raif said, "I have called you all together this morning with important news. The nature of our operation here is changing, maybe for a short term and maybe permanently."

There was some murmuring.

Raif continued, "The reason is simple. We found something more profitable than cattle ranching. It does however come with danger so we will need to keep it secret as long as possible. Miriam and I have decided to share our good fortune with this group. We think our new venture will be very profitable. We will put ten percent of the profits into a fund to be shared equally by each of the people here. At the end of the month, you will get your share or your wages, whichever is greater. I think your share will be much larger than wages. There are conditions. Anyone who leaves the camp over the next thirty days will lose their rights to share. Anyone who takes anything belonging to the company, loses their right to share and continuing breathing. You will only share in the profits as long as you work for us. We will keep the agreement for land for a home under the same conditions. If you do not want to be a part of this, please leave now."

No one left.

Hank asked, "What's happening."

Raif took out the nugget and said, "Pass it around."

It was passed around.

One of the men asked, "Did you find just this single nugget?"

Miriam took the bowl to the center of the group and took a cloth off the top.

Raif said, "One at a time, get up and have a look. Miriam and I panned this in less than a day."

Everyone took a turn looking at it and there was much talking among those present. Everyone knew there was a small fortune in the bowl.

One of the men asked, "Do the women get a share?"

Raif said, "Yes. They will be keeping the camp so we can work longer and when they are not doing that, they can pan too."

Hank asked, "How do we make sure everyone gets a fair share?"

"Everything we mine goes into a common poke. It will be shared out according to weight. I expect we'll need the carpenters to build sluices. Once they leave, the whole world will know."

One of the men said, "We'll spend all our time fighting off claim jumpers."

Raif said, "Not claim jumpers, thieves. Remember, I have the deed to these lands and the mineral rights. While we pan out the stream, I will get a mining engineer and a geologist in to advise us. My family can help with that and my uncles own the land next to this. I'll send someone with a letter to my uncles. Tom are you healed enough to do that?"

"Yes, sir. Knowing what's at stake, I'll keep my mouth shut."

Hank said, "We'll have to keep a guard day and night."

Raif said, "Yes and keep an eye on the carpenters."

One of the men said, "Why don't we bring them in on share. It would make our life easier."

Raif said, "It's your ten percent to divide. I'll let you decide."

The men discussed it while Miriam and Raif listened without saying anything. The group decided to bring them in as they would be needed long term and could probably help increase the amount of gold taken.

Raif ended the meeting with, "Then we'll concentrate on panning operations and live in tents a little longer. Dan and Cracker will assign work stations. Remember we all share so work together.

After the meeting, Raif penned a letter to his uncles. It read, "*Uncles, I hope this letters finds you in good health and spirits. Miriam and I and our band are doing well.*

I have good news. It is news you must keep secret as long as possible or it will cause great trouble, even perhaps to death. We have found gold here. I suspect there may gold on your land and I advise you to investigate. If word gets out about our find too soon, we will have trouble defending our land and its riches. I suggest you make further arrangements for the security of our holdings. We will be hard pressed to defend our land with the men I have. We need to at least double our force. I will guarantee the payment of their wages.

I also request you arrange for a geologist and mining engineer to come and assess the situation. Discretion and secrecy is of utmost importance. Tom who brought this letter can be trusted to bring your reply.

Miriam and I will probably come for a short visit once we have mined the surface gold.

Your loving nephew,

Raif"

Tom left with the letter on the next train. Two weeks later Tom brought the reply, "*Our dear Raif and Miriam: We were happy to hear you are well. Your news was indeed good and unexpected. It will take some time to make the arrangements you have suggested. Your friend Charles, the colonel, will be coming to assist you and will be bringing men to help secure our lands. It will take a few weeks to recruit and get men there. It will be necessary to go slowly in the recruiting of a geologist and engineer who can be trusted. In the meantime, we are doing all we can to keep our secret.*

We are concerned the initial investment for the venture
will be substantial. We can discuss it when you get here.
We look forward to seeing you.
   Your dedicated uncles,
   James and Edward."
Over the next few weeks, Raif and Miriam spent a
considerable amount of time panning gold and seeing to the
management of the camp. The group took off a huge
quantity of gold in that first month and found with sluicing
they increased the amount mined. The carpenters went to
work doing whatever they could to help increase
production. Everyone had "skin in the game".

One heated argument broke out and Cracker cooled it
down quickly. He walked to where the men were and said,
"Ya two idjits not yet reckoned ya's fightin' over what ya
already got anyway? You get kicked out for fightin' and
all of us lose by the less in what we haul out of here."

The men looked at each other then went back to work.
Mostly, everyone was too tired to fight and argue. At the
end of thirty days, they were still taking a lot of gold. They
weighed their gold and how much each share was worth.

The company wanted to keep right on. The group had
two more weeks of provisions and more if some of the men
went hunting. Raif sent two men out hunting. Game was
plentiful and so the group stayed in camp for another
month. By the end of the second month they had taken an
enormous amount of gold.

The company had a meeting.

Raif addressed the group, "Well, you all know the
accounting. There isn't anyone here who doesn't have a
substantial stake. We have to take the gold to the city.
Half the men will go with the shipment to help guard it.
Miriam and I will go. Either Cracker or Dan will stay here.
We have to get the buildings finished before winter and
there is still gold to be taken. I expect we will need to hire

more men to protect us while we work. The profits we share will be after expenses. Questions?"

There were some and some discussion. The mining bug had grabbed everyone and all but one of the Gunners decided to stay to increase their fortunes.

Raif approached Tom after the meeting, "I was surprised you didn't decide to stay."

Tom said, "You've seen Major. After my wound healed, I walk with a limp and I can't carry a heavy load. The leg won't hold up under weight."

Raif said, "But you can still shoot and ride and think. That's what we need now more than ever. Besides you've earned a place. Think about it."

Tom nodded. In the end he decided to stay.

CHAPTER 7 - CONFLICT

The following day Raif went into town to finalize arrangements for their rail travel. Miriam and two of the Gunners group were with them. They rode directly to the train station to inspect the car that their party would travel in. It was on the siding and would be hooked up to the next train leaving to bring back more rail laying materials. Raif had just finished and his little group was leaving the station. Will Parker was standing near their horses.

Will tipped his hat, "Good morning."

Miriam said, "Good morning, Mr. Parker," and turned to her husband, "Raif, this is Mr. Will Parker. He works for our railroad."

Raif smiled and played the game. He offered his hand and said, "I'm pleased to meet you, Will. Most folks call me Major."

Will Parker said, "I haven't seen you in town for weeks, Major."

Raif smiled, "We had no reason to come. We've been very busy. I am disappointed not to see more development here."

Will said, "I think the other owners expected your family to be more involved in opening businesses here."

Miriam said, "We are Mr. Parker."

Will said, "I meant mercantile businesses here in town."

Raif said, "As far as I know, the only land my family owns are the ranch tracts we purchased and the home site Miriam and I own at the edge of town. The land here all belongs to the railroad."

Will said, "But, Major, your family owns stock in the railroad."

Raif nodded agreement, "True. That however is not the same as owning the land. You don't build on someone else's land."

Will said, "I was under the impression there was an agreement."

Raif said, "I know of no such agreement."

Will said, "Perhaps you can talk to your uncles about it. It would be a shame if they missed an opportunity here."

Raif looked around, "What opportunity would that be, Will?"

Will did not know what to say so just nodded and said, "Good day, folks."

Miriam said as he walked away, "The poor man is in deep water and can't swim." After a pause she added, "And there's no one around to shoot who won't shoot back."

Raif smiled and said, "Seems so."

Two days later Raif, Miriam, and half the Gunners came to the train station with enough gear for the trip. Their passenger car would be hooked to the end of the train when it arrived. The carpenters had made small boxes for the gold because it was heavy and the plan was to move their cargo without attracting much attention. The loading of the numerous boxes went smoothly because there was no one there to notice.

The first few hours of travel were uneventful. Unfortunately for a group of criminals, their luck was about to run out. Their first attempt at train robbery would turn into their worst nightmare. They were successful in blocking the tracks and getting the train to stop. They approached the front of the train aiming at the engineer. Raif's men knew what was happening.

Inside the last car Raif said to his men, "They can't know about what we have. We hold this car and they aren't coming in. If they start shooting some of us will go outside and kill them."

Cracker nodded and said, "Yes, sir," and within seconds chose which men would stay and which would go. The men who would stay were the best close in fighters. The men going were the better with the rifle.

The train robbers were not prepared for what happened when one of their nervous members opened fire at the engineer when he leaned over to move a lever to let pressure off the boiler. The engineer was saved from serious injury by the frame of the engine, but he did scream as a bullet fragment hit him in the arm.

Raif ordered, "Go."

He and five of the Gunners got off the car and walking three abreast on each side of the track started calmly and methodically walking forward shooting would be train robbers. The robbers were taken totally by surprise. A few fired wildly in the direction of the Gunners, but as they were the ones killed first the rest gave up on that and decided to run. The few who survived the first two minutes made for their horses. Two were shot off their horses and of the eleven would be robbers only two escaped. The engineer's wound was minor. After his arm was bandaged, he declared he could operate the engine.

Raif took the conductor aside, "What was that all about? What was so valuable they wanted to rob this train?"

The conductor said, "I can't say."

Raif grabbed him by the collar, "You will say. My family own a lot of stock in this railway. My life, my wife's, and my men's were in danger. I want to know why? If you don't tell me I will beat you within an inch of your life then I will have you fired."

The conductor said, "Sir, ya gotta promise not to say."

Raif nodded.

"T'was gold ore. They found gold down the tracks away. There's four armed guards in the boxcar with the boxes."

Raif asked, "When did they find gold?"

"About six months ago."

Raif nodded, "We never had this talk."

The conductor nodded.

The tracks were cleared while some of Raif's men stood guard. The bodies of the dead attackers were gathered and put in a boxcar to be left at the next stop for burial. Raif's men boarded and the train started out again. It was the only incident during the journey.

Once the train was travelling, Raif took Miriam out onto the deck of the observation car. They leaned on the rail and he told her about the conversation with the conductor.

Miriam said, "That explains a lot."

"Doesn't it though."

The rest of the trip with the gold was tense if uneventful. Miriam seemed to have developed motion sickness. The men thought highly of "Mrs. Major" and her illness had Raif and the men worried. After one bad bout where Miriam had run out and stood on the observation end and threw up over the rail, Raif was concerned.

Raif had his arm around her, "I'm worried. You've never been sick because of movement."

Miriam said, "That's because I've never been with child before."

Raif smiled broadly and hugged Miriam, "I'm glad you're in the family way, but I wish you didn't have to be sick over it."

Miriam said, "My ma had sickness, but it went away after a few weeks. I s'pect mine will too." She smiled and said, "Besides it was bound to happen sooner or later given your lust for your wife."

Raif smiled, "I suppose. The men are worried about you. May I tell them?"

Miriam smiled, "Sure. They're going to see for themselves soon when my belly is way out there," and she held her hands out to show how big she'd be.

Raif laughed.

The men were relieved when they learned the reason for Miriam's "sour stomach". The news served to lift the men's spirits.

Everyone was relieved when they finally arrived in the city. They had the gold converted and their cash. Raif had a fortune on deposit in sound banks.

A shipment of supplies was purchased based on lists each man who had stayed behind supplied. Hank and Tom stayed with Raif and Miriam for the trip to Pennsylvania. The rest of the men headed back. Miriam's sickness became a little less random and more regular. Still, Raif felt better knowing once Miriam threw up in the morning she would be good for the rest of the day.

It was after a morning bout that Miriam said, "Husband dear, I'm going to need a woman to help when we return home. I have plans and I'll need help with the little one."

Raif was smiling, "You can have three if you want."

Miriam smiled, "No, I think two will be enough."

Raif was now laughing.

They arrived at their destination in the early evening. They had no sooner gotten off the train than Henry greeted them.

"Good evening, Major, Mrs. Gunnerson."

Raif said, "It's good to see you, Henry."

Miriam added, "Indeed it is. Have you been well?"

"Yes, ma'am. We have two carriages waiting to take you and your associates to the residence."

Raif did the introductions. Two men with Henry took the group's bags to the carriages. Hank and Tom got in one of the carriages. The business community was growing as evidenced by the fact it was a Thursday evening and the downtown core was still busy.

As the carriages pulled away, Henry said, "Your uncles are at a meeting at the club this evening. They are not expected until very late. I'm afraid it will be an informal meal for you and your Aunt Pauline. Your uncles would like to meet with you both at your Uncle James' office in the morning at half past ten. I will let your uncle know if that is agreeable. Your aunts have planned a family dinner for tomorrow evening."

Raif looked at Miriam who nodded agreement, "Very well."

Henry said, "With your permission, I will arrange for your associates to be put up in the guest house and have a carriage at their disposal."

Raif said, "Thank you, Henry."

When they arrived at the house, Raif got out of the carriage and helped Miriam down as a matter of affection rather than need. Miriam smiled broadly.

"Thank you, dear."

Raif smiled, "You are welcome, lovely lady. If you'll excuse me for a minute, I'll go talk to Tom and Hank before they are taken away."

Miriam got serious, "Please do."

Raif hurried to intercept the men and Miriam followed the servants through the front door. A servant girl said, "Mrs. Gunnerson, Mrs. Gunnerson is waiting for you in the parlor."

Miriam smiled, "It is quite a mouth full isn't it."

The servant girl smiled, "It is, ma'am."

Miriam went into the parlor and said, "Aunt Pauline, it is so good to see you."

"And you."

The two women embraced.

Pauline said, "Please sit. You've had a long journey. Would you like something?"

Miriam smiled, "It has been some time since I've had a nice cup of tea. Out west it's coffee, coffee, and more coffee."

Pauline laughed and looked at one of servants who left to get tea.

Miriam said, "It has been a very interesting few months."

Pauline said, "You'll have to tell me all about your experiences."

"I will. I do have news that I think will make you happy."

Pauline asked, "What is it?"

"I'm with child."

Pauline clapped her hands, "That is marvelous, grand, and very good news."

Miriam said, "It'll will be your news to tell everyone tomorrow evening."

Pauline said, "That will be so much fun. Our secret until then?"

The tea came and was served. Pauline decided to have a cup as well. It was being poured when Raif entered, "Aunt Pauline!"

Pauline said, "Well if it isn't the prodigal nephew."

Raif smiled, "Aunt Pauline, I am too happy to let your teasing me ruin my mood."

Pauline said with a smile, "Parenthood will do that to you."

Raif looked at Miriam and said smiling, "You just couldn't let me tell her could you?"

Miriam smiled, "Of course not. This is woman's business, my dear."

Raif sighed, "You have me there," and sat down.

Miriam said, "Pauline is to have the honor of telling the family tomorrow evening."

Raif said, "Of course. It is only right as Pauline has been like a mother to me."

Pauline said, "That is so sweet," turned to Miriam and said, "You are good influence on him."

Miriam smiled, "I told you I'd do my best to do honor to the family and he did need some civilizing."

Raif choked on the tea that was halfway down

then smiled broadly.

The three of them talked for a while and Pauline brought them up to date on what was happening in the family. Marjorie's pregnancy was going well and she was healthy. After about an hour the little gathering broke up and Miriam decided to walk around the estate while Raif met with Tom and Hank.

Miriam walked through the garden and then to the paddock to see the horses. She watched them for a while then went past the barn and that's when she saw her.

Miriam called out, "Sarah, is that you?"

The woman looked up and waved. Miriam went to her. Sarah had a black eye that was mostly healed, but still slightly swollen. She also had bruising on the sides of her neck.

Miriam said, "Sarah, what happened to you? Why are you here?"

Sarah broke down and started sobbing. Miriam put her arms around Sarah and held her. One of the other servants started toward them and Miriam waved her off. When the servant recognized Miriam, she left. Miriam stood holding Sarah until she stopped sobbing.

When Miriam had worked for the Pattersons, she'd met Sarah. Sarah worked for the Crawleys and the Patterson and Crawley families moved in the same social circles. As servants, Miriam and Sarah came to be in the same places at the same time. They had become friends. Miriam said, "Come sit down."

"I should get back to work. I can't afford to lose this job."

Miriam said, "Don't worry. I'll take care of that."

"How can you?"

Miriam said, "I just can. Trust me. What happened?"

The women sat on a nearby plank bench.

"It was awful Miriam. If it weren't for Mrs. Gunnerson's kindness, I don't know what I'd a done.

Young Ed Crawley attacked me. He was trying to force me and to have his way with me. I kicked him and hurt him bad in his man parts. Young Mr. Crawley wanted me fired. His mother didn't want a scandal. She talked with Mrs. Gunnerson, who out of the goodness of her heart, took me on and gave me a room."

It was well known that young Ed Crawley was the family's black sheep. He was a mean violent young thug. There would come a time that the family's money would not keep him out of trouble.

Miriam said, "Are you alright?"

"Yes. He didn't hurt me down there. I heard some time ago the Patterson's fired you. How did you come to work here?"

Miriam said, "I don't work here. I'm now Mrs. Major Raif Gunnerson."

Sarah said, "I didn't think that could happen for real."

Miriam said, "You'd be surprised how many of these great high and mighty ladies used to be workers. What work do you do here?"

Sarah said, "Anything the other servants don't want to do. I'm the leftover jobs person. I'm happy to have this job and not be out on the street."

Miriam said, "What would you think about moving away from here."

Sarah asked, "Where would I go?"

"With me, out west. I'm with child and I need a woman to help out. The life there is different than here. The work is not though. There are a lot of eligible bachelors there, but there is danger also."

"What kind of danger."

"The physical kind, Indians, thieves, and such, as you've already had a run in with. Difference is, out there you'd be armed."

"Armed?"

Miriam smiled, "You'd carry a gun. I'll teach you to use one."

Sarah asked, "And you live in such a place?"

"Yes, out in the territory."

Sarah said, "But I work here."

Miriam said, "I'm sure Aunt Pauline will agree to let you go with me."

Sarah asked, "Aunt Pauline?"

"Mrs. Gunnerson, my husband's aunt."

"Oh."

Miriam said, "Think about it. If you want to come, I'll arrange it."

Sarah said, "I have no future here and I trust you. Please, I will go and work for you."

Miriam smiled, "Good. You'd best get back to work until I arrange for you to be my lady."

Sarah said, "Yes ma'am," and rose. "I will work hard for you Mrs."

Miriam smiled, "I know. Out there," she pointed west, "you can work for me and still be my friend."

"Oh."

Miriam watched Sarah go back to work. Miriam thought what a strange world this was. She walked back to the house. She went in to find Pauline giving instructions for dinner. Miriam went and took a seat to wait for Pauline.

When Pauline came over she said, "You look like a woman with something on her mind."

"I saw Sarah Halse. It was a kind thing you did for her."

Pauline said, "That Crawley boy is going to come to no good. His mother won't be able to protect him forever. I understand his father gave him a beating over poor Sarah. I suppose he's about finished with the boy."

Miriam said, "Are you going to keep Sarah on?"

Pauline said, "I suppose I have to. It will be more a charity than a need on my part."

"You have a soft heart, Aunt Pauline. May I take her into my employ to go west with me. I need women to help me."

Pauline said, "I suppose you will need someone. You will be doing me a favor and I suppose a good turn for the young woman. I understand there are men out there looking for wives."

Miriam said, "There are. Sarah would also be useful to me there."

Pauline said, "Then it's settled, if Sarah agrees." She paused, "Will you bring the baby to visit?"

Miriam said seriously, "Of course! It will be important for the children to know their family. I expect as they get older, if the family is willing, the children will come for extended visits."

Pauline said, "You are as ambitious about family as you are about business."

Miriam said, "I suppose so."

Pauline said, "I approve. We need hardy stock in the family."

Miriam laughed, "Now you are the one sounding like a rancher."

It occurred to Pauline what Miriam meant and she smiled broadly.

Pauline said, "You know things are different here. James is old school and he does not discuss business with me. I know something big is going on, but even after all these years I can't ask James. I won't. It would offend his sensibilities."

Miriam said, "We need absolute privacy."

Pauline got up and said, "Let's go for a walk."

Pauline led Miriam out to a Gazebo away from prying ears. They could look over the lawns and see no one was close. They sat down.

Miriam said, "Anything I tell you, you must promise to keep absolutely between us. You can't mention it to anyone, not even Aunt Mary. You must not let even your husband know I told you."

Pauline paused, "Mary and I are so close."

Miriam said, "I know."

"Why not Mary?"

"She and I don't have the same relationship as you and I. I hope someday we will."

Pauline thought then said, "I agree."

"What do you want to know?"

Pauline sighed, "Are we going to be poor? Are we about to lose everything?"

Miriam smiled, "To the contrary."

Pauline said, "Are you sure? There's so much tension and secrecy. I've never seen James this tense."

Miriam said, "I'm sure. Raif and I found gold on our land. Well actually I discovered it by accident, a lot of gold. Pauline, we are talking major money. A vast fortune, perhaps several, may be made. The gold is probably on James' land too. The thing is, if this gets out before we're ready, it will be really dangerous. I mean killing dangerous. Gold makes men crazy. The men are working quietly to see what we will need to mine the lands the family owns. We have to hire more security or the place will be overrun."

Pauline said, "How much is involved?"

Miriam said, "The gold off the land Raif bought has multiplied our fortune several times over just in the last three months."

Pauline was for the first time since Miriam met her, absolutely speechless. The women sat quietly for several minutes.

Pauline finally spoke, "Tell me in terms I can understand, how much land does my husband own out there?"

"Enough that it would take a day for a rider to go from one end to the other on a good horse flat out."

Pauline was silent for some time. She finally said, "I did not know. I think I may now just have a little understanding. I will be patient with James."

Miriam said, "The men have a lot on their hands right now. They need us and our support more than ever."

Pauline said, "We'd best get ready for dinner."

The women walked back to the house. Raif, Miriam, and Pauline had a pleasant dinner. During the conversation Miriam told Raif that she'd hired a woman from Pauline's staff to help her.

Raif said, "Well, you just need one more."

Miriam smiled, "You said I could have three."

Raif laughed and Pauline looked at Raif and asked, "Why are you laughing?"

Raif explained the exchanges about help he and Miriam had shared. When he finished, Pauline was smiling. After dinner, the three of them had wine on the veranda. They all retired early.

Miriam was up and ready early in the morning. Her pillow talk with Raif included preparing Sarah for the west. Pauline, Raif, and Miriam had breakfast together. James had come in late and left very early. After breakfast, they sat on the veranda to drink coffee that Miriam had brought.

Pauline said, "I was always told this coffee drink was terrible. I think I could easily get into the habit."

Raif said, "I already have."

Sarah came up to the veranda and waited until Pauline signaled for her to come forward and speak, "I was told you called for me Mrs. Gunnerson?"

Pauline said, "I heard that you were thinking of leaving my employ, Sarah. Is that correct?"

"Yes ma'am. Mrs. Gunnerson, the Major's wife, has offered me employment."

Pauline smiled, "Well as of right now you no longer work for me."

Sarah had a shocked look.

Miriam smiled and added, "What she means, Sarah, is you now work for me."

Sarah's shocked look turned to a smile, "Thank you Mrs. Gunnerson, Major Gunnerson, Mrs. Gunnerson."

Miriam said, "You best get ready to go to town, Sarah. We will be leaving in about fifteen minutes. Wear your best."

"Yes, ma'am."

They watched Sarah rush away.

Pauline said, "I take it you knew Sarah before?"

"Yes. She's a good worker, dependable, honest, and has a good heart. I also know from seeing with my own eyes that she is very good with children."

Pauline nodded.

The carriage was waiting for Raif and Miriam when they finished having coffee. Sarah was sitting on the seat next to the driver. Raif helped Miriam up onto the carriage.

Miriam said to the carriage driver, "Good morning, Jake."

"Good morning, Mrs. Gunnerson."

Miriam turned to her husband, "I've known Jake for some time. He was always friendly to Jeremy and me."

Raif said, "I'm pleased to know your name, Jake."

"Thank you, sir."

"Please take us to my Uncle James' office."

"Yes, sir."

The ride was pleasant. When they arrived, Raif helped Miriam down.

Raif said, "Jake, you and Sarah wait here. I don't know how long we'll be."

Raif and Miriam went inside where they were greeted and taken to an office where James and Edward were sitting. Both rose.

James said, "I'm sorry I missed dinner last night, but Edward and I had an important meeting."

They all sat down.

Raif asked, "Who did you meet with?"

"The other shareholders in the railway. They made us an offer to buy our shares."

Miriam said, "I'm not surprised."

Edward asked, "Why?"

Raif told his uncles about the attempted train robbery and his conversation with the conductor.

James said, "Well it appears our new friends really are not."

Edward said, "Greed does funny things to men."

Raif told his uncles about what Will Parker had said to him.

After the telling, James said, "Well it appears there is no reason for us to continue to play nice."

Edward said, "We've discovered the Patterson bank holds the note on the money loaned to our scoundrel partners. Perhaps we could convince Peter to call the loan."

James said, "We would have to be in a position to buy the shares from the bank. That will require more money than we have if we are to start mining."

Raif smiled, "I'll loan you the money against your lands out west. I have no long term interest in owning a railroad. The share I now own is enough for me."

James said, "It will take lot of money to pay out the loan."

Raif looked at Miriam and she nodded. The fact that Raif looked to Miriam for approval was not lost to the uncles.

Miriam said, "The gold we already have taken off our land would pay for the shares many times over."

Edward looked at his brother, "This does not require a lot of thought."

James said, "Alright then, we'll see if we can persuade Peter to call the note. How do we convince him we can pay?"

Raif said, "Miriam and I have enough on deposit at Patterson's bank to almost cover it. Tell him I'll guarantee payment. The fact you know about my deposit and your name should be enough assurance until papers are prepared."

Edward said, "Then the next item of business is the mining assessment."

Raif said, "I suggest we do that as soon as possible. When will Charles be leaving?"

"Day after tomorrow."

"How many men is he bringing?"

James said, "Two Sergeants and forty well-armed and equipped men. All are veterans and trusted men."

Raif said, "I'll send one of my men back with him to do introductions as our people need to cooperate."

Edward said, "Agreed."

James said, "Then we have finished our business."

Raif said, "We'll take our leave then. We have things to do. We'll see you at dinner this evening."

When Raif and Miriam left, James said to his brother, "I don't know what I think about a woman involved in business?"

Edward said, "We've always said, if it works, use it. I suppose we could learn from their example."

James sighed, "I just can't bring myself to ask my wife's advice about business."

"No, but perhaps we should share more about what we are up to. I think our wives worry when we are very busy and hardly at home."

James nodded, "I suppose, but on the other hand they are used to it. I don't think I'd want to deal with a wife like Miriam."

Raif and Miriam got back to the carriage to find Jake and Sarah waiting patiently. Raif helped Miriam up and Miriam told Jake where she wanted him to take them. When they arrived, Jake stayed with the carriage while Miriam and Sarah went shopping. Raif went down the street in search of something he wanted.

Miriam and Sarah went into a woman's clothing store. Miriam was determined to have Sarah outfitted for the west as she had been. They first got what Sarah needed.

Miriam said, "Sarah, why don't you take your parcels to the carriage and come back. I want to look around some."

Miriam was inspecting a blouse when she heard the scream. Her reaction was instinctive. She ran out the door drawing her weapon. By the wagon Jake was lying on the ground bleeding and a young man was holding a knife to Sarah's throat.

"You little bitch. You thought …"

Movement caught his attention and he looked up to see Miriam. As soon as she fired, Miriam knew she had missed the mark. She'd been aiming for his right eye.

The last thing young Ed Crawley saw before going to meet his Maker was Miriam aiming her pistol at him. The bullet hit him square in the forehead. The knife dropped from his hand and he fell dead.

No longer held up by Crawley, Sarah collapsed.

Miriam saw Crawley's brains on the ground and threw up. She supposed it was the pregnancy that caused it.

She rushed to where Sarah was and applied pressure to her bleeding neck. Sarah was looking up into Miriam's eyes as she lay bleeding. Her blood was on Miriam's dress but Miriam didn't mind. She knew she'd come just in time to save Sarah. The wound had not cut the big blood tubes in Sarah's neck.

Sarah looked up to see Raif helping Jake.

Raif called, "He's been stabbed."

Sarah and Jake were rushed away for medical attention. Raif made it known the cost of care for the two injured would be paid by the Gunnerson family. Raif and Miriam had to stay to talk to the constables that came to investigate. There were lots of witnesses and it seemed the case was straight forward.

After the police took statements, Raif was allowed to take Miriam to the hospital to see Sarah and Jake. After seeing them and being told they would both most likely fully recover, Raif and Miriam left the hospital. Their excitement for the day was not over.

Five toughs were waiting at the carriage. The leader said, "So ya's the one's kilt poor Mr. Crawley."

The man brandished a knife and another a piece of wood while another had a mean looking hooked tool. The leader had barely finished speaking and both Raif and Miriam each had pistols drawn.

Raif said, "My wife here has already killed one man today and I'm in a foul mood over it. I'm Major Gunnerson of Gunnerson's Gunners and you have to decide if you want to follow young Crawley to hell this day or get the hell out of our way. Well?"

The men looked at Miriam's blood stained clothes, the pistols, each other, then ran.

Miriam said in a loud voice, "Wise decision."

Raif almost spat the words, "Probably some of Crawleys low life drinking and whoring friends." Raif looked at his wife, "Sorry, dear."

Miriam holstered her guns under her jacket, "No offense taken, love."

They drove in silence back to the house. It was late when they arrived. Miriam entered the house and Pauline came directly.

"My poor dear, you are covered in blood. I'll cancel the dinner."

Miriam said, "Aunt Pauline, don't you dare. I'm hungry and I haven't seen the family. I just need to get cleaned up."

Pauline was over being shocked by Miriam's strength to hold up under danger. She simply said, "Well then, you'd better hurry up. It won't be long."

Pauline started giving orders for the servants to prepare a bath for Miriam. Miriam rushed to get ready. Ten minutes before the guests were to arrive Miriam went downstairs with her husband.

Pauline was the ultimate hostess that evening. Miriam figured that Pauline had given orders that the events of the day would not be welcome at the dinner table. As a result, the family dinner that evening was very enjoyable and Pauline made sure it was light hearted. Marjorie's pregnancy was the talk of the family.

After dinner, just before the men and women went to their separate rooms, Pauline said loudly, "I have an important announcement."

The table went silent.

Pauline said, "My dear Miriam is with child."

There was a moment of silence because of the way Pauline had acknowledged Miriam. The silence was followed by chatter, congratulations, and good wishes. It was a few minutes before the men and women went their separate ways. Once the women were alone, all the ladies wanted to know about "the shooting" everyone in town was talking about. The talk had just started when Raif came bursting into the room.

He grabbed Miriam's arm, "We need to go right now!"

Miriam was used to Raif and went immediately. He led her out the back door where Hank had horses waiting. Miriam mounted though she looked a little out of place in the saddle wearing her evening dress. A lot of leg was showing but it could not be helped. Raif pointed and Miriam followed Raif's lead as he rode full speed away.

They rode for several hours on back roads before Raif slowed. They stopped in a small grove to rest the horses.

Raif said, "Your riding gear is in your bag."

Miriam dismounted took the bag behind some bushes and changed. She came out looking like a different person. Raif said, "We eat and then we ride until sunrise and hide."

Miriam asked, "What's going on?"

Hank said, "I was in town. A posse was being gathered to come and arrest you."

Miriam said, "No charges would stand up. There were too many witnesses."

Raif said, "You'd never have made it alive to a jail cell. Crawley was behind it. We need to stay away until things settle down. When folks find out Crawley set this up, there will be a high price he will pay. Right now, retreat is wisest."

Miriam just nodded.

CHAPTER 8 – NOT CIVILIZED OR LEGAL

When Raif spirited Miriam away James swept into action. Henry told him what was happening. James sent a rider to Charles calling for him and as many of his men as he could muster to come quickly. Charles and eleven of his men were at the house before for the "posse" arrived. The family was told what was happening and what they were to do.

The posse that came consisted of one constable who was indebted to Mr. Crawley and fifteen "volunteers". The posse pulled up short at the front of the house when met by Charles and his men who were heavily armed and blocking the entrance.

Constable Sibler called out, "Stand aside. I have an arrest warrant for Mrs. Miriam Gunnerson and a warrant to search the premises."

Charles said, "Let me see it."

Sibler handed it to Charles who read it and said, "Mills won't last long now, if indeed that is his signature. Miriam Gunnerson is not here."

Sibler said, "Stand aside. We are going to search the premises."

Charles said, "You have authority, but these louts do not. I doubt even Mills was stupid enough to formally deputize them. You can go up to the house and search. These ruffians stay here."

Sibler protested, "These men are with me. Stand aside."

Suddenly Sibler was facing down the barrels of guns held by men Sibler knew to be good at killing.

Charles said, "I repeat. You may proceed Constable, but these hooligans stay here. Of course, you can dispute this now with force. I and my men will be tied up in legal proceedings for some time, but that won't matter to you, will it now?"

Sibler knew the threat was real. He turned to the men, "Stay here. I'll go search."

Charles said, "I'll escort you," then turned to one of his men, "Sergeant, if these men try to advance, make sure it is the last thing they do."

"Yes, sir, Colonel."

Charles said, "Get down then, Constable, and come in."

Charles led Sibler into the house. A servant asked Sibler, "May I take your hat sir."

"No. Stand aside."

It was an awkward moment because the servant was not impeding the Constable and looked around.

Charles snickered and said, "Follow me, Sibler."

They went into the parlor where Charles said, "Constable Sibler is here on official business looking for Miriam."

James said, "She's not here."

Sibler said, "I have a warrant to search."

Edward asked, "Who signed it?"

Sibler said, "Judge Mills."

James said, "You mean Magistrate Mills. Not a smart man is he, Edward?"

Edward said, "I suppose this will be his undoing and the undoing of those who abetted this miscarriage." Edward looked directly at Sibler.

Sibler repeated, "I have a warrant to search."

James said, "Then please do but don't break anything. Charles, please go with the Constable so he can't be accused of stealing anything. We don't want his reputation tarnished now, do we? It's hard to find new employment with a bad record."

Charles said, "True," turned to Sibler who was beet red and said, "Where would you like to look first."

Sibler knew then he had lost. She wasn't there. Still he searched for two hours before giving up and going away with his "posse".

Charles watched his departure and then said to his sergeant, "The men will stay here tonight in case they try to come back."

The sergeant said, "Yes, sir. It would be a bit more fun this time if'in they do."

Charles smiled, "And unfortunate for them."

Charles went back into the house. He met with James, Edward, and Connor.

James said, "Pour yourself a bourbon, Charles. Nasty business this."

Charles went to the table and poured a drink and came and sat with the others. He said, "I still have the warrant Sibler gave me. I don't believe it's a forgery."

Edward said, "Why would Mills do such a stupid thing?"

Charles said, "Money. It's a minor post being a magistrate. It doesn't pay much and it would be easy to tempt him for a sizeable amount."

Connor asked, "When will Raif and Miriam be able to return?"

Edward said, "Probably a couple of days. James and I will talk to the district's supervising judge in the morning. I think it will be an interesting meeting."

James said, "It was a good thing Raif's man was gathering intelligence or we'd have had no advance warning."

Edward said, "I think we'd better set up our own spy network here."

Charles said, "To spies," and held up his glass.

Edward said, "Toast."

The men said in unison, "To spies."

Raif, Miriam, and Hank rode under the stars that night. Just before the sun rose they found a wooded area to hide in. It was not the first time they had slept under the open sky. They set up a watch schedule and slept in shifts.

Raif woke to the sounds of Miriam throwing up. He watched to make sure she was alright and went back to sleep. He woke about noon to find Miriam preparing a cold meal. He went into the woods and relieved himself. When he returned, Hank came into the camp.

"It seems quiet."

Raif nodded.

Miriam asked, "Why would they do such a thing?"

Hank said, "Revenge."

Miriam said, "But they were sure to be found out."

Raif said, "Then they just didn't care if they were caught as long as they had their revenge."

Hank asked, "How long will we have to lay low."

Raif said, "Maybe a couple of days. We'll wire my uncles tomorrow from our next stop. By then they will probably have this straightened out."

About this time Ed Crawley Senior was in a rage. He'd found out what his wife had done in his name and was yelling, "You've ruined us Evelyn. For what? Revenge over an evil man who deserved what he got."

Mrs. Crawley screamed, "He was my son! I won't rest until that little tramp that shot him is dead."

Mr. Crawley spat it out, "It seems he was indeed your son."

Ed Crawley Sr. was no fool. He walked out and went to Doctor Ment's office. That afternoon, Mrs. Crawley was detained. She was deemed to be a threat to herself and others. She was to be sent to the state home for the criminally insane having been involuntarily committed by her husband and her doctor with an order signed by a judge. Mrs. Crawley went kicking, screaming, and cursing, which just confirmed her unbalanced state of mind.

Mr. Crawley then arranged to go see the Gunnerson brothers. Once Ed Crawley had apologized and explained what his wife had done in his name, Edward and James agreed to let bygones be bygones. The matter would be dropped and everyone would be made whole except Mrs. Crawley, Magistrate Mills, and Constable Sibler.

Truth was, though he would not admit it to anyone, Mr. Crawley was glad to be rid of his shrew of a wife. Mrs. Crawley was likely to spend the rest of her days in a lunatic asylum.

The next morning, Hank went to the nearest telegraph office. He sent a coded message to James Gunnerson. "Is it fixed? Stop. Major. Stop." Hank waited for an hour and a half for the reply which simply said, "Please come home. Stop. Uncles. Stop. Bring child bearer. Stop."

Hank brought the reply to where Raif and Miriam were camped. They laughed when they read the reply.

While Raif, Miriam, and Hank were on their way back, Charles and his men left to go west. Connor though had hired some of his former comrades to provide security for the Gunnerson family. Under the circumstances, no one thought anything of it.

While Raif and Miriam were on the way back, Edward and James were meeting with Peter and Connor.

Peter said, "So you believe the men who borrowed the money to buy the stock are over extended."

Edward said, "We do. We share a common interest in this as we both have much to lose. You will know they are over extended if you call the loan and they can't pay."

Peter said, "The bank has no desire to own railway stock."

James said, "Raif alone has enough money on deposit here to buy the stock, but all three of us will guarantee we will buy the stock in equal portions for the amount of the loan and unpaid interest."

Peter said, "There is something here I don't know, isn't there?"

Edward said, "Yes. My brother and I found out about double dealing and that's all I want to say about that. We were betrayed by men we thought were honorable. They are not."

Peter said, "If you'll sign the offer to purchase the stock, I'll call the demand loan. The only reason I made the loan in the first place was because you were involved."

James said, "We had no idea."

Edward exclaimed, "The scoundrels used our good name!"

Peter said, "They will have thirty days to pay. We will serve notice this week."

Edward said, "Thank you, Peter."

The men all shook hands and the brothers Gunnerson left.

Connor said, "You know, father, they are on to something big."

Peter said, "Why do you say that son?"

"Well not all bankers keep their mouths shut about their customers' dealings. Raif has been making very large deposits elsewhere. "

Peter said, "How large?"

Connor sighed, "Best I can determine, in amounts and numbers of accounts only a very, and I repeat very rich man could. I think we have only a small portion of Raif's money on deposit."

Peter sighed, "It seems my friends are wealthier by far then we knew."

Connor said, "We always knew they were serious men. Marjorie told me her father and uncle have large holdings in the west. The brothers sent a company of experienced soldiers out west to protect their holdings."

Peter asked, "Did Marjorie say how large or what kind of holdings?"

"No. I don't think the women in the family know much about the business. Miriam may be the exception, but she is as tight lipped as any man."

Peter said, "Yes, and with all due respect to your sister, Raif knows how to choose a woman."

Connor smiled, "Smart, strong, loyal, pretty, young, and deadly."

Peter said, "Ah, but she has a kind heart, unless you cross her."

Connor said, "I'm glad she and Raif are family if only by marriage. They are both dangerous people."

When Raif's party returned to the Gunnerson estate, they found it was if the incident with the Crawley's had never happened. Everyone was going about their business. Miriam was greeted by Pauline in the front hall.

Pauline said, "My dear, you certainly do lead an adventurous life."

The women hugged.

Miriam said, "I've been on the trail and I need a bath and to get cleaned up."

Pauline said, "Yes, dear, you are a little ripe."

Miriam smiled, "You didn't have to agree with me."

Raif said, "Aunt Pauline, are you just going to ignore me?"

Pauline looked at Raif, "As much as I might try, dear boy, I don't think that would be possible. You men always seek to be the center of attention. After you get cleaned up, I'll have a light meal served on the veranda."

That evening James and Raif sat on the veranda with their wives enjoying the cool breeze.

James said, "Peter is calling the note that was made for the purchase of the railway stock."

Raif nodded acknowledgment.

James looked at Miriam, "The stock was collateral for the note. The debtors will have thirty days to pay. From what we've been able to uncover, they're unlikely to be able to pay or get the money. Few know what you found and they couldn't prove it if they did."

Miriam asked, "What about the cargo the others sent back? Won't that pay off the debt?"

James said, "Our sources indicate it was good quality ore, but it has limited content so little value except as assay material. It does however prove the presence of a vein of what they were looking for. It was not the pure thing you brought back. Their source will require intensive mining operations. That means heavy equipment and a large investment. There is no reason for investors to assume the risk on what is known at present."

Miriam added, "When it does become known, which it will eventually, the heavy mining will require rail transportation."

James smiled and nodded, "You catch on very quickly, my dear."

Miriam realized they were discussing business with Pauline present. Something had changed. James saw Miriam glance at Pauline.

James said, "I've told Pauline about our business plans."

Miriam just nodded.

Raif said, "So they won't be able to meet the demand to repay."

James said, "Not likely."

Raif said firmly, "Good."

Miriam said, "So the family will end up controlling both a supply and the means of transportation."

James looked at Miriam and said, "We really don't want to operate the railway in the long term, do we?"

Miriam looked at Raif, "Well do we?"

Raif said, "You better than anyone know the other business will be more profitable. Once the railway is doing well, I suspect we will sell the majority of the stock to another operator at a good profit. James and Edward will of course negotiate preferential shipping rates which is really what we want."

Miriam could see the wisdom in the plan and nodded agreement.

James said, "Raif, let's go inside and have a cigar."

The men had no sooner gone inside when Pauline said, "I see why the men like business. It is so interesting. I had no idea of the scheming, planning, and plotting."

Miriam said, "And danger, both financial and physical."

"Yes, there is that. Now that I know, I'm not so sure whether I'd rather know or not."

Miriam smiled, "Well that is a choice you and I no longer have."

Pauline said, "I came to that conclusion. I did discuss with James how I could be a sort of spy in the social circles. Some wives have no idea how important what they say during tea could be. It wasn't until the last few days that I started thinking about things I'd heard and paid little attention to. I wasn't even trying. James told me sometimes a lot of bits and pieces can give a good picture of what is happening. It is like working on a puzzle. You sometimes know what the picture is when only part of the puzzle is done."

Miriam nodded.

Pauline had a lot of questions about what it was like out west. They talked for some time and Pauline agreed she would talk James into coming to visit once things were safe and settled though that might be a few years. Miriam was tired and excused herself to go to bed early.

Miriam woke when Raif got into bed. It was soon thereafter that there was a loud crash.

James was pounding on Raif and Miriam's bedroom door, "Are you alright?"

James heard laughter and Raif said, "Go back to bed."

"What happened?"

"Your guest bed is not well built and it broke."

James said, "What?" He then said, "Oh! See you in the morning."

James went back to his bedroom to find his wife holding a pistol.

Pauline said, "What happened?"

"It seems our guest bed is not strong enough to support our nephew and his wife."

Pauline started giggling like a school girl.

James said, "I wonder if our bed is stronger?"

Pauline laughing put her pistol on the night table and said, "Let us find out, dear."

In the morning Pauline came down to find Miriam was on the veranda drinking the coffee Pauline was now addicted to. She called for some and took a seat beside Miriam.

"Where is Raif?"

"Out shopping for a new bed to replace the one we broke."

Pauline said, "Hussy."

Miriam said with a smile, "It seems yours is stronger, but it creaks something awful."

Pauline said dramatically, "Well, I never!"

Miriam smiled and said, "Oh yes, you did."

Pauline smiled, "I guess I did, didn't I." She sipped her coffee and asked, "Where are the men really. I didn't hear James leave."

"James left for the office an hour ago. Raif went with him. They are interviewing today."

Pauline sighed, "You decided not to go?"

"It was not appropriate. Here a woman involved in such a matter is unthinkable. It would create unnecessary problems and I could add nothing of value."

Pauline nodded, "I see."

"I learned as a servant that there are times to be seen and times to disappear, but to always keep my eyes and ears open. You'd be surprised what some of your brightest servants know that you don't suspect."

Pauline said, "Thank you."

Miriam said, "I am going to visit Sarah and Jake at the hospital this morning."

Pauline said, "I think I'll go with you if you'd like company. Afterward, we could have lunch out then go shopping."

Miriam asked, "What do you need?"

"I want those riding pant-skirt things and your advice on a new pistol. I'd like you teach me to use it. I've done some fowl hunting, but I suspect that is much different."

Miriam said, "The shopping we can do today. We'll have to go to the summer place for the shooting lessons."

Pauline said, "We could go tomorrow, maybe for a few days."

Miriam said, "It will be fun. I wonder if Mary would like to come?"

Pauline said, "We can drop by on our way to the hospital and ask her."

It turned out Aunt Mary wanted to join the ladies outing and the lessons with guns. So it was, the ladies with two of Connor's assigned security men set out on their adventure.

Sarah and Jake were surprised when the three Mrs. Gunnersons showed up to visit. The patients had heard of the recent adventures. Sarah and Jake were doing well. Sarah expected to be out in a couple of days. Jake would not be able to work nor get around for a while except on crutches.

The Gunnerson ladies ate lunch at the finest restaurant then went shopping for the special riding clothes. Afterward, they went to the gunsmith's shop. Mr. Miller greeted Miriam when she entered the shop.

"Good afternoon, Mrs. Major."

"Hello, Jed. I have my husband's aunts with me today. "Aunt Pauline and Aunt Mary this is Jed Smith, the finest gunsmith around."

Jed nodded, "I'm so pleased to meet you, ladies."

Miriam said, "Would you bring me three revolvers of different sizes, Jed."

Jed smiled, "Yes, Mrs. Major."

Jed hurried away and Pauline asked, "Why does he call you Mrs. Major?"

Miriam smiled, "The major is my husband, this is not high society, and I like Jed." It occurred to Miriam Jed had probably overheard their conversation.

Jed came back smiling broadly and handed the revolvers to Miriam. Miriam handed Pauline the larger and said, "Take this by the handle and hold it like this," and demonstrated.

Pauline did as Miriam instructed. Miriam was surprised at how long Pauline managed it before her arm started to quiver. Miriam took the pistol and said, "Good."

Miriam repeated the process with Mary. Mary had trouble right off with the heavy revolver.

Miriam said to Mary, "Well, we'll get Pauline fixed up while your arm rests."

They found a pistol for Pauline and then Miriam had Mary repeat the process with a lighter smaller weapon. Mary handled the medium sized revolver well. Jed and Miriam fitted Mary with the right pistol for her. It was a lighter pistol she would be able to control for some period.

Pauline saw it hanging on the wall, "Isn't that a rifle like yours?"

Miriam said, "Yes, but you won't need one like that around here. Something more like the shotguns you use for fowl hunting would be appropriate."

Mary said, "They would be hard to use in a wagon or house."

Miriam asked, "Jed, do you have any coach guns?"

"Yes, ma'am."

Jed brought a new one out.

Mary said, "They are so short!"

Miriam said, "And deadly at close range."

When the women had been outfitted with the pistols, holsters, ammunition, and two coach guns, Jed gave Miriam the total.

Pauline said, "Oh, my. We don't have that kind of money."

Miriam said, "I almost forgot."

Miriam added two pistols and holsters and another coach gun. She negotiated with Ned for a bit. When they had finished dickering, Miriam took out a wad of paper money and paid.

As the women walked to the carriage Pauline asked, "You always carry that kind of money around?"

Miriam said, "Sometimes more, sometimes less."

Mary said, "But women don't carry but pin money. It's an enticement to thieves to carry more."

Miriam simply said, "If a thief tries to rob me there will be one less thief in the world."

The security man who was helping with the boxes started to chuckle.

Pauline asked, "What's funny?"

The man stopped laughing, smiled, and said, "It's not likely anyone around here is going to challenge Mrs. Pistolero."

Mary looked at Miriam, "What does that mean?"

"Mrs. Gunfighter."

They were soon on their way to Mary's house. They stopped there to drink lemonade on the porch. They talked for a while then Pauline and Miriam headed back to Pauline's. They had been there but a short time when note was delivered by hand to Pauline. She read it and handed it to Miriam.

It was in Mary's handwriting, "*Pauline, my dear friend: I am afraid I will not be accompanying you to your summer home. Edward found out about the plans to teach me to shoot and he has forbidden it. Please pass on my regrets to Miriam. Mary.*"

Pauline said, "Please accept my regrets as well, Miriam. If Edward has taken this position then James will too. I can now tell James I have declined your offer before he forbids it."

Miriam nodded, "It never occurred to me when I was a servant that the women of the house were less free than I was."

Pauline gave Miriam a shocked look. Miriam touched Pauline's arm and got up. Pauline noticed Miriam was shedding a few tears. Miriam walked away.

When Raif got back to the house, he went looking for Miriam. He found her sitting in the Gazebo by herself. Raif could tell Miriam was upset. He went and sat down beside her.

"What's wrong?"

"I am sad for your aunts and grateful for you."

Raif said, "Why are you sad for my aunts?"

"They are like pretty birds in large cages. They can fly about a bit and they are taken care of, but they are not really free. They are just prisoners in a pretty little prison. They cannot really go where they want or do what they want, and they are totally dependent on their captors."

Raif took Miriam's hand and they sat there quietly for a while.

Finally Raif spoke, "What happened today?"

Miriam told him.

Raif was quiet for a few moments then said, "I have never considered a woman's life here. I just accepted things. Now that I think about it, the wives here are as much a prisoner of the circumstances as the servants who work for them. I suppose it is like that most places."

Miriam said, "So that is why I am grateful for you. You treat me more as your partner than your possession."

Raif said, "I love you."

Miriam put her head on his shoulder and said, "I love you too. I want to go home soon."

Raif said, "Alright."

Miriam added, "At home, I'm not a freak."

CHAPTER 9 - HOME

The next morning Miriam was up early and getting ready to take the carriage to town to fetch Sarah from the hospital. She had not gone to breakfast as she was avoiding James until she calmed down more. One of Connor's security men came out to get in the carriage.

Miriam turned on the man and said firmly, "You are not going with me. I don't need someone reporting on my every move."

The man looked at Miriam, "Please ma'am, I need this job. I just do as I'm told, like most."

Miriam hesitated, considered the situation, and then said, "Get in."

When Miriam arrived to get Sarah, she was presented with a bill for her treatment. Miriam had just enough cash to pay it, but was now essentially broke.

Sarah was brought out and given into Miriam's care. Miriam said, "You are looking good, Sarah."

Sarah's color had returned and except for the bandage on her throat, there was nothing to indicate what she'd been through.

Sarah started to cry, "Thank you, Mrs. Gunnerson. Thank you for saving my life. Thank you for paying for my care. Thank you for making a place for me in your life."

Miriam hugged Sarah then said, "Let's visit Jake for a few minutes," and they did.

On the drive back to James' estate, Sarah asked Miriam questions about life in the west. She'd had lots of time to think while she was in the hospital. Miriam was glad for the distraction and the ride seemed to pass quickly. Sarah asked when they would be leaving and Miriam told her it would be very soon. At the house, Miriam told Sarah to rest for the day.

Miriam did not go into the house, but rather walked out to the Gazebo and sat thinking. At about eleven, Raif came looking for her. Miriam saw him coming and rose to greet him. Miriam kissed her husband passionately and almost desperately.

Raif smiled, "What were you doing out here by yourself?"

"Thinking."

"About what?"

Miriam sighed, "This morning I had to pay Sarah's hospital bill. It took all the money I had. It occurred to me that I'm broke."

Raif said, "We have plenty of money."

Miriam said, "No dear, you have plenty of money. If, God forbid, you died, I'd be dependent. If you were incapacitated, I would have to depend on the charity of your uncles. I have no idea what would happen to your wealth, to you, or to me."

Raif said, "You are right. That must be corrected before we get home. We'll start this afternoon with matters here."

It was a busy afternoon. Raif and Miriam visited a lawyer and the banks in which Raif, now they, had deposits. Miriam also was given access to Safe Deposit Boxes. They would make several stops on the way west to deal with the accounts in other cities.

Miriam was in a much better mood when she and Raif were headed back to James' home. Miriam said, "Thank you, love."

"For what?"

Miriam had tears in her eyes, "Giving me freedom. You really do love and trust me."

They rode for several minutes in silence before Raif said, "You know you are going to have to forgive my uncles. They are products of how they were raised."

Miriam said, "I will of course forgive them. They are family. I think, though, that you make excuses for them, my dear. They have the same choice as you, but choose not to act. You must see that."

Raif sighed and said, "I do."

When they arrived at the estate, Pauline was sitting on the veranda. Miriam, looked at her husband and Raif nodded agreement, so Miriam went to sit with her. Miriam went to where Pauline was sitting and leaned over and kissed her on the forehead.

Pauline looked surprised. Miriam sat down.

Pauline asked, "Busy day?"

"Yes."

Pauline said, "You know, I'm quite content with my life."

"I know."

Pauline said, "But it's not for you?"

"No, it isn't. Raif and I are more suited to there than here. There are less social constraints on the frontier. Here the roles are pretty much already decided. I think in the established Midwest farm communities it is the same as here."

"It works though."

Miriam said, "I suppose for many it does."

Pauline asked, "Will what happened affect your relationship with James and Edward?"

"No. It changes my view of them. I see them more clearly so I understand their actions better. They are still family and I love them."

Pauline said, "Good. That will ease the tensions at dinner time."

Miriam smiled. No mention was ever made of the conflict. It seemed to Miriam that the family's way of dealing with unpleasantness was to put it out of mind.

Two days later, Raif and Miriam said their goodbyes early in the morning, and then their small group left for the journey home. When they arrived after the long trip and ahead of schedule, Raif was surprised to find the station was closed and the town site seemed abandoned. They all pitched in to help two railroad hands unload their belongings and the cargo they'd brought. It took the better part of a half hour. Once everything was off loaded, the train left.

Raif looked around and said to Miriam, "Interesting, isn't it?"

Miriam said, "I suppose it's a result of the demand for repayment?"

Raif nodded agreement, "Probably. We might as well make ourselves comfortable until our ride comes."

Ten minutes later a wagon came with three escorts and two saddled horses trailing a team pulled wagon. Dan was leading the little group.

Dan dismounted, "We missed you, Major. Mrs. Major."

Raif shook Dan's hand, "It's good to be home."

Miriam said, "Hello, everyone," and went around shaking hands and introducing Sarah. Everyone pitched in and loaded the wagon. Hank helped Sarah into the wagon and sat beside her. Raif and Miriam mounted and they all started the journey to camp.

Raif, Miriam, and Dan were out of hearing of the others riding out front.

Dan said, "I received an interesting telegraph about two weeks back."

Raif said, "That so?"

"It was from Gary Gates. He wanted to know what you were up to out here."

Raif looked at Dan.

Dan said with a smile, "He's still waiting for an answer."

"How do you know him?"

"Captain Patterson introduced us once. It don't sit right, Mr. Gates remembering me. It was one time and I didn't say much."

Raif said, "Interesting."

Dan said, "Charles paid us a little visit. Cracker and me showed him what we were doing here. He said what we were doing would be useful to know in the management and security of your family's lands. It is good he is now assisting you. We send riders back and forth every other day as a means of mutual support. If one of the riders doesn't show up, it means there's trouble."

Raif asked, "You get much more gold?"

"Yeah, we found another pocket. We've taken a lot of dust and nuggets. I figure we should work our way downstream checking all the settling places."

Raif smiled, "I guess we'll do alright money wise."

Dan returned the smile and changed the subject, "The buildings have roofs on them now and are mostly finished, but the windows never arrived. The stoves came though."

Raif said, "We'll get the windows eventually."

Dan said, "A few days ago all the workers in town left. What's that all about?"

Raif said, "A power struggle over ownership. I think my family will come out on top."

Dan said, "I'm glad you brought all that ammunition. It's the one thing in short supply that we can't easily get a lot of. We've been bringing provisions in by train with no problem. Between that and the game, we aren't lacking for much." Dan looked at Miriam, "How are you doing, ma'am."

"Well thank you, Dan."

Dan smiled, "The men will be some relieved to see you have a woman to help out. We've been riding the youngest fella about having to be midwife. He's about worried sick over it 'cause of the teasing."

Miriam said mockingly, "Men!"

Raif and Dan laughed.

In the wagon Hank, asked Sarah, "Would it be alright if I came to call on you once you get settled?"

Sarah said, "You don't waste any time."

Hank said, "In case you haven't heard, there is a shortage of women out here let alone a pretty lady like you. You'd stand out anywhere. You will have your pick of men who want to court. I'd just like to be first in line."

Sarah teased, "We'll see. There would have course have to be a chaperone. Mrs. Gunnerson warned me about the men out here."

Hank looked ahead, "Mrs. Major?"

Sarah said, "Yes. She hasn't taught me to shoot people for myself yet so she'd have to protect me."

Hank looked shocked and Sarah laughed.

Hank shook his head and said, "Miss Sarah, ya got me good."

When the little party reached the camp, work stopped and everyone came to greet them. After the greetings and introductions, the wagon was unloaded. The ammunition was distributed so it wouldn't all be in one place. When everything was unloaded, the porch of Raif and Miriam's house was piled with boxes.

Cracker came over to the wagon where they were standing and said, "It is good to have you back. You should look at your house. The men are right proud of the work."

Miriam smiled at Raif, "Would you like to accompany me, dear?"

Raif offered his arm and Cracker never one to miss an opportunity offered his arm to Sarah who smiled and took it. Miriam was looking over her shoulder and noticed Cracker seemed to puff up.

Cracker said, "Have you ever been out west before, Miss?"

"No, I haven't. May I be blunt, Mr. Cracker?"

"Miss, my real name is Carl Cummings, but everyone calls me by the nickname Cracker. You may be straight forward, Miss."

"Do all the men here smell as bad as you do?"

Cracker was stunned, "Miss?"

"I asked if all the men here smell as bad as you do. Is there no place for you to get water for bathing?"

"I didn't realize I stunk."

Sarah changed the subject, "I'm curious to see where I'll be living."

The four of them were at the cabin.

Miriam was surprised to find from the outside her house appeared done except for the windows. The logs of the cabin were a good foot above the ground sitting on large square cut stones. The cabin had a porch on the side facing what could be called the plaza.

Miriam opened the door and they went in. The house had rooms with plank walls and high ceilings. The door opened into a large main room where the cooking, eating, and socializing would be done. In the main room at the center of the house was a large wood stove. The house had two bedrooms, a large one for Raif and Miriam and a small one for Sarah. There was a small room between the bedrooms.

The main room contained an eating table with benches, several chairs, and a kitchen work table. Each of the bedrooms had a platform bed, a clothes hanging rod, wooden boxes for clothes storage, and a small bedside table for each sleeper.

Miriam inspected everything and said, "They did a very nice job."

Sarah said, "I expected a dirt floor, but this floor is very nice. It is set even and will be easy to sweep. Those little crosses on the shutters are a nice touch."

Miriam said, "Those are shooting slots." She explained to Sarah how when closed and barred, the shutters provided protection while allowing firing on attackers."

Sarah just said, "Oh."

They were standing admiring their new home when Raif put his arm around Miriam, "It's a good start, isn't it?"

"Oh, yes. I love it. I want to go thank everyone. Let's bring the boxes."

Miriam and Sarah found the right ones and enlisted three men to help them carry them. Everyone gathered in the open.

Miriam said, "I want to thank you all for the lovely home you built for us. It is the grandest gift we could receive that you looked after us even while we were gone. It is good to be home with my dear friends. I have gifts for everyone. Ladies first."

Miriam motioned to the married ladies and they came forward to much clapping. Miriam gave them each a parcel which they unfolded and opened. Miriam had brought them fabric with which to make dresses and curtains. The women were happy. They held the cloth up for everyone to see. There was clapping and hooting.

Miriam and Sarah handed boxes out to the men.

As they handed them out Miriam said, "There is something in here for the little boy in each of you."

Each small box contained matches, 2 bars of soap, tobacco and papers, a knife sharpening stone, and some hard candy. The packages also contained other items and what was in each was different. The men all shouted out their thanks. They started trading the different items.

Everyone walked around mingling and talking. Sarah was the center of the men's attentions. Miriam noted she was enjoying herself.

Raif said to his wife, "I hate to tell you, but we still have to unpack."

Miriam smiled, "Well let's get to it. Today is Sarah's day to shine."

The couple had started the unpacking when Sarah came running over, "I'm sorry, Mrs. Gunnerson."

Miriam smiled, "You go get to know everyone. We'll take care of this."

Two hours later Raif and Miriam had things put away. The last remaining things were on the table.

Raif said, "Let me guess, one for each of the ladies?"

Miriam said, "Yes and one pistol each. Two with holsters are for Sarah."

Raif said, "Are you going to teach the women to use them?"

Miriam said, "Yes. I'd like you to talk to the husbands about the need before I offer. If the husbands are against it, I think we should let it slide."

Raif said, "Ok. What's in the last box with the handles and the other one?"

Miriam opened the box and Raif said, "Makes sense. You never know when we'll need it."

The medical instruments were new and shiny. The other boxes contained bottles of various sizes.

Raif asked, "What's in the bottles."

"Laudanum and various medicines."

Raif said, "I hope you won't need to use it."

Sarah had come in and was standing open mouthed, "You do doctoring?"

Raif said, "She's already saved lives doctoring. She saved the leg of one of our fellows and the life of a woman who used to live in the railroad camp." Raif hugged Miriam, "I think I'll go talk to the husbands. If they agree, I will have them send their wives over to talk to you."

Fifteen minutes later both the wives, Maggie and Irene, showed up. Miriam explained to them and Sarah what she had planned and showed the women the weapons.

Maggie said, "I ain't never needed to use a gun before."

Miriam said, "And you've never been out west before. Rule one here is, you are never far from your long gun, and you have a pistol on you at all times to protect your person. If raiders come, you may have to help defend your homes and have your man's back. It's a matter of survival. I've kind of grown fond of you and I'd like to see you live to be rich old society wives."

Irene said, "Yeah, like that will happen."

Miriam said, "Half the grand ladies where you are from came from humble beginnings. It's money that will give your family a place but you have to live to enjoy it."

The women asked a few more questions. They would start lessons in the morning.

The camp fell back into its routine. Three mornings a week for an hour Miriam instructed the women. After two weeks all three of them could use the coach guns. The pistols were another matter. Sarah and Maggie took to it best. They got to the point they could hit most of what they shot at within twenty feet. Irene was iffy beyond ten feet.

Miriam worked with the men during the day panning, scouting, or standing guard. They were still finding surface gold in large quantities. The riders between Edward and James' camp came regularly. One day there was a break in the schedule. Raif gathered ten of the men and went to find out what was happening. The rest of the men would stay close to camp until it was known what was happening.

Those staying made sure the water barrels were full, the shutters were closed, and the watch was doubled. The camp was secure. Any raiders would pay a high price if they attacked.

Raif and his men rode all night and approached Charles' camp about dawn. They could hear shots before they ever got to the camp. They pulled up and Raif signaled to his men to stay put. He and Cracker went to the crest of a hill, being careful to stay hidden.

It was clear the attackers and defenders were in a standoff. The attackers weren't making progress and the defenders weren't going anywhere. Several attackers' bodies were lying in the dirt. Raif looked through his field glasses then handed them to Cracker. After scanning the area, Cracker handed the glasses back and Raif put them in their case.

Raif asked, "You thinking what I'm thinking?"

Cracker smiled, "I'm sneakier, so if'in ya agree, I'll take men down the gulley and sneak up on the ones can't be got from here. I'll leave the best four long shooters with you to pick off that lot we can see."

Raif nodded agreement and said, "We'll wait until we hear your first shots."

Cracker went down the hill. The horses were hobbled and four men took up hidden positions with two to either side of Raif. Like Raif they were judging wind and distance.

Raif could see Cracker's men sneaking down the hill for the first hundred feet then they disappeared. It was almost twenty minutes before the firing to Raif's left started.

The men with Raif began picking off attackers who had been firing on the camp. As the raiders tried to avoid the fire from Raif's men behind them, shots from the camp dropped some of them. The siege was broken within ten minutes. Several attackers escaped on horseback. Raif was not about to go after them right then.

His men set up a perimeter while Raif and Cracker went into camp. Charles came out to meet them.

Raif said, "Hello, Charles."

"Raif, your timing couldn't be better. We were running low on ammunition."

Raif dismounted, "Any wounded?"

"Three. One might not make it."

Raif offered, "Miriam can do some doctoring. Your wounded men would have a better chance at our camp."

"I'd appreciate it."

"We brought extra ammunition. We figured you'd need it."

Charles said, "Good. We'll set out after that lot that attacked us. We can't let them be wandering around to attack us later."

Raif asked, "How many men you have at this camp?"

"Eight if you don't count the wounded."

Raif said, "Take five of mine with you."

Charles nodded.

Raif looked at Cracker, "Set the men to making three travois and let's get the pack horse up and get some ammunition for the Colonel."

"Yes, sir."

Raif said, "You find anything yet?"

"Not yet. You?"

"We are still successfully mining. After you kill that lot, you are welcome to come visit for a bit."

Charles said, "I'll take you up on that. All our tents were burned. We'll get what's salvageable on our way back."

Raif nodded. Everyone got to work. Charles and his men set out within fifteen minutes. Raif and Cracker and their men headed back with the three wounded men.

Raif's men had learned to make travois for their wounded during the war. They consisted of two long poles with cross members tied between them. A wounded man or cargo could be laid on the cross platform. Two poles on one end of the travois went on either side of the horse's haunches and were harnessed over the horses back. The two poles on the other end of the travois dragged along the ground. It made for a bumpy ride on rough ground, but it worked.

Raif's party arrived back at their camp about nightfall. They were tired and hungry.

Miriam took one look at the wounded men and said, "Get them inside. Someone go bring the other women."

The night just started for Miriam. That night Sarah, Maggie, and Irene were introduced into the world of doctoring wounds. It was a trial by blood. It was almost dawn when covered in blood Miriam came out onto the porch.

Raif had been sleeping in a chair on the porch. He woke the minute Miriam came out.

"Well?"

Miriam had tears in her eyes, "I lost the gut shot one. He was just too bad shot. He died a few minutes ago. I suspect it was blood loss inside. He swole up something bad. I expect the other two will recover. I might have to yet cut off the one fellows arm. The tourniquet might have been too tight for too long."

Raif said, "Charles went after those that escaped."

Miriam did not realize Cracker was on the porch until he said, "Can you use some help?"

Miriam said, "I'm going to get cleaned a bit. I need the table taken outside and washed down good. The bloody rags need to be burned. The blood needs to be cleaned up. I need a pot of boiling water to clean the surgical instruments in. They just need to sit for a bit in the boiling water but care must be taken not to touch the working ends when they come out. The one fellow needs a grave dug. We need to move the wounded fellows somewhere else in case Charles brings in more wounded. I need sleep."

Miriam got a basin of water and went inside. She went into her bedroom and washed and changed clothes. She brought the blood stained clothes out and threw them in a pile with the bloody rags. Men were already washing down the table and the two wounded men had been moved.

Miriam went into her bedroom and collapsed onto the sleeping platform. She woke to a gentle shaking.

Sarah said, "It's afternoon and you need to eat. I made you something."

Miriam asked, "How are the men?"

"No fever. The one woke up a couple of hours ago and was hurting bad. I gave him a bit of laudanum. I read a little in the book you brought and reckoned it was long enough since he got some. The other is unconscious."

Miriam nodded and rolled out of bed. She brushed her hair and left the bedroom. She stood there for a moment looking around the room. The cabin was spotless, but the kitchen table had a dark stain. Miriam supposed she'd need a new table for eating. That one would be her surgery table.

Miriam had never been a religious woman, but just then she prayed, "God don't let there be more wounded. Protect Charles' men."

Sarah was standing to one side and said, "I didn't know ya was religious, Mrs."

Miriam smiled at Sarah, "I'll be back directly," and headed for the women's outhouse. When she came back, she washed her hands and went out on the veranda. Sarah brought out fried steak, cornbread, and beans. Miriam was very hungry.

Sarah said, "May I say the blessing?"

Miriam didn't know why, but she said, "Please."

Sarah bowed her head, "Thank you God for the food, this lovely day, and for our life. Amen."

Miriam said, "Amen," and started eating. The food was very good.

Miriam was still half in shock and the two women ate silently. When Miriam finished, Sarah asked, "Are you alright."

Miriam shook her head no then said as she saw Raif coming, "But I will be."

Raif came up onto the porch, "How are you doing love?"

"I need you to hold me."

Raif pulled a chair over beside hers and put his arm around her. She laid her head on his shoulders and quickly fell asleep. Miriam woke about a half hour later and said, "Thank you, dear. I needed the comfort of your closeness."

Raif said, "My pleasure, love."

"Where's Sarah?"

"She's checking on the wounded."

Miriam said, "I'd better go have a look."

Raif went with her to the storehouse where the wounded were being kept. One of the women was with them constantly. It was now partially a makeshift hospital. Both men were semi-conscious. After looking at the men's wounds, Miriam was of the opinion they would both recover. It seemed that the arm wound was healing.

When they left the building Raif said, "You seem relieved."

"I am. I was terrified about taking the arm quickly enough that the man would live. It appears now that he will keep it unless infection sets in."

Early the next morning a sentry sounded the alarm. It turned out to be Charles and his men approaching the camp. They rode into camp and Charles dismounted by Raif.

Raif said, "Did you get them?"

"All of them. One of the men is wounded. The bullet is still in his leg."

Miriam said, "Quickly. Bring him in the house." Miriam found herself praying quietly as she prepared him. Sarah brought the instruments and medicines and Miriam went to work. Charles was standing near the door watching.

Miriam carefully used chloroform before cleaning the wound and removing the bullet. She then stitched the wound, after putting a medicinal powder on it, and bandaged it.

When she was finished, Charles said, "Most impressive."

Miriam said, "He can be moved in with the other patients."

Charles said, "How are the others?"

Miriam said, "I lost the gut shot one to bleeding inside. I'm not skilled enough for that. I had no idea what to do. All I could do was relieve his suffering. I think the other two will recover. This latest one should be alright in spite of my lack of knowledge. Tom survived worse."

Charles asked, "You were the one who doctored Tom?"

"Yes."

Sarah had gotten four men and they carried the kitchen table on which the wounded man rested to the makeshift hospital.

Miriam said, "If this keeps up, I think we'll need a building to use as a hospital. I definitely need a new kitchen table."

Raif just nodded.

Charles said, "I'll make sure you get one."

Miriam said, "You can sleep here tonight Charles. We have plenty of floor space or a chair."

Charles said, "Thank you. It is dry and warm. It will seem like the best hotel after a few weeks in the field. Besides, I have a field bed on the wagon."

Raif said, "Let's go outside Charles and have a cigar."

"I'd like that."

Sarah looked at Miriam and said with a smile, "Now that one's a real looker."

"I suppose he is."

Raif puffed on the cigar, "I didn't use these before, but I enjoy the occasional smoke now."

"Your wife is quite a woman."

"She is that."

Charles asked, "Can we get a message up the line?"

"As soon as a train comes through. The telegraph lines will get here eventually and I'll be glad of it."

Charles said, "I'm expecting the engineer and geologist two days from now. I don't know what time, so I'll have a couple of men wait."

Raif nodded, "We are expecting a shipment so I'll send a couple of my men with wagons to bring them here along with my cargo."

That evening the two groups socialized in the plaza. Several men had been taking shifts turning two spits on which were cooking sides of venison. The smell of the open hardwood fire and the meat cooking had everyone's mouthwatering by early evening. They ate the meat with beans, fresh bread, and onions.

After the meal, a fiddle and harmonica came out and two men started playing. All four of the women, and the husbands of the three married women, were good sports. The women took turns having one dance with each of the men. After about two hours, the women were worn out and the dancing tapered off. The guard was doubled at dusk and that night everyone slept well.

Raif got up in the early morning and in the dark made a round of the sentry posts. He talked briefly with the men at each post and then moved to the next. He was back at the cabin an hour after he'd left. He didn't think he could sleep so he put his rifle beside a chair on the porch and sat down. He quickly dozed off.

Raif woke to the cabin door opening. Sarah was bringing the night pots to the outhouse.

Raif said, "Good morning."

Sarah smiled, "Good morning, Major."

A few minutes later Miriam came out and said, "Good morning, love."

"Good morning."

Miriam said, "I need a full bath today. Sarah too. Do you think you could come and stand guard?"

Raif said, "Certainly."

"We'll go before breakfast then."

The three of them had their weapons and Sarah carried a bag containing clean clothes, soap, and toweling. The women went to a pool that was mostly surrounded by bushes. Raif turned away as they undressed and went into the water.

The women, clean and refreshed were chatting on the path when Raif who was slightly ahead of them motioned and they went silent. He motioned for them to get down and they squatted. Raif moved ahead. He watched as two men snuck around, apparently scouting the camp. Raif watched them for a bit then motioned Miriam forward.

He whispered, "Cover me from here."

Miriam nodded and Raif snuck off. Miriam kept her rifle ready, but not in firing position. To do so would tire her arm needlessly and perhaps hurt her steadiness when the time came.

The men were about to retreat when Raif said, "Drop the weapons or die."

One man tried to turn and Raif shot him. The other dropped his gun.

Miriam saw the third man sneaking up on Raif and shot him. Raif was distracted for just a moment and the other man made to go for his gun. Raif was close so stepped forward and kicked the man in the face as he stretched to pick up the pistol he'd dropped. The man fell and reached for the pistol again. Raif stomped hard on his hand and the man screamed and withdrew his hand. He was holding it with his other and rocking back and forth when Miriam showed up with Sarah.

Raif asked, "How's the one you shot?"

"Dead."

Miriam went and checked the one Raif had shot and added, "This one too."

Sarah went to the dead men and took their weapons and looked for valuables.

Men were coming forward from the camp. Raif called out, "Over here."

Five men made a perimeter and Raif asked the man he'd captured, "Who sent you?"

The man spit at Raif and cursed. Raif kicked him in the head and the man's eyes rolled up and he fell unconscious. The group took the captive to the camp. They then had all the women except Miriam go inside.

The captive woke to find himself hanging naked, and upside down from a spit. His eyes went wide as he watched men bringing firewood and laying it under him.

Raif said, "The pain will build as the heat increases. You can save yourself a lot of hurt by just telling us who sent you."

"You'll kill me anyway."

Raif said, "If you tell us what we ask, I promise you'll live."

There was gunfire in the distance.

Charles was standing next to Raif, "It sounds like Dan caught up to some of this fellow's gang."

"Seems so. We'd could wait and let them watch us burn him so they'll know what they're in for."

Charles said, "I say start him to cooking now. They'll hear his screams by the time they get close to camp. Might have more effect."

The man started pleading in a whiney voice, "Please don't. I'll tell. I'll tell alls of it."

Raif squatted down and looked the man in the eye, "Who sent you and why?"

"Feller named Abe Martin. Don't know the why of it. He paid some up front and showed us more we'd git when we finished the job. He done said we could take the horses and valuables. He said we could have the women too 'cept for one we was to be sure to kill."

Raif looked at Miriam. They both knew who the one woman was.

"How much he pay you up front?"

"Two hunred dollars. That much agin when we got back."

Raif asked, "Where is he?"

The man hesitated and one of the Gunners lit a match. The man said, "He's hole up in Cartersville."

Raif said, "Get him dressed and chain him up."

Two men rushed to take care of it.

Charles said, "I guess we need to visit Cartersville."

Raif said, "Yes. If we don't find out who is behind this Abe fellow, it will certainly happen again. I'd rather go on offense."

Miriam said, "I wonder if there are any other prisoners?"

It turned out there were none. The seven men in the raider's camp had all died.

Raif said, "What do you think, Miriam?"

"We can hold down the camp with ten of the Gunners. Leave either Cracker or Dan and take the rest."

Raif looked at Charles, "What do you think?"

"We should head to Cartersville."

Raif said, "Then it's agreed?"

Charles nodded.

Cartersville was a town of about four hundred people. It was quite large for the area. The men had slipped into town in groups of two or three and went mostly unnoticed because they didn't wear their dusters and badges at first. They wouldn't be there long. Raif went into the saloon alone but three of the Gunners were already there. Raif stepped up to the bar and leaned his rifle against it.

The man tending the bar said in an almost demanding tone, "What do ya want?"

Raif snarled, "What have you got?"

"Whiskey or whiskey."

Raif slapped money on the bar with his left hand, "I'll have the real whiskey. None of that homemade rot gut."

Raif had his back to the door, but could see the reflection of everything going on in the dirty mirror behind the bar.

The bartender asked, "What's your business here mister?"

Raif was drinking with his left hand and reached with his right and took a pistol from his cross draw holster and pointed it backward around his left side without anyone noticing, "Looking for Abe Martin."

A man jumped up from a table near the door and started to draw a gun. Raif shot him. The move left a hole in Raif's duster, but it had put another in the man who had tried to back shoot him. Raif dropped his glass and had another pistol drawn before anyone realized what had happened. Raif now had one pistol in his left hand pointing toward the door and the other in his right pointed at the bartender who was leaning over.

Raif said, "You'd better straighten up and leave that scatter gun under the bar."

The bartender straightened and Raif motioned him away. Raif jumped over the bar and holstered one of his pistols and picked up the bartenders sawed-off shotgun and unloaded it. He put it on the bar. Raif walked over to the bartender and asked, "Where's Martin."

The bartender said, "Don't worry, he'll be coming for you."

Raif said, "Good."

The place had cleared out and it seemed there was only Raif, the three deputies, and the bartender left in the place. The three deputies went to the stairs and two went up to the second floor. Raif leaned against the inside of the bar and picked up a glass and poured another drink. He stood sipping it and the bartender stayed in the far corner of the bar hoping when the shooting started he'd be out of the way.

A voice from outside yelled, "Ya in dare come out or we'll burn ya out."

Raif looked at the bartender, "Go tell them we'll be out in a minute. You might still save your saloon."

The bartender headed for the door. He opened it and was riddled with bullets and fell forward. Raif reached over the bar, grabbed the barrel of his rifle and headed for the stairs. He was the last one up. Bullets were tearing into the first floor.

Raif's men each took a second floor room and standing to the side opened the door. The one Raif opened resulted in a scream. Raif looked at the half dressed woman and said, "Get out."

She did as she was told. Raif went to the window. The men in the street were reloading as the Gunners started shooting from the second floor windows. The street was suddenly littered with bodies and men were running in all directions. The Gunners loaded their rifles then they all met in the hall. They all ran downstairs. They went out the front door. No one was in sight.

Covering each other they found their horses and headed for the east end of town, but not as fast as they could have. They had just left the town when a group of nine men on horseback came chasing after them. Raif's men reached the rise about a half mile from town and turned their horses to face the men chasing them. It was open field here.

Abe Martin yelled, "We got 'em now boys!"

Once Martin's men were in range Charles brought the rest of the group into sight and they started cutting Martin's men down. Abe Martin had survived many shoot outs. He'd always tried to have the upper hand, but this time he realized too late he was badly out gunned. He turned his

horse to run, but it collapsed under him. It had been shot.
Martin was thrown hard into the ground. He lay dazed then
lost consciousness.

Several hours later Abe Martin woke in the saloon. He
was groggy and in pain. He shook his head. He looked
around. Three of his men were tied to chairs and Abe
realized he was too. Abe felt the pain. It was very bad. He
looked down to see a bone sticking out of his right leg. He
looked up at a man sitting across from him studying him.

Abe asked, "Why?"

"You sent men to attack our camp. We didn't like that.
Tell me who sent you and you'll die quickly."

Abe decided this was a serious man. He made no
empty promises of life, but just an easy escape from the
pain of torture. Abe heard a piercing scream outside. He
decided.

"Ya must be Gunnerson. Ya fit the description."

Raif nodded yes.

"Man named Gates paid to have ya done in and your
men kilt or run off."

Raif asked, "First name?"

"Feller with him called him Gary."

Raif asked, "You have a name for this other fellow?"

"Gates just called him Parker. Man looked to be a
shooter."

Raif couldn't believe his ears. Cousin Constance's
husband was behind this.

Raif asked, "What did this Gates look like?"

"Eastern feller, about five eleven, brown hair, wearing
a suit and funny hat that looked like a bowl. Talked real
fancy like. Citified and as we outnumbered them two
fellers, probably easy pickings, which is what I should'a
done."

"What did he pay you?"

"Not enough to face the likes of you lot. He gived me a thousand dollars silver. That much agin was promised when the killin' was done."

Raif said, "So you contracted the killing out."

"Yeah. I didn't think a bunch of eastern fellers would put up much fight. I suppose the men sent is mostly dead like my fellers."

Raif nodded.

Martin said, "I should'a knowed it was too good. It were too much money for an easy killin'."

Raif motioned and two men took Martin and his men away.

Raif said, "Bring me the whore."

Charles came to the table next to where Raif had his chair and poured two glasses of whiskey. There were several shots out back. They were drinking when the woman was brought to Raif.

Raif said, "Today's your lucky day. I need some information. You give it and we leave well enough alone. You don't cooperate and there will be a fire and you may die in it."

The whore was looking at Raif, more with curiosity than fear. She said, "What do you want to know?"

Raif asked, "What's your name?"

"Maude."

"Maude, tell me about this Gates fellow and the man with him."

"Not too smart. If Abe hadn't been so greedy for the second payment, he'd be alive and they'd be dead. I told him so, but he wouldn't listen."

Raif said, "So you run this place?"

"Well, Charlie was my husband, but yeah, I run it."

"How long were the men here?"

"Two nights. They came from the east. I heard them talking about eliminating a feller named Gunnerson and his woman. I take it that's you?"

Raif said, "I'm asking the questions, Maude."

The woman said, "Yes, sir."

Raif said, "You tell me all you heard and if it's useful I'll not only leave your saloon standing, I'll give you some of the money Abe had on him."

The woman smiled and began talking. When she finished Raif said, "Give her twenty dollars silver from Abe's money belt." It was done and Raif added, "Maude, if you ever hear anything useful to me, there's more money in it for you."

Maude said, "Yes, sir."

Raif said, "Charles, I think it is time we left, don't you."

"I think you are right, Raif."

Outside Raif said, "Charles, split Abe's money between your fellows."

Charles looked at Raif.

"We are here on our own business. The men with you work for wages."

Charles nodded and said, "I'll let them know it was your idea."

It was a long ride back to camp. When they arrived they were met by a half the men left behind.

Raif asked, "Where's Miriam?"

Dan answered, "She went to town with the wagons. We got notified supplies was arriving. The train went to the end of the line with supplies and it'll drop our cargo off on the way back."

Charles yelled, "Grab some ammunition and mount up."

Raif asked, "How long ago did Miriam leave?"

"Fifteen minutes."

Charles said, "We can catch them."

On the trail, Miriam knew they had lots of time before the train arrived so the party was taking its time. Raif and Charles caught up to her about four miles outside of town.

Miriam, who was being vigilant, spotted them first. She pulled out her field glasses to make sure who it was. She yelled to Cracker who stopped the group. They waited for Raif.

Raif rode up and leaned over and said, "Hi, love."

Miriam leaned over and kissed him then said, "I'm glad you're back. Any wounded?"

"No."

Miriam did not ask if they'd taken prisoners.

Raif motioned Cracker and with Charles and Miriam there, Raif said, "There will be an ambush at the train."

Miriam said, "And we'd of walked right into it."

Cracker said, "But now we know it's a comin', we can turn it back on 'em."

Raif said, "I think we have enough time."

When the train pulled into the station, the wagons were parked parallel to the train tracks as though waiting to pull up to unload cargo. It looked like some of the drivers and escort were sitting against the wagons on the shady side. One man, the only figure that was actually a human, got up as the train stopped and walked toward the last wagon in the row.

On the train Parker said to his men, "They aren't expecting anything. We have to take this lot hard and fast then move on to the camp." The men mounted their horses in the boxcars bending over in their saddles to stay clear of the overhead door frames as they exited. The doors of three boxcars were opened at about the same time and men jumped out then pulled out ramps. Horses started coming out, their masked riders shooting and heading for the wagons.

Parker was leading and only got about thirty feet when the return fire started. His horse went out from under him and he was thrown. Parker was about to try to stand when a flailing leg of his injured horse grazed his head and Parker was knocked unconscious. He was a lucky one.

The first few horses were down and blocking the other riders from exiting the cars. The cars were being riddled with bullets and horses and men were being hit. Horses were screaming and their riders trapped in the cars with the terrified horses died of bullets or flailing hooves or being trampled by the horses. No one inside could open the doors on the other side of the cars. It was over very quickly.

Only Parker and three of his men who had pulled out the ramps survived. Raif and Charles lost no one and Miriam had just a few minor cuts to bandage. All the train employees except the engineer were found murdered. Raif's cargo was not on the train.

Parker woke to find himself on the ground and chained to a steel rail. Three other men were chained near him. They were all glaring at him. Parker ignored them. He examined the situation and found that other than having a splitting headache, he was uninjured.

Two men were sitting about twenty feet away. One had a coach gun in his lap. It was he who said to the other, "Better go get the major and tell him Parker is back in the land of the living."

A few minutes later, Raif came and Parker yelled, "You murdering bastard. You killed all those railway security men."

Raif started laughing, "Will, Will. I know about you and Gary. These men are not railway men and you and I both know it."

Raif went over and looked at Parker's men and stated the obvious, "You threw in with the wrong side."

Two of the men had their heads hung low in the manner of defeated men. The third looked Raif in the eyes and shrugged. His actions did not impress Raif.

Raif said, "Let's take Parker aside."

Parker was taken away and chained to a hitching pole sunk in the ground. Raif grabbed a piece of log and used it for a chair. He sat in front of Parker.

Parker asked, "How did you know?"

Raif said, "I'm asking the questions."

Parker said, "But how..."

Raif got up and kicked him. Parker rolled over onto his side unconscious. Raif was called back when Parker regained consciousness. Parker now had a swollen face.

Raif took a seat, "Shall we start again? How has Gary got his hooks in this business?"

Parker seemed shocked and started to say something then stopped. Raif waited for him to speak.

Parker took a deep breath and started, "Gary was able to talk a group of investors to jointly make a big investment in the railroad. He got a piece of the action for putting the deal together. He had some sort of legal document that let him manage the investment behind the scenes. He was close enough to your uncles to manipulate them into helping without their knowing. I don't know how. He bought land in his own name with a loan from the railroad. He figured with a rail line here, he'd make a fortune selling land for ranching and selling town sites. Some gold had been found, but it needs expensive mining. I know he figured on using a rumor to create a gold rush."

"Go on."

Parker said, "Then his wife was eavesdropping and overheard about real gold being found. She told him about it. He figured a way to get money to finance his plans."

Raif asked, "How?"

"Take your gold."

Raif asked, "Why the massacre at rails end."

"To muddy the waters as to what was to happen here."

Raif asked, "What was his plan for me?"

"He thought to scare you off."

Raif shook his head and said, "Abe said he was hired to kill me and what really makes me angry, he was told to kill Miriam."

Parker did not respond.

Raif got up and walked away. He needed to think. He went and sat on the edge of the station deck. Miriam came with Charles and they sat beside him.

Miriam asked, "What's wrong, dear?"

Raif told her. Miriam didn't say anything for several minutes and Charles sat silently thinking.

Raif said, "Parker's understanding of things may not be complete or entirely right."

Miriam nodded and said, "Maybe and maybe not. Greed makes men crazy. Still, we know it's all Gary's doing. The problem is we can't prove anything. In truth, we can't be sure of what we know aside from the fact Gary apparently wants us dead and Parker stole a train. If Parker hangs we have no proof of Gary's connection to all this."

"True."

Miriam said, "What are we going to do?"

Raif said, "Write a long letter to my uncles about what happened here and what we've found out."

Miriam said, "You'll have to be careful about the details you include in case it falls into the wrong hands."

Raif nodded agreement, "What do you think?"

Charles said, "We can't do anything about the railway from here so let's leave that to your uncle's and get as much wealth out of here as we can."

Raif said to Miriam, "Do you think we'll settle here?"

Miriam sighed, "Love, I'd like to, but it may be out of our hands. We should wait and see what happens here. I don't think gold and cattle will mix. Until all the gold is taken, won't raising cattle be impossible? How do you guard a mine and take care of a herd?"

Raif said, "You're right. We should think about you going back to Pennsylvania."

Miriam said, "I'm not leaving. We are a team. Besides there's no guarantee I'll be safer there. You forget, I've killed men there. Gary's there and so I'd be in more danger there."

Raif nodded agreement then said, "I'll need your help to write the letter to my uncles."

Miriam added, "We need to decide who will be trusted to bring it to them."

They went back to the ranch where it took Raif and Miriam an hour and a half to decide on what should go in the letter and for Miriam, who had a neater hand, to write it. They sealed the letter and decided who would take it. They hoped the uncles would consider how to rid themselves of the viper in their nest.

Miriam had finished the letter when Charles came to the porch.

"Interesting few days."

Raif said, "Yes. Any idea of what to do with Parker?"

Charles took a chair, "Yes I do. Leave it to me. The only railway person Parker's fellows didn't kill was the train engineer because he was needed. He'll be a good witness at their trial. I have a plan that may help you deal with Gary."

Raif asked, "What is it?"

Charles told Raif and Miriam. It was a good idea and Raif said so.

Charles said, "I'll see if I can arrange it."

Raif asked, "What about the bodies of the raiders."

"I had the fellows bury them. The engineer witnessed it. I'll get a report to the territorial capitol. The engineer already made a statement and identified Parker and the others."

Raif said, "What do you think the territorial people will do outside of hold a trial."

"They may send someone to investigate and gather more facts, but it is what it is. We killed most of the ones that murdered the railway men and stole the train."

Raif said, "I wonder what Parker did at rail end."

Charles said, "The engineer says they murdered everybody. I sent a couple of men to confirm it."

I wasn't two hours later that the two riders returned. They were brought directly to Charles and Raif.

Charles spoke first, "What did you find, Les?"

"Bodies and ashes. Everything's burnt and everyone were kilt. Scavengers was already at the bodies. Too many bodies for us to do anythin'."

Charles looked at Raif, "I'd better send a rider to the nearest telegraph."

Raif nodded agreement, "We'd better ask for replacement supplies and men to bury the bodies to be sent."

For the next two days things were relatively quiet and mining operations continued. The one unusual event was that Parker and his three men were taken under guard to the territorial capitol to stand trial for murder. Charles sent a letter with the engineer who went as well. The prosecution was considered railway business and the engineer would be paid for his time in the capitol.

Several days later another train arrived. Raif, Miriam, and Charles were there to meet it with several men. They were waiting, the wagons between them and the train, with their rifles at the ready.

Three men wearing badges got off the train with a few railway employees. They saw the wagons and the armed deputies. Raif and Charles went to meet them.

The man who was the obvious leader said, "Good day, gentlemen. I'm Clint Crowe, U.S. Marshal and these are my deputies."

Raif said, "This is my associate, Deputy Sheriff Charles Bleeker, and I'm Raif Gunnerson, sheriff for these parts."

The men shook hands.

Clint said, "I understand ya was the ones who kilt the murderous scum who kilt all them folks at the end of rail." The marshal spit out some chewing tobacco.

Charles said, "At the time we did not know about the end of rail. The engineer told us after the attack here. They just came off the train shooting at us and we returned fire."

The marshal asked, "Any of 'em live?"

Raif said, "Just the ones we sent."

The marshal said, "Makes my job easier. I understand' ya sent two men to the end of track after the shoot-up here. I'd surely like to talk with the ones who went."

Charles said, "No problem." Charles looked at one of his men who without being told went to get the two deputies.

The marshal said, "All your people have them fancy rifles?"

Raif said, "Yes. My deputies are all issued them."

"I hear ya's all fought in the war."

Raif said, "You heard correctly."

"I can see where them raiders found themselves in a wasp's nest. You have anything agin them ya killed."

Raif said, "Yes. Aside from the fact they tried to kill us, they stole a train, murdered railway employees, and destroyed railway property. I take that personally as my family has a large interest in the railway."

Clint smiled, "I could see where ya would have no sorrow in the killin' of 'em."

Charles said, "And we don't."

The marshal asked, "Ya know why anyone would do this?"

Raif shrugged, "There has to be a reason. It won't stop the railroad. This delays the schedule and delay means money lost, but it certainly won't stop the line from going forward."

The marshal nodded, "I dun see how I kin find out why this were done with everyone dead." The marshal paused and looked at Raif, "It shore nuff seems they musta bin after somethin' special."

Raif said, "If you find out Marshal, I'd appreciate knowing."

The marshal looked at Raif and nodded.

The two men who the marshal wanted to interview came and Raif left to supervise the unloading of their cargo. Several men were getting off the train.

One came to Raif, "You know where they found the gold?"

Raif said, "I heard down the track a piece past where all them folks were murdered."

The man looked at Raif, "They try to run us off they'll have their hands full." The man turned to his friends, "Back on the train. The danger and the gold is further along."

Raif knew trouble was on the way. He headed back to where the marshal was. The marshal was just finishing his questioning of the men and said, "I'm obliged."

Charles had listened to the questioning.

Raif asked the marshal, "You know where these men got the idea there was gold down the tracks?"

"There's big rumors about gold bein' found. When I left, there was a passel of folks trying to git tickets to the end of the line. I s'pect some will be comin' by horse or wagon."

Raif said, "Is there anything we can do for you, Marshal?"

"Kin someone show me where the raiders is buried?"

Charles turned to Les, one of the men the marshal had just interviewed, "Show the marshal where the graves of them low-lifes are."

Les nodded, "Foller me, Marshal." The men set off.

When the marshal returned, Raif's people had just about gotten all their cargo off the train and into their wagons.

The marshal came to talk to Raif and motioned him aside, "I ain't got no problem with most of 'em murderous scum not livin'. I kin see everythin' here was legal like. Kin I 's'pect trouble in these parts 'cause of gold."

Raif asked, "Between us?"

The marshal nodded agreement and spat chewing tobacco onto the ground.

"Probably. I know some ore from down the line was sent for assay and it wasn't kept much of a secret. I suspect that's why some others tried to rob the train. We happened to be going east on business and six of us made quick work of the would-be train robbers. I did some asking around back east. I'm told the ore is the kind that will need engineered mining; lots of heavy equipment, and a big investment. That's profitable, but no get rich quick thing. Even so, there will be wild rumors and there will be trouble. I expect we'll have trouble keeping prospectors off our range. When they can't get gold, some will try to take what they need."

The marshal said, "And there's bound to be killin' all over as greed takes hold."

Raif nodded.

The marshal looked at Raif and asked, "How big a ranch ya got?"

"Over forty thousand acres. My two uncles each own the same size spread. When the ranches are stocked, we'll be able to ship beef direct to the cities back east. Good as gold and almost as profitable. I expect lots of farm goods will be shipped as well. If gold is mined then that won't hurt the railway."

The marshal asked, "Ya know ranchin'?"

"Yes. My branch of the family are ranchers. I have another ranch about half the size of this one that my pa and I built up."

The marshal just nodded then asked, "What ya need all these fightin' men for? Ain't no cattle here yet."

"You know the answer to that Clint. I can't protect what I've got or even get established without good men to keep the no-goods away. Being local lawmen we can protect others in the area. We've already fought off Indians and raiders. We've stopped train robbers and an attack on the railroad camp. We even had a shootout with a fellow who murdered a woman. It seems there are a lot who'd rather steal and murder than work."

The marshal nodded and smiled, "Still, it's a lot of deputies to protect cattle." Clint paused then when Raif didn't say anything continued, "I heard about all ur doin's. Word's gettin' around ya ain't no easy pickin's. Any truth ya had a run in with Abe Martin's men."

Raif said, "His outfit organized a raid on our ranch. It was not a good idea."

"Don't suppose I'll have to worry 'bout him no more. Why you agree to be sheriff."

Raif said, "When I realized how profitable my new ranch could be, I knew the future would be dependent on the lawless element being kept out."

Clint nodded, "Understand. I ain't complainin'. I has my hands full elsewhere. Like all the marshals, I'm run plum ragged all over the territory. I'm just puttin' out li'l fires while the whole kit and caboodle is ready to burn like hell."

Raif knew about Clint Crowe by reputation. In spite of his folksy ways, the man was no fool and was known to be a deadly fighter. He had a fierce reputation. He was also rumored to be as honest as a man could be. Raif could tell he'd probably figured out Raif had found gold here.

Raif said, "I could always use a man like you. Probably pays better than being marshal."

"Tell me."

Raif did and Clint said he'd be agreeable, but he had some matters he had to clean up first. Raif gave him money as a good faith payment toward future employment.

Miriam was standing by the wagons watching her husband talk to the marshal, when two men approached.

One of the men asked, "Mrs. Gunnerson?"

Miriam rested her hand on a pistol, "Yes."

The man said quietly, "I'm Carl Zimmer and this is Dave Peters. Mr. Gunnerson's uncles sent us. I have this letter of introduction for you."

Miriam took the letter, opened and read it, *"Raif and Miriam. These gentlemen, Carl Zimmer and Dave Peterson are the ones I promised to send to assess the situation on our lands. I suggest they start with your land and then move on. I would appreciate them always having security men with them in the field. Give our regards to Charles.*

James and Edward."

Miriam said, "Welcome, Carl, Dave." She offered her hand and they all shook.

After finishing with the marshal, Raif came to her and Miriam did the introductions.

Raif shook hands with the men and said to one of the men standing nearby, "Help these men with their things."

The reply was very military, "Yes, Major."

Miriam took Raif aside, "Your uncles sent this letter."

Raif read it and said, "Well we'd best get to work."

CHAPTER 10 – THE COMING INVASION

Over the next week, Charles and his men returned to James' land to continue to scout the area. They had to run off some squatters who had set up camp with the intention of starting a homestead. In fact they had run off numerous parties on the land. Charles' men also found two groups who were panning for gold. One had found nothing and the party was run off. One of the miner groups got ugly as they had found some gold.

They made the mistake of trying to shoot Charles' men. They were buried near their claim. The gold was confiscated and any sign of the campsite was removed.

Charles came to see Raif who was at the river. Dave Peters was showing the men how to efficiently sift the sediments for more gold. They were still taking out large amounts of dust and nuggets.

Charles approach was sighted by one of the look-outs and Raif was informed. Raif was waiting when Charles came with three men. Raif thought Charles looked tired.

Charles got off his horse and said, "Hi, Raif."

"You look tired. Your men too."

Charles nodded, "We have problems."

Raif motioned and they walked toward camp. Charles men followed.

Charles said, "You have any intruders?"

"We've had a few come from the area of the railroad tracks. We sent them packing. You?"

Charles said, "Some miners found gold and when we found them they tried to kill my men. They are buried near where they were mining. Not a day goes by we don't run folks off. I don't have enough men."

"How much gold?"

"Couple of pounds."

Raif said, "We'd better get serious. We'll recruit more security, but how do my uncles mine without having most of their profits stolen."

Charles said, "Similar to the way you do."

Raif nodded. They walked into the camp and to Raif's cabin. Miriam came out to greet Charles as his men went to find a place to rest.

She shook his hand and said, "It's good to see you Charles. You look dead tired. Would you like coffee and perhaps something to eat?"

Charles said, "Just coffee please."

Sarah who was standing in the doorway went to get it.

Charles said, "You are looking good, Miriam. You are showing, but you are still as pretty as ever."

Miriam smiled, "Thank you."

Sarah brought coffee. As she handed a cup to Charles they exchanged a look and both smiled. The men sat on the veranda with Miriam.

Raif said, "The telegraph line reached the station here. I'll send a telegraph to my uncles. I think a profit sharing arrangement would be good. I still think we need more men. I have an idea how to get some of them."

Charles said, "I'd like to hear your plan."

They talked for about half an hour then Raif drafted a telegraph to his uncles. It read, *"Profits to be had. Stop. Need more security. Stop. Ask Connor recruit thirty plus reliable security men for wages. Stop. Advise profit sharing Charles et al. Stop. Nephew."*

Raif also sent a telegraph to Clint Crowe. *"Need your help now. Stop. Need a dozen trustworthy deputies. Stop. Gunnerson."*

Raif had one of the men take the telegraph to town. When he had left, Miriam said, "Charles, you are welcome to stay here and rest up."

"Thank you Miriam, I'll accept your kind offer. If I am to stay here, I'd best get cleaned up. I'm going to wash up and shave."

Charles rose, mounted his horse, and rode toward the river.

Miriam said, "I wonder what that was all about."

Raif looked at Sarah, "It's not hard to figure out."

Miriam followed his look and saw Sarah smiling and blushing slightly.

Raif said, "I'd better get back to work," and after kissing his wife headed back to the river.

The next day a rider was again sent to town to wait for a response to the telegraphs. He returned midafternoon. He had two telegraphs which he brought to Raif who was at the river.

The first he read was from his uncles. It simply said, "*Agreed. Stop. Proceed as you think best. Stop. With our full authority. Stop. Connor agreed to help. Stop. Uncles.*"

Raif smiled and read the next telegraph. "*Can come with seven. Stop. More later. Stop. Need horses and new rifles. Stop. Arrive four days. Stop. Clint.*"

Raif sent the rider back to town to telegraph for certain things to be sent by train. Raif sent for Jeremy who came.

Raif said, "Jeremy, we are going to need more horses. I need you to go buy us about four dozen good ones."

Jeremy said, "I won't have to go far to get them. I'll take Hiram."

Raif nodded, "And take Tom for security."

Jeremy said, "Yes, Major."

Raif went looking for Charles and found him sitting by the river watching the work while talking with Sarah. Raif called out from a distance, "Hello."

Charles looked up and waved.

When Raif arrived where they were sitting, he said, "I've gotten a reply."

Charles said, "And?"

220

"I have full authority to act for my uncles so we'll go ahead with the plan. We need to meet with the men."

Charles smiled, "Good. I think I'll like living out here and raising a family."

Sarah blushed.

Raif said, "You know Miriam will insist on a proper wedding."

Charles said, "It is prudent given the dangers here. Sarah explained the necessity to ensure the family is looked after if something should happen to me."

Raif looked at Sarah, "Does Miriam know?"

Sarah said, "It was just agreed. Miriam knows though. I will stay here until after the baby arrives and Charles has a proper cabin for me."

Raif said, "We'll send for a minister. I understand there is a circuit Methodist preacher rides these parts, though I've never seen him."

Charles said, "We'll get married when he can come."

Sarah leaned over and kissed Charles, "I'd better go tell the Mrs. you finally got up the nerve to ask."

Charles smiled and nodded. After Sarah had left, Raif said, "She'll make a good wife."

Charles said, "I know. She's well suited for this land."

Raif looked around, "I need to go talk to my sergeants. Want to tag along."

Charles nodded yes.

Cracker and Dan met with Raif and Charles at the river. They all sat on some rocks.

Raif said, "I have some news. There is definitely gold on my uncles' land. Connor is recruiting more help because the invasion has already started. I have also hired Clint Crowe. He will have equivalent rank to you, but he is hired and not profit sharing. He will be responsible to keep the people from coming here from the railway and the future town site. He will be supervising the deputies he is bringing."

Dan said, "So he won't be working here?"

"No. I want to keep this area to just our people here. Charles' present people will be doing profit sharing as we do here and the new people will be hired and mainly secure the family property away from the mining."

Cracker said, "Makes sense. It will also mean we only have to be concerned about the main ranch and the area we are working at the time or where gold is likely to be found."

Raif nodded.

Dan said, "You want us to let the men know what's going on."

Raif said, "Yes. One other thing, I will have to go with Charles as my family's representative to tell his men about the deal being offered to them. Anything else?"

Cracker said, "I do has one thing to say," and looked at Charles, "You treat Sarah good hear, or Colonel or no, I'll box your ears." Cracker put out his hand and Charles shook it. Both men were smiling.

Charles said, "How did you know?"

Cracker said, "I ain't blind."

Raif said, "What have you learned from this, Cracker?"

"The better washed man gits the gal."

They all laughed. Still time would show Cracker took the lesson to heart.

The next morning, Charles and his men left with Raif and one of his men. Raif was gone two days before returning. He rode into the plaza at dusk. Miriam came out to meet him. Sarah stood on the porch.

Raif dismounted and Miriam hugged him tightly, "I miss you when you are away."

Raif said, "Believe me, my love, it is mutual."

Miriam said, "How did you stay so clean on the trail."

"I stopped at the river and bathed anticipating a warm welcome."

Miriam laughed, "And you will get that after you get settled and fed."

Sarah said, "I'll put something together."

The couple sat on the porch and Sarah brought coffee.

Raif asked, "How is production?"

"We hit extraordinarily rich silt and took off a record amount. It is time we took a load east. We have a lot of those small boxes. There's more than last time."

"We'll go after I get Clint settled. He is due to arrive tomorrow."

Miriam said, "Jeremy is back with the horses already."

"That was quick."

Miriam smiled, "It seems a lot of people came to the territory to get rich quick and when that didn't happen, had to sell possessions to raise money to return where they came from. He purchased other things as well. He has asked to go back with us on our next trip."

Miriam took a sip of her coffee. Raif looked at Miriam waiting for the rest of what was coming. She said nothing.

Finally, Raif said, "Tell me, dear."

"Jeremy had a girl he was sweet on. If she's still unwed, he'd like to court her."

Raif said, "Which family does she work for."

"She wasn't employed in a household. She is a store clerk."

"What do you think of her?"

Miriam said, "I hope she's spoken for. Jeremy can do better."

Raif just nodded, "If she isn't available, what then?"

"He's agreed to letting me do some matchmaking. I also have to hire someone to replace Sarah."

Raif said, "I'd better get a telegraph off telling my uncles we are coming."

Miriam said, "Please don't dear. Have it sent after we are well on our way. Who knows who might see those telegraphs?"

Raif nodded agreement, "Seems wise."

The next day Raif was at the station waiting when Clint arrived. Clint got off the train and went to Raif.

"Hello, Major."

"Glad to see you, Clint. Some of my people have your camp set up there on the hill. I'll be hiring carpenters to construct a small cabin, a stable, and a permanent bunkhouse. Meantime we have tents for you."

Clint said, "Better'n I s'pected right off."

Clint introduced the men with him to their new employer. Raif shook hands and talked to each of them a little. When they finished the introductions, Clint motioned and the men got in the wagon. They loaded their saddles and personal belongings.

Raif said to Clint, "The bay is for you."

Clint saddled the mount and they rode off. Clint said, "I'll get the men to choose a spot then I'll suppose you'll want to meet with them."

Raif said, "Yes. You'll get to meet my other sergeants and Charles when they're in town."

They arrived at the hilltop. Two large military tents had been erected and a small officer's tent.

Clint's men were getting out of the wagons and he told them, "Claim a space and drop your gear and come back for a meeting."

The men were surprised to find the tents had stoves and were furnished with military surplus field gear. They had not expected such comforts. They did as they were told and congregated.

Clint said, "Y'all might as well sit."

Raif said, "If Clint chose you that means you are all good at what you do. I'm glad you are here to help keep peace and order. After you're sworn in and get your badges, we'll provide your special gear. I'm sure Clint has told you the offer. So as to be sure there's no misunderstandings, you get paid once a month. As long as you stay at the sheriff's barracks, you get your board and provisions provided. You will be provided with horses. I will issue you a Henry repeating rifle which stays the property of the sheriff, me, so take care of it. If you leave, the horse and the rifle stays unless you buy them. To make sure you have pocket money, you will receive a one week advance on your first pay. Questions."

"Is Clint in charge of the deputies?"

Raif smiled, "Since he is the only one willing to deal with you lot of ruffians, he will be your sergeant."

There were some chuckles.

Raif continued, "You will report to him. I have two other sergeants and a former army colonel who is my second."

One of the men asked, "How many deputies is there?"

Raif said, "Including this group, we number just over sixty."

One of the men said, "Jiggers. How big a territory ya got, Sheriff."

Raif said seriously, "We police the entire county, over a hundred and fifty thousand acres. Most of it my family owns. Your part will be the control of the border on the rail side and especially here where the train stops. My family doesn't allow trespassers and part of your job is to keep them off our land. We also protect the railroad and people within the sheriff's area. Clint will show you a map of your area over which we have the right to enforce the law."

One of the men motioned and Raif pointed to him.

"Folks say ya's family owns the railroad. That true."

Raif said, "My family owns a major share in this line."

Another man made a motion and Raif nodded.

The man asked, "How long ya suppose we got jobs?"

"Assuming you are good at it and loyal, it could be many years and maybe even lifelong. For that to happen I need peace here. If I'm successful, everyone has a job. I fail, we all fail. It is no secret my branch of the family are ranchers and I plan to raise cattle here for a long time. I expect this will come to be a busy town. Other businesses will be here too."

The men looked around and one asked, "What if'in one of ur deputies gits hitched."

"That's your business. You'll mostly work close to here and make a good wage. I don't see why you can't support a wife and family. Save your money for a year and you can buy land and build a home."

Raif motioned to Jeremy who was nearby. Jeremy came over.

"This is my stock manager Jeremy who is also deputized. He's going to give you an advance on pay and have you sign or make your mark on the enlistment paper. He will also give you your equipment. Now let's get you sworn. Stand up and raise your right hand. You too, Clint."

After the swearing in, Raif gave each of the men badges and shook their hands.

Raif turned to Clint, "Let's go talk."

The men went to Clint's tent.

Clint asked, "Ya mean what ya said 'bout settlin'."

Raif said, "Yes. We all have a part in making it work though."

"Them are all good ole boys. They'll do what they're told."

Raif took out a wad of paper money, "Here's a month's pay and the recruitment bonus for each of the men you brought." Raif counted out the money.

Clint said, "I reckon' that's ta most money I ever had at one time."

Raif said, "You can have a nice thing going here, Clint."

Clint smiled, "I reckon' to make it so."

Raif counted out some more money, "This is for expenses. You keep a reckoning of what you spend it on."

"Sure thing."

Raif said, "Carpenters and laborers are coming on the next train to put up buildings for you. They know where they go. Keep an eye they don't wonder off. I'm taking my wife back east and we are bringing back more help. Charles will be in charge while we're gone, but he may or may not come by. I'll introduce you to one of the other sergeants tomorrow. You need something you can't get, you ask him. I'm relying on you to do whatever needs to be done. Try not to let anyone move them little flags. They mark the lots and streets of the town to be built."

Clint nodded.

Raif said, "I'm goin' to help my wife get ready for the trip."

Raif offered his hand and the men shook.

Clint went outside with a campaign chair and sat down. One of his men came. They watched Raif and Jeremy ride away.

"He on the up and up?"

Clint said, "Yup. Wouldn't ah tied my wagon to his horse if I did'n reckon so."

"Then we are goin' to have it good."

"Long as we kin stay alive. Same as always, only better workin' ways."

The man smiled, "And them rifles is some sweet piece."

"Yup. Load 'em on Sunday and fire 'em until Saturday."

The man smiled.

The next morning, Raif and his party arrived with three wagons at the train station for the journey east. When the train arrived there were no passengers to see Raif and his men load the boxes into the passenger car. While they were working, they heard gunfire in the distance. Raif looked up to see Clint ride down.

Clint dismounted and Raif went to meet him.

Clint said, "I has the deputies practicin' with them new rifles on ta other side of the hill. I thought it best them didn't see ya loadin' them heavy li'l boxes. No wonderin' about what's that heavy. My lips is sealed."

Raif just nodded.

Clint said, "I suppose the cattle comes later."

Raif said, "You reckoned right."

"Ya, I understand it always runs out after a while. Have a good trip, Sheriff."

Raif nodded and smiled, "Keep the peace."

Clint smiled and spat out some tobacco, "And keep my job."

Raif laughed and Clint mounted up and rode off.

The first leg of the trip was uneventful and as in the past they got their business done without any problems. Most of the men headed back west when Raif, Miriam, and Jeremy started the second leg. Raif was carrying a money belt full of currency and Jeremy wore another. Miriam looked even more pregnant than she was with more paper money, a lot, loosely bound around her middle.

When they arrived at their destination, they rented a carriage. They did not go directly to Uncle James' home but made some stops at various banks. Even after the stops, Raif still wore his money belt.

They arrived at James' home to find no one came out to greet them. Raif said to Miriam, "Stay here, my dear."

Raif knocked on the front door and a servant Raif did not know said, "Good afternoon, sir. May I help you?"

"I came to see Mr. Gunnerson."

"Mr. Gunnerson no longer lives here. The Pratley family bought this home most of a month ago."

Raif inquired, "Do you know where I can find Mr. Gunnerson."

"I understand they moved to the summer home."

Raif said, "Thank you."

Jeremy and Miriam had heard the exchange. They decided to eat before leaving town. They had just finished a nice meal at a restaurant and were drinking tea when a man approached them. He was a very thin man with gaunt features.

He looked at Raif and said, "Aren't you Raif Gunnerson?"

"Yes."

"I'm Alton Manley. I was sorry to hear about your uncle's bad luck."

Raif said, "Pardon?"

The man had what Raif thought was an evil smile, "I mean the fire at his business. Nasty that. Bad piece of luck. James is such a nice man. Give him my regards won't you. Remember, my name is Alton Manley."

The man left and Miriam said, "I wonder what that was all about?"

Raif said, "I have no idea."

Miriam said, "We should go look at James' place of business."

Jeremy said, "Why don't you do that and come back for me. I want to visit a certain shop. You can pick me up on the way back."

Raif and Miriam went to James' place of business. The building was heavily damaged by fire and unoccupied. They got out of the carriage and looked inside the shell through one of the windows.

Raif said, "The big safe is open."

Miriam said, "The building will have to come down."

They walked around the building looking at it from all sides. A constable happened by and stopped by them.

"Good day, sir. Mrs. May I help you?"

Raif said, "This was my uncle's place of business. We just came to visit and heard about the fire."

The constable said, "I recognize you. You're Major Gunnerson."

Raif held out his hand, "Guilty." The men shook hands and Raif added, "This is my wife Miriam."

The constable tipped his hat, "Pleased to meet you, Mrs. Gunnerson. I'm Constable Wright. Nasty business this. It was no doubt a work of arson. If anyone can figure this out the inspector can."

Raif asked, "When did it happen?"

"Three days ago. The fire volunteers, as you can see, did a fine job of keeping the fire from spreading. They also got it out hurry up quick like. Damage is not as bad as it looks, but the building will be easier to rebuild than fix."

Raif said, "Anything else you can tell me?"

"That's about it, sir."

Raif said, "Thank you, Constable. You have been very helpful." Raif shook the Constables hand again.

Miriam said, "Thank you."

The constable smiled and walked away.

Raif and Miriam went to the carriage and set out to get Jeremy. Miriam could tell by the look on Jeremy's face things had not gone well. They stopped and Jeremy climbed in.

He said, "Let's go."

Miriam said, "What's happened?"

"She's engaged to the son of the feed mill owner. When I tried to talk to her, she said she had no interest in being courted by a household servant."

Miriam said, "Ouch."

Raif said, "You didn't tell her about your new status."

"Why? She's obviously the wrong kind of woman. No future in that. What good's a woman just marries for what a fellow's got?"

Miriam said, "Well thought, brother."

Jeremy said, "I was sure she'd wait. She said she would."

Miriam said, "I will hold you to our agreement."

"Yes, sister. It seems you are better in romance than I."

On the ride to the summer home, Miriam and Jeremy discussed workers they knew who might be suitable as Miriam's new woman. They arrived at the summer home to find a flurry of activity. They tied the carriage team to a tree because construction was underway at the back of the house. They got halfway to the house when Henry came rushing out to meet them.

"Welcome home, Major, Mrs., Mr. Jeremy."

The trio smiled and greeted Henry.

Henry seemed all excited, "As you can see, a large addition is being constructed and stables and servants quarters. It is a large undertaking. Your uncle and aunt will be so pleased to see you. Please come, I'll send someone for your things. Mr. and Mrs. Gunnerson are at Mr. Edward's for lunch."

Raif said, "I hear there's been some excitement."

"Oh, yes. Mr. James will want to tell you all about it."

Once Miriam and Raif were shown to their room, Miriam partially undressed and Raif helped her unwrap the bundles of cash wrapped around her middle. They put the money into a carry bag. The trio met on the front veranda. A new servant girl came to the veranda.

"May I get you something to drink?"

Miriam said, "What's your name?"

"Callie, ma'am."

"Callie, please bring lemonade for all of us."

The girl said, "Yes, ma'am," and went into the house.

Raif said, "They are going into service younger and younger."

Miriam said, "I was her age when I started in service."

Raif said, "Yes, I guess you must have been."

The girl brought a tray with lemonade and some small slices of bread and cheese.

Miriam said, "Thank you, Callie. The bread and cheese was a nice touch."

The girl curtsied just a little, "You're welcome, ma'am." She left.

Jeremy asked, "What do you suppose your uncle is up to?"

Raif smiled, "I have no idea, Jeremy."

They had been sitting for about ten minutes when they heard gunfire. Raif looked at his wife and brother-in-law.

Miriam said, "Sounds to be about a half mile off. Practice of some sort. Too regular to be other. Could be where we used to practice."

Jeremy said, "True."

Raif said, "I'm curious. Let's go have a look."

They got up and Callie was just suddenly there.

Miriam said, "Tell Henry we will be back shortly."

"Yes, ma'am."

The trio boarded the carriage and Jeremy stuffed the carry bag under their seat. It turned out their suspicions were right. They came upon about three dozen men in a field. A man who was obviously in charge said, "It's no use havin' one of these bee-u-tee-full rifles if'in you are goin' to use 'em like single round rifles."

By then Raif was close to the man and said, "You are right about that."

The man spun on Raif, "And who might you be."

"Raif Gunnerson."

The man snapped to attention, "Major, sir. This your company that Captain Connor recruited. My regrets."

All of the men had snapped to attention.

Raif said, "No regrets necessary. At ease. Who do I have the pleasure of addressing?"

"Sergeant Nathaniel Pearce, sir, recently of the 83rd."

Raif turned to Miriam, "This is my wife Miriam and her brother Jeremy Cole."

The sergeant said, "My honor to meet you Mrs. A pleasure, Mr. Cole."

Raif asked, "Your men having a little problem with the new rifle?"

"Yes, sir."

"Would you like a demonstration?"

"Yes, sir."

Raif smiled, "Have your men take a seat."

Raif looked at Miriam who smiled mischievously. They did not have to speak.

Raif asked in hearing of the seated men, "The men a little intimidated by the new rifle."

"Yes, sir. This is their first time with it."

Raif held out his hand and the sergeant gave him a rifle. Raif turned to his wife, "Dear, would you do the honors."

Miriam said, "Certainly, dear," and handed her lace shawl to Jeremy. Much to everyone's surprise Raif handed her the rifle. She walked to the firing line. The men watched as Miriam, obviously in the family way, quickly fired all the rounds breaking targets in rapid succession. She broke targets with all but one of her shots, but most observers wouldn't realize it because of the rate of fire.

When she finished, she handed it to the sergeant and said, "It shoots a little low and to the right. Stock is a little too long for my arms, but it is quite serviceable."

The sergeant smiled, "Yes, ma'am."

Jeremy handed Miriam her shawl which she put over her shoulders.

Raif said, "Carry on, Sergeant. I'll drop by again and see if they are doing any better. I'd also like to see how good they are with a pistol."

The sergeant called the men to attention.

Raif said, "Carry on."

Raif and his companions got back in the carriage. As they rode away they chuckled as they heard the sergeant,

"You lot better get your miserable selves together. Ya jist been showed up bad by the major's Mrs. Ya got no pride if'in ya don't get hold of your manhood."

Miriam had trouble keeping from laughing.

Raif said, "Don't. It will be bad for morale." He looked at his wife and smiled broadly.

They arrived back at the house in good spirits. A servant came to take their carriage and they went into the house. Jeremy carried the bag. James and Pauline had returned and were waiting on the veranda.

Pauline rose as Miriam came out of the house.

Miriam said, "It is so good to see you", and hugged Pauline and then James.

Raif and Jeremy shook hands with James and then greeted Pauline.

James was first to say, "I assume you went to see the practicing."

Raif said, "Yes."

"What do you think?"

"Too soon to tell. I'm going back of course. I'll take Jeremy. Maybe we can help them become accustomed to the Henry."

James said, "Those things are terribly expensive. Do you think it's necessary?"

Raif smiled, "I wouldn't spend my money or yours if I didn't think so. What's the fire thing about and why did you sell your estate."

James said, "I think one of my competitors mistakenly thought I had fallen on hard times when I sold the estate. In truth, I secretly bought the old mill acreage. The mill is falling down but it's on a huge beautiful river parcel near the center of town. I plan to tear down the mill remains and build a grand house there. We are also enlarging the summer home to accommodate the whole family. For the time being, Pauline stays here most of the time and when I'm in town, I stay at Edward's. But I digress. It seems a competitor thought I was hard pressed and connived to put me out of business once and for all. He did not know the building was insured. Poor fellow was misinformed."

Raif thought his Uncle James was dangerously crafty. He made his competitor think he was vulnerable knowing the man well enough to know he would act. The end result was James was about to rid himself of a dangerous enemy.

James paused and looked at Raif, "Greed can draw some men into quicksand."

Raif said, "I agree. What about the building and the safe?"

"I don't think I'll rebuild there, but use one of my other buildings. Your strongbox is in Edward's big safe."

Raif said, "You think it was Alton Manley?"

James proclaimed, "My, but you are full of surprises, nephew. How did you come about that piece of information?"

Raif told about the encounter in the restaurant.

James said, "Cheeky little man will get his soon. Between us, the inspector has one of the arsonist's helpers in custody, the lookout man. It's only a matter of time."

Raif nodded, "And you'll have one less competitor."

"Yes. It was fortunate though that no one was hurt in the fire."

Raif said, "Indeed. I do need a private word uncle. Jeremy should come."

James said, "Of course," turned to his wife and Miriam and said, "If you will excuse us."

When the men left Pauline asked, "What's that about?"

Miriam leaned in and whispered, "Profits from your mine."

Pauline said, "Oh."

Inside the men went into the study and James poured whisky and gave one to Jeremy. He knew Raif usually didn't drink hard liquor.

"So nephew, what is the news?"

Raif said, "Give it to him, Jeremy."

Jeremy put the carry bag on the desk.

James asked, "What's this nephew?"

"Profits from your and Edward's mine after the share for your men was taken out."

James opened the bag. He looked at Raif and said, "This will be a lucrative venture." James pulled out the money and Raif could tell he was impressed. The bills were all large denominations.

James asked, "You bring more back?"

Raif said, "Considerably more than the last time. Your men have hardly started panning. They did find a placer though."

James said, "Placer?"

"Where there's surface gold. It's important I get the additional deputies trained and get back as soon as possible. We need to get more men on the perimeter. Where do we stand on the railroad?"

James said, "We redeemed the loan when the debtors couldn't pay and took most of the shares. We let the Pattersons take some as they were so helpful. Our spies tell us that Gary was behind the investors who took out the loan. He did indeed take a loan from the railroad and we now hold that note so his gold mining plans are in jeopardy. We still have no proof of the conspiracy so cannot take action against Gary. His time will come. It was hard to believe he contracted for your murder."

Raif said, "I was very surprised."

James continued, "On another note, we've had some initial contacts from various sources about selling the line. So far though, no one with the kind of money we are looking for. It'll come when the word about the gold gets out."

Raif said, "There are rumors now. It's not the kind of secret that can be kept for long. Soon we'll have enough men to protect our property and the news will definitely get out then."

James took a large envelope out of his desk and handed it to Raif.

Raif took it and asked, "What is it?"

"Deeds to property on the town site. Edward and I tried to split them up fairly. We paid the railroad a thousand dollars for the lot. It's now our town. You do what is necessary with our full backing."

Raif said, "I'll put these to good use."

James said, "I'll meet you on the veranda."

Raif and Jeremy left and James went to his hidden safe box and put the money in it. He had to arrange it carefully to get it all in. It was several minutes before he returned to the veranda.

While the men were meeting, Pauline asked Miriam, "How have you been feeling?"

Miriam put her hands on her belly, "Very good. The morning sickness has past. I am keeping very active and I feel good."

Pauline said, "You seem happy."

"Very. I forgot to tell you. Charles is getting married. He's taking Sarah as his wife."

Pauline said, "Oh, my! That is news. His is the poor branch of the family, but still she's a servant girl."

Miriam said, "Pauline don't be such a snob."

Pauline looked shocked.

Miriam said, "You know it's true, but I love you anyway. "

Pauline sat quietly for a bit then said, "I am sorry, dear. That was insensitive of me. I forget your beginnings."

Miriam said, "There is no shame in beginnings, just how you live."

Pauline looked at Miriam, "I suppose you are right, but my upbringing has made it difficult for me to accept that. It goes against everything I was taught. Enough of that."

Miriam thought, there's that if it's unpleasant avoid it thinking.

The men came out to the porch. The group socialized until dinner. Everyone retired when the sun set. When they got to their room, Raif touched Miriam's cheek, which led to a kiss, which led to hormones raging, which led to the couple making passionate love.

Afterward, Miriam just lay there with her husband spooning her and his hand resting on her bulging tummy. She was entirely content. She knew Raif was because he had almost immediately fell into a deep sleep.

Raif and Jeremy were at the practice range early. The men were just assembling. The sergeant came to Raif as he dismounted.

"Good morning, sir. The men are about to commence practice."

Raif said, "Good morning. Carry on, Sergeant."

Raif watched the men practice. It was obvious they were good riflemen, but most of them could not get the hang of rapid fire.

Raif walked up to where the sergeant was standing, "There are some fine riflemen here, but they haven't made the transition."

"No, sir."

"I'm capable with the rifle so perhaps some pointers would be in order."

The sergeant smiled and said, "Yes, sir."

The sergeant went to the firing line and called for cease fire and the men did. The sergeant called out, "Major, you use this rifle. Would you be so's kind to show this lot how it's done?"

"Certainly, Sergeant."

Raif said, "Gather around."

The men did and Raif said, "I see you all are good shots, but your experience and training with the army rifles and making every shot count goes counter to using this rifle. Here is what we are going to do. Every man is going to the firing line with a fully loaded weapon. Don't aim at anything. The first man to empty his weapon and hold it in the air get a small reward. Raif flipped a silver coin in the air. Questions?"

One of the men asked, "So we don' have to hit nothin' just fire until the rifle's empty?"

Raif turned to the sergeant, "I believe he understands, Sergeant. I guess you were wrong. This lot are not as dumb as a box of rocks."

The men smiled and chuckled.

Raif said, "Sergeant, let's see who can figure it out."

The men lined up and the sergeant said, "Wait for it."

The men pointed their weapons down range and the sergeant said, "Fire."

Six men seemed to finish simultaneously. All the men discharged all the rounds in quick time. They were all looking at each other.

Raif said, "See it's not so hard. You already have the speed. If nothing else that fire would have scared the enemy to death."

There was light laughter.

Raif added, "Probably a few would have accidentally hit the enemy just out of the sheer number of rounds going down range."

The men were smiling.

Raif said, "This was more expensive than I thought." He walked down the line and gave a silver coin to each of the six men who had finished at the same time. He then said, "Now gather round behind me."

Raif took up his rifle, "Now you know how fast the rifle will fire you just need to put together the accuracy you already have with the rapid fire you already have. I will do this slowly." Raif aimed the rifle and as he fired he said, "Aim, shoot, cock, aim, shoot, cock, aim, shoot," and continued until his rifle was empty. He had taken down all the targets he'd aimed at and it was not done slowly.

The men were waiting.

Raif said, "More rounds please."

They were handed to him and he reloaded the rifle, "It will go faster without the talk."

The men watched as Raif took the targets down much quicker on the next go round. This time the targets were further away and at an angle so harder to hit. When he finished he handed the rifle to the sergeant.

"I want you to practice putting together the aim and the speed you have already proved you have. I'll come back after lunch and see how you are doing. See how much ammunition and targets you can use up. Carry on, Sergeant."

"Yes, sir." The sergeant turned to the men, "You heard the major, back to it."

Raif and Jeremy headed back to the house. Jeremy said, "Some of those men can sure shoot. They were a distance off from those targets."

Raif nodded, "I would bet by this afternoon they will have pretty much mastered use of the Henry. You notice they were all using army surplus pistols and holsters."

"Yes. Most of them were ancient."

Raif nodded, "And not all the same caliber. We'd best go to town."

While the men were on their mission, Miriam was on one of her own. Miriam was sitting on a pile of lumber watching the construction and waiting. Jake walked toward her. Miriam smiled.

Jake said, "Mrs. Gunnerson told me you were looking for me."

"Yes, Jake. It seems you are fully recovered."

Jake smiled, "Yes, Mrs."

Miriam said, "Have a seat, Jake."

Jake looked strangely at Miriam and went and sat beside her. He waited for Miriam to speak.

"How old is your daughter Janice now?"

"Fifteen, almost sixteen, Mrs. She's turned out to be a right fine young woman."

Miriam asked, "She in service?"

"No. Mrs. Gunnerson has more than enough servants. Janice still lives with me and Martha. She works free at the hospital and helps her mother out here. Soon she'll have to find a position or a husband. There's not likely to be a spot here open up. Everyone knows Mrs. Gunnerson let's on she's hard, but she has a soft heart. She has more help than she needs. Sort of a charity for them's that fell on hard times through no fault of their own."

Miriam said, "Like Sarah."

"Yes, Miriam." Jake realized what he said, "I'm so sorry. I meant no offense. Old habits."

Miriam said, "No problem, Jake. No one heard and we are after all old friends."

Jake said, "Thank you. You was always kind."

Miriam asked, "How would you feel about Janice going out west with me."

Jake said, "I reckon that would be up to Janice, but if she stays here she will soon be between a rock and a hard place."

Miriam nodded understanding, "Been there."

Jake said, "I know. What do you have in mind?"

"Sarah is getting married. I need a lady to help me and probably two. There's a shortage of women out there and if I take her on she'll probably find a husband like Sarah did. I won't mislead you, there is danger. I will have to teach her to use guns."

Miriam neglected to tell Jake she was also matchmaking for her brother. It was best left unsaid.

Jake thought, "I would miss her something terrible, but it would be a more certain thing than she faces if she stays here."

"Tell her about the job and that I'm willing to interview her in the morning."

Jake smiled, "Thank you, Mrs. Gunnerson."

Miriam said, "In spite of the social issues here, I always, in my heart, will be Miriam to you."

Jake said, "Thank you," and whispered, "Miriam."

Miriam laughed heartily.

Jake nodded and left.

After lunch, Raif and Jeremy returned to the practice range. Raif remained mounted and watched the men firing. They were now firing rapidly and very accurately. Some of the men were good distance shooters. The sergeant was approaching and Raif dismounted.

Raif said, "I think they have it."

The sergeant smiled, "I reckon so, sir."

Raif said, "Most of them from the 83rd?"

"All but eleven are. Them eleven were cavalry, but if you is worried about the ones from the 83rd ridin', don't. All these boys, I swear, is half horse. They was assigned infantry 'cause they family couldn't afford to let 'em take a horse to war and the govermint didn' see fit to put 'em on one."

Raif asked, "Can they shoot from horseback accurately."

The sergeant hesitated, "Truth is 'bout half kin with rifle on the gallop, but most ah the other half can only hit what they's shootin' at half the time at the gallop."

Raif said, "With a Henry, half the time is good enough."

The sergeant smiled, "Sir, I never reckoned on that, so's it's as you say."

Raif said, "I want to see."

"Yes, sir."

It took about ten minutes to get everything organized. The men were sent in groups of five downrange toward targets. With the first group, by the time the horses were thirty yards off the mark and at full gallop, the targets were down and the riders veered off. To varying degrees the results were good or acceptable. Raif noticed three of the riders had not hit targets until they were almost in pistol range. That was not good.

Raif went and stood by the sergeant, "Your thoughts."

"There's four that shoot respectable afoot, but they's a loss on horse."

"Who are the four?"

The sergeant pointed them out and Raif watched them on the second run. Three of them he'd identified, but he now noted the fourth was indeed inaccurate on horse.

Raif said to the sergeant, "Good eye, Nathaniel."

"Thank you, sir."

After three practice runs, Raif was satisfied with the results and said to Nathaniel, "Let's do it with pistols."

"Yes sir."

As Raif expected, it was a mixed result. Some who were really good with a rifle were only acceptable with pistol and some showed the opposite. About a half dozen of the men were really good with both. After the assessment Raif had Nathaniel bring together the six.

Raif said, "It seems you gentlemen are the best shooters. I was only able to get eight of these in town." Raif handed out seven of the new pistols, one to the sergeant and one to each of the six. He added, "More will be coming. I want you to use them and then help the other men become more proficient. Nathaniel will assign each of you a man who is a poor pistol shot. Your first job is to help him get better. If Nathaniel tells me you were successful, there will be a reward. Carry on."

"Yes, sir." The men walked away.

Raif turned to Nathaniel, "How did the four last in the 83rd?"

The sergeant said, "They's deliberate."

Raif looked at the sergeant and said harshly, "Be plain sergeant!"

"Yes, sir. They is really good distance shooters with a rifle, but they's no good when fast is needed. They don't spook easy and keep their cool, but they just ain't fast like. There's a place for them types in the field. I don't know nothin' 'bout bein' a sheriff so's I can't say if they'd be good at it."

Raif looked at Nathaniel, "I don't take to pussy footing so be direct Nathaniel and we'll get along. No need to be catering to my feelings, but I won't tolerate disrespect."

Nathaniel smiled, "That suits me fine, Major."

"Ok, what would you do?"

"As I understand it you need a lot of fast riding, good shooters who have a head on their shoulders. If'in you need long shooters you have some of 'em, but I doubt you'll be able to make fast shooters out of 'em. One of the six is quick tempered and bound to git his self into trouble eventually. I'd send him packin'. Also one of the others I suspect of thievin' but I has no proof."

Raif said, "Bring me the two first."

"Yes, sir."

The men were called and came. One of them was a man from the group of six really good shots. Raif knew right off which of the two would have the temper.

Raif said, "Jeremy here will pay you for your time, but your services will no longer be required."

One said, "Ya can't do it."

The man rubbed Raif the wrong way and Raif said in a harsh tone, "Pack up and get gone and quick."

The man tried to draw his pistol only to find the barrel of Raif's pistol under his chin before he cleared his holster.

"Let it slip back."

The man let go of the pistol and Raif like lightening moved his pistol and hit the man in the head with it. The man collapsed. Raif took the man's pistol from him. The man was now conscious and groaning.

Raif said, "Consider yourself lucky to be alive. You're the only one ever tried to pull a pistol on me and lived."

Raif quite deliberately stomped on the man's gun hand breaking all the small bones in it. Raif then handed the new pistol to Nathaniel.

Raif said to Jeremy, "Stuff his pay in his pocket."

Jeremy nodded and complied. The other man being discharged was standing very still.

Raif said, "You want to take issue with me."

"No, sir."

Raif said, "Pay the man, Jeremy." Raif looked at the man on the ground and said, "Nathaniel get this pool of puss up and out of here. Make sure he gets his own pistol without shells."

Nathaniel said, "Yes, sir."

The four other men who Raif had called for were fidgeting nearby. Raif motioned them forward and they came.

"Take a seat, men."

They complied and Raif squatted down, "Here's the thing and you'll know it's true. You four are good shooters from a distance when you can be deliberate. You'll probably never be fast."

The tallest of the men was nodding in agreement.

"Thing is you are not suited for regular deputy duty." Raif could tell the men were disappointed. He continued, "But you would probably make pretty good guards, sentries, or if I need, distance shooters. You won't spook when the fighting starts. You could carry coach guns for up close work and I'll get you distance rifles. The pay will be two thirds that of regular deputies. Think it over and let me know. I'll still want you to be able to shoot a pistol but only for very close up. Think it over and let me know your decision. Questions?"

The tall one said with an accent, "Vill vee still train wit da udders so's to git bedder."

Raif said, "You'll train here, but some things you do special so you'll train separately for."

The tall man said, "So any fightin' we'd do mostly in close or far off."

"Yes."

The man said, "I don' hab to tink it over. I'm for it."

Raif said, "You others think it over. You are dismissed." The men left.

Raif knew Nathaniel had been listening. Raif stood and motioned to him.

When Nathaniel came over, Raif said, "I want them to practice long range shooting and close in with the pistol. Give the tall one, what's his name?"

"Jürgen."

"Give Jürgen one of the new pistols and share the other with the three so they can practice with it if they decide to stay."

Nathaniel was smiling, "Yes, sir."

Raif asked, "How are you with rifle, pistol, and horse Nathaniel."

"I'm as good as any here 'cept you and your Mrs., with the rifle. I'm not fast like you with the pistol but up to about forty feet I don't miss what I shoot at and I don't flinch if'in someone's shootin' at me. I reckon I can sit a horse better'n most."

Raif said, "Good enough."

"Yes, sir."

Raif signaled to Jeremy and they mounted and left.

One of the men said, "Sarge, seems the stories 'bout him is true."

The sergeant said, "Oh, they's true. I've bin told 'bout him riskin' his neck for his sergeant's and men on more'n one occasion. Few officers do that."

Another man said, "That's fer sure. One of those you kin trust, but best not cross."

Nathaniel nodded and said, "Well, we still got daylight you lot, so let's git at it."

As they rode off, Raif said to Jeremy, "I'll need coach guns for the ones who decide to stay as guards."

Jeremy said, "I'll take care of it tomorrow. I'll make sure we have lots of shells for them and bandoliers."

Raif said, "Right."

While Raif and Jeremy had been with the recruits, Miriam had gone to town. Jake was driving and one of the security men Connor had gotten for the family was sitting next to him. They took Miriam to a small market garden farm on the edge of town. Miriam used to come here to pick up the produce for the Patterson household. She had befriended a young woman here.

Miriam knew the woman's story. Tonia's mother had died birthing her and her father had never forgiven his baby daughter. Tonia had married young and her husband had died in the war and his family had never liked Tonia. Miriam never understood that. Tonia was a hard worker and extremely pleasant, both in personality and to look at.

Miriam suspected Tonia's dead husband's family's dislike of Tonia had little to do with her as a person, but her heritage. Tonia was short for Antonia and her family were Italian Catholic, which did not sit well with her husband's Presbyterian family. They had sent her away after her husband's death.

When Miriam's carriage pulled up a woman came out.

Miriam got out of the carriage and started toward the woman and as they got close the woman said, "Good afternoon, ma'am. How may I help you?"

Miriam said, "Two dozen eggs, a pound of butter, and a cheese please, Tonia."

The woman said, "Miriam, is that you?"

"Yes, Tonia."

The two women embraced and Tonia backed away, "Don't you look the grand lady? And in the family way."

"It's an accident of marriage."

Tonia said with a grin, "I'd heard a rumor you'd married some war hero named Gunnerson. Come to the porch and we'll have tea and talk. Father's in the field so I can take time."

The women went to the porch and Miriam sat down while Tonia went inside. She came out a few minutes later with tea.

Miriam asked, "How are you?"

Tonia sighed, "I am healthy."

"And?"

"I'm basically my father's slave. He is trying to marry me to one of his old friends, with the emphasis on old, and is threatening to throw me out on the street if I don't marry the man."

Miriam said, "I might have a fix for your problem."

Tonia said, "I'm listening."

"I am living in the territory and I need help. I am planning to hire two women to help me out."

Tonia said, "Tell me about it."

Miriam told her and Tonia had a lot of questions. The women talked for some time.

Tonia ended with, "So I work for you, get my room and board, and get to keep my wages. I go to a place where women are in short supply and I'll pretty much have my pick of men. I also get to be more independent. Only thing different is I have to learn to defend myself and your family."

"Yes, that sums it up quite nicely."

Tonia smiled, "I can be packed in twenty minutes."

Miriam said, "Don't you want to give your father some time?"

"The moment I tell him, I'll be out on the street."

Miriam said, "Then I'll help you pack."

Tonia's meager possessions were being loaded into the carriage when Tonia's father came in from the fields. He stopped his plow team and came to where the carriage was. Tonia was wearing her Sunday best.

Her father asked, "What's going on here? Tonia, what are you doing?"

Tonia went to him, "I have taken work with Mrs. Gunnerson. You are finally rid of me poppa." She hugged him and said, "In spite of all that's happened between us, I still love you. Perhaps I will get to see you again in this life."

Tonia turned and walked to the carriage and climbed in. Tears were streaming from her eyes. She waved to her father who was standing in the yard staring at her. The carriage started out. They were a fair piece down the road when Tonia turned and saw her father was still standing where she'd left him. She waved and turned around.

"I don't suppose I'll ever see this place or my older brothers ever again. Ah well, can't be helped."

When they got back to the Gunnerson summer home, Miriam introduced Tonia to Henry who offered to see Tonia settled. After dinner that evening, Miriam, Raif, and her brother were sitting in chairs on the lawn enjoying the view of the river while talking. Miriam had sent for Tonia who came as instructed in her Sunday best.

As she approached Miriam said, "Tonia, come sit."

Tonia smiled and did as Miriam directed.

"Tonia, this is my husband Raif and my brother Jeremy. This is Antonia. Everyone calls her Tonia. She'll be coming back with us."

Jeremy jumped right in, "I'm pleased to meet you, Tonia," and offered his hand.

Tonia leaned forward and shook it, "Thank you, sir."

Raif said, "Welcome, Tonia. I am pleased that you accepted Miriam's offer."

Tonia said, "Not as pleased, sir, as I was to be offered it."

Raif smiled and looked at his wife, "Cheeky isn't she?"

Tonia looked concerned until Miriam said, "Love, I know you like cheeky. You married me, didn't you?"

Raif laughed, "Yes I did and it was the best thing I ever did."

Miriam said, "Thank you, dear."

Jeremy said to Tonia, "You may eventually get used to these two lovebirds."

Tonia said quite innocently, "I expect so. In fact, I'm more than a little jealous of my friend's good fortune."

To Tonia's surprise Jeremy said, "Any wise person would be. A good wife is worth more than gold." Jeremy paused, "Or husband."

Tonia just nodded.

Miriam said, "Husband dear, let's walk down by the river."

"Certainly."

They got up and Miriam took Raif's arm and they walked away. When they were out of earshot of Jeremy and Tonia, Raif asked, "You matchmaking?"

"Yes."

Miriam looked over her shoulder and saw Tonia and Jeremy were talking. She looked at her husband and said, "Unlike you dear, Jeremy does not know the kind of woman he needs."

When Raif and Miriam were on their way back they saw Tonia and Jeremy walking and talking.

Raif said, "It seems Jeremy may be interested."

The next morning, Miriam, Jeremy, and Pauline were eating a light breakfast together. Raif had already gone off to the training site. Miriam received a message a young woman was asking to see her. Miriam asked for the young lady to be told to wait on the veranda.

Pauline asked, "What is that about?"

"I'm interviewing for help at the ranch."

Pauline said, "I see."

Miriam said to Jeremy, "Jeremy, perhaps you could sit in with me? I'd like your opinion."

"Of course."

They finished eating and Jeremy accompanied Miriam out to the porch. The young woman they were meeting with stood and Miriam said, "Good morning, Janice."

"Good morning, Mrs. Gunnerson."

Miriam smiled and went to Janice, shook her hand and said, "This is my brother, Jeremy."

Jeremy offered his hand and Janice took it. Miriam noticed that Jeremy and Janice held hands for just the required time needed to be polite before letting go. There was no chemistry there.

Janice said, "I'm pleased to meet you."

Jeremy smiled, "The pleasure is mine."

Miriam said, "Please have a seat, Janice."

Miriam saw that Jeremy was appraising Janice. Janice was completely different in appearance from Tonia. Tonia had a Mediterranean complexion and reddish brown hair. She was an attractive woman by any measure. Janice's complexion was pale and she had jet black hair. The stark contrast somehow worked with Janice's sharp features and made her strangely attractive. Janice was a woman of average height, lithe, obviously fit, and almost too muscular for a woman as the short sleeve well-worn dress she was wearing showed. Though modest, the dress left no doubt to Janice's womanly endowments.

Miriam said, "Well let's get to business."

The women talked for the better part of forty minutes with Jeremy listening intently.

In the end Janice said, "I'd like to go with you, Mrs. Gunnerson. There is no future for me here."

Miriam said, "Then you are hired. We'll be leaving in the next few days. This afternoon I will take you shopping for clothes suitable for out west. In the meantime, you should inform your family and start thinking about what you'll be taking with you."

Janice said, "Thank you, ma'am." and left.

Jeremy said, "Do you really need two servants?"

"Probably not until spring."

"Which one are you matchmaking for me."

Miriam smiled, "Your choice, but I suggest you make it before we get back or you'll have lots of competition."

Jeremy said a little too casually, "I know. They are both attractive in their own way and both seem to be strong women. I think they could both fit in out west and make a man a good wife."

"That is true."

Jeremy said, "I've just started to get to know Tonia."

"You think she'll accept?"

"I think you just have to complete the negotiation."

Miriam said, "No problem."

Jeremy said, "I was just joking, Miriam!"

"Oh."

"Sister, sometimes you get carried away. Remember, when it comes to family things, you are my baby sister, not my employer's wife."

"Yes, Jeremy. I will keep that in mind. I meant no disrespect, brother."

Jeremy smiled, "I am taking Tonia to eat at the restaurant this evening. I want to get to know her a little more."

Miriam said, "We are going shopping this afternoon and I'll make sure she has something suitable to wear."

"Thank you."

That evening Tonia came out to go to the restaurant wearing a dress Miriam had bought her. Jeremy felt his pulse race. She was indeed a pretty woman. Jeremy helped her into the carriage and the driver started away.

Tonia said, "I've never ridden in a fine carriage. It was always a farm wagon."

Jeremy said, "I was the same up until a year ago."

Tonia said, "If I am to be your sister's employee, why are you taking me out to a fancy place to eat."

Jeremy said, "I expect you have reckoned it out."

"So your sister is match maker as well as employer."

Jeremy smiled, "And she has good taste and judgment."

Tonia thought for a moment, "So either Janice or I might end up being courted by you. Is she the competition?"

Jeremy smiled, "I am not responsible for my sister's hiring decisions any more than her matchmaking."

Tonia said playfully, "Tease."

Jeremy laughed.

It turned out they had a wonderful evening. They talked on the ride about their likes and dislikes, about their lives, and their hopes. At the restaurant, they ate and talked and drank wine. Perhaps they had a little too much wine but just a little too much. They were a long time at the restaurant, so Jeremy left a large tip as he felt a little guilty about taking so long.

After dinner, the couple talked as they enjoyed the carriage ride. They were a short way from the summer home when Jeremy asked a serious question.

"How is it that you never had a child?"

Tonia said, "I was only married a week when he went off to war. I was just a child myself."

Jeremy said, "I will tell you now that I am quite taken with you. You are pretty, smart, and from what my sister says, industrious. You have a most pleasant personality and a smile that warms me."

Tonia said, "Thank you."

Jeremy said, "And being near you sets my blood on fire."

Tonia blushed, put her head down, and said in a low but firm tone, "Jeremy!"

"Well it's true and I'm not ashamed of it."

Tonia smiled.

"Do you fancy me at all?"

Tonia said, "Yes, I do."

"Would you consider marrying someone like me?"

Tonia teased, "Someone like you or you?"

Jeremy sighed, "Please go easy. I am sweating blood as it is."

Tonia said, "You'd probably make a decent husband. You are respectable, clean, from what I'm told, hard-working and gentle. You have gainful employment and you're not too bad to look at."

"Not too bad to look at?"

Tonia said, "That's not a bad thing. I tend to like regular looking men. Handsome can be trouble."

It hit Jeremy, "You are teasing me!"

"Of course I am and you are just too easy, Jeremy."

Jeremy smiled broadly, "I hope you like easy."

"An easy nature with his woman is the best thing a man can have in my book."

Jeremy asked, "How is it you know about me?"

"I asked. A lot of people here about knew you when you were working for the Pattersons. It wasn't a hard thing? I hope you don't mind."

Jeremy said, "Actually, it's to your credit. I think you were wise to do it."

They had arrived at their destination. Jeremy got out and helped Tonia out of the carriage and said, "Perhaps we could go for a walk in the morning after breakfast and have a serious talk."

Tonia said, "Of course."

Jeremy stole a kiss and Tonia blushed before saying, "By the way, you are quite handsome."

Jeremy watched her hurry away.

In the morning, Jeremy came down to find only Miriam was still in the house. She was on the veranda drinking tea.

Jeremy took a seat.

Miriam asked, "How did it go?"

"Amazing."

"No date for tonight?"

Jeremy said, "I don't think that will be necessary."

He had no sooner said it than Tonia came walking across the lawn. Jeremy went to meet her and they went walking arm and arm. Miriam intended to wait patiently on the veranda, but instead drifted off. She woke after a nap. Her first thought was that she supposed it was the baby causing her to be drowsy. Then warm memories of last night came flooding into her mind and she realized it was her husband not the baby that was the cause of her tiredness.

Miriam sat for another five minutes before her brother and Tonia returned. They came up on the veranda and took a seat.

Jeremy said, "Tonia has agreed to wed me."

Miriam exclaimed, "Wonderful! My good friend becomes my sister-in-law and my brother gets a good wife."

Jeremy smiled, "I expect so. I expect to be a good husband to her as well."

Miriam said, "I suppose we should arrange a wedding before we go back."

Tonia said, "It is what we planned. Jeremy said under the circumstances, as you were the matchmaker, you would not be offended if I left your employ to partner with my husband."

Miriam smiled and said, "True. But now I have to hire another helper."

Tonia asked, "Why?"

"Because out west, wives are in big demand. I no sooner hire a woman than she up and gets married."

Jeremy and Tonia were married by a Justice of the Peace. Miriam and Raif were witnesses. Miriam sent a telegraph ahead. Jeremy and Tonia would need their own cabin.

Things at the ranch were relatively quiet while Raif and Miriam were gone. The geologist and mining engineer had moved on to James and Edward's property. Now all three holdings were producing gold and a lot.

About the same time as Raif's new deputies were finishing their preparations to go west, Clint made a discovery. It was a chance thing. Clint was walking to the railway station to see if another telegraph had come from Raif. He saw a man who had but one bag with him and was waiting for the train. His horse was tied to the rail and it appeared the man was just going to leave it. It was a good horse.

Clint became suspicious. As Clint approached, the man bent to pick up the bag and had trouble lifting it with both hands. It was then Clint knew and drew his gun and yelled, "Sheriff. Put your hands up!"

The man dropped the bag and drew a pistol and fired wildly at Clint. Clint took deliberate aim and shot the man. The gun dropped from the man's hand and he fell to the station deck. Clint ran to check on him and picked up his gun. The man was still alive. Clint squatted next to where he lay.

The man said, "Almost made it."

Clint said, "Where'd you find it?"

"Promise to let me go?"

Clint knew the man was dying and said, "I promise if you tell me."

"Northeast slope, 'bout seven hours ride from here, high up in the trees between the three close peaks. I'm so tired."

The man coughed once and died.

When Clint's deputies brought the wagon for the body, Clint took the bag back to his tent. The thief was buried in an unmarked grave. When Charles and Cracker showed up in town, Clint, as honest as a summer's day is long, told them about the gold. Charles and Cracker took possession of it.

The men discussed finding the location where the thief had been mining. Scouts were sent, but even with the description of the location it took two days to find the place.

The thief had built a small basic lean-to at the site and his camp was pretty much intact. They found quite a bit more gold. The man had obviously a lot more than he could carry in one trip. There was now a new place to mine.

CHAPTER 11 - HOME

Raif, Miriam, and Jeremy returned with a lot more than they'd left with. They brought Jeremy's wife Tonia, Janice, thirty three deputies and a sergeant, three guards, carpenters and laborers, three boxcars of cargo, and forty horses. It was quite a group that got off the train.

Nathaniel and the men disembarked quickly. Nathaniel was immediately organizing the deputies and guards. The railway cars were being moved to a siding so the train could continue without waiting for the cargo to be unloaded.

Nathaniel dispatched the guards immediately to watch the box cars. They climbed on top of the cars and started their watch. Nathaniel took the deputies over by the boxcars and had them rest then came to see Raif.

Nathaniel said, "Where are your people?"

Raif said, "I don't know and I don't like it. Saddle up half the men to go with me. The other half will stay here with you to guard the train. Tell the men two days rations and lots of ammunition."

Nathaniel said, "Yes, sir," and hurried off.

Raif called out, "Jürgen."

The response from on top of the middle car came, "Ya, sir."

"Get your long gun and saddle up."

"Ya, sir."

Within minutes, the train was an armed camp and Raif was mounted and headed out. Raif got to the ranch to find a skeleton guard on duty. Tom came out to meet Raif.

Raif asked, "What's going on?"

"A large band of fellers decided to take Edward's lands. Everyone went to make sure it did'n happen."

Raif nodded and turned to one of his men, "Go let Nathaniel know what's going on. Tell him the workers can start on the Sheriff's station, but to keep an eye out for trouble. He's to hold down the town until I get back."

The man said, "Yes, sir," and turned his horse and rode away at a gallop.

Raif said, "See you later, Tom."

Tom said, "Good hunting, sir."

By the time Raif and his men got to spot of the battle. It was over.

Charles came out to meet him.

The two men shook hands and Charles said, "You missed the action."

Raif said, "It looks like you were up to the task. How bad was it?"

Charles said, "Short, but bloody. Twenty eight law breakers are dead, and three are dying. We have seven others tied up. I lost two men and two others were wounded. The prisoners will be tried for murder."

Raif nodded, "How bad are the wounded?"

Charles said, "I think they can be fixed if we can get them to Miriam."

Raif said, "It's a long way to cart wounded on a travois."

Charles said, "From here we can get a wagon to the rail and follow the rail right-of-way. I've taken a mule team and wagon from the trespassers."

Raif said, "If you have fresh horses we can take the wounded back and I'll leave you four replacements."

Charles nodded.

Raif pointed to four men, "You are with the Colonel." The men peeled off. Raif yelled, "Any of you good with a mule team."

Jürgen called out, "I vork some as muleskinner."

Raif said, "You'll take the wagon." He pointed to another man, "Get a fresh horse and go to the ranch and get the doctoring kit. Bring it to the rail station. Don't bring the medicine bottles. We have more on the train."

The man said, "Yes, sir," and hurried to change his saddle to a fresh horse.

Charles started giving orders and in no time Raif and his men were headed north to the rail line. True to his word, Jürgen was able to manage the two mules pulling the wagon. Raif and his men arrived at the train in the darkness of early morning. They were tired.

Miriam was waiting and had a makeshift infirmary set up in the train station. The rider Raif had sent had gotten to the station well in advance of Raif's group. The wounded were taken in and Miriam immediately went to work. Janice was assisting. Janice turned out to be a big help to Miriam given her volunteer work at the hospital back in Pennsylvania. She was not the least bit squeamish.

Nathaniel was allowed to watch.

When Miriam finished, she and Janice went outside. Tonia was left to keep an eye on the patients. Miriam and Janice sat on the edge of the station deck. It was not lost on Nathaniel that it was no accident Miriam had brought butchers aprons with her from back east.

Nathaniel said, "You've done this before Mrs.?"

"Yes."

"Kin I git ya somethin'?"

"If you could have someone bring coffee, I'd be obliged."

Janice said, "Me too, please."

Nathaniel nodded and left. Miriam thought Nathaniel was the army version of Henry the house manager, only deadly.

Janice said, "You did better than some of them doctors I seen work at the hospital."

Miriam said, "I do some good unless it's inside bleeding then I can't do much."

Nathaniel surprised Miriam when he brought two cups of coffee himself.

Miriam said, "Thank you, Nathaniel."

Nathaniel said, "You west women are the finest. It's enough to make me put my bachelor ways to the side."

Janice smiled, "Quite a compliment."

"It are that miss. That's a fact."

Nathaniel walked away.

Janice asked, "Where's your husband?"

"Sitting in the corner of the railway car we came in catching some sleep. I think we should finish our coffee and get some sleep too."

Nathaniel was watching from a distance and Miriam waved to him and he came over.

"Mrs.?"

"Tonia is keeping watch over the patients. Can you please have a couple of men stay with her in case she needs help and to keep her safe?"

"Yes, ma'am."

When the men were on guard, the women went to the railway car. Raif was sitting rather upright so Miriam sat beside him, cuddled up, and immediately went to sleep. She woke to find she was lying curled up on the seat and Raif was gone. She sat up and listened to the noise of men busy at work. Janice was gone as well. Miriam brushed her hair, put on her gun belts, took her rifle, and went to the station building.

When Miriam entered Janice was just taking a bandage off a wound. Miriam took her hat off and put it on a peg. She leaned her rifle against the wall.

Miriam asked, "How are they doing?"

One of the men said, "I'm jist fine, Mrs. Major. T'other's still sleepin', but he was always the lazy one."

Miriam smiled, "It's good to have you back in the land of the living, Albert."

"Thanks for easin' ma pain and doctoring me, Mrs."

"You're welcome. It's the least I can do for the brave men who keep the peace on my family's lands. You are like the knights of the west."

Albert smiled, "Ya shore nuff do have a way with words, Mrs. Makes me feel special."

Miriam said, "Good. Now rest up and don't move around too much right off. I don't want you ripping out those stitches and ruining my reputation for sewing people up."

Albert smiled, "I promise."

Miriam went to where Janice had the bandage off. Miriam said, "That's not looking good. I'll clean up. We have to lance that and drain it then put some salve on it."

The women worked for fifteen minutes concentrating on the work.

Janice said, "I don't think it's bad or in the blood."

"I hope not. We'd better arrange a twenty four hour watch."

Janice nodded, "I already ate so I'll stay. Tonia is with Jeremy."

Miriam nodded and left. She stood on the deck of the station. The railway clerk came and said, "Good morning, Mrs. Gunnerson."

"Good morning. I'm afraid we've turned your waiting room into an infirmary."

The man smiled, "Right now we don't have need for a lot of waiting."

Miriam smiled, "True. That will change and you'll be wishing for a quiet day."

The clerk tipped his hat and went to the office part of the station.

Miriam noticed Raif coming and went to meet him. She embraced him, "How is it going?"

"We are back on track."

Miriam said, "I need a bath, but I'll just have to wait. What are we doing for disposal of our disgusting stuff?"

"A couple of the men just finished a temporary outhouse for women on the other side of the station. There's a barrel with a step up and a seat on top. The men were so appreciative of the doctoring and nursing, they did it on their own without being asked."

Miriam said, "That was sweet of them."

Raif knew where Miriam was going when she headed that way. When she came back she washed her hands in the horse trough. Raif looked at her and she shrugged.

"It's cleaner than not. By the way, thank the fellows for the rags."

Raif just nodded.

Miriam asked, "So what's the plan?"

"Can the wounded be moved yet?"

"No, I wouldn't advise it. They should be left where they are for a while."

Raif said, "Then I'll have curtains put up in the passenger car for privacy, arrange some makeshift sleeping pallets, and we'll stay there for a bit."

Miriam said, "Any chance we could build a little fence over by the water tower and run a hose down so we could bathe in privacy?"

Raif said, "That's not a half bad idea."

Miriam said, "It's a great idea."

Raif smiled, "Dear, that's a grand idea."

Miriam said, "That's better," and kissed him on the cheek.

Raif asked, "What do you think about naming the place Gunners Town."

Miriam smiled, "Dear, that's a grand idea. You should put up a sign on the station."

Raif shook his head and walked away saying, "I've got work to do. I'll see you for lunch."

The little fenced in area was up within an hour and a pull chain was rigged to open a valve to allow water to flow through a small hose. Miriam and Janice were first to try it. Miriam went first while Janice stood outside with a coach gun. It was cold but Miriam thought it felt good. When she finished and changed, she took guard duty while

Janice got cleaned. Janice was just finishing when Tonia
showed up.

"My turn."

Janice was drying her hair, "I'll keep watch for you so
Miriam can get back to the patients."

At lunch, Nathaniel sought Miriam out. He had a plate
in one hand and a cup in the other. Miriam motioned to
him to sit on the makeshift bench with her and he did.

"What's on your mind, Nathaniel?"

Nathaniel sighed, "Some of the boys wanted to know if
they could use the bathing thing."

Miriam said, "Absolutely not."

Nathaniel was taken by surprise.

Miriam smiled, "I'll shoot any man found there. Now
if they want to build another one on the other side of the
tank I have no objection, but I'm serious about any men
being around the women's. No one's to be around the
women's one or around the tank when women are present."

Nathaniel smiled, "Ya's not just beautiful and deadly,
ya's smart too, Mrs. Major."

"Thank you, Nathaniel."

Nathaniel said, "I'll ask the Major for permission
then."

Miriam said, "No need. It's not Sheriff stuff, just
business, so my say-so is good enough."

Nathaniel looked at Miriam with a stunned expression.
He asked, "Truly."

Miriam said, "I value your loyalty Nathaniel, so I
wouldn't cause you trouble."

"Yes, Mrs."

Miriam asked, "You ever been married, Nathaniel?"

"Ya. Good women too. Loved her crazy like. I was
like mud in her hands."

Miriam asked, "What happened?"

"Her and the child died in birthing." Nathaniel realized this sharing might cause Miriam distress and said, "I'm sorry, Mrs."

Miriam said, "It happens and is part of life. Life is full of dangers and I'm not about to go around being afraid of what-ifs."

Nathaniel asked, "What means what-ifs?"

"What if this happens? What if that happens? People who worry about what-if can be frozen by fear to do nothing."

"I see what ya mean. Some men are like that in a fight."

Miriam said, "I wouldn't know about that."

"That's because ya's one of ta brave ones."

Miriam said, "I'm told you are too."

"I reckon. That Janice ain't afraid of the sight a blood."

Miriam said, "No she isn't."

"What's she like?"

"I think, Nathaniel, that's something you should find out for yourself."

"I reckon, but I'm sort of shy?"

Miriam said, "There's that what-if?"

Nathaniel said, "What?"

"What if she doesn't take to me? What if I don't say things right? What if? What if? I didn't take you for a what-if man, Nathaniel. I took you for a hard charger. If you lose one fight, you go on to the next."

Nathaniel paused, "I never reckoned on it like that."

Miriam didn't say anything. They just sat eating. When they finished Nathaniel rose.

"Mrs. Major, I surely do 'appreciate the way ya set me right. I surely do."

"You're welcome, Nathaniel."

Throughout the day workers swarmed over the town site working on the sheriff's barracks. Wagons came from the ranch and were loaded and several workmen went with the wagons to the ranch. Raif went with them to get the work started and give Cracker instructions. When he returned, he went to see Nathaniel.

Raif found Nathaniel at the water tanks telling some workmen where he wanted some work done. Raif waited until he was finished. Nathaniel saw him and came walking swiftly.

Raif said, "Let's take a walk."

Nathaniel out of habit fell into step with Raif. When they were out of hearing of others Raif said, "I'm going to share something we are trying to keep under wraps as long as possible. If it gets out before we want, it will hurt us and may cost lives. I am trusting you to keep it to yourself."

"Yes sir."

"We intend to have a large cattle ranch here in the future. Right now, though, we are mining gold."

Nathaniel said, "I heard tell the gold found down the track was a wild story."

"The gold we found here is real enough. It's why we need so much security and to keep people away from the ranches. I give rewards to those that give good service. I expect you'll be one."

"Yes sir."

Raif said, "The cat will be out of the bag soon enough, but for now you say nothing to anybody."

"Yes sir."

"You'll be leading patrols so I rely on you to use your wits. If you find thieves taking gold, bring it back. You'll get a reward. You come across gold in your patrols make a note of where. You'll get a reward."

"Yes, sir."

They walked back toward the camp.

Raif asked, "What are you doing at the water tower?"

Nathaniel told him. He didn't mention Miriam had said to go ahead.

When Nathaniel finished Raif said, "It's a good idea."

Nathaniel said, "It was original the Mrs. who thunk of it."

That evening Raif, Charles, and the sergeants had a meeting in a newly erected campaign tent that was on the hill apart from the others. They discussed deputy assignments. Four more of Clint's recruits had shown up while Raif was away. That put the total number of deputies he had at eleven. It was agreed that eventually the town would be the most likely place for people to come into the area. It was agreed to increase his number of deputies to twenty and assign him a guard. Raif would take Nathaniel, 8 of the deputies and two of the guards. The rest of the deputies would go to Charles.

Cracker would be responsible for Raif and Miriam's ranch compound and safeguarding cargo coming and going, Dan for mining security, and Nathaniel for patrols on Raif's ranch.

After the meeting Raif said, "Clint, I want you to stay."

The others took the hint and left.

Raif said, "I have something for you."

Clint said, "Sir."

Raif handed Clint and envelope and Clint opened it. Inside was a document. Clint looked at it.

Raif said, "It's a deed to a town lot. It's yours all legal."

Raif took out a wallet and handed it to Clint. Clint undid it and saw it was stuffed with paper money. Clint just stood staring at the money.

Raif said, "I reward loyalty and honesty, Clint."

Clint seemed speechless for another moment then said, "Thank ya, Raif. I was jist doin' what was proper."

"I know and that's why I appreciated it."

Raif offered his hand and the two men shook.

Clint asked, "Where is the land?"

"The lot number is on the deed and the town map."

"Thank ya, sir."

When Clint left, Charles came in and sat down.

Raif said, "We are taking a lot off."

Charles said, "Yes. We are all getting rich and the cattle ranching won't get started for some time yet, perhaps years."

Raif said, "We have a lot to do before winter sets in."

"Yes, we do. Do you think we have enough workers?"

"No. Let's talk about how to manage that."

They spent some time planning on how to get the necessary work done before winter. The next item was keeping a flood of trespassers off the ranches.

Raif said, "Word is going to leak out."

Charles said, "If we can keep the get rich quick types on the train, we'll keep the number of thieves down. Basically the town is privately owned. It's a company town. We could just put up no trespassing signs at the station and have deputies meet each train. We only let those who have business here off."

Raif nodded, "It might just work. I also think we should start sending smaller shipments more frequently. "

Charles nodded agreement. They continued planning.

The next day just before noon, one of the deputies assigned to Clint came in with a rider. The man was brought to Raif.

The man was carrying a book when he came. The deputy who brought him was standing waiting.

The man approached Raif and said, "Mr. Gunnerson?"

Raif said, "Yes."

The man put out his hand, "I'm Pastor Allen. I received a message you needed me to come to marry someone."

Raif smiled and put out his hand, "I'm pleased to meet you."

The preacher said, "Most folks call me Brother Allen."

Raif smiled, "And you may call me Major or Sheriff, unless of course you'd rather be on a first name basis."

The man's laugh was booming. Raif had to smile.

The reverend said, "My given name is Paul."

"Raif. Please have a seat."

Raif waved to the deputy who came. He was sent to fetch Charles and Miriam.

Paul said, "This seems to be a busy place. You are building a town I see."

"You are very observant."

Paul shook his head and smiling said, "You always this ornery?"

"Only with people I kind of take a liking to."

Paul asked, "Where's the church going to be?"

"There is not one in the plans."

"Should be. A town with a church declares it is a respectable and law abiding place. It also is proper for a community to have a place for worship, weddings, funerals, and such."

Raif thought then said, "I'll think on it and we'll talk more."

Paul asked, "You have a place for me to sleep?"

Raif said, "I'll arrange it. How long can you stay?"

Paul smiled, "Depends on how well the plans for a new church are going."

Raif looked at Paul who was smiling broadly and said, "Paul, I think we'll get along just fine."

Miriam and Charles came in and Raif introduced them to Paul.

Raif said, "Charles is the groom."

Paul said, "So when do I get to meet the bride?"

Charles said, "I will take you to meet her. She lives just a short ride from here. Perhaps you can have lunch with us and after I'll take you to meet her."

The group enjoyed a pleasant meal that Janice prepared over an open fire. After lunch, Paul went with

Charles to the ranch. They came back about two hours later.

Charles came to find Raif. Raif could always tell when Charles was on a mission. They had served enough together that they knew each other's manner.

Charles said, "The wedding is arranged. Will you and Miriam be witnesses?"

Raif said, "Where and when?"

"Tomorrow in the ranch plaza at eleven in the morning."

Raif said, "Alright."

Paul spent the afternoon walking the town site and talking with workers. At supper he approached Raif and Miriam where they were eating. He had a plate and cup in his hand.

"Mind if I join you?"

Miriam said, "Please," and Paul sat down with them.

Raif said, "I hear you did a lot of visiting today."

"Yes, I did, but I tried not to disrupt the work."

Raif nodded.

Paul said, "You have a problem If I hold an open air service this evening?"

Raif said, "Have at it."

Paul turned to Miriam, "When is the baby due?"

"Spring. I'm glad of the timing. It would be harder on me to be carrying the baby inside in the heat of summer."

Paul nodded.

Raif said, "Are you married Paul?"

"Yes."

Miriam asked, "Are you away from home much?"

"About two weeks every month. I try to alternate weeks and sometimes I'm just gone a couple of days. I'm fortunate that my brother and his wife live next door."

"You have a church building?"

Paul shook his head no, "We have worship at our house. We've talked about having a church raising, but that won't happen for a while yet."

Raif asked, "Does being a preacher pay well?"

"No. I get some help from the society and collect some love offerings. I am fortunate to have other income. My brother and I have a general store and I work there when I'm home. It provides a modest living. I'm one of the few ordained circuit riders. Many are laymen."

Miriam asked, "If it doesn't pay, then why go to the bother?"

Paul smiled as he looked at Miriam, "Because God has called me to do this work."

Neither Raif nor Miriam knew how to respond, so Miriam asked, "Do you have any children?"

Paul said, "Two boys ages nine and twelve. They are a blessing to me and my wife."

The three of them talked and Paul found out a little about the couple, where they were from, their families, and how they had met. Paul also talked to them about the need for salvation, but he wasn't pushy. After they finished eating, Paul left to go prepare for the service.

Miriam asked, "Would you take me to the service. I'm curious."

Raif smiled, "How can I deny you, my dear."

Miriam leaned over and kissed him. There were about twenty five people who came to hear Paul that evening. The service lasted about forty minutes with half taken up by Paul's preaching.

As they were returning from the service Miriam said, "I never heard any proper preaching before. I enjoyed it. I have a lot to think about."

Miriam looked at her husband who seemed to be lost in thought. He just nodded.

Raif asked, "Are the wounded well enough to be moved now?"

Miriam said, "If they go slow and easy."

Raif said, "Then we'll go home in the morning and they can follow along."

The next morning they set out for the ranch about eight in a wagon with their horses trailing behind. Raif was concerned about Miriam riding a horse in her condition and Miriam agreed. As they were travelling, Raif said, "Paul asked me to provide land for a church."

Miriam said, "And?"

"He made a good argument about it being a symbol of a respectable and law abiding town."

Miriam said, "I think we should do it, but with conditions."

Raif said, "Conditions?"

"He comes every other Sunday to hold service once the town has permanent residents. We'll pay him to do it."

Raif surprised Miriam when he said, "All right."

They arrived home to a warm welcome. Miriam introduced Janice and Sarah. They started the unpacking. Janice's things were moved into the room Sarah was leaving. Sarah's things were already packed in a wagon to take to her new home. They had just finished unpacking when a light rain started.

Sarah said, "Of all the days for this to happen."

Janice said, "I expect it will clear off soon. The clouds do not look heavy."

Janice was right and the rain stopped shortly. Janice left for a few minutes and came back with a small bouquet of wild flowers for Sarah. That set Sarah to beaming.

The wedding went off without a hitch. Over twenty deputies attended the wedding. Afterward, everyone ate a light lunch and Charles and Sarah said their goodbyes and headed off.

Raif looked at Janice, "I hope you take a while to decide which one you want."

Miriam chuckled.

Janice said, "No worry, I am particular."

Raif said, "I have business to attend to, if you ladies will excuse me."

Raif went to where Cracker was waiting.

"Are you ready?"

"Yes. The boxes is loaded and ready to go. The boxes is marked so we knows which is from where."

Raif nodded and said, "Well you'd best get going. Be safe, my friend."

Cracker nodded, "See you in a few days."

Sixteen deputies accompanied the shipment to the train and ten went with Cracker on the train. The other six returned to the ranch.

Raif went back to the cabin to find Paul and Miriam drinking coffee on the porch.

Paul said, "Nice couple. You and Charles serve in the war?"

"Yes."

Paul said, "But now the war is over and the colonel works for the major."

Raif shrugged, "Life is like that."

Paul asked, "You think any more about donating land for a church."

"Yes, but my wife and I have conditions."

Paul seemed surprised, "Conditions?"

Miriam said, "Yes," and told him what they were.

Paul smiled and the negotiations started. An arrangement was finally agreed to. Paul stayed the night and slept in the bunkhouse with the deputies. He left the next morning for home after giving Raif and Miriam a Bible for winter reading.

Cracker delivered the cargo and returned without incident. The following weeks were a beehive of activity. Cracker made two more trips and they went without incident.

The days got shorter and the weather colder, but work progressed. The hired men built the sheriff's buildings in town. A lot of wood was cut and made into lumber or split for firewood. The deputies continued to have some encounters with trespassers. As the winter approached the number of intruders declined, but did not stop.

Though the nights were cold, the men could work during the day though they needed warm jackets. A few hearty workers on the town site stayed in the military tents with the stoves inside stoked all the time. The men living in them built wooden half sidewalls. The pay was good and they were saving a goodly sum to take back home, so they kept working. Clint also paid to have a house built on his lot.

The patrols kept up and occasionally there were clashes. Clint on the other hand was busy every time a train arrived. Even in winter people came looking for quick riches. They often became angry and attacked the deputies when they found out they were not to be let off the train into Gunners Town which was a "private" company town.

Word soon got around fooling with the deputies was not a smart or safe thing to do. The deputies just defended themselves and put the trouble makers on the train going out. Usually the trouble makers who put up a fight were the worse for their encounter with the deputies.

Christmas at the ranch was a quiet time. Many of the deputies stayed in for the holiday. Miriam had shipped in presents for everyone and took great pleasure in giving them out.

Raif received word by letter that lands south of the track were being apportioned. It was good land for farming, but Raif wondered how many of the one hundred and sixty acre tracts would really become profitable family farms. Though the land was good, it would take hard work and knowledge to make it produce.

As spring broke, two things happened. The mining started again and Miriam went into labor. Janice and Tonia were with Miriam. Raif was on the porch pacing and sweating in spite of the cool weather. Jeremy was sitting patiently.

They heard Janice saying loudly, "Push, Miriam! Push!"

Miriam let out one shrill piercing scream which made Raif's hair just about curl.

Janice yelled, "There's the head. Push again, Miriam!"

Raif's hair on the back of his neck did stand on end when Miriam screamed again. Raif thought he was going to die when there was a moment of silence then he heard a baby cry.

Tonia came outside, "You have a son, Raif."

Raif started to go in and Tonia put her hands on his chest, "It will be a little bit yet. Miriam isn't fit for visitors."

Raif nodded agreement.

A while later Tonia opened the door, "Raif, you can come in now." and motioned for Jeremy to stay.

Raif went in and saw his son laying with his head on his mother's breast. Raif thought it was the most beautiful thing he'd ever seen. Raif went and kissed his wife.

Raif sighed and said, "Thank you, love."

Miriam smiled, "You owe me, husband."

Raif smiled and nodded.

Miriam covered up and said, "Would you like to hold your son?"

Raif nodded yes.

Janice asked, "Do you know how?"

"No. I've never done it before."

Janice demonstrated how to do it properly.

As Miriam handed Raif his son, she said, "Joshua, this is your daddy."

Raif realized as he held the baby, he was the happiest he'd ever been.

That afternoon a telegraph was sent to Pennsylvania, *"Miriam delivered a son Joshua. Stop. Mother and son well. Stop. Raif."*

Miriam was fit so was up and around the next day. It was obvious that Tonia had kept warm on the cold winter nights. She was already starting to show. Jeremy seemed happier than Miriam had ever known him to be.

When Joshua was only a week old, the meeting took place in Raif and Miriam's cabin. Carl and David had finished their survey of the areas and were to finalize their report. With them at the meeting were Raif, Miriam, Charles, Cracker, Dan, Nathaniel, and Clint. Cracker and Dan were there representing those who were profit sharing. Once everyone had coffee, Raif started the meeting.

"Well let's get to it. Carl, as rock man, tell us what we've got."

Carl said, "I expect it will take years to mine out the area. There are a lot of deposits. You've taken a lot of gold that's easy to get at, but my study shows that we've only got a fraction of what's here. This is a fairly gold rich area. I'll leave Dave to tell you the bad news."

Dave looked at Raif who nodded.

"Well, I have to tell you it's bad news for the cattle ranching plans. Getting the gold out will make this place unsuitable for cattle ranching for decades. You aren't going to want the cattle drinking the water after we hydro lick the area."

Charles asked what that was and Dan explained the use of high pressure water hoses in mining. Raif was looking at Miriam and they knew what this meant. He then listened to the rest of the report and the questions the others asked.

When the professionals were done, Raif said, "So there's going to be gold mining work for years, but probably never any cattle ranching in my lifetime."

Dave said, "That pretty much sums it up. There's still enough gold that can be taken by panning and hand sluicing for maybe a few months, but production will no doubt start to decline. It's time to start getting ready for commercial mining. The deputies you have here will have their hands full just keeping the gold secure. Not only will we be concerned about thieves from outside, but workers skimming off the gold."

Raif said, "Well that means that all those men I made promises to will end up well off over the next several years."

Carl said, "Yes."

Dave said, "I have prepared a report of what will be needed and a few skilled men that will have to be hired. I've prepared an estimate of costs for each of the holdings." He slipped the papers to Raif.

The men stayed and talked for a while then started to drift off. Raif looked at Miriam and said, "Let's go for a walk."

Miriam took her husband's arm as they set off around the plaza.

Raif said, "I never set out to be a mine manager."

Miriam said, "I know. That's work for someone like Dave. You have men who can safeguard the family's profits. Charles could do that."

Raif said, "Yes, he could. We could also sell the town lots."

Miriam said, "I suppose we could move to your other ranch to raise our family."

Raif said, "I think I would be happier doing that."

Miriam said, "Then we'll sleep on it."

CHAPTER 12 – ON THE MOVE

Charles would be in charge while Raif, Miriam, Jeremy, and Tonia, went to Pennsylvania. Raif came to realize in some things he was not as observant as he thought he was. Raif had just announced the planned trip when Cracker came to the porch where Raif was drinking coffee.

Cracker asked, "Can I sit and chew, I mean talk, a spell?"

Raif smiled, "Want some coffee?"

"Please."

Raif didn't realize Janice was at the door and she said, "I'll get it."

Raif asked Cracker, "What's on your mind?"

Cracker said, "I'd like to talk with the Mrs. too, if ya please."

Raif said, "It must be serious. I've never heard you speak so formally." Raif looked over his shoulder, "Miriam, would you join us please?"

A minute later Miriam came out with a cup of coffee and Janice was bringing one for Cracker and had one for herself. She handed a mug to Cracker.

Raif asked, "So what's on your mind?"

"I want to go to Pennsylvania with you."

Raif saw his wife smiling and asked, "You know what this about, love."

Miriam shook her head no and said, "I have my suspicions."

Raif said, "Would someone please tell me what's going on?"

Cracker said, "Well I've been visitin' and talkin' a lot with Janice. I don't know why, but this pretty lady has agreed to be wed to me. I want to go visit her family with her and make my intentions known and maybe get hitched there."

Raif said, "Oh, no."

Cracker said, "I can't go?"

Raif said, "Of course you can. I meant now Miriam will have to find a new lady to help her."

Cracker said, "Ya," and paused then said, "I mean you had me sweatin' for a hair's breath, Major."

Raif said, "Well congratulations, Cracker. It's about time some good woman made an honest man of you."

Cracker smiled, "Yes, sir," paused then asked, "Kin I ask you somethin' personal?"

"You can ask, but I may not answer."

Cracker said, "You don' strike me as the miner type. You gonna go back to t'other ranch? Durin' the war you always talked about doin' it."

Raif looked at his wife then Janice and said, "The walls in my cabin have ears."

Janice broke into a wide smile.

Cracker said, "I ain't got no friends, but you and your Mrs. I was wonderin', when ya, I mean you, go back to t'other ranch if me and Janice could go with you and the Mrs. You know I got means and I'd like to build a little home and maybe help you out a little, raise some kids, and maybe grow old with my wife."

Raif said, "That would be good. I won't get lonely and we can teach our sons, daughters, and grandchildren, what they need to know."

Miriam said, "You should know Cracker that my brother is going with us."

"Yes, Mrs."

They had finished their coffee and Miriam said to Janice, "You can go for a spell with your fiancée. Just stay in sight. I don't trust this Cracker fellow as far as I can throw him."

Cracker smiled broadly and said, "Yes, Mrs."

When Cracker and Janice were out of earshot Miriam asked, "Did you discuss the new arrangement with Charles."

"Yes. He was well pleased with the opportunity. Clint has also agreed to his new arrangement."

Miriam sipped her coffee, "Then just about everything is in place."

"It seems so."

Three days later the Gunnerson party left for Pennsylvania. It was a pleasant trip. During a lay-over Cracker bought two suits and shirts suitable for city wear. He also went to a barber, bought Janice an expensive engagement ring, and paid for some very nice dresses that Miriam helped Janice choose. Cracker also bought a pocket watch and gold ring for himself. He also bought shoulder harness holsters like the major's.

Not to be outdone Jeremy and Tonia did a little shopping of their own. When they arrived at their destination, they looked as they needed to in order to fit in. Carriages were waiting for them at the train station and Henry was there to greet them. He had two men with him and they hurried to get the party's bags

Henry said enthusiastically, "Where's the newest Gunnerson?"

Raif said, "Not even a hello for us, Henry."

Henry smiled, "Sir, you are old news."

Raif said, "I understand. I expect Joshua will be the center of attention during our stay."

Miriam introduced Henry to Joshua. After everyone had greeted Henry, they set out for the summer house. It was as if they were on vacation and to some extent they were.

They arrived to find the addition to the summer house finished and the new stables built. It was quite impressive. They all got out and were shown to the main house. It seemed that Janice had suddenly become a little intimidated. Miriam could tell she was fighting her past experience here.

Miriam leaned over and said, "Take Joshua. He'll be the center of attention."

Janice smiled.

Inside, Pauline came out to meet them in the new entryway, "Where's the newest Gunnerson."

Janice smiled, "Here he is, Mrs. Gunnerson."

It was obvious that Pauline was pretending not to recognize Janice. Miriam thought that it was to be expected. Janice had changed. She'd filled out and no longer was she ivory white, but rather a golden beauty. She hadn't changed so as to look entirely different.

Pauline hugged Miriam and then went and took Joshua into her arms, "He's adorable."

Miriam introduced Cracker to Pauline as Mr. Cummings, a friend of Raif's.

Servants came and took their hats and coats and Pauline said, "Come. Come," and they all followed Pauline into the parlor.

Pauline had no sooner sat then she motioned to a servant who came and got Joshua. Miriam recognized the old woman who had been nanny to all the Gunnerson children. She smiled at Miriam and left the room.

Pauline said, "You are looking good, Miriam. Western life seems to agree with you."

"It does, Aunt Pauline."

Pauline asked, "Would anyone like tea or coffee?"

Everyone wanted something and Pauline rang a little bell and a servant came and Pauline asked that it be brought.

Pauline looked at Cracker, "Mr. Cummings, how is it you come to know my nephew?"

Cracker smiled, "We was in the army together in the war. The major saved my life mor'n once."

Raif added, "And he mine."

Pauline said, "I see. What do you do for a living, Mr. Cummings?"

Cracker smiled, "I s'pose I'm retired. My associatin' with the major has bin very rewardin'."

Pauline said, "I see. What did you do before the war?"

"I farmed. I still own the farm, though I s'pose I should sell it. It's not a life I reckon to return to."

Miriam added, "My friend Janice is engaged to Mr. Cumming. They plan to be wed soon."

Pauline said, "How nice. Congratulations, Mr. Cummings."

"Thank you, Mrs. Gunnerson."

The group made small talk until the nanny came with Joshua who was fidgeting. Miriam knew what he needed and said, "If you'll all excuse me. Janice, would you help me please."

Janice smiled, "Of course."

Pauline called for someone to show them to their rooms. Once they were in Miriam's room and she was sitting feeding Joshua, Janice said, "She doesn't recognize me."

Miriam said, "Oh, she recognizes you. She just doesn't want to admit she does. It's part of her coping. If it's unpleasant to her then she pretends it didn't happen or isn't what it is."

Janice said, "Most of the women around here are like that."

"Yes. After supper, we'll go for a little walk and you can visit your parents."

Janice nodded agreement.

Once Joshua was fed, the women went back downstairs leaving Joshua sleeping in the care of the nanny. James came home with Edward and Mary who had come to see the western branch of the family and to meet the newest addition. It was a very pleasant meal time.

After supper, Miriam and Janice went for their walk. They were surprised to find Cracker was already at Janice's parent's place, sitting on a wooden bench talking with Jake and his wife. Both Jake and Cracker were smoking pipes while Martha was sitting in a rocker gently going forward and back. As Janice approached, her parents got up and came to greet her. There were firm hugs and Miriam was included. Jake went into their small one room house and brought out two chairs.

Jake said with a smile, "Cracker has asked for my blessing to marry you, dear."

Janice smiled, "Isn't it grand, father?"

Jake puffed on his pipe and looked at his wife, "I think our daughter is smitten."

Martha said, "It seems they both are."

Miriam said, "You are both looking good."

Jake said, "Thank you, Mrs."

Martha said, "Mr. Cummings was telling us he'd take good care of our daughter."

Cracker said, "I expect she'll do most of the takin' care of. It's a credit to ya that ya raised your daughter to be very strong woman."

Jake said, "She comes by it natural. She's like her mother."

Martha smiled.

Miriam said, "My friend here is a dependable man and a man of his word. I believe he will make Janice a good husband."

Jake said, "Good enough. You have my blessing."

Janice got up and hugged her father then sat down again.

Jake said, "I suppose you'll be living where you came from."

Cracker said, "No. Raif and Miriam are going to their ranch and we are going to buy a place nearby and live there."

Jake said, "Buy?"

Miriam said, "Mr. Cummings is a man of some means."

Martha said, "Oh."

Jake asked, "Where and when are you planning to have the wedding."

Janice said, "We thought to get married here and as soon as we can arrange it. We have to find a preacher."

They started to discuss possible wedding plans. While they were talking, Raif was meeting with James and Edward. The men were smoking cigars in the library.

Raif asked, "Whatever happened to that Manley fellow?"

"He's in prison. Unfortunate that. His family had to sell his business interests. I was able to help them out."

Raif just smiled and nodded.

Edward said, "The arrangements you made for the overseeing of the mining operations are good. We are going to send two accountants to keep track of things and keep an eye on finances. We assumed you'd agree."

Raif just nodded agreement and said, "Charles and Sarah moved into the ranch when we left. It should work out well."

James added, "The new equipment will be going out within the next week along with the men to work it."

Raif asked, "How is the new estate coming?"

James said, "We have the old Mill down and we salvaged a lot of brick and stone as well as timber that can be used in the new buildings. The foundations are completed for the new home and the servants' houses. The new servant's homes will have two rooms."

Edward asked, "How long are you planning to stay?"

"Perhaps three or four weeks."

Edward said, "We still haven't figured out how to deal with Gary. We have no proof he did anything wrong here."

Raif said, "I've done something," and handed an official document to James.

James read it and handed it to Edward.

Edward asked, "Is it enforceable?"

Raif said, "If there's a federal marshal anywhere around. I had something else in mind though. I'd like your thoughts on it."

The men discussed it for a bit and it was agreed Raif's plan would be best for the family. Later that evening, James told Pauline they would have a family dinner Friday evening and everyone was expected to attend. On Saturday evening, they would have a dinner for their closest friends.

The next morning Miriam and Janice went searching for Janice's wedding dress. Jake drove the carriage and they had an entirely enjoyable time. Janice found the dress she wanted and was fitted for it. They ate lunch in a restaurant and took Jake along. It was Jake's first time in a restaurant. They returned to the summer home in the late afternoon.

After dinner, Raif and Miriam went for a walk.

Miriam started the conversation, "You know we'll need new help at the ranch."

Raif asked, "Would you like to tell me who we're going to hire."

"I was thinking Jake and Martha. They would be close to Janice and Cracker, but not in an embarrassing position."

"You mean being employed by their son-in-law or taking his charity."

"Yes." Miriam paused, "They are strong and healthy. They probably have a lot of working life ahead of them and they're industrious and nice."

Raif asked, "Are you going to do the talking?"

"Please."

Raif nodded yes and said, "We'll make room for them."

Miriam said, "I was thinking about building proper houses this time. We can certainly afford it and it won't disrupt Ross and the men already there."

Raif just nodded, "I suppose."

Miriam said, "Thank you, dear."

Miriam started to steer her husband toward Jake and Martha's home and Raif just smiled.

Martha was surprised when Raif and Miriam came to her door. She said, "Good evening."

Miriam asked, "Martha, we would like to talk to you and Jake."

Martha said, "Certainly, Mrs. He's out back in the garden. I'll go fetch him. Please have a seat."

Martha hurried off and Miriam and Raif took a seat on the little porch. They had hardly gotten seated when Martha returned with her husband.

Jake said, "Good evening sir, Mrs."

Raif smiled, "It is a beautiful evening isn't it?"

Jake said, "Yes, sir."

Martha and Jake took a seat.

Miriam said, "We have a proposition for you."

Jake said, "Yes, ma'am."

Miriam said, "We are going to live at Raif's ranch and he has not been back since before the war. We'll need help there. We would like you to come to work for us. If you decide to come, Raif will talk to James about releasing you."

Martha looked at her husband.

Jake said, "Is this because of Janice's being wed to Mr. Cummings?"

Miriam said, "No. With Janice getting married, I'd need help in any event. You know I have a habit of hiring people I know. This was just natural."

Jake asked, "Are we the only help?"

Raif shook his head no, "I have a bunch of ranch hands that take care of the cattle and Jeremy and his wife will be living at the ranch and he is bringing a couple of helpers."

Jake looked at Raif, "What is the pay?"

Raif looked at Miriam who answered, "The same as here. The big difference is we do not deduct for housing and food."

Martha asked, "Is it as dangerous as where you were before?"

Raif said, "Not as dangerous, but there is always some danger. If you decide to come it would be wise to learn to use a gun just in case."

Jake asked, "May we think it over?"

Miriam said, "Of course.

Raif said, "We'll leave you to talk it over," and got up and so did Miriam.

Miriam said, "Good evening," and she walked away with her husband.

Martha said, "We should ask Janice what they're like to work for."

Jake said, "There we could actually save money. No deduction from pay. Can you imagine?"

Martha said, "I'm going to find Janice."

When Martha returned, Janice was with her. The women sat on the porch. Jake started the conversation with his daughter.

"It's not for talking about with others, but Mr. and Mrs. Gunnerson have asked us to come work at their ranch. You have experience with them. What will it be like?"

Janice said enthusiastically, "That's wonderful. I didn't know. They are good people to work for. They expect good work, but they are easy with the industrious and they are fair. They would be easier to work for than Pauline and she's pretty good from what everyone told me when I lived here."

Martha said, "And we'd be close to you."

Janice smiled, "Oh, yes. I expect very close. It won't be like here though. Out west everyone calls Mr. Gunnerson major or boss. The soldier types say sir or major and the others say boss. Miriam has authority over the home and some part in the business."

Jake said, "Mr. Gunnerson sure let her have her say."

Janice nodded.

Martha said, "Let's have tea and you can tell us what to expect."

Miriam was up early the next morning to feed Joshua and change him. She supposed she needed a nanny. She had no ideas about that. She decided to talk to Martha.

After breakfast, Miriam found Martha working in the garden and stopped to talk to her.

"Good morning, Martha."

"Good morning, Mrs."

"It's a beautiful day to be working in the garden."

"Yes, it is."

Miriam said, "I'd like your advice."

Martha seemed surprised but said, "About what, Mrs "

"I need help to find someone who might make a good nanny for Joshua and the children to follow, God willing."

Martha said, "I know just the person, Abigail Ebbe. This has to be a God thing. She worked for the Crain family. She raised their daughter until she was six years old, but the family recently sent the child off to family in England to be educated. The Mrs. can't have no more children. Abigail would be a fine nanny for yours and they just let her go. She has to be out by Sunday and she has no family to go to."

Miriam said, "Thank you, Martha. By the way, would you get along with her if you decide to come?"

Martha smiled, "Most certainly. She is a very pleasant young woman."

Miriam nodded and left to make arrangements. Jake brought a carriage around and one of the security men was sitting in the front seat.

The security man said, "Good morning, Mrs. Gunnerson."

Miriam said, "Good morning."

Jake came to Miriam to help her into the carriage. He said, "We accept."

Miriam said, "Good."

Twenty minutes later Miriam pulled up at the Crain family home. Miriam went to the door and knocked. A servant answered.

"Yes, ma'am?"

Miriam said, "I'm Mrs. Gunnerson and I've come to see Mrs. Crain. Would you announce me?"

The servant looked at the fine carriage, the uniformed driver, and the other man in the carriage then said, "Yes, ma'am. Please come in and I'll tell Mrs. Crain you're here."

Miriam took a seat in the hall. A couple of minutes later, a well-dressed lady approached. The woman was smiling. She was an average looking woman prone to be a little on the plump side.

The woman said, "Mrs. Gunnerson, I'm pleased to meet you. I'm Ann Crain."

The woman offered her hand and Miriam shook it.

Mrs. Crain said, "Please come in," and she led Miriam into the parlor and they sat.

Miriam noted that the furniture was very nice, but worn. It occurred to Miriam that Abigail's release might not have everything to do with the family's daughter going off to school abroad.

Mrs. Crain asked, "How may I help you?"

Miriam said, "I am in need of a nanny. I heard that your daughter was fortunate enough to be going abroad for school. I understand that, as a result, you are releasing Abigail Ebbe."

"Why yes and of course I'll arrange for you to talk to Abigail if you'd like."

Miriam said, "Thank you, Mrs. Crain."

"Ann please."

"Miriam."

"Would you like tea, Miriam?"

Miriam smiled, "Always."

The china the tea was served in was of fine quality, but slightly chipped. Miriam did not let on she noticed.

Mrs. Crain said, "Abigail is delightful and she was very good with Alexis. What does your husband do?"

Miriam said, "We are cattle ranchers."

Mrs. Crain said, "I see," but Miriam figured Mrs. Crain had no idea what that meant.

Miriam asked, "What does your husband do?"

"He's a doctor of medicine."

Miriam said, "It's a noble profession."

"Yes, quite."

Mrs. Crain asked, "What did your family do Mrs. Gunnerson?"

"My mother and father were farmers. They have passed."

It suddenly occurred to Miriam that she did not know what happened to the family farm. She and Jeremy were just children when they were put off it. Yet she remembered how proud her father had been that he had owned the piece of land outright having inherited it from his father. She put it out of her mind for the moment knowing that she'd have to look into it later.

After tea, Mrs. Crain arranged for Abigail to meet Miriam. Miriam suggested to Abigail they go for a walk and talk.

As they walked, Miriam said, "I understand you need a position and I need a nanny. The mother of my friend Janice, Martha Dodd, recommended you."

Abigail asked, "Ma'am are you saying Martha's daughter Janice is a friend of yours?"

"Yes and I have known Jake and Martha for some years."

Abigail said, "Then you know my troubles."

"Yes, but I won't take advantage of your situation."

The women talked at some length and Miriam offered Abigail the position and she accepted with everything that went along with it. She was, like the others, surprised to find there would be no deduction in pay for food and lodging.

At the end of the meeting, Abigail asked, "When do you want me to start?"

"As soon as possible."

"It will take me about fifteen minutes to pack."

Miriam smiled, "I'll wait."

Abigail hurried off and Miriam went to see Mrs. Crain and tell her. Abigail left in the carriage with Miriam and a few meager possessions. Miriam thought another shopping trip would be in order.

When they arrived back at the house, Henry came out to meet Miriam and said, "Mrs. Gunnerson, your husband has returned and he'd like to take lunch with you."

Miriam smiled, "Thank you, Henry. I have hired Abigail to be my son's nanny. Would you have someone get her situated, please?"

Henry smiled, "Of course. It will be my pleasure."

Miriam went into the house to find Joshua. She knew because she was feeling full that it was time and he'd be looking to be fed. Miriam thought as she suckled her child that this was one of the true joys of motherhood that no man would ever understand.

After being fed, Joshua quickly went to sleep and Miriam called for Abigail and left Joshua in her care.

Raif, Jeremy, Tonia, Cracker, and Janice were waiting for Miriam on the veranda. Miriam went to Raif and kissed him lightly and he smiled and asked, "Were you successful?"

Miriam said, "In both cases. You need to talk to James and Pauline."

Janice said, "I am so pleased."

Cracker was smiling, "We were able to arrange a church and preacher to wed us on Saturday."

Miriam said, "That's marvelous."

They spent some time talking about the wedding and eating lunch. When they finished, Miriam said, "I have something serious to talk about."

Raif said, "What is it?"

Miriam told Raif about her family farm. When she finished, Jeremy spoke.

"It never occurred to me, but Miriam is right and I now suspect we were defrauded."

Raif said, "Then we'd best have someone look into it for us. I take offense to someone stealing my wife's inheritance."

Jeremy said, "Agreed and I'm not too happy on my own account either."

Later that afternoon, Raif and Miriam arranged to talk to Pauline when she came home after visiting Mary. They met on the veranda and Pauline had beverages served.

Once they were all settled, Pauline asked, "What is it you wanted to talk to me about?"

Raif said, "A gift for us on the occasion of our first born."

Pauline said casually without thinking, "Anything within my power, dear boy."

Raif said, "Good, then we will take Jake and Martha into our employ and to the ranch with us."

Pauline looked at Raif, "Nephew, you have become as wily as my husband. That is altogether too sneaky."

Raif said with a smile, "But seriously, we would like you to give your blessing for them to come with us."

Pauline said with a smile, "I half expected this with Janice marrying your associate Mr. Cummings. I just didn't think you'd manipulate me so easily. I intended to make you sweat over it."

Miriam said, "All's well that ends well."

Pauline said, "Quite. I'll have Henry tell Jake and Martha I approve."

Raif said, "Thank you."

Pauline said, "It's the least I can do seeing as you two have increased our family fortunes greatly. I suppose it will be easier for me to find help here than for you to find it there."

Miriam said, "That is true. It's why we came up with the plan to trick you."

Pauline gave Miriam "the look" which caused Miriam and Raif to laugh. It was all good natured.

Miriam told Pauline about the informal wedding and Pauline said in a way that indicated she was teasing, "Well it's a good thing the Dodds are now in your employ. I'd expect otherwise I'd have to pay them while they were off attending their daughter's wedding."

It was Miriam's turn to shake her head in mock disbelief.

The next day was a day of errand running. Miriam left Joshua with Pauline's nanny so she could go shopping to get her new help outfitted for the west. Tonia and Janice went along as they wanted some new things as well. Jeremy and Raif went to have the Cole farm matter investigated. Cracker went to send a telegraph to a lawyer back near his farm to arrange to have the farm put up for sale.

They were all back at the house well before the family dinner was to start. Cracker had decided to take Jake and Martha for their first restaurant dinner in town.

The Gunnerson family started arriving from town and soon the house was abuzz. Everyone wanted to see Joshua, who having been fed just before the arrivals, slept through the oohing and ahing.

The dinner was a pleasant affair and even Raif's cousin Paul was there having returned from his European business trip. After the meal, as was their habit, the men broke off to meet apart from the women. All the Gunnerson males and the men married to the daughters were there; Raif, James, Edward, Paul, Connor, Dennis and Gary. In the library James poured whiskey for everyone including Raif.

It was Connor who had the honor, "A toast, to uncovering treachery in our midst."

The men raised their glasses and everyone but Gary said, "Hear, hear."

Raif handed Gary a paper, "This is for you, Gary."

Gary unfolded the document and read it as he turned redder and redder. Finally he said, "This has no legal basis."

Raif said, "Actually, it does. Your co-conspirator, Will Parker agreed to testify against you to keep from hanging. He's in a territorial prison."

Gary looked around and saw nothing but hostility. "There's some mistake."

James said, "And you made it."

Gary tried to be dismissive, "This has no meaning here."

Raif said, "Again I say, it does. That is a federal, not state, arrest warrant and any federal marshal can arrest you. Fortunately for you there is no marshal here, yet."

Edward said, "I suppose you could escape and go abroad. I'm not sure if I would like Constance watching her husband be hung for murder."

James said, "Now we know about the warrant, we'll be obliged to tell the authorities. I suppose it will be later in the morning tomorrow, so you'll have something of a head start."

Connor said, "I'd do it quickly. No telling when a federal marshal will show up."

Gary was standing speechless. After a second, he put his drink down and left the library and the house without Constance. Gary did not realize he was being followed.

James said, "That was actually quite enjoyable."

Edward asked, "Does anyone think it's a certainty he'll do the smart thing and depart across the ocean?"

Connor said, "I figure there's a fifty-fifty chance that he'll do the smart thing."

On Saturday morning, while Raif and Miriam witnessed the wedding of Cracker and Janice with Jake and Martha watching, James received a terse telegraph, *"Heading to New York. Stop. Further report to follow. Stop. J."* James figured, on the basis of the telegraph from his man Joel, Gary might yet prove to be smart enough to know when to cut and run.

It was later in the morning that a note addressed to Constance was delivered to the Gunnerson summer home. James had Constance and Pauline come to the library and sit down.

James said, "Constance this note came for you."

Constance opened and read it then said, "Thank God!"

Smiling, she handed the note to her father. It said, *"Constance, I have had all I can take of the Gunnerson family and the place you call home. I'm leaving for Europe. I will not be coming back. Gary."*

James handed it to Pauline and she started reading.

James said to Constance, "That was not the reaction I expected."

Constance said, "I'm glad to be rid of the pig. He beat me, but was careful it didn't show. I've lost two babies because of that whoring monster."

James was the one to be shocked, "Why didn't you tell me?"

"What would you have done?"

"Had him killed."

Constance's mouth dropped open and Pauline was sitting with a stunned look on her face.

James said seriously, "I didn't mean to give voice to the thought." He changed the subject, "If you can prove extreme abuse you can get a divorce."

Constance said, "My doctor can attest to it."

James said, "I'll get our lawyer started on it Monday."

Constance asked, "You'd really have done that for me?"

James just looked at his daughter and she knew he'd have done it.

She said, "Thank you, father. I love you, too."

She went around the desk and hugged him tightly for a moment, then left the room her head held high.

Pauline was looking at her husband and was still speechless.

James broke the spell, "Dear, don't you have things to do to get ready for this evening?"

Pauline said, "Yes, of course," and got up and left. She now understood that Raif was not the only dangerous Gunnerson.

The Saturday evening social in celebration of Joshua's birth was a fine affair and a good time was had by all. Peter was in good health and Ellen was as delightful as ever. Their daughter Kate seemed happy hanging on the arm of a rich merchant's son.

Connor and Marjorie compared notes with Raif and Miriam about their babies. Marjorie told Miriam she wished she could have been there when little Nelson James Edward Patterson was born.

On Sunday morning, much to Pauline's surprise, Miriam, Raif, Janice, and Joshua left early in a carriage. Pauline could not believe that of all places they were going to church which was a result of reading the Bible all winter. This had resulted in many discussions about the material and they were eager to find out more.

In New York, Gary woke early on the day his ship was to leave. Something was wrong. His valise was unlocked and open. He rushed to it. His ticket was still there but some of his money was gone. He counted it. Exactly half was gone.

Gary thought. This was most certainly the work of Constance's family. A thief would have taken it all. He thought about getting revenge then quickly discarded the idea. If they could get to his money they could just as easily have murdered him in his sleep. He locked the bag and got ready to go to the ship that would take him to a new life.

James received a telegraph later that day, *"Cargo on board for Europe. Stop. Commission taken. Stop. Returning. Stop. J."*

Gary wasn't the only one to have a surprise that week. Mr. William Colter, Attorney at Law received unexpected visitors. His assistant Ben came into his office.

"Sir there are four men here to see you," and handed his employer a business card. William looked at the card and recognized the name. Whoever had hired Franklin White, Attorney at Law, was very rich. Mr. White was among the three most respected attorneys in the state.

William said, "Show them in, Ben."

"Yes, sir."

William stood when the men came in. He said, "Good afternoon, gentlemen. Please have a seat. I'm William Colter," and offered his hand to Mr. White who ignored it.

The four men took chairs around the table in William's office.

Mr. White said, "I represent Mr. Raif Gunnerson and Mr. Jeremy Cole," and he motioned to the men in turn.

William's heart skipped a beat. He thought Cole, it can't be the same one. He controlled his emotions and said, "How may I help you?"

White said, "Correct your criminal behavior and right the injustice you did to my clients."

"I do not know your clients and I resent the charge."

White said, "Mr. Gunnerson is the husband of Miriam Cole. Jeremy here is Miriam Cole's older brother. I have proof you defrauded and displaced the children illegally from their inherited property that was rightly theirs. You forged documents and with the help of the former county clerk, registered false deeds. Now this can go two ways. I have a quit claim deed here you can sign returning the property to its rightful owners."

Colter protested, "I have invested considerable sums improving the property."

White said, "Using stolen income from the property. My clients are willing to waive their claim against your other assets, at least some of which they will get if they sue, and no one can be sure how much. In any case, it will most likely put you in the poorhouse. If all this comes out in civil court, your days as an attorney will be over."

Colter said, "You have no proof."

"There is a paper trail at the county courthouse. My juniors found it within an hour of starting their search of records."

Colter said, "I need time to consider what you've said."

White said, "We're not fools, Mr. Colter. We are not inclined to give you the opportunity to attempt to destroy evidence or flee."

Raif moved so part of his shoulder holstered weapon showed.

Colter said, "Let me see the papers."

He read them while the others sat patiently saying nothing. The signatures on the releases were signed by Miriam and Jeremy and notarized. When Colter finished he said, "I'll sign them."

White turned to Cracker, "Would you ask the notary to come in."

Cracker got up and went outside and came back with the notary. The documents were executed and Raif and his party left. As they exited the building, White said to the two county sheriff's deputies, "He's all yours."

Raif smiled.

Mr. White said, "As an officer of the court, I have an obligation to bring all criminal acts I become aware of to the attention of the proper authorities. If he was half the lawyer he thought he was, he would have seen this coming. I'll have the Cole deeds registered."

Raif said, "Thank you, Franklin."

"My pleasure, Raif. My firm has done business with your uncles for many years."

Jeremy offered his hand and Mr. White shook it. He then went to his carriage. Raif started to mount his horse when the deputies brought Mr. Colter out in handcuffs. He sat on his horse watching the deputies put Colter into a jail wagon.

Raif and his friends rode away. They were not heading directly back to the Gunnerson family home. They went to the Cole family farm. From the road on top of the hill overlooking the Cole farm, Jeremy could see the fertile fields spread out before him. The crops in the fields were already growing. The buildings were in much better repair than Jeremy remembered them. The farm was also much larger than he remembered.

The men rode down to the farmhouse. A woman came out to meet them, "Can I help you gentlemen."

Jeremy said, "Hello. I'm Jeremy Cole. My sister Miriam and I own this farm."

"Sir, I believe you are mistaken. Mr. Colter owns this farm and my husband and I have been crop sharing it for him for many years."

Raif asked, "Since when."

"Since he bought the place."

Cracker said, "Ya suppose they were in on the stealin' of the farm?"

The woman suddenly looked afraid.

Jeremy said, "Could be. I recognize her as the one that packed me and Miriam up. She was none too kind about it either."

The woman said, "I think you should clear off."

Raif said, "Colter was dragged off to jail less than half an hour ago. If you were in on it, I imagine it will come out."

Jeremy said, "We are not leaving."

As the men dismounted, the woman went into the house just inside the door. She came out with a shotgun. She realized the men had moved apart and all three of them had fancy rifles pointed at her. She put the shotgun down.

Cracker said, "She's pretty smart."

Jeremy said, "Are there children here?"

The woman shook her head no.

Raif said, "Where's your man?"

"North field."

It wasn't long before the man and the woman left the farm on foot carrying their personal belongings.

Jeremy said, "I'm hungry. Let's see what we can scare up to eat."

Cracker said, "Sounds good to me."

The men went inside and found the house was well provisioned. It was a very nice house and well furnished.

The men slept comfortably that night. In the morning, two deputies showed up looking for the man and woman Jeremy had run off. The deputies had coffee with Jeremy and his friends before heading out to look for the couple. When the deputies left, the three men sat out on the farmhouse porch drinking coffee.

Jeremy said, "I think the farm will bring a good dollar. I just have to figure out how to sell it."

Cracker said, "There's fellers that specialize in selling all kinds of stuff. I had one such feller looking for someone to buy my farm and it sold right off for top dollar for the land, but I didn't get anything for the buildings because they needed tearin' down."

Raif said, "We should go to the nearest town and ask around."

Cracker said, "Wagon comin' down the lane."

Jeremy said, "Seems so."

They watched until the wagon came into the yard. An older and younger man were in the wagon. The older man called out.

"Mind if we come talk?"

Jeremy motioned, "Come on."

The men got out of the wagon and walked to the porch. The older man looked right at Jeremy, "You might not remember me, Jeremy, but your pa and I were friends. I'm Clive Moore and this is my son Greg."

Jeremy smiled and said, "I remember you, sir, and especially Greg. How are you Greg?"

"Good, Jeremy."

Jeremy shook hands with the elder and hugged the younger.

Jeremy said, "This is my brother-in-law Raif Gunnerson and his associate Carl Cummings."

The men shook hands.

Jeremy said, "Take a load off. There's coffee if you'd like some."

Clive said, "That would be nice."

Jeremy got up and went and brought two cups back.

Clive said, "Word is already around about what happened to you kids. Everyone believed you went to stay with kin and lawyer Colter bought the farm right and proper. It was the usual kind of thing would happen. No one guessed what Colter had done."

Jeremy just nodded.

Clive asked, "You gonna stay?"

"No. I'm going to sell the place. Seeing as you have the place next to this, are you interested?"

Clive said, "I'm interested. We'd pay the fair going price and this is a top notch farm. Greg is getting hitched and this is a nice house. He's saved a considerable sum."

Jeremy looked at Greg. "How much is considerable?"

Greg told him.

Jeremy said, "I reckon that's nowhere near enough."

Greg said, "I know. I'd give a mortgage for the rest on payments. The banker said he'd give the loan. This is good land and I can earn a good living if I can buy it fair."

Jeremy said, "I'm not sure what the fair price is."

Clive said, "The acre price around here is pretty much the same as all the land is good for farming. You have nicer buildings than most, so you'd get more, especially if you're selling furnished and equipped."

Jeremy said, "We are."

Clive asked, "Who's we."

"My sister and I."

Clive said, "Of course. Can you speak for her?"

Jeremy said, "Yes."

Clive looked to Raif who nodded agreement.

Greg said, "We can have a price give by the ones who sells farm equipment and come to agreement on the furnishings."

Jeremy said, "Sounds reasonable."

After two hours the men had agreed on terms. Jeremy and Miriam were going to become wealthier by the sale.

By the time the group was ready to go south and west, their business matters had been completed. Between what he made with Raif and the sale of the farm, Jeremy and Tonia would be quite well off. Cracker who had been wealthy because of the money they'd taken from the confederate payroll wagon, had become even wealthier with the sale of his farm land and his small share of the gold. He and Janice did not expect to have any money problems.

CHAPTER 13 – HOME AT LAST

It was about two weeks after Jeremy had sold the farm that the Gunnerson party was boarding the train heading to the ranch. The trip to the railway station closest to the ranch was long, but relatively uneventful. At first Miriam had a little trouble finding a way to feed Joshua on the train without having men gawking at her. Raif suggested the poncho and it worked extremely well.

They arrived in town at midafternoon. Roy Callum, who was Edward and James' man and had been helping with the business end of the ranch, was there to meet them. He came forward, "Hello, Major. Roy Callum. We've been expecting you."

Raif said, "Hello, Roy," and proceeded with the introductions.

When Raif finished, Roy said, "I have horses and wagons with teams ready. I suggest we stay in town tonight and start out in the morning. I have rooms reserved at the hotel."

Raif was suddenly distracted. He called out, "Hey, Toby," and went to see a man who was by the wagons. The men shook hands and embraced. Raif brought Toby to meet everyone. Raif explained Toby was the one who watched over him on the cattle drives when Raif was very young.

The men went with Raif to offload their cargo and the women climbed in the wagons. Miriam could see the trouble coming and said to Abigail, "Stay up here in the middle of the seat with Joshua."

Miriam got down from the wagon and moved toward Janice who also got down off the other wagon. The three men approached the women.

The leader said, "Lookie what we got here. We's goin' to have us some fun, fellas."

Miriam threw back her poncho with her left hand revealing her guns, including the one in her right hand, and Janice was suddenly holding her coach gun pointing at the three men.

Miriam said in a firm and serious voice, "Do you fellows really want to die today?"

The man who was the leader was momentarily speechless. He had been caught by something he had not expected. Suddenly to the side Raif said, "Dear, do you need some help?"

The leader turned to see Raif with all his holsters and holding his Henry pointed at the men.

Miriam said, "No, there's only three of them and they won't be hard to kill."

Raif lowered his rifle and said, "Mister, ya ought to know better than to get between a mama bear and its cub."

The leader looked back at Miriam, then Janice holding the coach gun and decided. He raised his hands shoulder high and turned and walked away. His two companions followed him.

Janice came over to where Raif and Miriam were standing.

Raif said, "That fellow didn't know how close he came to looking up from six feet under."

Miriam said, "If he'd gone for his gun Janice would have cut them all down and I'd have finished them."

Janice simply said, "Yup."

Raif said, "We are ready for the wagons."

Miriam climbed up with Abigail and drove the wagon to where their cargo was. Janice climbed up with Martha and drove the other wagon.

Martha said, "I didn't know you could manage a team."

Janice said, "I've learned to do a lot in the past months."

Martha said, "So I seen. Does that kind of thing happen often?"

Janice said, "Nah, maybe a couple times a year where we were. There was some low-lifes there that needed killing. After a while, people knew our reputation and gave us a wide way. Here it's likely we could be challenged because people don't know us by reputation yet."

Martha looked at the coach gun and asked, "You know how to use that thing?"

"Yes, mother. I'll teach you."

They were by the cargo and Janice set the brake and got down. Martha watched her daughter load cargo and was surprised to see Miriam helping. Martha got down and helped. Once the cargo was loaded and fastened down, they all got into the wagons and went to the hotel. Martha, Abigail, and Jake had never stayed in a hotel and it would be a first.

Before they went inside the guard shifts were decided. There would be two guards with the wagons and cargo at all times. It turned out their planning was for nothing. The hotel had overbooked and there were not enough rooms for them.

The wagons were heavily loaded and would travel slow. It would take several days to get to the ranch with them and Raif had wanted everyone to have a night in the hotel before they left. He was put out and made it known.

Roy was very angry and let the owner know. Roy had prepaid for the rooms. He demanded a refund. The hotel owner took one look at the heavily armed group and decided not to be greedy. The hotel manager's "mistake" would turn out to be very fortunate.

Raif decided the women would double up and the men would sleep by the wagons in the lean to and a man would stand guard in the hotel hall outside the women's rooms. The sentry shifts were arranged and the women were helped to get settled in.

The members of the party ate in the hotel restaurant in shifts. The food was basic and filling. Everyone was tired and they turned in early.

Raif and Cracker happened to be standing guard in the early morning hours when Raif became aware of the men sneaking up on them. He and Cracker turned the tables and when the man closest to Raif entered the lean-to, Raif introduced him to the butt of his rifle. Three others were taken without a shot being fired. The men were trussed up and Jeremy went for the sheriff just about the time the sun was coming up.

The sheriff came into the lean-to about fifteen minutes later.

Raif said, "Good morning, Sheriff. Seems that we have some fellows who thought to steal our cargo."

The sheriff introduced himself and Raif did the introductions of the men with him.

The sheriff asked, "You any relation to the Double G Ranch Gunnerson."

Raif said, "That's my ranch. I've been away since I went to war."

The sheriff looked at the men with him, "That explains these men bein' taken."

The sheriff went and looked at the men. He came back and said, "Two of 'em have wanted posters. There's reward money. These boys ain't use to havin' run ins with hard men. They usually look for easy prey."

Raif said, "Criminals most often do."

The sheriff said, "They reckoned wrong this time. Can one of your men help me get them to the jail? My deputy is off investigatin' a rustlin'."

Raif said, "Of course, Sheriff."

Cracker said, "I'll do it, Major. I'll take care of claiming for the reward."

Raif nodded.

Raif's party started out very early in the morning. That first day they travelled almost fifteen miles before making camp. The sky was clear and Raif decided they'd hobble the horses and sleep under the stars. They parked the wagons parallel to each other and started a fire between them. Two sentries were on duty at all times.

The following day the party made about twelve miles before making camp. On the third day they made only nine miles, but reached the town closest to the ranch. Everyone was still in good spirits. They all slept in beds at a hotel that evening and ate a good meal. They were able to wash in their rooms using basins. Raif was also able to sleep most of the night alone with his wife.

The next day and after a late start, they reached the ranch boundary at mid-morning. There was a gate on the trail. It was built of two tall vertical poles topped by two horizontal poles between which were mounted two forged metal interlocking G's that were the Double G brand. A closed wooden gate barred the way.

Miriam looked in both directions and as far as she could see was fence stretching for miles. She could see large groups of cattle here and there grazing. She also saw what looked like two windmills a long way off and a large distance apart.

Miriam pointed at the closest windmill and Raif said, "They pump water from the underground aquifer for the cattle."

Miriam said, "Aquifer?"

"Like an underground river."

Miriam nodded.

Toby opened the gate and the group moved through as he waited to close it.

Miriam asked, "What does the double G stand for?"

"It stands for Gunnerson and Gunnerson. First it was for my mother and father and then for me and my father. Now it's me and you."

Once they passed through the gate, it took another hour to get to the ranch house because the wagons moved so slow, loaded down as they were. They climbed a long rolling hill and at the crest they saw the ranch buildings on another hill. It was not what Miriam expected. There were over two dozen buildings. Even at a distance she could tell these were not like the log cabins at the mine site. These were mostly single story whitewashed buildings sided with clapboard. There were two stables, two barns, a large two story main house, a long narrow building, and other buildings of various sizes.

On the far side of the house, below the hill on which it sat, a stream flowed. She could follow the path of the winding stream for some distance.

Miriam looked at Raif, "Husband, you've been keeping secrets."

Raif smiled, "I just wanted to surprise you."

A single rider was coming out to meet them. Raif's group started forward. When they met with the rider, Raif moved to the side and Miriam followed.

The man stopped and said, "It's been too long, Raif."

"Yes it has, Ross."

The two men shook hands from the saddle then Raif said, "This is my wife, Miriam."

Ross tipped his hat, "Pleased to meet you, ma'am."

Miriam smiled then said, "Thank you, Ross, for all you did while Raif was gone," and offered her hand which Ross shook.

Ross turned to Raif, "Boss, how did a homely dog like you capture the heart of such a fine looking woman?"

Raif smiled, "Just lucky I guess. Our son Joshua is in the wagon there with Abigail who is coming to help Miriam."

Ross said, "I see you brought some new help. I suppose they are house people?"

Raif nodded.

Ross said, "Well boss, let's get you settled in. We kept the main house in good repair while you were gone. It will need a good cleaning though. This time of year we didn't really have time."

Raif said, "I understand. We have help for that."

The three of them turned their horses and followed the wagons. As they got close to the main house, Miriam realized it was larger than she first realized. She exchanged a look with Raif and he smiled.

The wagons stopped in front of the main house and those on horse dismounted.

Miriam was surprised by the size of the house. It was as large as many of the homes of the family in Pennsylvania. The entire house was surrounded by veranda. It had a metal roof.

Raif called out, "Everyone gather round. First things first, introductions."

Raif introduced everyone to Ross and explained he managed the ranch's cattle operations. He also told them Ross would later take them on a walking tour of the ranch buildings and explain the operation.

Raif said, "Let's tour the house."

Miriam was pleasantly surprised when they entered the house. The house was finished with painted vertical planking throughout and the floors were of some sort of waxed wood. Furniture with covers on it were placed throughout the house.

As they toured the main floor, Miriam noticed each room on the main floor had windows as well as either a fireplace or a stove. The main floor consisted of a very large formal living area, a large dining room, a good size kitchen, and a small two room servants' quarters. There was a pump in the kitchen and Martha tried it and it worked. The water ran into a sink and Martha looked into the sink.

Raif said, "There's a drain runs outside and away from the house downhill."

Martha said, "That's nice."

Raif took them out the kitchen door. There was also a separate outdoor summer kitchen across the porch at the back. Raif explained that allowed the cooking of meals separate from the main house to help keep the main house cooler in hot weather.

Upstairs there were five bedrooms off a broad hall. The owner's bedroom was twice as large as the others. Every bedroom had at least one window and Miriam noted the layout of the windows would allow cross breezes from any direction when they were all open. Throughout the upstairs there were heavy curtains on rods to cover the windows and grates in the floors.

Miriam stood over one of the grates, "What are these for?"

Raif said, "Downstairs in the ceilings you'll see the same thing. Hot air rises and in winter the heat from the fireplaces and stoves rises through those to the upstairs. In summer it rises and the cross breezes carry it away."

Miriam said, "Good idea. Is it cold upstairs in winter?"

"On the coldest days a little, but we have lots of blankets."

Miriam said, "Well, tonight we get to sleep in beds. Let's finish the tour."

She heard Joshua start to cry and the fullness in her breasts meant it was feeding time. She said to Raif, "You go on without me. You can give me a private tour later."

Miriam took a cover off a rocking chair in the big bedroom and Janice gave Joshua to Miriam who took him. Janice closed the door after everyone and Miriam fed Joshua. She fell asleep. She woke to gentle knocking on the door. Miriam covered herself and said, "Come."

Martha said, "Mrs., we are about to unload the wagons and the Major wants to know where you want everyone situated and the things put."

Miriam smiled, "Of course."

Martha and Henry were given the downstairs servants' quarters, Abigail was put in one of the upstairs bedrooms and so were Cracker and Janice, Jeremy and Tonia. Hiram and Horatio were moved into the bunk house. It was decided to unload only the baggage. Everyone was tired from travelling and there was no reason to hurry. It was decided the cargo would be unloaded in the morning, so Jeremy sent Hiram and Horatio to move the wagons into one of the large barns.

They all ate a light meal on the veranda and afterward they all sat drinking coffee.

Cracker said, "It's a nice place. How big is it major?"

Raif said pointing, "About seven miles that way and four and a half that way."

Jeremy said, "It's sure a lot of land."

Raif said, "If you want to build here, I can give you the land. There's some nice land by the gate where we came in. There's a little creek there. We aren't far from town here. Private, but close."

Cracker looked at Janice who nodded and Cracker said, "I'd like to go take a look."

Tonia spoke for Jeremy, "We'll go along with, if that's ok?"

Janice said, "For sure."

Raif said, "Well, I suppose now is as good a time as any."

So it was Raif, Miriam, Jeremy, Tonia, Cracker, and Janice set out. On horse it took no time at all to get to their destination. In less than twenty minutes, they were dismounting above the small creek.

Janice said, "It is pretty here."

They dismounted and led their horses. They walked following the creek for about ten minutes. They then turned and headed back to the trail.

Cracker said, "This sure is pretty land."

Jeremy said, "For sure."

Janice said, "I'd like to go into town tomorrow and really get a feel for what they have."

Jeremy said, "That might be a good idea."

Miriam said, "We could all go together."

It was agreed. They returned to the ranch and put the horses up.

Raif was leaving the stables when Ross came to see him, "Boss, can ya take a li'l while to talk?"

Raif said, "Sure, Ross. Let's go sit on the veranda."

They had no sooner sat then Martha appeared, "Can I get you something, Major?"

Raif smiled, "A glass of cool well water would be nice."

Raif looked at Ross who said, "That sounds good."

Martha went inside.

Raif said, "You have done a very good job while I was gone."

Ross said, "I've saved just about all my pay and them bonuses you gave me, which I am rightly 'preciative of."

Raif said, "You deserved them."

Ross asked, "Now that you are here, what am I supposed to do?"

Raif said, "Continue as you have. I couldn't do better, so I can't see any reason to change, can you?"

Martha brought the water to them and Raif said, "Thanks, Martha."

"You're welcome, Major."

Ross said, "Well there is one thing."

Raif looked at him.

"I have a gal in town. Young widow who lost her husband in the war. I been courtin' her and I'd like to wed her. The problem is a place to live so's I can still do my job here. The little house I share with Roy ain't going to do it."

Raif said, "Easy to solve. I can have a house built down the stream a bit or I'll deed you land down by the gate for a house if you want to build your own."

Ross said, "I'll talk it over with Della."

Raif said, "Let me know what the boss says."

Ross smiled, "She surely does have a bridle on my heart."

Raif raised an eyebrow, "It must be love with you talking like that."

Ross grinned, "I reckon. Thanks, boss."

Ross got up and walked away.

Miriam came out on the porch, "When we go to town tomorrow, I will need to pick up some seed to start a garden so we can grow our own vegetables. Maybe we can even grow some berries."

Raif said, "There are lots of wild blueberry and strawberry patches not far from here. You can just go pick 'em by the pail full."

Miriam said, "Then we'll make preserves and can it for winter. On hot bread it'll be wonderful."

Raif said, "The trouble with just men living here is that it never occurred to us to do something like that."

Miriam smiled.

Raif caught a bit of the odor of what Martha had cooking and asked, "What's that delightful odor?"

"Martha's made stew and fresh bread."

Raif said, "I hope she made extra because I expect that odor will cause us to have company drop by and hint."

Miriam said, "It's a very large pot. Martha's middle name is hospitality. What do the ranch hands do?"

"They have their own dining hall with a kitchen and a good cook. Dad and I always used to eat there. The hands, when they come in, won't come by. I expect Ross and Roy will."

Miriam said, "One day soon, perhaps we can ride the ranch and you can introduce me."

Raif said, "All right. It'll be a good thing for me as there have been new hands hired while I was gone."

Miriam said, "You think we can build a small version of the railway water tank so I can have a fenced in bathing enclosure."

Raif said, "That sure was nice, but it would be easier to build a privacy fence down by the swimming hole."

Miriam looked at her husband, "That wouldn't provide much privacy from somebody watching from the hilltop."

Raif said, "It would if it had a roof on it. A dock could be built to walk into it so you could change out and into dry clothes."

Miriam said, "Ok by me. Does the stream flood in spring?"

Raif said, "Not with a current strong enough to do any real damage."

Miriam said, "It's only a couple of hundred yards down the hill, so that will work."

Raif was right. They had drop by guests for dinner and everyone had a good time. After dinner, Ross suggested they go down to the dining hall so he could introduce everyone to the hands. Roy went ahead to tell the men and the little party walked to the hall. The dining hall was larger than Miriam expected. The introductions went well. Everyone was chatting.

One of the men said in a fairly loud voice, "Is it true ma'am what Hiram told us about ya shootin' injuns and such, and doctorin'."

The room went silent. Miriam was certain a pin dropped would be heard. Everyone was waiting for Miriam's reaction.

Miriam said quietly, "Yes. My husband the Major taught me the shooting and my mother the doctoring. I was much honored by the company called Gunnerson's Gunners to become an honorary member to which Mr. Cummings, a former sergeant in the Gunners, a hero himself and who saved my dear husbands life on occasion, can attest."

The men were looking around.

Cracker said, "Ya fellers don' want to make Mrs. Major upset, hear. She can shoot ur ears off 'fore ya can say sorry ma'am."

There was general laughter and things returned to normal.

Miriam looked at Hiram who looked somewhat sheepish. She smiled at him and she could tell from across the room that he sighed deeply. She supposed it was relief.

The men seemed happy the boss and his Mrs. and their friends shared coffee and conversation with them. Many of the hands went to see Joshua, though Miriam suspected it was more to talk to Abigail than to see the baby. The socializing broke up after about an hour. The Gunnerson clan and friends walked the two hundred plus yards to the main house.

Everyone went to bed and as Miriam was undressing, Raif came up behind her and started kissing her neck. One thing led to the next and the couple found their blood heating, their hearts pounding, and Miriam was carried away. She was loud in the throes of passion and she didn't care. Afterward as she lay there content, she heard giggling.

Raif whispered, "You were screaming like a wildcat fighting a bear."

Miriam giggled like a school girl. She had just started to drift off when they were woken. Miriam rolled over and Raif spooned her and whispered, "Seems Janice is learning your ways."

Miriam whispered, "Shush. Go to sleep."

Raif said, "I can't sleep with that going on."

Miriam rolled over toward Raif which turned out to be
a mistake, or not. Afterwards, Miriam acted like a man and
fell into a deep satisfied sleep.

In the morning, Miriam tried to ignore the gentle
knocking on the door. She felt Raif get out of bed and pull
a blanket off of it. The door opened. A minute later Raif
put Joshua at her breast. Miriam was very happy as she lay
there half awake.

When Miriam finally came downstairs with Joshua,
everyone was up and had finished breakfast. Martha was in
the kitchen when Miriam came in.

Martha said, "There's still fresh coffee."

Abigail came into the room, "You want me to take
Joshua?"

Joshua was now sound asleep so Miriam gave him
over and poured herself a coffee. Miriam went out on the
porch, but nobody was there. She sat down.

Abigail came out and sat holding Joshua. She was
looking at Miriam.

Miriam said, "Something on your mind?"

"Woman to woman?"

Miriam's curiosity was peaked, "Yes."

"My mother always let on that," she paused, "the
goings on between a man and a woman was duty and
maybe disgusting. I never knowed it was enjoyable. My
mother never showed it was so. After last night, you and
Janice have me thinking it can be pleasurable."

Miriam said, "With the right man it can be the most
pleasurable thing you can imagine."

Abigail said, "Then why don't women do it all the time
with fellows."

Miriam said, "Most men want the pleasure, but they
don't want to take a wife that is used goods. You know,
have given themselves to other men. It's especially so if

she has another man's child. You fool around outside marriage, you get a bad reputation because men like to brag about such, your chances of finding a good husband drops to about nothing, and your chances of being scorned, homeless, and poor because you had a child outside marriage goes way up." Miriam sipped her coffee then added, "Some men once they have their way with a women figure they aren't worth anything if they give up their innocence for few kind words. Your innocence should be for your husband only. The best gift you can bring to your marriage bed is your first time. "

Abigail asked, "How do the war widows get other husbands then."

Miriam sighed, "Because they lost their innocence rightly. They are not seen as women of lax morals. The new husband also knows he's never going to be in the embarrassing situation of running into the man that was there first."

Abigail said, "So men will take innocence when they shouldn't, discard the one that gives it away, and mostly leave a woman to fend for herself if she is with child outside of marriage."

"That's about it. There's only one rule which is only give up your innocence to your husband on your wedding night. The Bible says God outlaws fornication."

Abigail said, "That's plain enough."

Miriam smiled, "After you're married, have all the loving with your husband you can."

Abigail's jaw fell. She sat there open mouthed.

Miriam said, "Close your mouth, Abigail, before you catch flies."

Abigail did. Then giggled when she realized what had happened. She sat there looking at Miriam.

Miriam said, "What?"

"I don't know what to do when the time comes."

Miriam said, "When you get engaged, I'll tell you what to do the night before you marry."

Abigail just nodded.

Raif came out of the stables leading his and Miriam's horse. Both were saddled. He came and tied the horses at the rail in front of the porch steps.

He said, "Good morning, ladies."

Miriam replied, "Good morning, husband."

Abigail said, "Sir."

Joshua started to fidget. Janice said, "I think someone needs to be changed and cleaned." She got up and went off with Joshua.

Cracker, Janice, Jeremy, and Tonia came following with their horses.

Miriam said, "I'll go get my hat and rifle."

Miriam came back out of the house to find the others mounted and ready to go. She put her rifle in her saddle sheath and mounted her horse. The group headed out.

Ravensville was a short horse ride from the ranch. The group arrived to find the town bustling. Ravensville was the county seat and the party expected to find a number of shops, but to their surprise there wasn't much. Miriam was able to get her vegetable seeds and she found a leather worker who would make her a double cross draw holsters on a belt with cartridge loops.

What passed for a general store had very little stock and there was not a gun shop in the town. There was a cattle sales barn, a horse sales barn, a farmers market, and a courthouse. The only place to buy a meal was at the one hotel's dining room. After visiting the few shops and exploring the town, the little group met at the dining room for lunch.

After they had ordered, Cracker said, "I think there are lots of business opportunities here."

He looked at Janice who said, "It would be fun to be a shopkeeper and we could keep a proper stock. We wouldn't have to worry if things were slow. We could live above the general store."

Cracker just nodded.

Jeremy started to speak, "I suppose we..." and was cut off by sound of gunfire and screams.

The group looked at each other and went outside. Riders were coming from the courthouse randomly shooting at people. They sent one shot in the direction of Raif's group breaking the dining room's window.

Suddenly the six had guns drawn and were returning fire. Four riders and a horse were down and the remaining five riders turned back toward the courthouse one picking up the rider whose horse had been shot. Five of the six instinctively went to their horses and drew out their rifles. There was firing up the street and four of the six were headed back toward Raif's group. The five walked out into the street and calmly at a distance of about a hundred yards shot the four riders out of the saddle. Suddenly there was dead calm.

Tonia was standing by the horses reloading her pistol her hands shaking. Jeremy went to her and said, "You did good."

Tonia said, "I need one of them fancy rifles and you need to teach me to use it."

Jeremy said, "Yes, dear."

Tonia threw up in the street.

Miriam said, "I did the same thing after a gunfight when I was pregnant."

Tonia nodded and looked for something to wipe her mouth with. Miriam took her bandana from around her neck and said, "I need a new one anyhow."

Miriam left and started walking up the street with the men to check the fallen. Raif got to the first one and kicked his gun away. Miriam and Cracker had their rifles ready and scanned the men that were down.

Jeremy said, "This one's dead."

Raif said, "This one too."

They made their way up the street. They found one man alive, but he was gut shot and swelling up from internal bleeding.

Miriam kicked his gun away and said, "Who are you?"

The man said, "Remember the name. Keefer. My kin will come fer ya." He coughed and died.

Raif came to Miriam, "What did he say?"

Miriam told him. They continued to check the bodies. No one else was alive. Miriam went to a wounded horse took out her pistol and put it out of its misery. She holstered her pistol. Several men were coming from the direction of the courthouse with rifles cradled or over their shoulder. One of the men had a badge on.

Raif and his little group put their weapons in non-threatening positions.

The man with the badge came to Raif, "I'm Sheriff Stan Holt, Colby County."

Raif held out his hand, "Raif Gunnerson, Double G Ranch. This is my wife Miriam, my friend Carl and his wife Janice, my brother-in-law Jeremy is over there with his pregnant wife. He went to her after the shooting was over."

Miriam said by way of explanation, "She threw up after the gunfight. It's because she's with child. Same thing happened to me once. Killed the fellow and heaved all over the street."

The sheriff looked at Miriam, then her guns, and shrugged.

Raif asked, "How come you are over here?"

"Some of the Keefer boys and friends kilt some folks over my way. It's been a curse since they moved here about. I only caught the one Keefer and two of his friends. The others escaped my county. They was supposed to stand trial in Colby County, but his honor Judge Brant and his whole family was kilt. I suspect it was done by the

Keefers. The murderous lot was brought here to stand trial, but some of his other kin tried to break him out jist now during the trial.

They kilt the judge and the sheriff and two deputies from here. I was takin' a piss at the time or I might be dead. They snuck in a back window and bushwhacked everybody. They wounded a couple of the jury and generally shot the courthouse to hell. They would have got away if it weren't for y'all. You'll have trouble with the Keefers now. They is known for their blood feuds."

Raif looked at the sheriff, "They got what they deserved."

The sheriff said, "They kilt their own sheriff about two years back but the why of it no one knows. It was knowed the sheriff was bought and paid for by the Keefers. There's no law there now. Ain't nobody wants the job."

Raif said, "That most likely suits the Keefers."

The sheriff said, "They'll come lookin' for you and me both. They'll be lookin' to take it out on the town, too."

Raif looked at the bodies, "Then there will be a lot more dead bodies." Raif looked at the sheriff, "I don't like the idea of looking over my shoulder. You ever thought the best defense is an offense."

The sheriff said, "I like your thinking."

Raif said, "Let's gather up these boys' guns then let me buy you a coffee at the hotel dining room."

Cracker knew what to do and immediately went to work. He and Janice gathered all the weapons and valuables. Shortly after, over coffee in the hotel dining room the plan to bring down the Keefers was hatched. Afterward, Jeremy, Miriam, and Janice took Tonia back to the ranch.

Raif and Cracker, together with Sheriff Holt, went to see the presiding county commissioner of Raven County. After a lengthy discussion, he promised to call the other

322

commissioners together the next day. Raif invited Sheriff Holt to stay at the ranch and he accepted.

In the morning after breakfast, Raif, Sheriff Stan Holt, and Cracker rode into town. They met with the county commission which approved the recommendation. A telegraph was drafted and agreed to. The commission also appointed Raif as Sheriff of Raven County until the next county election and swore him in. Raif immediately swore Stan and Cracker in as deputies and Stan swore Raif and Cracker in. They now had at least two counties covered.

A fast rider was sent with two horses to have two telegrams sent on from the nearest telegraph office.

Raif returned to the ranch with Cracker. Raif had a barn cleared out to serve as temporary quarters. It took two days for the results of Raif's message to bear results. That day two men showed up together and three others came alone.

It was fortunate that the Keefer's spy was an impatient man. After finding out the five men had arrived, he rode to report to Elroy Keefer, the patriarch of the Keefer clan.

When Elroy heard the news he laughed and said, "When all the kin folk arrive there'll be near thirty of us. We'll burn Ravensville and the Double G Ranch to the ground and kill them what murdered our kinfolk."

Five days after the telegraph went out, Raif had twenty one men staying in his barn. That was the day the message came that the commission had received a reply. Raif, Stan, and Cracker went to town with five other men. Those men stood guard around the courthouse as the commission met.

The news was good. Their request had been granted. The special commission had been given and the warrants issued from the capitol. After the formalities were observed, Raif returned to the ranch and swore in the twenty one men.

Seven of the new men had repeating rifles of their own. Raif had fifteen new repeating rifles in three wooden cases. He issued fourteen of them to the others and gave one to Tonia. They weren't the Henry, but the new Winchester 66. The deputies drew lots of ammunition and rations and then set out. Twenty three heavily armed lawmen set out with five spare horses. They went to serve arrest warrants on the Keefers.

Jeremy, Hiram, Horatio, Ross, and the women, along with some of the hands, would stay to protect the ranch.

CHAPTER 14 – FULL CIRCLE

Raif sent two experienced scouts ahead of their column. They each took an extra horse with them. The main group was halfway to the Keefer's place when the scouts came back to report. The Keefers were headed directly toward Raif's deputies.

Raif asked, "How long do we have before they get here."

"Ten to fifteen minutes. They're coming hard wasting their horses."

Raif asked, "What's the terrain ahead of us like?"

The scout who had gone out the farthest said, "It's flat open country ahead."

Cracker said, "There's that gully we passed a bit back. We might use it to advantage."

Raif said, "Here's what we are going to do."

Elroy and his men were riding high on emotion and riding fast. They were anticipating rape and pillage. Elroy saw the nine men ahead of them. He knew it was Gunnerson, Holt, and the hired guns. Elroy figured he'd just ride over them. He drew his rifle and the others did the same. They were too far off for an accurate shot, but one of the men on his right fired. As Elroy expected it had no effect, at least for a moment.

Elroy saw Gunnerson's men raise their rifles. Three of his men were shot from their horses and one horse cart wheeled forward crushing its rider.

Elroy cursed but he was not about to turn back. Another volley from the Gunnerson men changed his mind. Five of his men went down. Elroy was no fool. He yelled for his men to turn about. He looked over his shoulder and saw the nine were setting out after him and his men. They were firing at the gallop.

Elroy was surprised when his cousin Job was shot and fell forward in his saddle. Elroy figure he'd rather take some of them with him and pulled up. His men did the same and they put their horses down and got behind them. To his surprise the Gunnerson men pulled up and turned back and dismounted just about out of range.

Elroy was stunned. His world was shaken when the man next to him slumped forward from a shot from behind. Elroy looked around and saw men firing from a gully not a hundred yards away behind them to the left. They had repeating rifles. It was then Elroy knew he was probably going to die anyway. He got his horse up, mounted quickly, and rode perpendicular to the men in the gully and parallel to the men just out of range. Some of his men followed his lead. Only seven of them made it out of range. He rode hard away from the slaughter behind him.

Raif knew the immediate job was to kill as many of the Keefers as possible. He ordered two scouts to follow the escapees at a distance and report back. They each took an extra horse. Raif and his men got into distance shooting positions and started shooting at the few men still putting up resistance.

When it was all over, the superior fire power of Raif's deputies had won the day. One deputy had been shot in the side, but it was a through and through flesh wound. It was a painful bleeder, but once bandaged was unlikely to cause a long term problem. There were three other deputies with minor wounds that required bandaging. All of Elroy's men had died from multiple gunshot wounds, but one. He was gut shot and unlikely to live more than a few minutes. The deputies put the badly injured horses out of their misery.

In order to bring the bodies back, they would have to put two bodies on each of the remaining Keefer horses. It would be slow going.

Cracker said, "I guess this means we will be hunting again."

Raif said, "Looks that way."

Stan said, "Still, it's a good day's work."

Cracker agreed, "It is that."

The party was just getting ready to pull out when the scouts returned. They came directly to Raif.

One said, "They split up into three groups. There were seven in all. They were still headed west when we last saw them."

Raif said, "They'll steal horses and circle around back to their own county thinking they'll be safe there."

Stan said, "Why don't eight of us go directly to their hide. The rest of the deputies can go protect Ravensville and the ranch just in case."

Cracker said, "It makes sense as much as I hate to admit it 'cause I know who you're goin' to send back."

Raif smiled and Cracker said, "Consider it done."

Raif and Stan set out with six deputies. Raif was wrong in anticipating what the remaining Keefers would do. After the scouts dropped off, the Keefer men gathered together and raided a small ranch, killing the family and hands. The Keefers stole fresh horses, but they did not head home.

Miriam was standing guard sitting on the roof of her two story home from which she had a commanding view for miles in the light of the full moon. Hiram was asleep on the roof next to her. Miriam saw the riders. She took up her field glasses. It wasn't any of their people. Miriam shook Hiram who woke immediately.

"Go quickly and raise everybody. We've got raiders coming. Night-time plan."

Hiram scurried off the top roof entering the attic through the only dormer opening. The riders were still a half mile off when Miriam went into the house. It looked like they were coming straight in. They would find themselves in a shooting gallery with a three way crossfire.

Elroy was angry and intended to go straight into the main house and kill everyone in it before they realized what was happening. He and his men went into the yard at full gallop. They were ten yards from the front door when a shotgun blast took Elroy's horse out from under him and then it seemed the world was filled with rolling gunfire.

There seemed to be fire coming from every direction and as he rolled over he saw his men being riddled. He crawled forward and jumped up on the veranda and ran full speed into the front door and it burst open under the weight of his shoulder. He just straightened up in time to see her gun barrel pointed at his head and then he died.

Miriam stood looking at the man. Tonia was looking at the corpse and started to heave. Miriam yelled, "Not in here."

Tonia ran onto the porch and threw up over the rail. Miriam was beside her and said, "Being with child will do that to you."

Tonia just nodded her head.

Miriam went to where Elroy's horse lay dying and fired her pistol into its head. She hated to see animals suffer. She walked around the yard. All the Keefer men were dead as were their horses.

Miriam thought, "This is going to be a mess to clean up."

The Keefers had been so surprised and subject to such fierce fire that they had not managed to do anything but break a few panes of window glass with the few rounds they did get off. For that they had lost their lives.

The fire had the effect of bringing in ranch hands from all over. They were needed, not for fighting, but for cleaning up the carnage. The men now knew firsthand the stories about Mrs. Major were not exaggerated.

Miriam had instructed the men and horses be stripped of anything valuable to pay for the cost of the clean-up. Ross was not about to cross Mrs. Major and did as instructed. The horse carcasses were disposed of. Miriam had the bodies of the Keefers loaded into wagons and she took them into town.

The following day Cracker showed up in Ravensville to the news about the attack on the Double G. Miriam had brought her bodies in first. The town was abuzz when it became apparent the Keefer gang had been wiped out. It seemed anti-climactic when Raif and Stan brought the only two Keefers who would stand trial. They were wanted for murder and been at the Keefer home.

The Keefer women had been dumbstruck to find lawmen at their door. One woman had shot at a deputy and been killed by return fire. The other women suddenly realized these men were not townies, but professionals that would not hesitate to respond to deadly force with death. They quickly surrendered on promise they and their children would not be harmed if they gave up their weapons and surrendered. They did and were not arrested. The two men were found hiding under one of the houses.

The two Keefers were tried, found guilty, and hung. The circle was complete.

Raif decided he liked being county sheriff and left the running of the ranch to Ross. Raif and Miriam continued to live in the big house. Raif kept the best of the Gunners, who had come to rid the area of the Keefers, on as deputy sheriffs. A couple of others stayed on as hands as they were experienced in ranching.

Jeremy and Tonia bought a ranch adjoining Raif and Miriam's and turned it into a horse breeding and training operation. They made a comfortable living. Tonia and Jeremy's first child was a boy who they named Joel.

Cracker and Janice bought a small shop on a large lot on the town square, tore it down, and built and stocked a large general store with a living space above. They carried all types of dry goods including an inventory of guns and ammunition. They did it to have a place to pretend to work. It turned out to be a huge success and kept them very busy.

Raif and Miriam started going to the local church regularly and brought their friends with them. They were beginning to understand what Christianity was about.

The Gunnerson family sold its railway stock for huge profits when the settlement in the west continued. The Gunnerson mine continued to produce gold for half a decade before running out.

It turned out that the Double G would be the longest lasting, if not most profitable, of Raif and Miriam Gunnersons' businesses.

The legacy of the rancher Gunnerson branch of the family was firmly established.

The End